THE DARK DOMAIN

Gratefully I sank into a rear seat of the car. How good the smell of the leather upholstery, how comforting the sound of the V8 engine! Looking about me as we glided down the narrow road I saw the unchanging outlines of the fells that less than an hour ago I had seen as they had been four centuries earlier. And the enormity of what had happened hit me. I had been directed to witness a specific event which had taken place in the past. The possibilities this opened up made my thoughts spin.

'I know you're not feeling very well at the moment,' said Geoffrey, turning round in the front passenger seat, 'but can you tell us – was there . . .'

'Yes, Geoffrey,' I said. 'I heard Madeline Auber curse your line before she was burnt alive.'

Mark Ronson

THE DARK DOMAIN

Hamlyn Paperbacks

A Hamlyn Paperback

Published by Arrow Books Limited
17-21 Conway Street, London W1P 6JD

A division of the Hutchinson Publishing Group

London Melbourne Sydney Auckland
Johannesburg and agencies throughout
the world

First published in Great Britain 1984
by Century Publishing Co. Ltd
Hamlyn Paperbacks edition 1985

Printed and bound in Great Britain by
Anchor Brendon Limited, Tiptree, Essex

ISBN 0 09 937050 6

For Shirley Russell

I

Derwentwater!

The name was magical. In the years ahead it was to have many connotations for me – not least that of horror – but as I sat in the back of the highly polished Morris 1000 that long gone spring morning, the name of our destination sang in my imagination.

On my knee was the manuscript of my historical novel *Black Days in Dark Ages* – which owed more to Scott than to my inventiveness – and notes on Derwentwater which I had copied out in the Notting Hill Gate library, with that obsessive need to collect information shared by children and journalists.

'Keswick – the town at the top of the lake – used to be called Ketel's Wyke because that was where a Viking called Ketel came in his dragonship,' I announced.

'I can see we won't be needing a guidebook,' my mother said without enthusiasm.

'But how could he have got there?' I asked my father.

'Inland along the river Derwent, through Bassenthwaite Lake and on into Derwentwater. The river must have been deeper in those days. The last time I saw the stretch connecting the two lakes it would have been too shallow for a Viking boat.'

As an adolescent my father had cycled round the Lake District, and it was his memory of its pure air and scenic grandeur which prompted him to take me there for my recuperative holiday.

Eighteen months earlier I had climbed a forbidden tree, a branch had snapped and I had plummeted to the tangle of half-bared roots below, bruising my back so vividly that it was regarded as punishment enough. But soon I was being reprimanded for being an old slouch, my physical education teacher referred to me as a letter C and, when it became obvious that the condition was not a result of wickedness on my part, the family doctor ordered me to be X-rayed.

As a result I spent a year in hospital, confined by sticking plaster and pulleys to a frame designed to mould me back into shape while the tuberculosis which had attacked the injured area became quiescent under new bone layers. The only movement I was allowed was with my hands – even my head was held in a padded helmet. But while my body was immobilised my mind found freedom in the inner space of the imagination, stimulated by books supplied by my father. These ranged from the Dr Dolittle stories to Dennis Wheatley's *The Devil Rides Out*, a curious mixture for a thirteen-year-old but one which I found highly satisfactory.

Halfway through *Ivanhoe* I lost my ambition to become a helicopter pilot – I was going to join the ranks of the story-tellers.

During my incarceration, my father – bravely hiding the possibility that I might not walk again – talked about the holiday we were going to take when I was cured, how I could use his old camera to photograph Derwentwater as he had done. And when the visiting hour was over, and the light dimmed to a single green-shaded lamp in the centre of the ward, the Duc de Richelieu and Dab-Dab the duck were interwoven with the Lake District in my fantasies.

It turned out that I made a good recovery, and when I came home to the flat in Pembridge Square I felt surprisingly healthy. Delighted to see me walking, albeit somewhat drunkenly at first, my father promised that as soon as he could get a fortnight's leave from the publishing house where he was a layout artist we would take the promised holiday. He knew I needed time to adjust before resuming school life. My body had been returned to normal with the help of physiotherapy but my mind had not caught up with it.

Looking back to that time I am still surprised at how

receptive I was, how ready for the impressions I was about to receive in the enchanted domain of the children I thought of as Hansel and Gretel . . . Gretel, who turned into the thief princess and stole my heart with a grave smile, leaving a memory which grew like an illusionary corridor created by mirrors held opposite each other.

'Soon be there,' said my father.

For the last hour he had become more and more boyish at the prospect of returning to the Lakes, telling us about his cycle tour, how the tent had leaked, and the saga of a puncture in a remote pass. My mother was not interested and I leafed self-importantly through the novel I had started writing some months earlier in an exercise book poised awkwardly above my face. At that time I had no doubt that my purple prose would appear in print, believing that when a writer did not achieve publication it was because he lacked the tenacity to finish his story.

'Here's Keswick,' my father announced. 'No Vikings today.'

A slender church spire rose above grey stone houses. In narrow streets early tourists in fell-walking boots gazed into shop windows displaying Herdwick wool sweaters, clocks set in green slate, and chunks of amethyst and fool's gold for amateur geologists. Suddenly I was looking over Derwentwater, its islands so low that trees appeared to grow out of the sky-tinted water.

Minutes later we were hefting suitcases into a guest house on the other side of the town, and – for an active boy – only five minutes from the lakeside. It was run by a bantam of a woman named Mrs Ridley, watched by bulky Mr Ridley whose lameness provided an excuse for a vast inactivity. This disability proved to be to my advantage. Hearing that I was newly discharged from hospital, he regarded me with fellow feeling and said I could use his rowing boat – in which he occasionally slumped over a fishing rod – provided my parents agreed. They smiled their consent. As swimming had been part of my physical rehabilitation, they knew I would be at home in the water should I fall in.

9

'It'll do him good to go off on his own sometimes,' I heard my father saying in their room down the corridor. 'He needs to regain his confidence. He's been shut away for a year – a terribly long time for a chap of his age – and soon he'll be entering a new world.'

Prophetic words.

The next night I dared myself into an adventure. That morning the three of us had gone for a cruise round Derwentwater in the launch *Princess Margaret Rose* and, while my mother rested through the afternoon, Dad and I trekked over Cat Bells. But it had not been enough to satisfy me. I was impatient to set off by myself and explore the lake.

After supper I lay in my odd-angled attic gazing at a windowful of stars, and was seized by the thrilling notion of a midnight row. Still exhilarated by the sense of freedom which had bubbled through me since I was unstrapped from the orthopaedic frame, I felt that anything was possible. The idea became a dare, and within a minute I had pulled on my clothes and crept out to the shed where Mr Ridley kept his oars.

Reaching the lakeside, I was awed by the theatrical effect of the moonlight. I was a product of London and had never suspected the moon could be so bright – when I found the boat nudging its jetty, I was able to read the name *Pandora* displayed across its transom in flaking gold transfers. As I untied the painter and fitted the oars into rowlocks, I was deliciously scared, not only by my first attempt at such a clandestine enterprise but by the water I was about to set out on. In this light – which gave everything the sharpness of old plate negatives – Derwentwater was a mystery.

The surface was like black glass, yet as I thrust away from the bank *Pandora*'s wake shone with dissolving swirls of mercury, and pearls dripped from the blades of my oars.

After rowing parallel with the west bank for some time I

paused and gazed about me, trying to identify distant patches of darkness which marked islands. Although I had pored over maps of Derwentwater for the past week, I was disorientated in this black and silver world. Tomorrow's daylight would return the lake to the reality of the guide-book, but tonight it was outside the normal laws of perspective. Above *Pandora*'s stern Skiddaw was etched sharply against the luminous sky, a reptilian cloud flowing glacier-like from its summit – a mist-lizard stalking Keswick.

The boat turned idly so that the mountain slid from view, and I found myself gazing at the darkly wooded shore in the shadow of Cat Bells. And then I saw the lights.

Fairy lamps were strung between the trees. Beyond an expanse of lawn, drained of colour by the cold radiance of the moon, were tiers of illuminated windows. A fancy-dress party was in progress. Figures in extravagant costumes performed a minuet, while couples strolled beneath the glow-wormed branches. A jester shambled after an eastern queen holding a bottle, a cat embraced the Red Shadow, a Grand Inquisitor knelt before a witch. At the margin of the lake masked Columbine regarded her reflection, while a Ruritanian general lounged against a tree with unmilitary patience, a glass halfway to his lips.

From the black water I watched with hungry eyes, spell-bound by a scene almost too beautiful to be real, and puzzled by its silence. There was no music for the dancers, no laughter from the revellers, no cry from the figure which ran over the grass with waving arms.

The world tilted and the vision was lost. The boat spun and I had a flash sensation of soaring. As *Pandora* neared the summit of the huge wave she was hurled forward like a surfboard.

The swell which carried me through the night was with-out foam, a moving mound of dark water, as smooth as the back of a whale, whose only sound was a distant hiss where it overflowed the bank.

My acceleration was brief. *Pandora* lost her impetus as the peak of the gigantic ripple slid beneath her, and she wallowed down the rear slope, smacked by wavelets left in the wake of the phenomenon.

Luckily I had clung to the oars and it did not take me long to regain control and begin rowing back to Mr Ridley's jetty. The excitement of the wave eclipsed my glimpse of the fairyland scene and on the return journey I did not see any lights on the bank. This did not strike me as strange – I was too elated that I had experienced the mysterious 'bottom wind' of Derwentwater.

Next morning my back ached from the unaccustomed work with the oars, but this did not dampen my enthusiasm for setting out to locate the site of the masquerade.

As I hurriedly ate my cornflakes in the Ridleys' over-bright dining-room my mother peered at me and said, 'Martin, you're pale. I think you should rest today instead of larking about on the lake.'

My father must have caught my dismayed expression, for he said in his usual placatory way, 'I think fresh air will soon bring his colour back – he's been cooped up too long.'

My mother gave her resigned look and a few minutes later I was carrying the oars down to the jetty, along with a bottle of Lucozade (for my strength) and a huge packet of Marmite sandwiches courtesy of Mrs Ridley.

The air was still and the water unruffled, and the solitary wave which had hoisted me in the moonlight seemed as improbable as a dream. But the memory was too vivid, and I knew from my reading that the sudden swell was the result of an unexplained disturbance in the lake known locally as the bottom wind. Some authors dismissed it as yet another picturesque Cumbrian legend, but I now knew differently, and I was saddened that I could not tell my parents about it – I had a great sense of guilt in boyhood. So I consoled myself that I still might legitimately find Derwentwater's floating island.

In the morning sunlight *Pandora* seemed like an old

friend, and I was soon rowing down the lake, frequently resting my oars as I tried to pick out landmarks with the aid of a map. Far to my right I recognised Lord's Island, where James Radcliffe, the third and last Earl of Derwentwater, had lived before losing his head on Tower Hill for his part in the 1715 Jacobite rebellion. The 'bonnie lord' had become a great favourite of mine in the last week, and I wondered if I could incorporate a character based upon him in my *magnum opus*.

Ahead of me lay St Herbert's Island, once the home of a disciple of St Cuthbert who had retired to a life of contemplation, living on vegetables and fish he caught in the lake. His sanctity was said to be endorsed when, in 687, he breathed his last at the exact moment when St Cuthbert died on Lindisfarne.

This manifestation of holiness left me sceptical. How could they be sure that the hermit expired at the same instant as the saint when people did not have watches?

Passing tiny Otterbield Island, I saw the *Princess Margaret Rose* trailing diesel fumes close to the eastern bank, a toy boat beneath a pine-covered rampart which soared against pale sky in imitation of the Canadian Rockies. Although I had seen plenty of illustrations in library books, the actual scenery of Lakeland made me feel I was in some wild country far beyond the shores of prosaic England.

My flight of imagination was interrupted by the need to go ashore and get behind a tree.

I swung the dinghy towards the bank and, turning my head, saw that I was heading towards an inlet so sheltered that it would be hardly noticeable from craft going at any speed. The dilapidation of the jetty told me that years had passed since it had been in use.

As I rowed, *Pandora* became aligned with a gap in the woods which grew down to the lakeside, revealing an avenue of black yew trees and distant walls of stone pierced with lancet windows. For a brief moment I thought I had found the scene of last night's silent revel, but as I drew closer to the bank I doubted it. The grass growing on what had once been a landscaped garden was so rank that I guessed the place had been long abandoned.

I ran *Pandora* into the reed margin and, without bothering to unbuckle my sandals, squelched into the undergrowth. A minute later I returned to the boat for my packet of sandwiches and the Lucozade, having decided that this would be a fine place to have a solitary picnic.

I was certain the house beyond the avenue was deserted, and now I recognised it from yesterday's hike over Cat Bells. While we had taken a breather, my father had pointed to a jumble of slate roofs rising from the sea of trees below, explaining how the house must originally have been a peel-tower where the locals found protection from the northern reivers. Later, wings with gabled roofs had been added, and windows cut in the ancient walls.

'Few can afford to live in places like that today,' said my father with some satisfaction. He was a rare cheerful social-ist and one of the original Aldermaston marchers. 'Think of the heating bills . . .'

I was irritated by his mundane remarks when he could have been telling me about the reivers, but he was to be no rival to Sir Walter.

Now I entered the neglected avenue and went stealthily towards a little stone house not far from the lake shore. I had to push my way through waist-high briars and clumps of purple willowherb, from which rose explosions of butter-flies. No one had been using DDT here.

The small building had no windows, but when I circled it I found verdigris-stained doors between two marble pillars like those I had seen in illustrations of Greek temples. Above the lintel was a carving of a lady in what looked like a nightdress, grieving over an inscription which I could not read because of lichen, and I came to the conclusion that it must have been a place where they put the dead in olden days.

I sat on the cracked step, undid the rubber band round the sandwiches and unscrewed the Lucozade cap, and then I saw them. Hansel and Gretel.

2

The names sprang to my mind as soon as I saw them dwarfed by the great black trees, walking hand in hand through the long grass. They were about my age – perhaps a little older. The sun turned the boy's fair hair into a halo, while the girl was even fairer than he. Her hair was palest gold and it flowed down each side of her face in long tresses. Somehow they made me think of lost children, holding hands to give each other courage against what might be lurking in the surrounding forest.

Had they strayed into this place like me, or was I wrong about its being deserted? I took a bite of sandwich to show my nonchalance.

Fingers still linked, Hansel and Gretel came close and stood regarding me on the step.

'Hi,' I said. 'I'm just having my lunch. Like a sandwich? They're jolly good – Marmite.'

The boy took one and bit into it with relish.

'Who are you?' he asked through a mouthful.

'I'm Martin Winter, and I'm on holiday with my mum and dad.'

'You're on our land but it doesn't matter. I'm Geoffrey Auber, and this is my sister Leila. Do you know if Captain Shepherd got into space? The battery of our radio has run down and the witch won't get us another.'

'He blasted off all right,' I told him, savouring the expression. The word 'witch' made me think of Hansel and Gretel again. 'Who's the witch?'

'Mrs Forster. At the moment she's looking after Auber – and us.'

I was to learn that the estate had belonged to the Aubers

for so long that the family name and the house had become synonymous.

'Mrs Forster hates having us on her hands – she says. But our father's in Venice and mother's in a nursing home. That's why we were sent up here.'

He said it in such a positive way that I could think of nothing to say, and because children have to accept so much without question it only occurred to me later that I never found out where it was they had been sent from.

'She's got the right name for a witch too,' said the girl gravely. 'When there were witches in England there was one called Anne Forster over at Riding Mill. She used to meet with other witches in a house which is now a pub, and they had a Devil's rope. When she pulled it, all sorts of food dropped down.'

'I wish our Mrs Forster had a rope like that,' muttered Geoffrey. 'May I have another sandwich?'

I avoided looking at Leila in case she noticed me blushing. She was the most beautiful girl I had ever seen and already I was fantasising about her – saving her from drowning in the lake or leading her to safety from a blazing forest. I looked at the dense woods beyond the wall of yews, but they seemed unlikely to burst into flame.

For a while Geoffrey talked to me about space and ate my sandwiches, and then I felt it was time for me to leave, though I was desperate to be invited back.

'What is this place?' I asked, trying to spin out the conversation.

'In the old days they used to put coffins in here instead of burying them,' said Geoffrey. He walked over and kicked the door. A dull echo came from within and the three of us drew back.

'*'Tis the vault of thy lost Ulalume!*' chanted Leila.

'Lost who?' I said.

'We're reading Edgar Allan Poe at the moment,' said Geoffrey. 'I like the stories best, but she likes the poetry.'

'A funny name,' I said with a stupid giggle, 'for a Poe-et.'

Brother and sister watched me in silence.

In hospital there had been a craze for making puns, but now I burned with shame at having made such a weak one.

'Must be going,' I muttered.

'Come back tomorrow and I'll teach you to play chess,' Leila said.

'I'll try,' I said casually, suppressing an urge to leap and knock my heels together, an expression of enthusiasm at which I had been proficient before my accident.

Now I wanted to get away quickly while her invitation hung in the air, while the magic in the yew tree avenue – which *she* referred to as the 'alley Titanic' from her *Ulalume* poem – was still upon me. I blundered through the briars, an awkward prince hastening from enchantment.

As I rowed away from the secret inlet I looked back and saw them watching me, and once more I thought of Hansel and Gretel – a tale which until recently filled me with fear.

Next morning I rowed back to Auber and Leila taught me to play chess, though the truth was that I had learned a couple of years earlier from my father and now could have won at least half the games we played. I tried to let no hint of this appear, though at times I worried in case my deliberate mistakes were too clumsy.

We played in a large, untidy downstairs room with stone walls and a huge fireplace at one end above which was a shield with rampant heraldic animals. I saw very little of Mrs Forster, who appeared to be too young and attractive for my notion of witches, though her expression was as severe as the bun into which she pulled back her hair. In our brief meeting I knew that I had joined Geoffrey and Leila in her estimation. She had a sweetish smell about her which later I was to remember and recognise as the breath of the gin drinker.

She would appear to announce that lunch was on the huge scrubbed table – of a size suitable for a refectory – and disappear again with a sniff of disapproval. The food she set out reflected this emotion, and when I came to Auber I always brought a plentiful supply of sandwiches which we ate secretly.

Leila played chess solemnly and with few words, her long hair sometimes brushing the crowns of her King or Queen when she leaned over the board. In the background Geoffrey slumped in an ancient club chair, a leg dangling over the arm and a leather-bound volume in his hands. At first he was unhappy to be outside our zone of concentration, but this wore off when he turned the musty pages.

The delight of Auber was that its two occupants lived in the world of books and stories and self-created fantasies just as I had during my immobility. And I was ripe for this world which, in 1960, was something I was not likely to find among my schoolfellows whose entertainment was ready-made on television.

My new companions enjoyed reading aloud to each other, and to me. Leila was particularly fond of the King Arthur stories – not a child's version of the Knights of the Round Table, but Malory. She read from a volume taken from the dusty library which to my eager eyes seemed to contain thousands of books.

Stretched out in the shade of the mausoleum, my contentment was complete as I listened to her read such tales as 'How Sir Gawain came to the Lady Ettard and lay by her, and how Sir Pelleas found them sleeping'.

I rowed to Auber almost every day. Our mornings were devoted to chess, playing in the grounds or exploring Derwentwater in *Pandora*.

One day we crossed the lake and, running the boat on to marshy ground where the Derwent flowed in from Borrowdale, saw the silver skeins of the Lodore Falls glimmering against the sombre rockface. Then we walked to the Bowder Stone, a 2000-ton boulder balanced delicately on one corner, near the Jaws of Borrowdale. This astonishing rock – transported from Scotland by the glacial ice sheet which had crept southwards during the Ice Age – stands over thirty feet high, yet its base is so narrow that it is possible for two people to join hands round it.

The first time I touched Leila was that morning when we lay belly-flat beneath the stone, which I half-believed would roll on us at any moment. Geoffrey climbed the wooden steps attached to it and stood aloof, surveying the surrounding birch forest, while below I held Leila's left hand in my right as we struggled vainly to get our free fingers in contact.

'When we've grown a bit more we'll come back and do it,' she laughed, as we stood up and brushed earth from our clothes.

It became one of our instant traditions that after lunch Geoffrey asserted his right to be the centre of attraction, and this he did by story-telling. His stories were all scary, and years later I was to recognise M. R. James as his main inspiration.

He had a strong sense of effect, even then. He would lead us up to the great attic beneath the gabled roof of the wing which had been added to the peel-tower. Here in the hot triangular space he perched on a broken Victorian rocking-horse. Leila and I sat facing him on a tin cabin trunk which had once accompanied an ancestral Auber to Mombasa, if the dim wording beneath its layer of dust was to be believed.

'There was this chap – a professor – who went to the east coast – to a place called Burnstow – to play golf,' Geoffrey began on the first day.

Surrounded by the lumber of the past, his words took on an immediate creepy note which they would never have achieved in the open air, where – as the highly critical author of *Black Days in Dark Ages* – I would have dismissed them as affected. But in the attic it was different, and soon my fingers left trails in the dust as they stole towards the girl sitting beside me, rather like Geoffrey's best story about a severed hand which took on a life of its own.

At first Leila sat primly upright in the airless gloom, her hands folded in her lap, her hair hiding her profile from me. Then I had the pleasure of feeling her fingers touch mine. For a moment I feared the contact was accidental and wondered whether the correct thing to do was to move my hand, but her cool fingers grasped mine firmly.

There was always a silence after Geoffrey's dénouement: he had the ability of the natural story-teller to allow his tale to affect him as much as his audience. And we shared a sense of relief as we trooped down the narrow staircase to the corridor with its rows of blank varnished doors behind which languished the ghosts of exhausted servants.

'Of course, that was only a story,' I said after one of these sessions, as we walked the overgrown terrace garden between a double row of statues overlooking the yew avenue and the forest beyond. I had been coming to Auber for three or four days but it seemed to me that half my life had been spent here, so quickly had I absorbed its *moeurs*.

'But there are such things,' Geoffrey protested.

'Rubbish,' I said. I was hostile because he had teased me about my legs in front of Leila. He said they looked like white matchsticks beneath my shorts. I dared not explain that it was 'hospital pallor' because it would sound as though I was seeking sympathy, and besides I had no wish for her to know I had been ill.

'But there are.'

'Rubbish,' I repeated, and Geoffrey looked dismayed.

'I'll take you for a row,' I said. 'Let's go and look for the floating island.'

'All around us,' said Geoffrey in a whisper, 'there are *forces*.'

'Oh, yes,' I said. 'Radio waves and things like that.' And I began to whistle, skipping down the steps whose lichened balustrades curved outwards towards a pair of weed-filled urns.

On the top step Geoffrey turned to Leila.

'Shall we tell him about the Murder Room?'

She nodded.

That night my father and mother went out for dinner. I lay gazing at my square of night sky and wondering if Geoffrey's tale about the Murder Room could be true.

'No one ever goes in there,' he had told me as we sat on

the jetty, dangling our legs over peat-coloured water. 'It's a room at the top of the old peel-tower, and it was there – centuries ago – that a lady had her throat cut. It was never used after that but when someone went in in our great-grandfather's time there was still blood on the floor, and it was sticky . . .'

I turned to Leila.

'Is he kidding me?'

She gave a little shrug.

'There's a room which has always been known as the Murder Room in the oldest part of the house,' she said. 'One of our ancestors was supposed to have killed his wife up there so that he could marry someone else. I don't know much about it, but all old places in Cumbria have creepy stories.'

'The day after he married his new wife, the murderer looked out of the window of the Murder Room and saw the name of his dead wife cut into the stonework,' continued Geoffrey. 'And so he knew there was a curse on them. The name – Madeline – is still there.'

'How do you know if no one ever goes into the room?' I asked.

'You can see the letters with binoculars,' he answered glibly. 'It's written upside down and it's in a place no human hand could have reached unless scaffolding had been put up. It was the work of the Green Lady.'

'Green?'

'She appears as a sort of greenish shape in the Murder Room, seeking revenge from anyone who enters it, and she has two spindly arms that reach out to her victims . . .'

'You should be an actor when you grow up,' I said, impressed by the enthusiasm with which he told the story.

'I think I'll be an artist or a musician,' he answered. 'It runs in the family.'

'You want to be a big rock star?' I said innocently and Leila giggled.

It was easy to tease Geoffrey, and I tended to do this when he was relishing morbid topics. He spun stories about the spirits of the dead to impress us, but I had seen death. When Henry had collapsed in the bed next to mine, that had been true horror.

It had been easy to dismiss the story of the Murder Room as we sat peacefully with our toes in the water, but as I lay in bed I could not get it out of my mind. I think a lot of what I felt was due to the gothic atmosphere of Auber. Used to a London flat, I was dwarfed by the dimensions of its rooms; and the passages and staircases leading to goodness knew where would have been appropriate settings – I thought – for Frankenstein or Dracula. The house even had a chapel which my companions took me into one day.

We left footprints in the dust, and the air seemed as stale as in an Egyptian tomb. Splotches of colour marked the walls from rays filtering through stained-glass windows, and on the floor lay pathetic skeletons of birds who had entered through a broken pane and then starved to death. As we looked about us, trying to make out the dark paintings on the wall, a clattering noise made our hearts race. It was a bird beating its wings against the transparent face of a saint.

'Why doesn't your dad get it cleaned up?' I asked. They explained that the family had not lived in Auber for ages.

'This is the first time we've been here since we were small,' said Leila.

Yes, Auber had captured my imagination, perhaps because it was such a contrast to the spotless hospital ward with its chromed equipment and floral-curtained brightness. But it also made me an outsider. It was a world which Geoffrey and Leila inhabited naturally, its strangeness taken for granted. A sadness grew with the understanding that I could never share it fully with them, a feeling which was intensified when it dawned upon me that they were twins.

I was still awake when the door creaked and my father looked in to see that I was all right.

''Night, old son,' he said when he saw that I was awake. 'Your mum and I had a smashing meal. You'll have to give your posh friends a miss tomorrow. We're going for a drive into Scotland. Gretna Green and all that. OK?'

I nodded.

'Dad, are there such things as ghosts?'

'Probably, but I don't expect they're what we think they are.'

I heard my mother whisper down the corridor.

'The War Department's calling.' It was my father's traditional joke. 'We'll talk about ghosts and all sorts of things when we have a bit of time together, if you like. You haven't seen one, have you?'

'No. I sometimes wonder if Henry became a ghost. But what made me think about it tonight is that Auber House has a Murder Room which is supposed to be haunted.'

'All these old houses have something like that. Glamis Castle is said to have a secret room and a monster, isn't it?'

Next day photographs of marriage parties round an anvil looking at the sepia dicky bird, and then a drive to Burns' birthplace at Alloway, did little to compensate for being away from the secret world, but I also got a perverse pleasure out of thinking that the children of Auber might be missing me.

3

With what relief I pushed my way through the briars of the 'alley Titanic' and saw Auber looming beyond the ornamental steps. It had taken on a dreamlike quality in my mind, and I was anxious to return to the dream.

Mrs Forster told me that Geoffrey and Leila were somewhere in the peel-tower and – sniff! – I could go up if I wished.

I climbed the curving staircase which once had been the symbol of Auber's grandeur. Years must have passed since its woodwork was oiled, but the filigree of its balustrades was as remarkable as ever. Curious creatures from English mythology – woodwoses, cockatrices, wyrms and such – lurked in the metal foliage or peered at the passerby through long-stemmed metal grass. The latter had been cast so delicately that air displaced by someone hurrying up the stairs would make these blades vibrate realistically and emit a 'tinging' sound.

On the landing stood a large clock with a carved ebony case – a massive grandfather whose face, with its phased moon and zodiacal characters, must have been designed by an astrologer. Leila had told me that its pendulum had not swung this century.

'I remember Grandmother saying it had a very loud tick, which used to sound through the house like a heartbeat,' she said. 'I suppose it wore out and my father couldn't be bothered getting it repaired.'

That clock was typical of Auber – something very fine which had run down, a once powerful rhythm allowed to become inert. But such thoughts were far from my mind as I entered the part of the house which had once been the peel-tower, calling, 'Geoffrey, Leila!'

There was no response. The house had a quality of absorbing the human voice, of soaking it into its masonry, so that in later years one of my most vivid memories of Auber was its silence.

I came to the cast-iron staircase spiralling to the upper storey. To search there would mean passing the Murder Room, and this made me pause. Yesterday I had dismissed the story as one of Geoffrey's grotesque flights of fancy – until nightfall! I was annoyed it had affected me, and here was a chance to show that I was no longer scared by going up to the door – not inside the so-called haunted chamber, but as close to it as possible.

Reaching the top floor I found myself in a passage lit by a dirty skylight. There was still no sign of the others, and I momentarily forgot them when I saw the carved door whose bas-relief of a chained monkey – Auber's Ape – told me that this was the Murder Room. And on the other side of it was – what?

I wanted to go back, but the imp of the perverse was tempting me to turn the wrought-iron handle and prove that I had been a fool to take Geoffrey seriously. And it would demonstrate my valour to Leila, an important consideration.

The handle held my gaze.

I had only to turn it, take a quick glance inside and run.

How satisfactory it would be if I was to find it locked. That would remove the onus I had put upon myself, but I had little doubt that the handle would turn. When Geoffrey had told me about the Murder Room I'd asked if it was sealed, and he'd said, 'Of course it's not locked. No one would ever go in there.'

Time ticked away like a pulse, and at last I could stand the self-generating tension no longer. I grasped the handle and the door swung slowly inwards. Beyond worm-drilled pilasters was a large room whose gloom was pierced by slender shafts of sunlight slanting through lancet windows. Rent tapestries draped its walls, and the few pieces of furniture beneath them were shrouded with webs.

Squinting into the darker recesses I saw nothing to make me frightened, and I walked forward softly. With the creak of ancient boards came the thought that I might be the first to tread this floor for a century. I would trace my initials on the grime of a window pane as evidence of my boldness.

Halfway across the room I glanced down and my yell echoed about me. A pool of crimson, irregular like a horrid map, seeped over the floor. And in a ray of sunlight it had a liquid gleam – *wet* and spreading. Turning, I beheld a green and spectral shape. A spirit of evil buzzed in the air about me, and my heart felt as though it was jumping in my chest, the only part of me capable of movement. Then the Green Lady – the thing called the Green Lady – advanced.

Panic surged along my nerve filaments and my muscles responded automatically. I spun down the spiral staircase, stumbling along a corridor of blank doors, and set the metal grass whispering on the grand staircase.

The buzzing in my head was louder. I raced into a landscape which – on recollection – had changed in the last few minutes. It appeared in monochrome: the faces of satyrs and gods lining the terrace had lost their lichened softness, and the trees ahead formed a tunnel as their upper branches reached towards each other.

I entered this tunnel, swerved round the Auber mausoleum and floundered through the briars towards the jetty. The entrance to this menacing realm which was also my escape route.

Too terrified to look over my shoulder – because I knew the ghoul was close behind – I ran on to its rotting boards and dived.

The shock of cold water stemmed my fear. Even the slimy weeds caressing my legs did not hold their usual dread as I followed my bubbles to the surface and, treading water, saw Geoffrey and Leila on the bank, wide-eyed. The boy still held the green garden net with which he had draped himself.

'All right now?' asked Leila as I waded ashore. I nodded, my teeth chattering with cold.

'Get a blanket for him while we dry his clothes in the sun, otherwise the witch'll find out,' she said to her brother.

'OK.'

Geoffrey turned to me. 'It was just a joke. I knew you'd have to go into the room but I didn't think you'd scare so badly.'

It was the wrong thing to say at that moment. I threw a clumsy blow which made him stumble backwards with a satisfactory look of alarm.

'Who's scared now?' I jeered. I took a step forward, eager to punch those delicate frightened features.

Leila stepped in front of me.

'Forgive him,' she said. Her words drained my anger and I turned away feeling weak.

'Get that blanket, Geoff,' she said and he ran.

'And you must get these wet things off.'

I was still shivering as she slipped my Aertex shirt over my head. Then she undid the S-shaped buckle of my elastic belt so that my clammy shorts slipped down, leaving me embarrassed in my junior Jockey shorts. These would have to dry on me – the freedom from shyness so painfully acquired in hospital had deserted me on my return to the outer world.

For a moment Leila stood motionless opposite me. Then she leaned forward, clasped her hands together behind my neck and pulled my head forward so that our lips touched. The enormity of what was happening made me tremble. This beautiful girl was kissing *me*!

For a long moment I stood like a dummy while Leila's lips remained soft and magical against mine. My eyes closed themselves. The world and the stupid terror of a moment before was lost in the awareness of her mouth, of the strands of her hair caught between our faces, and the heat of her body radiating into mine.

The impossible had happened. Leila shared what I had felt for her since our first meeting – so long ago – last week.

During that long moment, like a larva becoming an imago, I was conscious of shifts within me. Things were happening to my body. Breathing was difficult and there was a rush of blood to my loins.

It was not just my body that was in a season of change. Seconds ago I had been a boy who had been very scared and then very angry – and suddenly a new dimension had been added to that boy standing on the bank of Derwentwater.

He was in love.

I do not know how long we remained while waves of this new, awesome emotion swept me, but it dawned on me that I should respond or Leila would think I was some silly kid who did not understand what was happening. My fingers locked behind her waist and there was a cruelty in the way I pulled her against me.

And so we stood amid the reeds.

Several times we had to pull our mouths apart to gulp air before resuming the frantic if inexperienced embrace, clinging to each other with the intention of never letting go. And then I felt her fingers slip away from my neck and our lips separated for the last time.

Leila took a step back and regarded me gravely with her clear eyes. I felt tears welling behind my own.

'There!' she said.

'Leila . . .' I began, and then saw that Geoffrey was standing with a blanket over his shoulder, his face unnaturally blank.

'We must wrap you up,' Leila said as though nothing unusual had happened. She took the blanket from her silent brother and swathed it round me. 'It wouldn't do for you to catch a cold on top of everything else.'

The three of us sat down, watching a triangular sail far out on the lake, and waiting for my clothes to dry.

'That was a jolly good ghost, Geoffrey,' I said shakily, wishing to restore the harmony. And then I noticed a stain of red paint on Leila's fingers.

That night in bed I watched tatters of cloud drift past a moon which, like everything else that day, had assumed new significance – Leila's kiss had unlocked a Pandora's box of premature emotions. I knew the basic facts of life, thanks to school biology, and I knew how adults 'did it', but what had taken me by surprise were the fictions of life.

What appalled me that restless night was the thought of having to part from Leila. How would I keep in touch with her when my holiday was over? And when she and Geoffrey left Auber, would they be going to some exotic setting from which I would be excluded by my very ordinariness? Remembering that Venice had been the theme of a conversation, I saw them in my mind's eye walking through a Canaletto scene.

As the stars turned I grew desperate. It was so unfair that I had entered this new dimension only to find it slipping away. And to soothe the pain I pressed my lips against my wrist as a reminder of Leila's kiss.

And so I drifted into sleep, to dream of climbing the circular staircase to the door with the chained monkey on its panel. Geoffrey had mentioned that the heraldic creature and its enigmatic motto – 'He without Honour beware the Ape' – had once been a significant tradition of the house, but now its story was forgotten.

In my dream the carving bared its little white teeth and gibbered at me while the door opened inch by inch. I knew that something horrible was waiting for me beyond, yet I was compelled to enter the dim room. To my relief there was no Green Lady, only a long white box on trestles in the centre. Fear returned as I found my legs taking me towards it completely against my wishes. My progress was slowed by a sticky red tide spreading across the floor.

Then I was looking down into the silk-lined coffin in which lay Leila. But surely she was not dead. I saw the hands demurely crossed on her chest begin to twitch, and then her arms reached towards me and the door of the room clanged shut like the stroke of doom . . .

My shout brought my father to my room, followed by my mother in her candlewick dressing-gown.

'A nightmare, old son?'

I sat up in soaked pyjamas and nodded. The relief I felt that I was back in my room and Leila was not in her coffin!

'It must have been because of your ducking,' he said. My damp clothing had not gone unnoticed, and I had explained that I had tripped while mooring the boat.

'You shouldn't go out on the lake alone,' my mother said while my father wiped my face with the corner of the sheet.

'I wasn't alone. I had my friends from Auber House with me.'

My mother looked disapproving but said nothing further. Did she know something about Auber which I did not, some titbit of adult gossip, or was it normal parental fear of my adventuring?

'What was the dream?' my father asked.

'I dreamed I saw a dead person.'

My father gave my mother a significant look I was not supposed to see, but I understood – it referred to Henry.

'Dreams go in opposites,' he said. 'I'm always dreaming I'm going to be rich, and look at me.'

I laughed, and the aftertaste of the nightmare faded with the certainty that a few miles away Leila was well and sleeping like a king's daughter in her palace, no longer Gretel but the Snow Princess.

The following days were as near perfect as I could have wished. I sensed a shift in my relationship with the brother and sister. Her favour had elevated me in Geoffrey's eyes, but although he appeared anxious to be friendly he did his best to see that Leila and I spent as little time alone together as possible.

We did manage to exchange a few stolen kisses. They were 'stolen' because of the unspoken apprehension of Geoffrey's catching us, a fear which gave an added excitement to the game. I wanted to tell Leila all I felt about her, but when I began she smiled and put her forefinger to her lips. Was it that she did not want to know? Was she afraid of her brother overhearing, or was it that she understood my feelings without the need of words?

Looking back in this attempt to analyse these childhood events which were to have such an effect on my life when I returned to England as a young man, I recall how I wanted to believe in a bond between lovers which gave them understanding of what went on in each other's minds, yet I had not an inkling of what Leila really thought.

In spite of the undercurrents caused by my feelings for Leila, we were happy as a trio. We spent hours talking, at least Geoffrey and I did when curtains of rain hid Derwentwater. We speculated on whether there was an end to the universe, had King Arthur been a real person, would a NASA probe someday find life on other planets, what happened to us when we died and did telepathy work.

We experimented with the last, using a pack of shuffled cards whose colour one of us would try to 'project' into the mind of another suitably blindfolded. No doubt because they were twins, Leila and Geoffrey achieved scores far beyond random possibility, and went on to have some success in the transference of the cards' numbers and symbols. To my secret chagrin Geoffrey was better than Leila at transmitting these images to me.

'You two ought to go on to the stage as a mind-reading act,' she said.

When we tired of such experiments, we played in the grounds of Auber, lit campfires in the woods to roast stolen potatoes and explored the surrounding countryside.

One day Leila said, 'Come, and I'll show you something pretty.'

With Geoffrey dogging us, she led me through the woods to where willows veiled a decaying boathouse on the lakeshore. Inside reflections of wavelets beyond a wooden portcullis danced on the black hull of a boat whose prow curved into a shape which made me think of a musical note.

'A gondola!'

'Yes,' said Leila. 'Grandfather brought it back from

Venice. He used to take Grandmother out on Derwent-water in it at night time.'

'Couldn't we use it now?' I could picture myself in a straw hat, rowing Leila round the islands while the distant roofs of Keswick were transformed into the Venetian skyline.

'Probably sink. It's a very old boat,' said Geoffrey.

'Auber must have been fun once,' Leila said wistfully. 'The gardens gardened, parties with coloured lights in the trees, and music, and the gondola . . . Wish I'd been born then.'

'I don't,' said Geoffrey. 'I'd have had to go to the trenches when I grew up, and get killed at Le Cateau like Grandfather.'

One morning at breakfast my mother remarked, 'I can't understand your obsession with going to that old house every day. You used to get bored so easily. And I think your dad's disappointed that you don't want to come out with us.'

My father and I were stricken with guilt. The last thing he wanted was to be seen as a possessive parent; equally I was distressed at the thought of hurting his feelings.

'Perhaps you can spend some time with us this morning,' my mother continued. 'We're going over to Ullswater to see Wordsworth's daffodils – at least the descendants of his daffodils – and then we're going to have a picnic . . .'

'I'd love to come,' I lied.

'It's all right, Ann,' said my father with his easy-going laugh. 'Our son has become a Grand Meaulnes, and Auber is his Les Sablonnières . . .'

'As long as there's no Mademoiselle de Galais,' retorted my mother, who at times liked to prove she was as 'literary' as her husband. 'And he won't be able to visit his world of lost content after Saturday,' she added. 'Even he must learn that holidays don't last for ever.' This was the only part of the conversation which I understood.

'I never thought they did,' I muttered in misery. Beneath

the tablecloth I calculated on my fingers – only four days left, counting today.

Later, having lunched with my parents in the centre of the Castlerigg stone circle, I rowed down the lake to find Auber spotlit by sunlight pouring through a rent in the clouds. My friends had been watching from the mausoleum and came racing to meet me.

'Let's go and look for the floating island,' I called from *Pandora*.

'It hasn't risen from the lakebed this year,' Geoffrey said. 'It's always in the papers when it comes up to the surface.'

'Maybe it's just a story to attract tourists, like the Loch Ness Monster,' I said contemptuously. I was so angry because my time with them was running out that I had become quarrelsome, perversely wanting to dissolve the illusion which was Auber and add to my unhappiness.

'Oh no, it's real,' protested Leila. 'It appears every three or four years.' She gazed up the avenue to the terrace, the lawn with its two ranks of weathered statuary and the grey house beyond. 'Here everything is *real*!'

The sudden hint of desperation in her voice shocked me. It was the only time I had known her to be upset. I could not understand why, and this added to my frustration.

'Oh, come out on the lake anyway,' I said.

I rowed them to Otterbield Island, a tiny islet of rock on which a few trees had managed to take root. I tied the painter to one of these and we sat on the summit. I handed out the bars of chocolate I had bought for them that morning.

'I wonder if anyone ever hid gold here,' I said, seeing Otterbield as a miniature Treasure Island.

'There's supposed to be a treasure in the lake,' Leila said.

'The Derwentwaters lived on Lord's Island,' Geoffrey said, pointing to an island close to the Friar's Crag on the east bank. 'They used to have a big house there, but there's only the foundations left now. After the last earl was imprisoned for trying to get England's rightful king on the throne . . .'

'We're Jacobites, of course,' said Leila with a slight smile so that I did not know if she was teasing or not.

'. . . his wife Lady Anna took the family jewels from the island in the hope of buying him a pardon, but on the crossing the jewels were lost in the lake.'

'When the earl's body was brought up from London to Dilston Hall in Northumberland there was a great display of the Aurora Borealis,' added Leila. 'Up here they're still called the Derwentwater Lights.'

'And it's said that the ghost of Lady Anna haunts the ruined tower of Dilston Hall, holding a lamp at a window as a beacon to guide her lord home,' Geoffrey concluded.

'Here we go again,' I groaned. 'You and your rotten old spooks. Don't you get bored making these stories up?'

Geoffrey looked hurt.

'I've told you,' he said. 'There are such things.'

4

'You've said that before,' I said. 'I think you just like saying it.'

Leila looked at me reproachfully and my hostility began to be diffused by guilt. They had been two of the best friends I'd ever had, and I was stupidly spoiling that friendship through frustration at my approaching departure. And – as I now see it – there was a double element of jealousy affecting my immature emotions. I envied Geoffrey because he was Leila's twin, and the years that he was able to spend with her while I had known her for only ten days.

And as the aspiring author of *Black Days in Dark Ages*, I envied his story-telling ability. How laboriously I wrote each page, how many sentences were scored through and rewritten in red ink in the crowded margin; yet Geoffrey told his tales so effortlessly, almost as though he were talking about things he had experienced.

Now my unkind remark upset him.

'Look, supposing I told you about something sort of supernatural, and then could prove it to you,' he said. 'Would you think I was telling the truth then?'

I nodded, anxious for the old mood to be restored.

'I read about something very odd the other night in a book I took from the library,' he continued. 'It was all about the folklore of Cumbria, like the phantom army which was seen on Souter Fell, the ghostly skulls of Calgarth Hall, and the witch who was put to death in the Castlerigg stone circle . . .'

I wanted to ask him about that. Had something horrible happened where two hours ago I had leaned against a megalith munching my sandwiches while my father took his holiday snaps? But Geoffrey ignored my interruption.

'The best story in the book was about the vampire of Croglin . . .'

'A Dracula story?'

'This happened before Dracula was thought of. When I'd read it I asked Mrs Forster about it. She comes from the Eden Valley where it happened, and she'd heard about it.'

'I'll bet,' giggled Leila. 'She's probably the vampire of what-do-you-call-it herself.'

She and I roared with laughter while Geoffrey continued earnestly.

Who can say why a particular picture remains vivid in the lumber of one's memory when others more significant fade to nothing? I carry a mental image of Geoffrey as he was on that day far clearer than any which I formed of him when he was a man. The breeze flowing over Derwentwater blew his hair like pale golden flames and his eyes took on the same quality of light as Leila's. I wonder if unconsciously I was in love with both of them – or with my vision of them.

What I did not realise then was that, although my body was out of hospital, my imagination – which had developed abnormally through the long night watches – was still a distorting crystal through which I viewed the world: a crystal which inevitably was to become a dark glass.

Strangely, my memory of Leila that day is less detailed, an impression of beauty which may have owed a lot to the eye of the besotted beholder. How would she have appeared to an adult? A thin young girl with hair unfashionably long and an unusually grave face. I did take snaps, and looking at them now they tell me little because of inaccurate exposure. But they do show that she was still a child not above putting her tongue out at the camera.

'. . . and because they liked Cumbria so much these three Australians – Edward, Michael and Amelia Cranswell – rented Croglin Low Hall,' Geoffrey was saying. 'They must have been quite rich because they were over here on holiday for a couple of years. I suppose that in those days, before aeroplanes, travel took so long that when you got to a place you made the most of it.

'Anyway, one summer night in 1875 they had a picnic supper, and they sat on the grass watching the moon, and they were very happy being on holiday and living in the old farmhouse which must be as old as Auber.

'It was nearly twelve when they said goodnight to each other and went to their rooms. Amelia didn't feel sleepy, so she sat up in bed, looking out of her window at the old farmyard. There was a super moon in the sky and with all the shadows and everything it was all sort of mysterious.

'Suddenly she saw something . . . two little lights that seemed to be moving about the yard. She had no idea what they could be unless they were the eyes of an animal. But it couldn't be a cat or dog: they were too high off the ground.

'Then, for a moment, they vanished – just like that. Amelia wondered what could have happened to them. But she soon knew. A moment later they appeared close to the window, and Amelia could see that they were real glowing eyes – but what of she couldn't say. The head they belonged to was in the shadow.

'Amelia wished she had fastened the shutters outside her window. There was something that chilled her with horror about those glowing eyes and that shadowy face. She should have called out to Michael and Edward, but instead she sat up in her bed as though she was hypnotised.

'Then came a horrid sound. It was made by long nails scraping against the small window panes. The owner of the eyes was trying to get in.'

'Ugh!' said Leila with a shiver. Her hand tightened over mine.

'Ugh is right!' Geoffrey whispered. 'It was a terrible moment. Amelia jumped out of bed in her nightie and ran to the door. She tried to unlock it, and she was so flustered and scared that she dropped the key!

'She went down on her knees, feeling for it with her hand, and while she was trying to find it a new noise came to her ears. The thing at the window was unpicking the lead strips which held the panes of glass together. She looked over her shoulder and saw a face like sort of wrinkled leather looking at her from the hole it had made. Then it put its long skinny arm through and turned the handle and opened the window.

'The creature jumped inside and grabbed Amelia by her hair. She managed to scream once and then it bit her throat.

'It was very lucky for Amelia that she did manage to scream, because it woke up Edward and Michael, and they came running. When they found the door locked they got a poker and forced the lock. Bang! The lock burst, and they tumbled into the room.

'A nasty scene met their eyes! There was their sister lying on the bed with all blood running from her neck. While Michael wiped the blood away Edward raced to the window and in the light of the moon saw a tall thin shape vanishing through the archway in the farmyard wall.

'Well, one of the brothers rode off for a doctor, and the other stayed with Amelia. Luckily the bites were not very deep and there was no danger of her bleeding to death or anything like that.

'When the doctor came I guess he put iodine on, or whatever they used for Dettol in those days. When the brothers asked what could have made those bites he could only think it must have been a big monkey that had escaped from a travelling circus. Or maybe it was a lunatic. He told Edward and Michael that, because she had been upset, she ought to have a holiday. So they all went to Switzerland.'

'Is that all?' asked Leila.

He shook his head.

'That's just the first half. They had a super time in Switzerland. And when the summer was over Amelia's brothers asked her where she would like to go next. She said she wanted to go back to Croglin. She wasn't scared any more. If it was some old monkey it would have starved to death in the countryside by now, or if it was a madman he'd have been caught and locked up.

'So the three Cranswells took the train back, and in Croglin they were quite happy again, although Amelia always closed her shutters at night, and Edward slept with a pistol under his pillow, just in case. I think he must have bought it in Switzerland.

'Then one winter's night the next year Amelia woke up in a panic. There was the sound of fingernails on glass. Somehow the thing had managed to open her shutters and it was trying to get in again.

'Well, Amelia shouted for her brothers and Michael ran to her room while Edward – pistol in hand – went into the farmyard and saw the tall thin figure in a funny old cloak running away from the farmhouse.

'Edward raised his gun and fired in the moonlight. The monster thing staggered and then went on running, with Edward running after it. The chase went across the fields until they almost reached Croglin village, and the last glimpse Edward had of it was it limping into the Croglin churchyard.

'At dawn Michael and Edward, and a couple of neighbours who were friends of theirs, went to the old graveyard. It was very creepy. There was mist everywhere, and the tombs were overgrown and everything. Anyway, as it got lighter they spread out and began searching among the gravestones.

'Suddenly one of them yelled out. The others crowded round and he pointed at a slab that was out of position, with a sort of grave beneath it in which lay the horrible vampire. It was like a mummy, its flesh all dried out, but in one leg was a hole that had been made by Edward's pistol shot.

'It seemed to be in a sort of trance, so the men got a lot of wood and paraffin and built a bonfire in the corner of the churchyard, and before the sun came up they lifted the thing out of its grave and threw it on the fire.'

For a minute we sat in silence. In spite of myself I had been impressed by Geoffrey's story, but since that trick in the Murder Room I was cautious.

'Is there really a place called Croglin?'

He nodded.

'I looked it up on the map and it's there all right. Even Croglin Low Hall is marked. I say we should go over and talk to the people there, and if they know about the Cranswells then you'll know that there is truth in these things.'

We agreed to take a bus to Croglin village and walk to the Low Hall the next day.

We spent the remainder of the afternoon on Cat Bells. At the highest spot we gazed down at Derwentwater, spread out like a jagged mirror, and the wind pressed Leila's unfashionably long dress against her in a way which I found wonderfully erotic. For once she disregarded Geoffrey and put her arm round me. He stuck his hands in the pockets of his duffle coat and strolled along the skyline, whistling his indifference.

Leila gave me one of her curiously solemn smiles which made me yearn to tell her all that I felt, but she raised her finger to her lips – Geoffrey was returning. Silently I vowed that somehow on the Croglin expedition I would get everything sorted out between us.

As my most vivid recollection of Geoffrey is of him engrossed in his story on Otterbield Island, so the child Leila remains with her finger held in warning to her lips.

Having tied *Pandora*'s painter to the ramshackle jetty, I began my routine trek up the yew avenue, carrying an extra large parcel of sandwiches for the Croglin expedition. Dew had been heavy during the night and webs festooning the willowherb sparkled in the morning sun. Wisps of vapour rose as the earth warmed, some curling from the roof of the Auber mausoleum. And here it was I found Leila waiting, the lower part of her long dress soaked from her walk through the rank grass.

'We can't go to Croglin today,' she said. 'Geoffrey's not well.'

I felt my heart bump. It could be that my moment of truth was upon me.

'What's wrong with him?'

'He says he has a sore throat, but he'll be well enough to go tomorrow.'

'It'll have to be the day after,' I said, sobered by the flight of time. 'I've got to go off somewhere with Mum and Dad, or there'll be more trouble.'

I rolled my eyes upwards in dumb comment on my parents.

'Then I'll see you the day after tomorrow,' Leila said. 'Unless you'd like to spend the rest of today just with me.'

'What do you think?'

She laughed.

'I'd have been hurt if you didn't stay. Want to visit the patient, or play chess, or . . .'

'Let me take you out in *Pandora*.' I waved the sandwiches. 'We can have a picnic on one of the islands.'

She took my hand as we pushed our way through the diamante veils to the jetty, and a minute later she was lounging in the stern seat while I slowly pulled on the oars, trying to control the panic rising in me. There was so much that I wanted to tell Leila, yet I could not think how to begin my declaration. She was content to say nothing, trailing her hand in the water and sometimes humming a tune high in the pop charts.

I rehearsed several futile openings, then decided to count to ten and plunge in. As I did so I was fearful that, surprised I had taken a few kisses so seriously, she might laugh.

. . . *five, six, seven* . . .

What to say? 'Since I've come to Derwentwater I've got very fond of you.'

Not *fond*!

. . . *eight, nine* . . .

The skin above my upper lip beaded with perspiration.

. . . *ten!*

'I love you,' I almost shouted, and caught a crab, so that I tumbled into the bows with my legs pedalling the air.

41

'Martin, what a funny boy you are,' Leila said and collapsed in a giggling fit while I struggled upright and grabbed for a retreating oar.

My face burned with embarrassment and I muttered an apology.

'What are you sorry about – making me laugh, or saying you love me? You should have seen yourself with your legs waving in the air.'

Her laughter was infectious and I felt my mouth twitch, then I was laughing as well. *Pandora* swung in a circle while we sparked each other to further outbursts and then lay exhausted with tears drying on our cheeks.

'Let's go to St Herbert's Island,' Leila said at last. 'And if you must plight your troth, Sir Galahad, wait until we're on dry land or we might get shipwrecked.'

I adjusted the oars in the rowlocks and swung towards the island in the centre of the lake.

'You're a strange boy,' Leila remarked. 'You've hardly told me anything about yourself. You're a mystery – do you know that?'

Me? A mystery? I was amazed. Compared with the Auber twins there could not be anyone more commonplace.

'I'm serious,' she continued. 'Who are you? Do you have any brothers or sisters?'

'I'm an only child,' I admitted with the usual feeling of shame, and waited for the inevitable comment about being spoilt. When Leila said nothing I added, 'Mum says she couldn't have any more babies after me.'

'It must be dreadful for you,' she said. 'Having a brother, I can't imagine what it must be like to be alone – to have no one to think with.'

I shrugged.

'I'll be your sister from now on,' she said but I could see that she was teasing.

'Geoffrey wouldn't like that,' I said, teasing in return.

'No. I suppose being on your own so much has made you grown up . . .'

42

'I've had plenty of company at times . . . when I was in hosital.'

'You've been ill?'

I nodded. In silence we approached St Herbert's Island and I moored *Pandora*.

'Let's find the old hermitage ruins,' said Leila, stepping ashore.

We wandered through trees until we reached the remains of the stone habitation which had been an object of pilgrimage in the fourteenth century.

'There's a funny old legend that some stones from the saint's home were used in the building of the Auber peel-tower,' said Leila. 'And this caused a curse to fall on our ancestors.'

'You sound like Geoffrey.'

'He can't help being an Auber,' she answered. 'Old tales and traditions are in the blood. There *is* supposed to be a family curse but I don't know if it was anything to do with the stones. Anyway, one of them is called the Weeping Stone of Auber. When something bad is going to happen to the family drops of water run out of it like tears.'

'How does the curse work?' I asked as we sat down and I unpacked the sandwiches.

'Father only laughs when we ask him about it. But I think what happens is that an unknown boy comes in a boat and gets soppy. Tell me about hospital . . .'

I began to talk about the funny things – how one boy put a smuggled brick into a bedpan, to the mystification of a nurse who had to remove the covered object during a visiting hour. And I told her about Christmas Day, when the doctors came round in paper hats and there were carols, and a panto by the nurses for those who could leave their beds.

Talking about it brought back memories which had been checked by my new experiences. To my shame tears ran down my cheeks.

'What is it?' Leila was startled by my change of mood. 'Was it something bad?'

I managed to say, 'Henry.' And scrubbed my eyes with a handkerchief and blew my nose.

Leila took my hand and led me back to the boat.

'Sorry about that,' I said as the business of rowing restored my self-control. 'I've never mentioned him before.'

'He was a friend?'

'Yes. For months he was in the bed next to me. The two of us were in a sort of alcove – a mini-ward, they called it. I don't know what was wrong with him – something to do with his chest, I think. He was so thin. Some of the kids called him the Skeleton. We used to talk a lot, especially at night, and we became each other's best friend. Although he couldn't sit up much, he was always full of fun.'

'Was he the one who played the joke with the brick?' Leila asked as *Pandora* entered the inlet.

'Yes. He liked to play tricks when he was having a good spell.'

Walking towards the mausoleum, I found myself telling her about the terrible day.

'After we'd been given our porridge one morning Henry told me he'd peed the bed. I started to tease him but his face was white and sweaty. He asked me to call Sister.

'I yelled for a nurse, and two came running. One pressed an oxygen mask over Henry's face while the other drew the curtains in front of our alcove. A doctor came and gave him a big injection. Sister said it might be best if they wheeled my bed to another part of the ward. Henry said in a sort of gaspy voice that he didn't want to be by himself, and Sister let me stay.

'So we lay in our beds side by side, and he sweated so much that they kept changing his pyjamas, and giving him more injections. While a nurse was fitting up a plasma stand, he whispered to me that he thought he was going to die. I told him he wasn't, but I was terrified. The thought of him dying was just too awful, and I hated myself because there was nothing I could do.'

'Let's sit down,' said Leila, pointing to the steps in front of the bronze doors of the mausoleum.

'The time went awfully slowly,' I said as I sat beside her. Memory of that day was returning so strongly that I had difficulty in controlling my voice. 'Henry slept a bit, and Sister would look in every five minutes to take his pulse and count the number of times he breathed in a minute.

'When Henry was awake again I had an idea – there was something I could do, after all. If I read aloud to him it might take his mind off how bad he felt. I asked him if he'd like that, and I think he nodded his head. I began to read from *Doctor Dolittle*. I read and read but I don't know what – I was just saying the words on the pages, but I couldn't stop.

'All of a sudden Henry sort of raised himself up on his arm, which had a tube plugged into it, and said, "Can't you bloody shut up? It's bad enough to be like this without having to listen to you . . ."

'I dropped the book and turned my head away. It had been silly to read aloud, and I was afraid I'd made him worse. After a couple of minutes I turned my head back and saw bubbles coming from his mouth. I screamed for Sister, and then there were a lot of people around his bed . . . a couple of orderlies lifted him on to a theatre trolley, and a doctor was doing something I couldn't see, and Sister had the mask over his face again, but I knew that . . . that . . .'

My voice failed me. Tears again.

'He was dead,' said Leila.

I nodded.

'How awful,' she said, and put her arms round me.

I can still feel the sensation of comfort as she held me tight and I pressed my face into her silky hair which dried my tears and hid my shame of them. I had never spoken of Henry's death – my parents knew he'd died and it had upset me, but something had prevented me from talking about it as I had to Leila. Probably it was my guilt at irritating him during his last minutes of life. I knew they would tell me I had not, but I knew differently.

It was twelve weeks since Henry had been taken away

with tubes trailing from him, and the passage of time was frightening me. I had a mental picture of an astronaut drifting in space while the ship from which he had been separated glided on until he was a tiny glint in the starshine. I, and the world, were being distanced from Henry.

For a while I did not think of Leila as Leila but just a sympathetic fellow being to cling to during this treacherous spasm of evocation.

We no longer sat on the steps, but lay side by side in the grass in front of the mausoleum, our arms tight round each other. The effect of this brought me out of the past; the image of the orderlies lifting that form – whose head lolled so horribly – faded as reality returned.

And what must Leila be thinking? She had been kind, but from now on she could not help but see me as a cry-baby.

'Sorry,' I murmured in her ear.

'Why be sorry because you miss your friend?' she whispered back. 'Our father says he pities people without the imagination to grieve . . .'

'But I don't want you to pity me.'

'Pity you!' she exclaimed. 'Poor Martin, there's so much you don't understand . . .'

My face moved across hers, pushing the tresses to one side so that our mouths met. And I was aware her cheeks were also tear-moist.

Suddenly there was a shift of emotion within me as I felt currents of sexuality passing between us. The image of dead Henry was replaced by living Leila, and my temporarily displaced yearning for her returned with renewed intensity. Those cathartic tears had left me defenceless against the genes whose paramount objective – it seems to me – is their own duplication in the sequent hosts they create.

My heart beat as though I was running a race, and this pulsation was reflected in the throb of an agonising erection of which Leila must have been well aware, yet to my innocent surprise it in no way repelled her. While I pressed against her, her kisses rained on me so that our

46

faces were sheened with tears and saliva. And my hands—seeming to have desires of their own – slid over the silky material of her dress until a vast sensation of pleasure indicated that they were cupping her small breasts.

I heard her give a small cry – my name, I think – and briefly I felt a pang ·of shame at my roughness, but only briefly. Extraordinary and irresistible forces had been set in motion. The fingers of one hand relaxed, strayed down her body to the hem of her dress and then returned along her leg, a sensuous glissade over smooth skin.

We had scant knowledge of the physical technique of love but it was unimportant. Instinct bore us headlong to our objective with the sureness of that immemorial automatic pilot which steered Adam to joy and death. There was only one thing in the world that mattered, and that was to feel myself fused with Leila.

I took my hand from her to my zip to ease the agonising constriction, and for a second her fingers brushed against me and the blood roared in my ears. My hand returned beneath her dress, finding its way between her thighs, expecting to touch her underwear, but instead there was only the sensation of swansdown and warmth.

That she was wearing nothing beneath her long dress was the final trigger. I knelt above her while she lay back in the grass and together we pulled the dress above her navel. Dizzy, as though about to faint, I fell upon her and, after a moment of despairing failure, she helped me to enter her.

My body responded automatically, carrying me forward as inexorably as the freak wave that had taken possession of *Pandora* on Derwentwater. Stars spun within my head and I felt that my life was bleeding into her.

The wave passed, leaving only contented exhaustion and the conviction that, while Leila was truly mine, she had equally possessed me.

'I do love you,' I murmured.

'Of course,' she said softly as we rolled apart. A plant

with black berries – deadly nightshade, I think – had been caught between us and had left violet stains on our bellies.

Leila shook down her dress and then, as she looked beyond the long grass around us, I saw her stiffen.

I sat up and saw the small figure of Geoffrey on the top of the ornamental steps, swinging a pair of binoculars by their strap.

5

Waking in my attic, I was excited at the prospect of the trip with Leila and Geoffrey after the eternity of yesterday when my father had taken me to Glasgow. He had wanted to see Salvador Dali's *Christ of St John of the Cross* in the city art gallery, and the painting was the only thing I remembered clearly of the outing. I had been fascinated by the crucified figure floating high above the lake, and the minute figures on the shoreline reminded me of other figures on the margin of Derwentwater.

After a fish and chip lunch we drove through the Gorbals, so I could see a very different side of the city. As an object lesson it was wasted: views of grimy streets and black tenements were filtered through erotic recollection.

The only flaw in my happiness at what had passed between Leila and me was a feeling of guilt towards Geoffrey. If he had seen us through his binoculars I knew that he would be shocked – not just shocked but hurt in a way I could sense but not understand. But when we went to him his only remark was that, feeling better, he had brought the old binoculars to show me the mysterious name carved high on the peel-tower. His voice sounded strange, but I told myself it was the result of a sore throat.

Now I wolfed the usual generous breakfast in record time and raced to where *Pandora* was moored, a gift for Leila burning in my pocket. I had spent many hours considering what sort of memento I should give her. With youthful sentimentality I had first considered a ring, but good sense prevailed. It would have suggested an engagement ring, which might have made her burst into laughter. Or she would be embarrassed at having to invent a suitable explanation when it was noticed on her finger. But a small gold cross on a fine chain could be worn secretly and, using cash which had been saved from my pocket money in hospital, I bought one in Keswick.

Rowing towards Auber I suffered none of my previous nervousness at the thought of a serious conversation with Leila. Today there was nothing I could not say to her. I believed that the physical intimacy which had taken us unawares – and which I ached to repeat in more suitable surroundings – had been inspired by a new depth of feeling between us.

Sir Galahad, Leila had called me.

My confidence lasted until I tied the boat to the tilting jetty and walked to the Auber mausoleum. Then, suddenly, I was swamped by a feeling of depression. Despite the sunlight, the house was as sombre as when I had first glimpsed it. It infected me with a psychic chill which sent a physical shudder through me. I knew the magic had gone, that I would not see Leila.

Usually the twins came down the yew avenue to meet me, or I would find them on a paint-peeling garden seat deep in their books. Now the garden was deserted and I had a wild fear that I had been the victim of an illusion, that Auber had been the setting for a sequence of dreams. Then I remembered Leila lying beneath me in the sweet grass, and I knew there was nothing illusory about her smooth skin and secret warmth.

I trudged up the steps to the terrace garden and into the great kitchen. The fire which had always glowed in the old-fashioned stove had withered to a mound of ash. Dirty dishes had been left in greasy piles on the refectory table. Soon, I felt, these would be covered with cobwebs, and dust would settle on the tiled floor as in the palace of the Sleeping Beauty.

I went to Geoffrey's bedroom to confirm what I already knew. His bed was unmade, but his clothes, books and comics were gone, as was his old Ted which had sat in a place of honour on the now empty wardrobe. Had his mysterious father suddenly arrived from Venice and spirited him and his sister away?

Yet the door had been open, which must mean that Mrs Forster was still in residence. Although I knew she disapproved of me as much as she disapproved of the others, she could hardly refuse to tell me what had happened and perhaps I could wheedle their address out of her.

I walked nervously to her sitting-room and found the door ajar, and froze. Mrs Forster – her normally puritan hair hiding half her face – was sprawled on a faded *chaise-longue*. She had no clothes on and was careless about keeping her legs together. Bottles stood on a little circular table nearby, and she was regarding the glass in her hand with a lopsided grin.

Then, from a hidden part of the room, there came a man's laugh.

I ran down the staircase into the great hall, through the cold kitchen and out on to the lawn. Once more I fled down the 'alley Titanic' and I went waist-deep into the water to pull *Pandora* clear. Only when I had to stop rowing to get my breath back did I look up. Above the treetops I glimpsed the gables of Auber as sinister as an illustration in a fairy-tale book.

Hansel and Gretel had gone, and the witch had come into her own.

There is no point in dwelling on that long-ago agony of mind the child I was suffered as we drove south. Behind us was the holiday which my parents had hoped would 'normalise' me before returning to school, and which had carried me to a stranger shore than I had ever dreamed of in hospital.

Already I had posted the first of the letters I wrote to Miss L. Auber with 'please forward' dramatically underlined on the envelope. I believe that years later some were discovered at the back of a dresser drawer in the kitchen of the old house. The question which tormented me as I sat in the back of the Morris was: had Leila and Geoffrey known they would be leaving Auber the day I was to go to Glasgow, or had the sudden departure come as as much of a surprise to them as it had to me?

'Well, son, I hope you enjoyed your holiday,' said my father, parking in Pembridge Square.

'Smashing, thanks,' I said automatically.

'I must say I liked being at Derwentwater again,' he said, satisfied with my efforts at enthusiasm. 'Perhaps we'll have our next holiday there.'

A glimmer of hope!

Because I had missed so much schooling my father sacrificed his socialist principles and enrolled me at a private school in Holland Park, hoping that smaller classes and an old-fashioned philosophy of hard work would enable me to catch up. I began my first day with misgivings, but the teachers must have been aware of my problem because they did what they could to put me at ease and arranged extra lessons while the other pupils were at sport. My homework was increased, and this additional work was welcome as it reduced the time I could spend brooding on the lost world of Auber.

Sometimes a rogue memory would take me by surprise. I might be in a chemistry class, pipette in hand, when I would suddenly see Leila, her finger to her lips as she had placed it that day on Cat Bells. And sometimes my cheeks glowed crimson as recollection became erotic.

Such sudden fits of abstraction provided amusement for my classmates, and I am sure I had a reputation for being peculiar. This was doubtless reinforced by my need to grasp the basics which they had long absorbed. Often I would have to go out to the teacher's table with my textbook and ask him to explain some aspect of an exercise which I could not comprehend. In my eagerness to show him that I was following his explanation – whether I was or not – I formed a habit of continuously repeating 'I see! I see!' which must have been infuriating for him. Nor was it lost on the rest of the class, and I earned the detested nickname of 'I-see'.

Another aspect of those days was my obsession with the postman. Each morning my first action was to see if there was a reply to the letters which I had been sending secretly to Auber. If the postman was late I would dawdle until I knew for sure that I would not be hearing from Leila that day. Oddly enough, I had never seen her handwriting, and on several occasions my heart missed a beat when a letter in a strange hand fluttered to the floor of our hall.

As far as my letters were concerned I might as well have been throwing bottles with messages into the sea. In final desperation I took the little gold cross I had bought for my love in Keswick and posted it to Auber with a letter so passionate that I blushed whenever I thought about it afterwards.

It was my last throw.

After that I did not write again. At school I was gaining ground, and my exclamations of 'I see' diminished, and so did thoughts about Auber. Perhaps I had concentrated so much effort on trying to retain its image that it lost reality. One night I overheard my father say to my mother, 'He certainly seems to be getting back to normal.' And I accepted it as an accolade.

But I was to have one more encounter with the House of Auber before my life changed completely. When the autumn half-term holiday came my father took me back to the Ridleys' guest house outside Keswick, only this time my mother did not come with us.

His literary zeal led him to make pilgrimages to the haunts of the Lake poets. Saying that these might be boring for me, he suggested I might like to go off on my own, perhaps in *Pandora*. Later I was to realise that his need for solitude was greater than mine.

There are fine autumns in the north. Although the mornings and evenings preluded winter, there was still sunshine to encourage late holiday-makers. Once again I was captivated by the moods of Derwentwater, sometimes sombre, cloud-shadowed, and then sparkling when a sudden wind cleared the skies.

As soon as I could I took *Pandora* out and rowed in the direction of the hidden inlet which led to Auber. That morning the surface was a mix of brown and blue, curling and coiling like the colours of an oil slick – the result of a flock of altocumulus clouds drifting over Cumbria.

Once more I tied up at the old jetty, and then walked between the ancient yews. Blackberry bushes clutched at my clothes like cats' claws, and without thinking I chewed their berries, my eyes on the house and wondering if it could be possible that the others had returned.

The familiar door was locked. The downstairs windows were sealed by heavy shutters and the garden had an air of desolation which fitted perfectly with the melancholy seeming to seep from the very stones of the house.

'What d'yeh want, lad?' came a rusty voice.

I turned to see an old man standing behind me. From his clothes and the rake he held I guessed he was a gardener.

'I used to come here, in the spring,' I said. 'I was wondering . . .?'

'Things hev changed sen then,' he said, shaking his head so that a fringe of white hair fell in front of his eyes. 'T'hoose is shut up, and likely teh be, Ah shouldn't wonder. It was in t'papers – don't yeh read t'papers? T'reporter wanted teh talk teh me, but what Ah kent wasn't for him. Nor naebody else.'

'Do you know the address of the Aubers?'

He turned and began to walk away. It seemed to me that he was what used to be called simple.

'Nae address Ah can give,' he said, turning his head. 'It was in t'papers and noo it's best forgitten. Ah'm nobbut employed by t'agent teh keep an eye on things. It's nut a job Ah like – but it helps t'pension. But there's nae address Ah can give yeh, and it's better that way for yeh, young fellow my lad.'

'But surely, someone must know . . .' I said. But the old man had disappeared among the jungle of rhododendrons at the side of the house.

I plunged after him, but he was gone as though by magic

and I returned to the terrace garden. Something within me did not want to find the old man. Obviously he could not help me, and I did not want to hear any more of his talk. I wanted my idyll left intact, and I dismissed his words as just another part of the enigma which was Auber.

I returned along the 'alley Titanic' and stood for a moment by the steps of the mausoleum, looking at the overgrown spot where a few months before Leila had lain beneath me. Now there was nothing to mark my frantic urge to become part of her, no slight monument to what had been the greatest moment I had ever experienced. The grass which we had flattened in our inexpert exertions had grown tall, the bracken which had caught a strand of her hair was withered.

It seemed to my young mind that something of such importance should have lingered, even a psychic ripple in the air, but the ground was dead, as was the whole of the landscape about it. I strained my ears, but even the birdsong was missing. In fact this was nothing particularly unusual for that time of day at that time of year, but to me it seemed like a terrible omen and I hurried to *Pandora* and rowed away with smarting eyes. The feeling of desolation was only lifted when a handful of passengers aboard the *Princess Margaret Rose* waved cheerfully to me.

There was one other journey to be made under the influence of the fading voice of Geoffrey – a final gesture to the past. On the third morning my father seemed relieved when I announced that I would like to go off on my own on the guest house bicycle.

'Have a good time,' he called as I set off with my lunch packet tied to the rusty carrier. It seemed that we were almost embarrassed by each other's company, and had I been less obsessed with the past I would have realised that this return to Derwentwater was as traumatic for him as it was for me.

From Keswick I took a crooked route towards the Eden Valley. To my southern ear the places I wobbled past had a hint of alien adventure . . . Greystoke – wasn't Tarzan really

Lord Greystoke? Unthankend – did that mean thankless? Thiefside Cottages, Blaze Fell, Baron Wood . . . all places where strange happenings must surely have taken place.

Finally I ate my lunch wearily under a sign which pointed towards Croglin Low Hall.

The old grey farmhouse was easy enough to find. There was a drive lined with large trees, and I came to a stop where a small brook gurgled close to a stone arch leading into the walled farmyard.

I wheeled my bicycle through it and saw a lady in a floral dress throwing food to her peacocks.

'May I take a photograph of your house, please?' I said, holding up the old camera.

'Of course,' the farmer's wife replied. 'It's an interesting place – used to be fortified once, and not so long ago we found a priesthole.'

I listened politely as she told me about her home, but I dared not mention the vampire story – she would think I was silly. I took photographs and felt disappointment that nothing was mentioned to confirm Geoffrey's story. I began to think that he had seen Croglin on a map – certainly it was an evocative name – and made up the story to fit it.

I put the camera away and thanked the lady. Just as I was turning to go I suddenly noticed that a ground-floor window had been bricked up. Seeing my interest, she said, 'That was done after Miss Cranswell was attacked by the vampire.' And she related the story Geoffrey had told us on Otterbield Island.

As I started the long journey back to Keswick with aching calves I felt happier than I had since the day I had found the others gone – in some way this corroboration of Geoffrey's story confirmed their reality. And it was something that I was to bless years later.

When we returned to Pembridge Square there was an envelope on the kitchen table with my father's name written in my mother's hand.

'Mum's left you a note, Dad,' I called as he brought the suitcases in. Instead of taking up the envelope, he carefully put water in the electric kettle to make tea.

'I'm afraid there's going to be some bad news,' he said. 'Put your things away in your room while I read this.'

I became aware that the flat was not quite the same. There were gaps in the bookcase, the pile of records was missing – then I saw that the radiogram had gone as well, and in my parents' bedroom the open door of the wardrobe revealed its emptiness.

'Dad!'

I ran into the kitchen, and saw that my father's bottom lip was trembling.

Horror filled me. Was I going to see him cry?

Instead he turned and poured me a cup of tea. When he faced me again I felt a sense of relief – he was not going to break down and my illusion of him was safe.

Quietly he told me that Mother had left and would not be coming back.

'I wasn't right for her,' he said, more to himself than me. 'And of course this is no surprise. I think I went to Derwentwater to give her the chance – she didn't have much courage when it came to confrontations.'

He sighed.

'We got married for the wrong reason . . .' And it seemed to me that I must be that reason.

'But where's Mum?' I asked, dizzy with the realisation that our family pattern was broken.

'She doesn't say, but I expect she's gone to a chap she used to know at art school. I suppose it's best for one to be happy rather than both miserable . . .'

But what about me? a voice shrieked in my brain.

'Of course, you'll be seeing her . . . once the dust settles . . .'

That never happened. A couple of months later my father and I flew to New Zealand where he had arranged to be transferred to a publishing house which was a subsidiary of the company he worked for in London.

And so my father and I began a new life in Wellington.

From the first I loved the city, with its tier upon tier of white houses rising up steep hills around the world's most beautiful land-locked harbour. My first sight of it was from the Air New Zealand DC10 and, as we had flown into the antipodean summer, the upper slopes of the hills were ablaze with the wild gorse which is the city's natural livery.

Riding in from the airport to the terminal in Customhouse Quay, we were delighted with the verandah-covered streets, the trams and the crowds of people who, to our alien gaze, looked as though they were all on holiday in their light summer clothing.

We settled in a small wooden house perched in an alarmingly-angled garden in a hill suburb called Kelburn. Its picture windows gave us a breath-taking view of the city, especially at night when it looked like a galaxy above which we were drifting in a starship. Another of my joys was the cable car which my father rode each day to his work in Cuba Street – the Oxford Street of Wellington.

He buried himself in his new job, and my regret over the break-up was dulled by new impressions. I was happy to exchange the hated nickname 'I-see' for a few good-natured jibes about Pommies. My school mates were friendly – they were used to immigrants in that area – and it was natural that I tried to emulate them. Within a few weeks my vowels began to lengthen and after a year I was a dinkum Kiwi.

As my teenage years passed I thought less and less about England. Sometimes I wondered about my mother, who never missed sending me a card for Christmas and birthdays, but the strongest images to remain were those I had absorbed during my highly receptive state after leaving hospital, images which were focused on Derwentwater.

New Zealand is a land of mountains and lakes, and such scenery inevitably invoked my Auber dreamscape. During the long hot Christmas holidays I went camping in remote places where the dark green bush was as it had been for thousands of years, and I enjoyed a growing empathy with these solitudes. At first I went with my father, who had become a great outdoors man, and when high school was changed for the Wellington teachers' training college I went with companions of my own age.

English became my favourite subject and I joined the Poetry Society – the childish author of *Black Days in Dark Ages* still lurked somewhere in my mental background. I had several light-hearted affairs with fellow students – girls who came with me in group outings to Day's Bay beach, the Trentham Races or college dances – and in my final year I began to go steady with Dawn, one of those golden-skinned children of the Pacific to be found on the beaches down under or along the Californian coast.

It was with Dawn that I got an unwelcome inkling there might be something psychic about me. One wintry Sunday afternoon we were wandering the windswept streets of the city when we came to a spiritualist church where, according to a placard, a meeting was in progress.

We went in, partly out of curiosity but mainly to escape an onslaught of rain carried by the cruel southerly wind which is the winter scourge of Wellington. The hymn in progress made us giggle into our handkerchiefs.

'*Knocking . . . who is knocking?*' was one of the gloomy lines.

After a sermon in which sheets of automatic writing – said to have been transmitted from the world beyond by Queen Astrid of Belgium – were displayed, a cadaverous medium, Mr Flett, was invited to pass on spirit messages. He had a spirit guide called White Feather who was so eager to communicate that at times Mr Flett tersely asked him to 'slow down'. Dawn and I were nearly in hysterics as he surveyed the congregation and then pointed out a lady. 'Does the name Eva mean anything to you?'

She pondered for a minute and then agreed it did.

'Wait a minute, White Feather' – to the invisible brave –

'yes, I have it. You are to remember the 25th of next month. Does that mean anything?'

The woman shook her head.

'Never mind, it will. Just hold it in your mind. Now, I have a message from Babs – does anyone have a dear departed by the name of Babs, Barbara . . . Bob?'

Someone knew a Robert who had passed over, and an inconsequential communication via White Feather was relayed.

Dawn caught my eye.

'Phoney!' she mouthed.

'Too true,' I mouthed back.

Suddenly my humour evaporated as I saw a tiny old woman gazing at him with hope in her eyes. A sense of sadness filled me and I felt aghast at the loneliness which drove people to come to this charade and pray for ambiguous messages. 'Your dear departed remembers you and surrounds you with love . . .' 'Your wife? Yes, White Feather says it is. She will be waiting for you . . .' 'James – is that right, a brother? Yes, it's your brother. He's worried about your health. He wants you to have a check-up.'

I felt anger against the obnoxious Flett. So many of his statements were really questions which, when answered, seemed like affirmations to those desperately anxious to believe, which seemed to be everyone in the hall.

I felt a nudge from Dawn as he regarded me.

'Young man, I am getting a strong communication for you . . . White Feather is giving me a picture, a lake, and a humped hill behind it – something to do with a cat . . . belling the cat . . .'

'Cat Bells!' I exclaimed involuntarily.

He nodded.

'I have something to say to you, privately. Please see me after our meeting.'

At the end of the service Dawn and I waited until the handshaking and the donning of damp raincoats was completed, then we found ourselves in a little room at the back of the hall with Mr Flett.

'I am given your name as Martin,' he said. 'Is that right?'

I nodded.

'Martin, are you a spiritualist?'

'No. I was just interested and came in.'

'Perhaps you were led, who knows? Our destinies are moved by mysterious forces. I asked you to see me like this because the message which came through was perhaps unsuitable for a public meeting. You have a strong psychic streak. Have you been aware of it?'

I tried to answer, aware that beside me Dawn was trying to control a giggle.

'I don't think so,' I said.

'Hmm. You may find that you have certain powers as time goes on. I feel you have this possibility, and with application you could develop it . . . However, does the name Henry mean anything?'

I looked puzzled for a moment.

'Hold that, then. He has a message . . . he says that you must beware the lake . . .'

'Henry!' I exclaimed. 'I once knew a Henry . . .'

'And he passed over?'

I nodded. 'And the lake?' I said. 'What lake?'

'Just the lake . . . and a room . . .' He looked at me closely. 'I sense a room in which a wickedness took place – there is an old evil there. Death.'

'The Murder Room,' I said.

'Murder – yes. Does this mean something to you?'

'Not much.'

'No matter. We are establishing credentials, as you might say.'

For a moment he closed his eyes.

'White Feather brings a message from your mother . . .'

'But my mother's not dead.'

Mr Flett shook his head impatiently. 'She wants you to know she is sorry . . . yes, sorry. She loves you, she wants you to know that, but she failed you. This thought will not let her have peace . . . forgiveness. She wants forgiveness.' He opened his eyes. 'I hope White Feather's message has not disturbed you too much. Please come again. I am sure there is a great potential.'

Outside the hall Dawn said, 'Was that all junk or was there something in it? You certainly went pale.'

'When I was a kid, in England, I got a big fright in an old room they called the Murder Room.'

'That's it, then. It's not spooks, but some sort of telepathy.'

'But I wasn't thinking about the Murder Room, or poor Henry.'

'No, but they were filed away subconsciously and old Flett has some trick of – of picking your memory bank. I wonder if he realises that or whether he really believes in White Feather.'

'What puzzles me is that business about my mother,' I said. 'Surely Dad would have heard if she'd died.'

'Unless it's only just happened,' said Dawn with a slight shudder.

For the next few days I ran anxiously to the tin letterbox mounted on our gatepost, but nothing arrived from England, and the sound of the telephone – which made my heart bump unpleasantly – never heralded bad news. Finally the arrival of my usual birthday card convinced me that my mother was still among the living. I never went back to the spiritualist church.

That summer college days came to an end. It had been a time which I greatly enjoyed. Apart from a wearying pain in my back after long hours swotting for exams at my bedroom table, there was nothing I could complain of. The shadow cast by the House of Auber had long faded into limbo, and there was an unreal quality about my old life in England, as though it was something recollected from a dream.

Now the adult world of having to fend for oneself, of having to make a living, was upon us students. My companions would be scattered to do their probationary years in the four corners of the dominion, and there was a touch of sadness in our end–of–term revels.

Perhaps to make our carefree life spin out longer, a friend in my section named John Richardson invited Dawn and me to spend a few days on his father's boat on Lake Waikaremoana.

With his girlfriend Helen and another student couple, we travelled north by railcar. It was a jolly party. We liked to think we were 'bohemian' – a sadly missed word now – and, after making an inroad into our supply of DB Lager, began singing unofficial college songs.

> 'Oh, be kind to our web–footed friends,
> 'Cause a duck may be somebody's mother . . .'

Looking back, it was all very innocent. Some passengers joined in with us so that a movable party developed while the carriages flashed over the alluvial plains and up the eroded ranges of the east coast.

John's father was a prosperous wine–grower on the Poverty Bay flats. He took us on the last leg of the journey to Lake Waikaremoana where his thirty-foot cruiser *Hinemoa* was moored.

'You look after her, Jonno,' he cried, when we had climbed aboard with our grips and were casting off. 'There's a couple of harvests invested in her.' With a wave he drove off in his truck, a pall of pumice dust marking his progress down the rough country road. He had loaded several cases of his wine aboard. 'In case of snakebite,' he explained. There are no snakes in New Zealand, but as *Hinemoa* began her cruise round the great lake we still took precautions against them.

It was a glorious blue day, the boat seeming to hang between a vast sky and the water reflecting it. The girls cooked sausages and kumaras – ugly sweet potatoes with delicious yellow flesh – and we took turns to steer and fish, and drink the wine, usually referred to as Poverty Bay Plonk or PBP.

It was also an important day for Dawn and me. Without talking about it, we both knew it was a point of departure – so far we had not slept together but now our bags were stowed together in the small forward cabin.

When the sun dowsed itself in the western waters, we glided into a small bay and John threw out the anchor. After supper we sat drinking PBP, laughing over our favourite college recollections and playing pop tapes on the cruiser's hifi system. It was an idyll, three pairs of lovers in a world of their own beneath the crystalline arch of the Milky Way.

As the others began dancing on the sundeck, Dawn and I went to the bows and leaned on the pulpit rail. I slipped my arm around her and we pointed out constellations to each other and made wishes when meteors ruled silver lines across the sky.

Suddenly she turned to me.

'Is it going to be all right, Martin?'

'Of course.'

'Then kiss me.'

She turned to me and as I bent towards her I noticed the lights of a small Maori settlement.

Her arms tightened round me but I did not respond. The lights reflected on the water in a way that took me back to the night I had rowed out on Derwentwater and glimpsed the mysterious gala.

And then it seemed that I was back there, back in *Pandora* while the costumed figures moved to unheard music, and someone was running, and I knew that in a moment I would be torn away from the sight by the bottom wind . . .

'Martin,' Dawn was saying. 'Where have you gone?'

In the starshine her face came back into focus, but for a moment I did not recognise her. I was still a boy on a lake on the other side of the world.

'I'm Dawn, remember me? – the sheila who's going to give her all for you.' There was a note of anger underlying her mockery.

'Sorry,' I said, shaking my head.

'You OK?'

'Yes. Something seemed to come over me.'

'I'll say. I hope it's not too much PBP.'

I laughed and kissed her and soon the incident was dismissed as one of my 'weirdo moods' – something which Dawn attributed to my Pommy origins.

That night in our little cabin I committed my only infidelity to her. After kisses and caresses a surge of passion locked us together, and as I felt her moving eagerly to receive me it was no longer Dawn I held in my arms but a grave-faced child with silver-gold hair.

6

My probationary year passed at a junior school in Lower Hutt, a suburb to the north of Wellington whose bungalow-type houses, each with its individual garden, provided a setting which later made me feel at home in California. I saw Dawn constantly and I knew that our friends – and my father – expected the announcement of our engagement when we finally qualified as teachers. I knew Dawn was hurt that I had not proposed after our idyll on Lake Waikaremoana, for, despite the ripples of the women's liberation movement lapping our shores, the expected way to prove one's love to a girl was to marry her and provide her with what her parents would acknowledge as 'a lovely home'.

Her unspoken disappointment made me feel increasingly guilty. At times I was desperate to conform to what was expected of me, and make her – and therefore us – happy. Yet I was held back by a stronger instinct which, had I tried to explain it to Dawn, I would have found almost impossible to put into words. Then I could not recognise warning signals from the unconscious, and I really believed I was being cruel and perverse. If only we could continue as part-time lovers, yet as we entered the third term I accepted that changes in my life would be inevitable.

Not only would Dawn and I have to come to a decision about our relationship, but if I was to remain a teacher I would have to sign an agreement to work for the Department of Education for at least three years. I had the feeling that I was about to enter a cul-de-sac. And with my feeling of panic came the conviction that before I committed myself I should return to England.

I told Dawn that I wanted to see my mother again, and do the Young New Zealander's grand tour of Europe, before settling down.

'Why not come with me?' I said enthusiastically. 'We'll buy a Vespa and travel the Continent on it. We'll see what swinging London's all about, and after a year we'll come home.'

She was tempted. It was the fashionable thing for young people to do, and we finally decided that I should go on ahead to get everything organised and when she had saved up her fare she would join me. I had enough money to leave when the term ended, because I had spent the previous summer holidays as a labourer in the freezing chambers of the Petone meat works. The seasonal influx of sheep to be slaughtered and chilled sent overtime pay soaring.

The day my school broke up Dawn and I had a farewell supper at the Moonlight – our favourite Chinese restaurant – which we both found heart-wrenching. As we tried to make jokes and speak light-heartedly, a voice in my head was urging me to call the whole thing off – to settle comfortably with this highly attractive girl and enjoy the good life which I might be about to lose.

I was opening my lips to announce I had changed my mind when a second voice swamped the first with my old fears of entrapment and the absolute necessity of returning to England. And even then, while a victim of this conflict, I wondered what it was that was really drawing me back.

Next morning my father drove me to the airport.

'Good luck, old son,' he said as I joined a queue with my new passport at the ready. 'Keep in touch, and make the most of your travels. When you see your mother . . . no, it doesn't matter. Send me a card from Derwentwater if you should go that way. It was rather good there.'

I nodded, not trusting myself to speak, struck by the reality of parting from my father, who had been so important in my life.

'I'll be back in Godzone in a year, Dad,' I managed to say at last. He just smiled, and then I was moving through the barriers into a new life.

It was snowing when I arrived in London, and with so many Christmases celebrated with barbecues or beach parties, I was delighted with the Christmas card effect. I found a room in a street of terraced houses in Hammersmith whose very seediness struck me as 'atmospheric' – what a pity fogs and gaslamps were a thing of the past! – and already I was choosing adjectives to describe it in an aerogramme to Dawn. It was only when I made my pilgrimage to Pembridge Square and gazed at our old flat amid dancing snowflakes that I comprehended that the city had once been my home. I sought out my old school and a few shops which I suddenly recalled with affection, but I remained a stranger between two worlds.

This feeling of unreality was not helped by a visit I made to Eastbourne to see my mother. Feeling highly nervous when I caught the train at Victoria Station, I wondered how I should greet a parent I had not seen for ten years. A sedate taxi took me through streets with pink pavements to a block of flats which overlooked the downs.

When the door opened I stood foolishly silent and thrust the pot of miniature roses at the woman who stood on the threshold. My awkwardness was caused by the momentary panic of not knowing whether it really was my mother. Obviously I had expected her to look older, but it seemed there was nothing in common between this thin nervous woman and the mental image I had carried for so long.

'Martin, is it really you?'

I nodded and stepped inside. How she had altered, grey threads in her hair, skin that had become paper-textured, and a suspicious, birdlike movement of her head.

'Mother?' I managed to say. For a moment her eyes glistened. Then she quickly ushered me into the living-room where I recognised our old radiogram and several paintings.

'Robin has gone – he won't be back,' she called from the kitchen where she had hurried to make tea. I did not know whether she meant he had tactfully gone out for the day, or whether he had left her for good. I was too embarrassed to ask.

Over tea, as I told her something of my life in New Zealand, her expression showed disapproval of my accent.

'I should imagine it suits your father,' she said. I replied that it did, and went on enthusiastically about his appointment to the board of the publishing company and how he was becoming a name in local politics.

'I'm surprised he's not remarried.'

'He has a good friend.'

'He would have. He's all right, isn't he? Nice and comfortable. But what about me?'

'I hardly know anything about you,' I said. 'As I grew up I hoped you had found what you wanted with – er – Robin.'

'You don't know the problems I've had, Martin. All your father's fault. If I hadn't been forced to leave him, if only he had been different. Of course, you're a man now and couldn't understand. Men are all the same – so bloody egotistical. Even Rob . . .'

I began to see that her interest in me was as someone to complain to about my father, and I had not come all this way to listen to ancient bitterness.

'You gave me quite a scare a couple of years ago,' I said to change the subject, and I went on to describe the 'message' relayed to me at the spiritualist church by the odious Mr Flett. She became interested in this and asked me the date.

'I was ill at that time, Martin. Things had got too much and . . . well, never mind that. I was really unwell, and naturally I was thinking about you. The medium must have picked up my thought waves.'

'I'm sure that was it,' I said. 'I was scared you were in the spirit world, but I think that all that business was merely telepathy. I was quite good at it as a child . . .'

'When was that?'

'I experimented with it with those friends I made at Derwentwater. We used to get a pack of cards . . .'

'Oh, wasn't that a boring holiday! All that countryside, and your father behaving like a Rover Scout.'

When I left my mother's flat to catch an evening train it was not the snow which made me shiver but the sense of human isolation which I was thankfully leaving behind me. Robin, I sensed, had not lived up to my mother's expectations. And nor had I.

In London I became a supply teacher, and after my orderly class in Lower Hutt I was stunned by the anti-social behaviour of the classes which I took over, sometimes for a few days and sometimes for several weeks – frequently, it seemed, when the usual teacher was having sick leave. I could see why nervous breakdowns were an occupational hazard. It only took the first morning to lose my treasured college theories along with my belief that education should be an enjoyable experience for both pupils and teacher. All the headmaster required of me was to keep order – any sort of order would do provided the shouts and jeers of my riotous class could not be heard in the corridor. What shocked me more than the swearing and abuse of my pupils were the defeated faces I saw in the staffroom and the pettiness which replaced lost illusions.

Each morning I dreaded what I knew would be, in spite of my best efforts, another wasted day – a day of pretending not to hear when I was sworn at and struggling through lessons while the pupils chatted or vied with each other to give comic answers. Perhaps I had been unlucky with the school – perhaps the next would be better. Meanwhile I carried on to earn the money for the grand tour with Dawn.

Three months after my arrival I found a letter waiting for me addressed in her handwriting. The moment I picked it off the mat made ragged by my landlady's smelly labrador I knew to expect bad news. Her letters, which had arrived in batches to begin with, had slackened off of late. This one began, 'Dear Martin, I am sure this will not come as a surprise to you . . .' And she went on to tell me that she was going to be married to John – good old Jonno who had taken us to Waikaremoana.

It did come as a surprise, and as I vainly endeavoured to get drunk in a cheerless pub that evening I burned with self-hatred for throwing away my chance of happiness with Dawn. I was tempted to make a desperate telephone call to Wellington and 'talk it out' with her, but thankfully the flask of brandy I smuggled into my room when the pub closed saved me from making a maudlin fool of myself.

Next day I was suffering from a throbbing head and a broken heart, and when a mini race riot erupted in my classroom I hardly had the energy to quell it.

The headmaster blamed me, probably rightly, for not being able to control the youngsters – and I retorted that I could not be expected to keep order when the system itself regarded discipline as a dirty word.

'This is the bloody play-way gone mad,' I said through a mist of black spots from last night's lonely debauch.

'Discipline!' he retorted. 'A proper teacher can keep a class happy without *discipline*. I suspect that your failure is because you can't use a *sjambok* in this country.'

The headmaster had it fixed firmly in his mind that I was South African.

A few minutes later I trekked over the vast concrete playground, the only consolation in my life the knowledge that my teaching career was over.

A few days after my resignation I became a journalist in my father's old publishing company.

'Nothing like a spot of nepotism to open the right door,' said the editorial director, 'but once the door is open it's up to you. All that counts is the number of good column inches you provide.'

The nepotism paid off. I fell in love with my new career – I had always wanted to write and now I was being well paid to do it. I sent Dawn a cable of congratulations.

I had been working on *Newsview* for nearly a year when I looked up from my typewriter one morning to see the features editor shuffle through the office door with a fan of invitations in his hand.

'Free drinks with this lot,' he said. 'Anyone interested?'

'Any for Buck House?' asked the Canadian girl who wrote the television column.

'Not today, but there's the opening of a new boutique in Bond Street with pink champagne guaranteed. There's a party to launch Poxy's new LP – there'll be spirits there. And an artist named Auber is having a preview of his exhibition at Leighton House – rotgut sherry . . .'

'Who did you say the artist was?' I asked.

'Auber – Geoffrey Auber – an up and coming young man in the art world.'

'I'll take it,' I said, holding my hand out for the invitation printed in gold on a pale grey card.

'You Aussies really are culture vultures,' the features editor said, making his ritual joke of pretending to think I was Australian.

'Too true, cobber,' I replied dutifully. 'If it wasn't for the flamin' culture I'd be back in Blue Mud Creek.'

My mind filled with a crowd of jostling memories conjured up by the name Auber. And for the rest of the day I was haunted by the question – would Leila Auber be at her brother's preview?

That rainswept evening I was glad to enter the strange calm of Leighton House after an unpleasant walk from the Underground station. Once the home of Victorian artist Baron Leighton – exalted for such paintings as *The Bath of Psyche* – the house retained his exotic decoration with its dark carved wood, Gothic stained glass and Moorish tiles, and proved to be a highly suitable setting for the paintings I was about to see. I found my way along a dim hall to the brightly lit gallery used for exhibitions. From the hall it looked like a stage peopled with tightly-knit groups of actors with drinks in their hands. Only a couple of loners were prowling the walls and actually looking at the paintings.

For a moment the group centre stage parted. A girl with a tray of sherry, which was far from rotgut, briefly broke it up, and I saw a slim young man with a halo of fair hair round his fine, sensitive face. Geoffrey Auber.

He was dressed in black – velvet had just become fashionable for men – with a white turtle-necked shirt, and even from this distance I could see that he retained a gracefulness which I suddenly remembered he had possessed as a child. And from the animated faces surrounding him it appeared that he had not lost his gift as a raconteur.

On Geoffrey's left, and half a step behind him, stood a beautiful young woman. Everything about her was an invocation of the Pre-Raphaelites – her russet-hued un-fashionable yet sensational silken dress and heavy golden chain, her tall, slender body, elegant limbs and cascading hair whose colour matched that of King Cophetua's beggar maid, and, above all, her pale delicate face with large greenish eyes so capable of expressing mystery or sorrow. From the expression with which those eyes regarded Geoffrey her devotion to him was obvious. Together they made a magnificent couple.

The sight of them made me conscious of my own mediocrity. Along with childhood memory returned my childhood awkwardness, and I remained in the shadows watching the stylish guests so alive with an intellectual confidence left over from the sixties.

On Geoffrey's right stood a man I recognised from an illustrated feature which had appeared in *Newsview* on the benefits of hypnotherapy. Oliver Penthorne was a highly successful practitioner in this field, and in the mohair suit which perfectly fitted his rotund body he looked highly successful. In his mid-fifties, the smooth skin of his plump face, eyes as innocent as two blue marbles and receding hair gave him a curious baby look. One felt if one was close to him he would smell of milk and talcum powder.

The group closed again and for a moment I felt like turning away. Was it that I did not want my freshly awakened recollections of Derwentwater to be overlaid by new impressions of Geoffrey Auber? But a girl, one of those cool Bond Street beauties who seem born to inhabit the world of expensive art galleries, checked me against her list and gave me a glass of sherry and a catalogue. Curiosity overcame my reluctance to join the crowd of critics and art journalists, and I stepped into the light. In the catalogue – whose prices told me how highly Geoffrey was regarded in the field of contemporary art – a section headed 'Subterraneans' caught my interest. I saw the reason for the group title when I joined the loners gazing at the paintings.

These Subterraneans gave me that *frisson* which comes with the emotional recognition of one's empathy with a work of art, a passage of music or a natural view which is perfect in itself. I felt a surge of admiration for my boyhood friend, and I remembered him saying lightly that he would be an artist or a musician – 'it runs in the family' – and I wondered whether if he had turned to music it would hold the same hint of menace. Geoffrey's art had the same elusive, disquieting quality as de Chirico's surreal colonnades.

A typical picture, entitled *Subterranean 5*, was executed in smooth tempera and showed an immensely long rectangular tunnel with low uninterrupted walls dwindling into the perspective. Without any other detail it gave the claustrophobic impression that it was far below the surface of the earth, but what made it so striking was that, although there was no light source visible, the cavity was pervaded by an intense luminosity as though it had the capacity to create its own illumination.

'Phantasmagorical!' exclaimed a lady with burnished

copper jewellery behind me. 'A perfect expression of the unconscious.'

Later, when I combed all the art journals to see how Geoffrey's work had been received, I saw that she had used the same words in her review in *Icarus*.

A whole wall was devoted to the Subterranean series, and each picture was a variation on the theme of the angular catacomb. The one which affected me most depicted a tunnel with that curious sterile light, in which a human shadow was hinted at so cunningly that I could almost picture the figure which had just vanished round a distant corner.

'What a perfect illustration for Lovecraft,' a man with a New York accent remarked to the lady from *Icarus*.

'It's pre-natal memory,' she replied. 'And a virtuoso example of chiaroscuro.'

'To me it's creepsville,' he said. 'I expect to see Vincent Price coming into view at any second.'

I recalled the young Geoffrey telling me the story of the Croglin vampire on Otterbield Island.

Moving to another wall, I found the paintings less *outré*, being landscapes which I recognised with growing nostalgia. On every scene Geoffrey had managed to put his individual stamp, that anxious hint of menace which in these paintings suggested nature holding its breath prior to some extraordinary occurrence. When there were human figures in these landscapes they were dwarfed by Lakeland features – a solitary walker made insignificant by Skiddaw's bulk – and yet it was not merely accomplished by contrast in size. In a painting of the Castlerigg stone circle there was a human figure in the foreground, but such was the skill with which the old stones were delineated that an impression was created – at least for me – of the human spirit made Lilliputian by the immensity of unknown forces and undreamed dimensions.

If I had had the perception to analyse those paintings in Leighton House instead of accepting them at face value how different this story would have been!

With my back to the chattering crowd I came to the third wall and was immediately attracted to a painting of the House of Auber – an Auber slightly out of focus, if one can apply a photographic term to a work of art, and yet so evocative that I could almost hear the surf-sound of the forest behind the walls of yew. The painting had been done from the avenue, with the mausoleum in the foreground. A wild poppy glowed where Leila and I had once lain slaking our childhood passion.

I looked up the painting in the catalogue and found that it could be mine for five hundred guineas – a nice old-fashioned touch – and it was entitled *Ulalume*. What else?

The last picture listed was not for sale and was the only portrait in the exhibition. A young woman stood against a seascape whose vividness suggested the Mediterranean, blue sea merging into blue air, and a strong wind held a strand of silver-gold hair across her face while she regarded the artist with a faint smile expressing a complicity which could never be put into words. It was, of course, Leila Auber a decade on.

'That's neat,' the American said beside me. 'The *Mona Lisa* had better watch out.'

I stood for a long time in front of the portrait, a little disturbed by the images it recalled which, in truth, I had believed were safely buried under layers of new experience.

'You seem to be very interested in that portrait.'

'Yes,' I said, turning to Geoffrey. The Pre-Raphaelite girl stood half a step behind him like an acolyte.

My face puzzled him.

'You're from . . .?'

'The past,' I said with a smile.

'The Boy!' he cried. 'You're the Boy!'

We looked at each other not knowing what to say next – how to resume a conversation left off half a lifetime ago?

I wanted to shout, 'Why the hell did you and Leila leave without a word to me?' Instead I said inanely, 'You've hardly changed . . .' And we both laughed.

'Anyway, congratulations,' I continued, waving my hand round the gallery. 'You've certainly accomplished what you said you'd do.'

'The child is father of the man. And you?'

'Fleet Street. Is . . . ?'

Did he know what I was going to ask, or was I being over-sensitive? For he turned quickly to the girl and said, 'I'm forgetting my manners. Dian, this is Martin Winter, a childhood chum. And this is my very good friend and mentor, Oliver Penthorne . . .'

The introductions were exchanged. Dian Derbyshire merely inclined her head. Oliver Penthorne extended the most carefully manicured hand I had ever seen and, calling me 'dear boy', spoke enthusiastically of Geoffrey's work.

Over his shoulder I saw a beautiful black girl in a white trouser suit approaching. What appeared at first glance to be her shoulder bag turned out to be a tape recorder, and I recognised Charity Brown of Radio City. Geoffrey was certainly doing well to have such a celebrated radio reporter cover his show.

'Hi, Mr Auber,' she called. 'Can we have a few words?'

'Of course,' said Geoffrey. Turning back to me he said, 'Sorry, Martin, I'm rather on duty here. Give me a call at this number and we'll arrange to meet for a meal.'

He scrawled a telephone number on my catalogue.

'Now, Charity . . .'

I took a final look at Leila's portrait, retrieved my trench-coat and went into the winter night. I was elated at having met Geoffrey again, and yet the prospect of learning more about Auber gave me an unexpected pang of unease akin to the feeling inspired by the Subterranean paintings.

7

For several days I hestitated to dial the number Geoffrey had given me, yet I could not say what it was that held me back. I puzzled myself – I had been genuinely pleased to meet him again, and it would be interesting to learn what had happened to him after that unexpected departure from Auber which had filled me with secret grief. And by seeing him I would have news of Leila . . .

Was that it? Was I afraid of what he might tell me about her – her love affairs, or even marriage?

Sitting in the reporters' room, watching dribbles of rain creep down the window panes, I was filled with a sense of shock. Could it possibly be that in some secret recess of my psyche I was still in love with a grave-faced child I had once thought of as Gretel – a child who no longer existed?

'Rubbish!' I said aloud, to the amusement of my colleagues. I picked up my telephone and asked the switchboard for an outside line.

'Martin, I was hoping you would ring,' said Geoffrey. 'I say, where did you get that dreadful accent? We must meet as soon as possible. I'm staying with Oliver Penthorne, so why not come round here tomorrow evening, if you're free? Do you know Frognal, off Finchley Road?'

I found that Oliver Penthorne's apartment consisted of two upper floors of one of those huge houses of Edwardian brick which line Frognal, a spacious setting for a man who obviously enjoyed playing the role of host.

'Enter, dear boy,' he said cordially as I shook his manicured hand. The other held a slender glass of champagne. 'You'll find Geoffrey holding court as the Great Artist,' he added as he ushered me into a hall which was as large as most normal-sized rooms. It was expensively and effectively decorated with rose wallpaper which had the texture of raw silk, and oriental rugs scattered on highly-polished parquet. Illumination came from a number of ornate Persian lamps hanging from silver chains. There was a whiff of Scheherazade in the air.

Setting out that evening I had expected to find Geoffrey alone, but when I entered a large drawing-room – one wall of which held Oliver's collection of Russian icons – I found that he was in fact holding court. A semicircle of guests was hanging on his words while the beautiful Dian Derbyshire sat at his feet on a large cushion. Seeing me, he jumped to his feet and shook my hand enthusiastically, then quickly introduced me to a dozen people, none of whose names I managed to catch but who I gathered were associated with the art world.

'And you remember Dian?'

'Of course.'

She inclined her head in recognition and then smiled up at Geoffrey as he resumed his seat and anecdote. I had looked forward to a meeting where we could chat freely, and I wondered if he had deliberately invited me when a party was in progress to prevent my becoming too inquisitive. But before long I learned that this was not a party by Oliver Penthorne's standards. He had visitors most evenings and I guessed that his practice was socially orientated. Now he took me by the arm and led me to the far end of the room.

'Do have some champers,' he said. 'And while Geoffrey is in full spate let me show you my new St Nicholas which I got at Sotheby's last week. I'm still thrilled with it.'

While he poured my drink I examined the icon. It showed only the face and body of the saint, the rest of the picture being covered with a silver riza decorated with gilt wire.

'Isn't it exquisite?' he said with his wide-eyed baby smile. 'Here's cheers, dear boy.'

'You're very kind.'

'I like to keep in with the press,' he replied, and I knew he meant it. 'Newsview treated me very kindly in that article on hypnotherapy. My waiting list increased as a result.'

'People who want to give up smoking and that sort of thing?'

'Most of my patients are male, and mostly middle-aged to elderly. I treat them for lack of confidence, hypertension and what are euphemistically referred to as "personal problems" – in other words they can't get it up, dear boy. The spirit is desperate but the flesh languid.'

His candour made me laugh.

'The profit from impotence allows me to continue my private researches into hypnotism, a subject which is like an unknown continent where the explorers have only set foot on the beach so far. Do you know anything about it?'

I shook my head.

'Later I'll be giving a little demonstration which you may find amusing. Meanwhile let me show you some icons – you'll probably be bored, they are an acquired taste – but I love talking about them. Here we have a rather fine example of the *Unexpected Joy*. You see it depicts a sinner having a most undeserved vision of the Virgin Mary. What a sense of veneration – we lost grace as well as superstition when Mr Darwin stood the world on its head. Those artist-monks were too humble to sign work that was for the glory of God, and they mixed their pigments with holy water . . .'

Before long Geoffrey rescued me from the icons. The conversation had become general and Geoffrey, flanked by the silent Miss Derbyshire, came over and physically led me away from Oliver who was in the middle of an exposition on a black-faced Madonna known as *The Mother of God of Kazan*.

'Old Oliver does love to gallop his hobby-horse,' Geoffrey said as he poured me a fresh drink. 'But I can't complain about his artistic appreciation – he has been truly helpful to me, and it's very convenient to have a room here.'

'Is he an old friend?'

'I met him a couple of years ago at Galaxidhion on the Gulf of Corinth, when I was doing my Greek landscapes. It was early spring, before the tourist invasion. I had gone up to Delphi to watch the sunrise behind the temple of Diana, and out of the glory stepped Oliver. Typical of him to make such a theatrical entry into someone's life. I think he had been trying to get in tune with the ancient vibes. But tell me, what's been happening to you? By the sound of you, you haven't stayed in this country since you used to row around Derwentwater in that little boat.'

I condensed the last decade of my life into four or five sentences.

'That's no good,' Geoffrey said. He turned to Dian Derbyshire. 'He's a strange one. When I was a kid, up in Cumbria, he made a mysterious appearance in our little domain, then he vanished, and now he gives his auto-biography as a throw-away line.'

'It was you who vanished . . .'

'You could at least have written to us.'

'I . . .'

'Hush,' said Dian. It was the first time I had heard her speak and her soft clear voice was a delight. 'Oliver is about to perform his magic.'

While the guests settled back in their luxurious chairs Oliver carried a small blackboard into the centre of the room.

'Some of you have been kind enough to express interest in my work,' he said. 'So I intend to show you a little hypnotism, of the sort which my predecessors performed in ancient temples, in Victorian music halls and on television until it was banned. Once during a TV demon-stration thousands of viewers went into trance. Switch-boards were jammed by indignant relatives – you can picture the scene. Now only entertainment programmes are permitted to send us to sleep!'

There was dutiful laughter and Oliver regarded us benignly. In no way did he match my mental image of a hypnotist. I suppose I pictured someone of impassive mien with uncanny eyes wrapped in a Dracula cloak like a stage magician.

'Not everyone is a suitable hypnotic subject,' Oliver continued. 'The ratio of good subjects is about two in five, though in medical hypnotism non-receptive patients can be helped by certain drugs. However, tonight we are concerned with instant hypnosis and to discover who's suitable I'll conduct a few quick tests. I assure you there's nothing to be alarmed about.'

Looking at the eager faces about the room I realised that Oliver Penthorne must gain many new patients as a result of these soirées – no need for him to depend on 'personal notices' sandwiched between advertisements for haemorrhoid cures and norti-nite glamourwear in local newspapers.

'When I give the word I want you to place your hands on your heads and lock your fingers together,' he said. 'Although you may try to release them when I tell you, you will not be able to do so until I clap my hands. As I said, there will be nothing to worry about but your hands will remain on your heads as though paralysed until I clap. Are you ready? Good. Rather like going back to school, isn't it?' He gave a reassuring chuckle. 'Hands on heads!'

Dutifully most of us followed his command and linked our fingers, a procedure which to me smacked of a childish party trick.

'Excellent,' said Oliver. 'Press your skulls as hard as you can and keep your fingers tight. In a moment I am going to say "hands down", but you will not be able to move them until I clap. Let's do it on a count-down – three, two, one, hands down!'

The room filled with laughter as everyone loosened their grip and dropped their hands to their laps. So much for Oliver's experiment! Then I was aware that all eyes were on me, and I realised that the palms of my interlocked hands were still pressing my hair. Feeling foolish, I fought to let go but, stupid as it seemed, I had lost control. Only when Oliver clapped was I able to relax my hold and lower my arms.

'Congratulations, Martin,' he said reassuringly. 'You are obviously a most receptive subject.'

'Does that mean I'm weak-willed?'

'Dear gracious lord, no! There used to be a fallacy that the lower the IQ of a subject the easier it was to put him or her into trance. In fact we know it to be the exact opposite. The hardest person in the world to hypnotise is the village idiot. I would like to try another test, if you don't mind.'

Despite my scepticism I was curious about the work of this urbane magus, so I nodded my agreement.

'Excellent, excellent,' he said. 'All I'm going to do is give you a prick. Nothing to worry about, just a test of your reflexes.'

From his lapel he drew the largest darning needle I have ever seen and quickly passed the point through the flame of his golden Dunhill.

'Please stand up and hold out your left hand palm down, and keep your eyes fixed on Dian over there.'

I did as I was told and the girl gave me a very faint smile of encouragement while Oliver gently took my wrist, which was out of my range of vision, in his fingers.

'Martin, in a moment I am going to jab you with that needle you saw. I sterilised the point so there is no danger of infection when I pierce the flesh. Ready? Now!'

'Bloody hell!' I jumped as the needle stung me. I had not expected the pain which shot up my arm. The lunatic must have driven it right through my hand and I turned on him in anger – to see him holding a matchstick against my unmarked skin. There was a ripple of applause.

'You are remarkably receptive,' he said, putting the unused needle back in his lapel. 'What you have all seen is the most basic form of hypnotism – the achievement of a physical reaction to a mental suggestion. Martin felt a spasm of pain because I had made him expect to feel it. Non-subjects would have felt nothing more than the touch of the match I substituted for the needle. Would you like to go further, Martin?'

I said I would. The pain had been so real that I had become intrigued, and I could see the possibility of a future article on my experience.

'It is absolutely necessary that the subject should be relaxed and have complete faith in the hypnotist. Therefore, Martin, I will show you the routine with someone who is already a subject. Dian, please.'

Geoffrey rolled an easy chair into the centre of the room and dimmed the lights. Dian Derbyshire settled into the chair, her legs stretched comfortably and her hands loose on the arms. Oliver adjusted a standing spotlight so that it shone on him while Dian remained in shadow.

'I have hypnotised Miss Derbyshire before,' he explained. 'This makes the process very easy – I could put her off by merely speaking to her – but I'll do it the conventional way to give you the idea. Everyone, please, as quiet as possible. A cough can disturb the concentration of the subject. Ready, Dian?'

She inclined her head. Oliver produced a crystal pendant on the end of a thread, which he dangled a couple of feet in front of her face.

'Watch the pendulum, Dian,' he said.

Obediently her eyes followed its movement while the guests settled back to watch and several cleared their throats in fear of coughing at a critical moment.

Oliver swung the glittering pendant gently to and fro until complete silence had fallen, then he spoke to the girl in a soothing voice.

'Watch the pendulum, Dian. With every swing it makes you are feeling more drowsy . . . more and more drowsy. Soon you'll be floating down into sleep . . . deep . . . black . . . sleep . . .'

Her eyelids began to droop and flutter as she tried to follow the crystal's arc.

'You want to drift down into that sleep . . . there you will only be aware of my voice . . . my voice which will tell you what to do . . . my voice which you will obey even though you sleep . . . sleep . . . sleep . . .'

Dian's eyelids ceased to flutter.

'You sleep?' said Oliver.

'Yes.' Her murmured response seemed to come from a long distance.

Oliver pocketed his pendant and said in a matter-of-fact way, 'There, she's hypnotised.' He lifted her hand, then released it. It fell lifelessly to her lap.

'A subject has to be talked into a hypnotic state rather like an aircraft being talked down to a runway,' he explained. 'Although my words may sound rather mellifluous, they are chosen to implant suggestion. There are three levels of hypnosis. Dian is still in the first and before we try a few experiments I shall take her down to the second where no extraneous sound can influence her and where her mind will accept only my voice as her link with reality. Such is the power of suggestion that if a bomb exploded she would not hear it, yet she would respond to a whispered word from me.'

He turned back to the prone figure.

'Dian, I want you to sink farther into sleep – to go down and down so that it is only my voice you can hear, and only my voice that can wake you. You are going deeper?'

'Yes,' she sighed.

'Now try and wake her.'

'Dian!' somebody shouted, but she remained like a statue. 'Dian! Dian!' the others chorused. It had no effect on her.

'We are ready now,' said Oliver. 'As you are probably aware, everything that happens to us from birth onwards – and, I tend to think, for some time before birth – is recorded in our memory cells. Not a single experience, no matter how mundane, is missed. To be aware of these billions of recordings would be too much, would blow our minds, so to speak. Therefore, to protect us, our memory mechanisms have to be selective, and they also tend to block out what we do not wish to remember. Yet, no matter how poor you may think your memory is, the incidents of your life are all stored like information in a computer bank. Through hypnosis one can bypass conscious memory and unlock the stored information.

'I'm now going to talk Dian back in time, and you'll see what I mean.'

I sensed a rustle of unease among the guests. The girl lying supine in the chair seemed so defenceless before this baby in adult clothes who displayed such bland conviction of his powers. There was a hint of indecency in one person having such control over another, and yet we continued to watch in fascination.

'Dian, do you hear me?'

'Yes.'

'Dian, the years are falling away. You are getting younger and younger, are you not?'

'Yes.'

Was it my imagination, or had her voice become different, rising in pitch?

'You are going back through your teens, and now your birthdays are single figures.'

'Yes.'

'You are aged eight. Yes, you are a little girl of eight, and now it is your birthday . . .'

Suddenly Oliver's tone became that of a jolly uncle.

'Dian, what day is it today?'

In a little-girl voice the young woman answered, 'It's my birthday.'

In reply to Oliver's questioning she listed her presents and who had given them to her, the names of a dozen children invited to her party, and gave detailed descriptions of the dress her mother wore, a programme on television and the weather outside.

'Dian, tell me what you like best about your birthday.'

'Lucy.'

'Lucy?'

'My new doll.'

Oliver then coaxed her to write her name. I noticed her eyelids trembled as he gently raised her up and led her to the blackboard, but they never opened. He placed a piece of chalk in her hand and she painstakingly wrote 'Dian' in what children call 'joined-up' writing.

'You are going further back in time,' said Oliver. 'You are now six, and I want you to put your name on the blackboard.'

This time she printed it with the 'a' back to front. Oliver led her to the armchair.

'You are outside time now,' he said. 'And you are returning to the event which made you happiest.'

'I can't believe it. I'm so lucky. Thank you ever so much, Daddy . . .'

There was a longish pause, presumably while she listened to something her father said, and then, 'I'll call him Dapple – you lovely boy, Dapple . . .'

'You are returning to the present day,' said Oliver. 'When I count to three you will wake up gently and feeling refreshed.'

A moment later Dian's eyes opened and she smiled as though she had awoken from a pleasant sleep.

'I feel marvellous,' she said with a yawn. 'What did you make me do this time?'

Geoffrey pointed to the blackboard and she laughed.

'You've taken me time-travelling again,' she said. 'How nice it would be if I was conscious and could live over again the best bits of my life.'

'Who was Lucy?' asked Oliver.

'Lucy? Of course, she was a Victorian-style doll, my favourite. I wonder what became of her. Mummy bought her at Hamlyns.'

'And Dapple was obviously your pony.'

She nodded.

I took my turn in the easy chair.

'Unlike Dian, Martin has never been hypnotised before,

and it's only natural that he should be a little nervous,' said Oliver. 'So to reassure him that we shall not do anything undignified like the old so-called theatrical mesmerists – getting people to bark like dogs or act as though they were drunk – I shall leave this tape recorder running. Then he can hear everything that happened on playback. Ready, Martin?'

I nodded. He told me to relax, to try and empty my mind and concentrate on the crystal which glittered in the spotlight as it swung rhythmically before my eyes.

For a short time I was distracted by tiny noises in the room, but I found it increasingly difficult to keep my eyelids open, and Oliver's soft voice was getting further and further away. My body became limp and heavy and I floated down into soothing darkness . . .

My heart was pounding and my shirt was soaked with sweat when my eyes opened. I felt ill and disorientated, as though I'd escaped from a ghastly nightmare.

'Drink this, Martin,' said Geoffrey, putting a glass of brandy into my hand.

'What happened?' I asked. 'I don't feel so good.'

'I'm afraid it's the result of waking you too hurriedly,' said Oliver, his face that of a solicitous cherub. 'Dian is used to the waking process but when it's someone's first time I have to use a very gentle approach. Unfortunately you suddenly got very upset and I decided it was best to recall you immediately.'

'What did I do?'

'Listen to the tape.'

At first it was merely the voice of Oliver talking about 'deep black sleep' which came out of the machine, then he took me down to a lower level of unconsciousness and this was followed by my going back in time like Dian. I found it rather eerie to hear my own voice getting more and more childish, describing incidents like a Christmas with my parents at Pembridge Square, or a long-forgotten sports day at school.

Then Oliver's voice said, 'Martin, you are now going back to the day which was most important to you, and I want you to relive it for us. First, how old are you?'

'Thirteen and a half.' I sounded like someone talking in his sleep.

'Where are you?'

'In bed.'

'You are entering that moment which had special meaning.'

There was a pause on the tape, then I was aghast to hear my boyish voice trying to contain a note of hysteria as I said, 'Henry, would you feel better if I read to you . . . ?'

8

For several days following my visit to Oliver Penthorne's flat I was in a sour humour. I was resentful that a sad fragment of my past had been used to make a Roman holiday, and I formed a dislike of my hypnotherapist whom I now saw as a twentieth-century conjure-man, a latter-day Cagliostro with his carefully contrived decor and parlour demonstrations. I understood why he had made himself so agreeable to Geoffrey – how many wealthy patients was he gleaning from his art world contacts?

Yet I had to admit that as a hypnotist he was impressive. My taped boyish voice, taut with fear, still haunted me as it read a Dr Dolittle story – stumbling over a word here and there exactly as I must have done a dozen years ago – until I had screamed, 'Sister! Sister!' and my distress had made him jolt me into the present.

In fairness I admitted to myself that when he had taken me back to a moment of 'special meaning' he could not have known I would return to that traumatic hour when I felt compelled to entertain my dying friend. I also had to admit that Geoffrey had contributed to my chagrin. When at the exhibition he suggested a meeting I had imagined the two of us enjoying a pleasant meal at some bistro-type restaurant. In reality the few words I had been able to exchange with him at the Frognal apartment had been disappointing.

As soon as I had recovered from the shock of the abrupt awakening I bid a curt goodnight to Oliver and his guests, and Geoffrey took me to the door.

'Sorry you were upset,' he said. 'I remember Leila telling me once about something ghastly that had happened to you in hospital . . .'

'How is she?' I asked. Hadn't the fool realised that I had come in the hope of hearing about her?

'From her last postcard I gathered she was enjoying life.'

'Where is she?'

'Travelling,' he said vaguely. 'In Europe. She doesn't write often.'

I was about to ask more questions when Oliver's voice boomed through the large hall, 'You are needed, dear boy.'

Geoffrey pulled a face of comic resignation.

'His master's voice . . .'

Outside, as I waited for a cruising taxi to take me to the small flat I rented in Hampstead, I decided that for some private reason Geoffrey had not wished to see me alone or get into any but superficial conversation. Probably he had no wish to renew our brief boyhood friendship, and it was most likely that tonight's invitation had been at Oliver's behest with an eye to a further hypnotherapy story, this time devoted entirely to Oliver Penthorne. Although I had only been with *Newsview* a short time I was no longer surprised at the efforts some people made to get free publicity, even to folds of notes being proffered as an 'appreciation in advance' for a 'nice write-up'.

Several days passed during which I hoped I might hear Geoffrey's voice when I picked up the telephone on my desk, but he never rang.

I was staring at my typewriter, wondering how to transmute dross into feature stories, when my telephone made a welcome intrusion. A beautifully modulated voice said, 'Mr Winter? This is Dian. Dian Derbyshire. I would be grateful if we could have a short meeting.'

I felt annoyance. I had believed I had finally shed that curious obsession which had for so long linked me with the short period in my life when Derwentwater had infected me with an uneasy enchantment, but this unexpected reminder of Geoffrey awoke an imp of curiosity, perhaps the most dangerous of all temptations. Ask Madame Bluebeard.

'If you could find a little free time – this afternoon perhaps – we could meet for tea,' the soft voice continued.

'I could get away from the office,' I said. 'One of the perks of being a reporter.'

'That would be very kind of you. Shall we say three thirty at Fortnum's?' Where else for the cool and elegant Miss Derbyshire?

After the slush of Piccadilly Fortnum's was warm and comforting, an emporium of exotic produce presided over by men who would be taken for butlers in the outside world. It was a suitable setting for Dian Derbyshire who, when I saw her at a table in the tea-room, might have been waiting for Rossetti.

At first she was ill at ease and this made her formal – 'May I call you Martin?' 'If I may call you Dian' – and we merely made sociable sounds until she poured the tea.

'I worry a lot about Geoffrey,' she said. 'Although he looks well enough at the moment there are times when he suffers . . . with depression. Perhaps you are aware of that?'

'Dian, I know nothing of Geoffrey. I knew him and his sister for a short time, when we were children . . . Auber was a child's world, though there was a touch of the Brothers Grimm about it. But I expect you know about Auber?'

'I've never been there. Geoffrey's hardly ever mentioned it. Sometimes I have the feeling that the place had a rather traumatic effect upon him.'

'Do you know Geoffrey's sister?'

'It was through Leila that I met Geoffrey two years ago. After that I didn't see her. She went travelling, when – when . . .'

'When you fell in love with Geoffrey?'

'Yes, after I fell in love with Geoffrey. She was – is – very beautiful. You must have had a crush on her at Auber.'

'I rather think I suffered from a premature love affair. Did Leila get married?'

'Not that I know of. I wonder how you would feel if you saw her now. I can imagine she meant a very great deal to you. People like Leila are few, and you cannot forget them.'

In her formal manner Dian covered ground quickly. What I was recognising about her was a natural sympathy of character. At first I had dismissed her as being artificial, suspecting her of playing up the Pre-Raphaelite role, the beautiful silent maiden who gained everyone's attention by her air of patient submissiveness, but I had been mistaken. She had no need to wear masks like most of us. Everything about her was genuine.

While she poured me a second cup of tea I considered her last question.

'I felt very deeply for Leila,' I said. 'But it was an odd time in my life, and it affected me more than it should. On the surface we were just three kids playing round a lake, yet behind the scenery, as it were, there was so much more . . .' I let my hands drop, not knowing the right words to describe what I felt. 'Perhaps I was in love with them both, or what they represented – or perhaps it was a spell that fell upon me when I found Auber. Whatever it was, though, it felt like love.'

'Love,' Dian said. 'A game which we pawns have to play without knowing the rules. Only the Leilas and Geoffreys of the world know them.'

We had both said more than we intended, and I broke the uneasy silence. 'You asked me here because you were worried about Geoffrey? I don't know what I can do. I've only seen him at Leighton House and at Penthorne's flat, and then we only exchanged a few sentences.'

'Although Geoffrey gives an impression of great self-confidence – especially since he's starting to be recognised as an artist – he is very sensitive behind that façade. At times he's greatly troubled, I'm not exactly sure by what.'

'The family curse,' I suggested lightly.

Dian gave me a quick look.

'What do you know about it?'

'Nothing much. It was just something that Leila mentioned to me. Auber reeked of that sort of thing. There's a stone in the wall which is supposed to weep when doom is about to befall the house. And there's something weird about the Auber coat of arms, a chained ape which I remember as rather demoniacal. Then there's the good old Murder Room — did Geoffrey every tell you about that?'

'I told you, he's hardly ever mentioned Auber to me. Over some things he's a very secret person. I suppose it goes with being a genius.' She actually used that word.

'So?'

'He needs a friend, Martin. He was very hurt that you didn't ring him after that evening at Oliver's.'

I must have shown my surprise.

'Oh, don't laugh. It's true.' Dian was upset. I envied Geoffrey's having someone like her to care so much.

'I think you must have meant quite a lot to him once.'

'I doubt it, although I was quite a good audience when he used to tell his creepy stories . . .' (in the hot gloom of the attic Leila's hand crept downwards to mine while Geoffrey spoke about ghosts in a low voice) '. . . and if he had really wanted to see me he could have easily telephoned me.'

'You don't understand,' said Dian with a hint of irritability. 'But then, how could you? All I can say is that Geoffrey needs you as a friend — to supply some element that I suppose I am not able to provide.'

I realised the effort it had cost her to say that and I saw that she was under the spell of an Auber as once I had been. The knowledge made me feel like a fellow conspirator.

'If it'll help I'll see him,' I said. She smiled her relief and briefly held my hands over the table.

'Thank you.'

'I'd like to see him away from Penthorne.'

She inclined her head.

I asked her about herself, and she told me that she came from 'the suburban wilderness of Harrow', that she was studying music in the hope of becoming a professional pianist.

'Come up Bond Street with me and I'll show you something interesting,' she said as we rose. 'Thank you for my
tea. I have fulfilled my ambition to have afternoon tea at
Fortnum's. A student grant doesn't go very far these days,
even with some family help.' Later I learned that her
expensive-looking clothes were the result of her own skill
with a needle.

As we walked she told me that when I rang Geoffrey
she'd arrange it so that we all met at her place – 'terribly tiny,
just off Russell Square' – the following Sunday.

'I'll look forward to it,' I said, conscious that heads turned
as she walked with unconscious elegance past London's
most exclusive shops.

'Look,' she cried. Turning my head, I thought for a
moment that Leila was gazing at me from the window of
the Alessandro Gallery. It was, of course, Geoffrey's portrait of her.

Dian explained with pride that following the success of
the Leighton House exhibition the Bond Street gallery had
taken a lot of his paintings.

'Her eyes are so like Geoffrey's,' she sighed as we stood
close to the glass, like poor children gazing at riches beyond
our reach.

When I returned to my office I dialled Oliver Penthorne's
number, hoping that he would be away at his clinic instill-
ing confidence into his patients, and that Geoffrey would
be at home. My talk with Dian had whetted my curiosity,
and because I felt we were *simpatico* I would try to help in
her concern over the man she adored.

At the other end of the wire the receiver was lifted and
Geoffrey repeated Oliver's number in a listless voice.

'Hello,' I said. 'Martin here.'

'Martin!' His voice became enthusiastic. 'Martin, you are
the Winter of my discontent.'

'I thought I had a monopoly on terrible puns. I'm sorry I
haven't rung before.'

'I was afraid I wasn't going to hear from you at all, after that silly hypnosis business.'

'It wasn't your fault. When can we meet?'

'A Bond Street gallery has hung some of my paintings and I want to take you to a celebratory supper at my favourite restaurant. So how about tomorrow night at La Capannina? Do you know it? In Romilly Street.'

'I'm sure I can find it.'

Geoffrey chatted light-heartedly for another minute and then once more I was gazing at the blank page in my typewriter. I was surprised at how pleased he had been to hear me, and rather than get on with my story I reviewed what Dian had told me about him. At the same time the curious claustrophobia of his Subterranean paintings returned. I wondered about the mental state of my friend.

Geoffrey and I arrived at the restaurant together, and it was obvious from its warm and intimate atmosphere why it was his favourite. Waiters welcomed him with what appeared to be genuine pleasure, a traditional cowbell was clanged as we took our corner table, and the proprietor came and congratulated Geoffrey on the recent interview on Radio City.

Our talk was trivial while we drank our *Punt e Mes* and Geoffrey guided me through the menu. Then we settled back and he said, 'The other day you asked about our departure from Derwentwater – it was completely unexpected. Our father turned up that day you went somewhere with your parents, and we were immediately bundled off to stay with a perfectly horrible aunt. It was all rather ghastly. I believe Father was going mad and wanted to be alone at Auber . . .' He paused. I remained sympathetically silent, but I had a flashback of Mrs Forster's room, and the laughter of an unseen man in the background.

'That summer at Auber was our last really happy time as children – childhood's end, in fact,' Geoffrey continued. 'And you were special because you shared some of it with us. The Mysterious Boy in the Boat, Leila used to call you. She was very hurt that you didn't write – after all that happened she thought a postcard was the least she could expect.'

He closed one eye and regarded me through his wine-glass. From a table across the aisle I heard someone whisper, 'Why, that's Geoffrey Auber.'

'But I did write,' I protested. 'I wrote and wrote, addressing my letters to Leila care of Auber House. If anyone was hurt it was me – you see, I couldn't understand what had happened, and when I never got an answer . . .'

'Auber was shut up. I suppose whoever looked after the place didn't bother to forward your letters, or if he did our aunt was quite capable of destroying them. The family taint took her in the form of insane respectability – have you ever thought how it was the Puritans who banned the maypole and burnt witches? Aunt would certainly have seen sin in letters from an unknown youth to her niece. So we weren't as callous as you thought. Auber makes everyone its victim.'

'That's a curious thing to say.'

He shrugged.

'Didn't you feel the place wasn't just stone and mortar? Weren't you aware of – of a presence?'

'I was one day in the Murder Room.' We laughed. 'What's happened to the house?'

'Despite financial misfortune it still belongs to the family – just. It's been empty ever since our father . . . ever since we left. Martin, do you know why I'm elated when my pictures sell in Bond Street, or get a free plug on the radio? It's no ego-trip. It means money – and I hunger for money so that I can bring Auber back to life, tear down the boards from the windows, clear the garden of weeds, and exorcise it.'

He might have said more but our main course arrived.

'Exorcism,' I said as I began on my *Pollo alla Linda*, 'that takes me back. You still have a taste for the supernatural. I shouldn't have thought that Auber needed an exorcist. I

97

remember it had an atmosphere I've never come across again, and to me it was utterly magical, not evil – a feeling that one had entered a place where anything was possible. But that was probably my over-vivid imagination.'

'When I was abroad I learned that magic is like a prism,' said Geoffrey. 'It can focus a whole spectrum. It's not Auber itself that needs an exorcist, rather something it focuses.' He laughed. 'You'll think I've gone back to making up legends – I'm sure you never believed my stories. What funny kids we must have been. All that business about the Green Lady.'

'At least you didn't make it up about Croglin,' I said as he went on laughing. 'The farmer's wife told me the same story.'

'You went back – you went to Croglin?' he said in surprise.

'Yes, not long before Dad and I went to New Zealand.'

He beamed at me.

'I wasn't wrong about you, Martin. Even then I knew – Leila did, too.'

'What do you mean?'

Instead of answering he poured more chilled wine into my glass.

'Lovely wine,' he said. 'Do you know that in Bernkastel on the Mosel the inhabitants were saved from the plague by a wine produced by one Dr Thanisch, and it's still know as the Bernkasteler Doktor?'

'You haven't altered, Geoffrey,' I said. 'Even the wine you drink has to have a tale attached to it.'

'I can't escape my ancestry,' he said. Then he asked me about New Zealand, and in return I got him to talk about his life. He told me how he had hated the school he had been sent to by his aunt, where everything was judged on one's ability as a Rugby player, and he was regarded askance because of his artistic interests.

'When some books of poetry were found in my kit the story went round that I was a bloody queer,' he said. 'And more than one prefect tried to test it out for himself. Foul place! In the end I ran away and – having some money of my own – was able to study art.'

'Which art school?'

'None. I wanted to learn like all the old masters as an apprentice to someone I respected. I went to Italy and somehow persuaded Silvolli to take me into his atelier. It was bliss after that beastly school. Even when things are bad I wake up in the morning thinking, "At least I'm not going to have to mix with our future leaders today." Do you know, Martin, someday I'm going to fulfil an ambition to return to Derwentwater and become a recluse.'

'I don't think Miss Derbyshire would relish that,' I said.

'That reminds me, she asked me to invite you to her place next Sunday.'

'I'd like that. You're very lucky, Geoffrey. She's a lovely girl. What a model she must make!'

'I daren't paint her,' he said. 'I'd be accused of trying to start a neo–Victorian movement.'

Just before we left the restaurant Geoffrey said, 'Oliver was most impressed with you as a hypnotic subject. He'd rather like to have another session with you. He thinks there are great possibilities . . .'

'Never,' I said. 'When I woke up from his trance I felt as though I was going to have a heart attack.'

'That was unfortunate. I can promise it would never happen again. You hardly know Oliver. He really is a most remarkable man. What you saw the other night was nothing, an elementary demonstration for people with no knowledge of the subject. But his real work is fascinating. Hypnosis is merely his tool to explore the psyche, and he is on to something which one day could make him as important as Freud. Truly! But he needs subjects he can attune to his ideas, and he says you would be ideal. What a chance to be in on such important work!'

'It's an opportunity I'll pass up.'

Geoffrey still looked disappointed when we said good-night on the pavement.

'I go to Leicester Square station,' I said.

'And I'm cutting through Soho.'

'See you on Sunday.'

He appeared to brighten at this and said how much he had enjoyed our meeting. At the end of the street I looked back over my shoulder and saw a light-coloured Rover pull away from the kerb and pause at the corner beyond La Capannina for Geoffrey to climb in. Against the green glow of the instrument panel I saw the silhouette of a face, and recognised the soft, bland features of Oliver Penthorne.

9

The following Sunday I trod in the footsteps of Rossetti and his friends along Bernard Street to Dian's flat. I rang a bell at a door beside which was still mounted a black iron cone from the days when linkmen used it to extinguish their torches. As she opened it I thought again – with a niggle of jealousy if the truth be told – of Geoffrey's good fortune to have the devotion of such an attractive young woman. She wore a dress of pale oyster down to her ankles with a loosely-tied girdle low on her waist, and this with her braided auburn hair gave the impression of a Burne-Jones painting come to life.

'You're ahead of Geoffrey,' she said as she ushered me through the hall into her 'studio apartment' on the ground floor. Half the living-room was taken up by a Blüthner piano, the other furniture consisting of a stool, a marble-topped coffee table and an old sofa which had seen better days. The only wall decoration was one of Geoffrey's pictures, a powerful painting of the Castlerigg stones with Souter Fell in the background.

'The megalith painting was a birthday present,' she explained from her tiny kitchen as she poured water on instant coffee. 'Do you recognise it?'

'Yes. I was taken for a picnic there once. I might not have enjoyed it so much if I'd known it was the site of a witch-burning.'

'Geoffrey did enjoy his supper with you the other night,' Dian said, reappearing with a tray. 'I'm awfully grateful to you. It got him out of a depression which had been going on too long.'

'I thought he seemed in fine form,' I said. 'Are you sure you're not a little over-anxious about him?'

'You'll understand if you see more of him. Now that he's having this success with his painting I thought it would release him from certain things, from his obsession with the past.'

'You mean the unhappy time he had at school?'

'No, it goes farther back than that. I mean the past stretching back to – to the beginning of Auber, I suppose. At times it haunts him; he feels like a sort of puppet whose strings reach into antiquity.'

'That sounds like a question which worries a lot of people – me included, when I think about it. Whether there is such a thing as free will, or whether we have the illusion of free will while in reality all our acts and attitudes are predestined by genetic memory and glandular secretions, and formative environment.'

'And what do you think, Martin?'

'I would dearly love to believe in free will – in having choice – but, much as I like the idea, it seems to me that we are programmed. Even the Christians who dodge the question of God being responsible for sin by blaming man's free will are merely expressing an idea they have been preordained to express.'

'How horrible.'

'I agree. To me it's very horrible.'

'So you think that if I work myself to death to become a concert pianist it'll make no difference . . .'

'You may feel that your ambition has been achieved through extra work, but you have been programmed to work extra hard, to make sacrifices – and to believe that by your actions you have influenced your destiny.'

'You make it sound so bleak. Like those people in India who step over the dying without a thought of helping them, because they believe it is karma. Oh, I do want to believe that I am the captain of my soul. Have you no hope in your horrid fatalism?'

'A slight one,' I said. 'I got it, strangely enough, from

reading the Norse sagas while I was at college. The Vikings were complete fatalists, believing that at the roots of the World Tree were the Norns, three women who controlled the fate of men. One spun out his life, and another cut the thread when the time came for him to die. But there was one aspect that mortals did control, and that was their *attitude* to what the Norns decreed. Events were predestined – even their gods were predestined to die in a final battle – but at least a man could choose how he accepted them.'

'You should talk to Geoffrey about that. I am sure that he believes we are slaves of the past, though once he said that if we had the right magic we could break free. My father's a clergyman. I must talk to him . . .'

She was interrupted by a chime announcing the arrival of Geoffrey.

He came into the room smiling. Wearing white casual clothes, and with his fair hair still wild from the winter wind, he looked a romantic figure in the sense of the *fin de siècle* artists, or perhaps a young Shelley. Dian's pride in him showed in her eyes. The thought 'ideal couple' came to my mind – she with her music, he with his art, both so attractive, the epitome of the decade just passed which had cherished youth and been vitalised by it, and perhaps been ultimately betrayed by it.

It turned out to be a charming afternoon. We drank a little sherry and chatted light-heartedly, and then Dian was persuaded to sit at her keyboard.

'In a few weeks she'll be making her debut at the Wigmore Hall,' Geoffrey said. 'You must rope in all your friends. There mustn't be an empty seat.'

Dian cut short my congratulations.

'I'm not the only one in the concert.' She sounded nervous of Geoffrey's enthusiasm, afraid that she could not live up to the image he projected of her. It was something she need not have feared. I recognised her ability, her instinctive feel for music, the moment her slender fingers rippled over the Blüthner's keys and she began the haunting *Valse Triste*.

Later we chatted – or Geoffrey did, regaling Dian with tales of my visits to Auber, of the trick he and his sister played on me in the Murder Room, our 'potato barbecues' in the wild woods beyond the yew-tree walls and our adventures in *Pandora*. Dian laughed delightedly at his extravagances, and occasionally glanced at me as though approving of my role as the source of such animation.

'How wonderful if we could all go for a holiday to Derwentwater,' she said. 'You could take me to all your favourite places, the Lodore Falls and the Bowder Stone and up on Cat Bells.'

'Not yet,' said Geoffrey. 'No, not yet.'

'More sherry,' Dian said quickly, as though fearing a shift in his mood. But his cheerfulness returned and I began to wonder whether Dian was morbidly sensitive about her lover's depression.

As dusk thickened over Bloomsbury, Dian drew her old curtains across the window and we listened to records. Geoffrey became rapt as the majestic sounds of Sibelius's *Swan of Tuonela* filled the little flat. I could imagine how his inner artist's eye must be turning the music into images of the great white swan floating on the dark river of death, serene despite the inevitability of fate, or perhaps serene because of it.

Afterwards Geoffrey said, 'That music confirms what I have begun to fear, that painting with pigment can never compare with painting with sounds. It's something I must think about.'

Soon afterwards I left them. As I walked to the Russell Square tube station I smiled to myself at the thought of Dian's brief look of gratitude when she clasped my hand at the door. I could not see what I had done to earn it by renewing this friendship. I now believed that if anyone benefited from it, it was I.

I next saw Geoffrey at Oliver Penthorne's flat. I had completed a story sooner than I had expected and, with this bonus of a couple of hours, I rang Geoffrey. He was busy painting but I was welcome if I did not mind watching him work. Oliver had turned over an airy room in the top floor of his flat to Geoffrey as a makeshift studio. Its windows looked out over a field of dark roofs with occasional oases of treetops.

I found my friend, in paint-spattered jeans and stained jersey, standing in front of an easel holding a canvas which he had been blocking in with pale blues and greys. Appropriately, from a portable radio the Third Programme provided what used to be known as *musique concrète*.

'Be careful where you sit. A tube of rose madder would play havoc with that natty Fleet Street suiting,' he called. 'If you feel like a shot there's some brandy in that bottle next to the turps.'

I helped myself and wandered about the room, examining paintings in various stages of completion.

'I feel rather as though I'm working on a conveyor belt,' Geoffrey said, stepping back to regard his canvas. 'At the moment there is a demand for Aubers and I'm going to fulfil it – with every picture I sell a bit more of the house is saved.'

'Geoffrey,' I said. 'What about Leila? She can't be travelling for ever.'

There was a clatter behind me and I turned to see his palette knife on the floor. I was not sure whether it had fallen or whether he had thrown it down in anger.

'I don't know about Leila,' he said. 'Her work is connected with films, and she's on the move a lot. I don't know where she is and she never comes to England. Don't expect to see her again by banging round me.'

His anger hung in the air like a dying musical note, and I was sure that when Oliver Penthorne appeared at the door he sensed it. I saw his eyes, as innocent as two blue marbles, give a curious flick, but he radiated bonhomie as he walked into the room.

'How's the daubing, Geoff? I'm exhausted. If I'd had one more patient it would have been me that went into trance. Where's that brandy you keep hidden up here? Martin, it's good to see you again. Don't be alarmed. I'm not going to pester you to be my star subject. Geoffrey told me you were adamant, and I know when I'm beaten.'

His laughter was infectious, and I found the frost of my mistrust thawing slightly. I was grateful for his timely entrance, as I have always had a morbid aversion to verbal anger. While many people enjoy the adrenalin boost that a quarrel gives them, my reaction is to dry up.

'You always find refuge in silence,' Dawn used to accuse me, herself an emotional street-fighter when in need of some release of tension. Our one-sided quarrels had never been about anything important, merely the misunderstanding of a remark, the wrong emphasis on a word, or the lack of an expected response. Now she was Jonno's wife she would have no cause to complain. He had the makings of an adrenalin addict himself. And, thinking along these lines, I realised that the last time I had lost my temper was when I threw a punch at Geoffrey after I had fled from what I thought was the Green Lady.

Oliver said, 'I hope you will be able to stay for supper, Martin. Geoffrey and I are so frazzled we need the influence of your monumental calm. Filomena has consented to make us one of her curries this evening.'

Filomena was a sad-eyed Asian refugee who acted as Oliver's housekeeper. He had known her family in Cambodia before the revolutions began. Later, when she was arrested as an enemy of the workers, he saved her from the motorised tumbrels by a business-like bankdraft to one of the new officials.

This I learned from Geoffrey when Oliver left to change out of what he called his 'business duds', meaning his blue Savile Row suit. By the time he reappeared in a cream cashmere sweater, the compass needle of my regard had moved several degrees in his favour. I realised I had been unfair to judge him so quickly, and I had to admit that my opinion of him had been prejudiced by my painful experience as a hypnotic subject. Now that there were no guests to impress, his formidable charm was diluted to an acceptable level. What finally won me over was his sincere enthusiasm for his studies in the field of hypnosis.

'I can understand your antipathy to it,' he said, as we concluded our supper with a cloying dessert. 'But what you saw was the merest tip of the iceberg. There are so many aspects to be investigated, physical as well as mental. When I was exploring the possibilities of self-hypnosis I was able to slow my heart rate down to six beats a minute. Try as hard as you might while you're in your conscious state, you cannot alter your pulse by a fraction.'

'Can you actually improve a person's intelligence or talent?' I asked.

'One can only work with what is inside the skull,' Oliver answered. 'If I were to hypnotise Geoffrey I couldn't make him paint one whit better than he does already. But what hypnosis can do is concentrate the mind – and the body – in quite remarkable ways. I first got an inkling of this when I was at university. It occurred to me that hypnosis might be useful as an aid to passing examinations. And it was. I hypnotised some of my friends who were poor at memorising and made them read key pages, or look at diagrams, while in a trance state . . .'

'Surely that would have meant opening their eyes?'

'Oh, yes. Nothing difficult about that once they've been taken down to the third level. So, having read the material, it was no problem for them to give themselves a post-hypnotic command when they had to tackle certain questions. Then they would see the page with the formulae or whatever just as though it was printed on the paper in front of them. My section had quite a surprisingly high marks-average in the finals. But I could only help with information retrieval. If my friends wrote a criticism or an original essay there was nothing I could do for them, apart from steadying their nerves if they were apprehensive.'

I asked what he meant by a post-hypnotic command.

'It's a signal-word introduced into the unconscious of the subject while he is in trance,' he explained. 'For example, I could tell the subject that after being awakened he would be aware of a scent of roses whenever the word "rose" was said. And he would accept the suggestion when he was wide awake and free from my control. The word does not need to be related in meaning to the effect it produces. With post-hypnotic suggestion a subject could be induced to sing "Land of Hope and Glory" when he heard the keyword "sausage".'

Geoffrey burst into laughter.

'If I allowed you to hypnotise me, could I have a post-hypnotic suggestion that when I drank a glass of water I would taste brandy?'

'Of course. Music-hall tricks like that are perfectly possible. You could also get gloriously drunk. Now I suggest we try some non-illusionary cognac. Why the grimace, dear boy?' he added, as I rose from the table.

'Just a back twinge,' I replied. 'An old trouble which returns from time to time, especially when I've had a day slaving over a typewriter.'

'When I met Martin he'd had a gruesome year in hospital,' said Geoffrey. 'But it was a long time before he admitted it to my sister. Always the stoic, our Martin.'

'What was the trouble?' Oliver asked.

'Potts' Disease,' I said. 'Imagine being struck down by something with such a boring name. When I was a kid I longed to have something with a glamorous Latin title, or at least anything a bit more upmarket than Potts. Penthorne's Syndrome would have done quite well.'

'And what do you think would be the symptom of such a complaint?'

'Hallucination!' Geoffrey and I cried simultaneously.

We spent the rest of the evening with balloons of Napoleon brandy, listening to Oliver's collection of Glen Miller records.

The following weeks were the most enjoyable I had spent since my return to England. As far as my work was concerned I had come to the conclusion that the way forward was through specialisation. Keen-eyed youngsters were coming along all the time, and on Fleet Street a general reporter burns out quickly. It seemed to me that the way to avoid the retreat into PR in one's thirties was to become a columnist who, as an expert in his field, would be cherished by his editor and need have less fear of the British obsession with age. Our film correspondent had given me a hint that she was negotiating for a job with one of the prestigious Sunday papers, and if that came off I was determined to try and replace her.

To this end I began to absorb everything I could about the cinema, and to catch up on films I had missed in New Zealand I joined the National Film Theatre. Amid the concrete art bunkers below Waterloo Bridge I became an overnight film buff. My obsession, which was to become one of the most important factors in my life, began from the moment I watched the knight playing chess with Death in Ingmar Bergman's *Seventh Seal*. Here was wine for the imagination.

And yet, as I wrote my first practice column for my self-critical eyes only, I wondered if my wish to become a film correspondent had been begotten by Geoffrey's remark that Leila worked in films. Looking back, it was sinister how my thoughts continued to relate to the Aubers.

Frequently Geoffrey and Dian came with me to the NFT, and it was at this time that I glimpsed the side of my friend's character which caused Dian concern. Sometimes he would wrap himself in sullen silence, a mood so intense that we could almost feel it as a physical chill. On one such occasion, as we approached Waterloo Bridge from the cinema, Dian took his hand and asked, 'What's the matter, darling?'

He shook her away and cried, 'What the hell should be the matter?' It was the tone of his voice rather than his words which made her flinch as though slapped by an invisible hand. I knew she was about to apologise to him, to feel guilt for something she did not understand, and I was determined not to let Geoffrey have the satisfaction that comes to those who use the technique of making someone else miserable to ease their own depression.

I seized her by the wrist and, pulling her behind me, began to skip over the bridge in the slow motion way popular with children in the playgrounds of infant schools. At first Dian hung back, concerned for the gloomy figure stalking behind us, but I was too strong for her and she was forced to skip after me.

Waterloo Bridge at night is probably the best stretch of pavement for skipping in London. On our right St Paul's was bathed in a halo of floodlights, to our left the illuminated Parliament buildings and Big Ben were equally impressive, while below the Thames flowed like black oil. The night breeze chilled our faces and ran its fingers through Dian's hair, and the night-walkers we encountered smiled at our exuberance.

When we reached the other side we collapsed against some railings, I gasping for breath and Dian speechless with laughter. She was still giggling minutes later when Geoffrey reached us, and I was delighted that she did nothing to placate his wounded dignity.

Everyone is entitled to his off moments, and I took little notice of Geoffrey's increasing moodiness or the fits of abstraction which would cause him to fall silent in the middle of an animated conversation. I had become selfishly involved in my own affairs. It seemed more and more likely that our film correspondent would be leaving, and the more I saw of the cinema – at that stage I was going half a dozen times a week – the more determined I became to take over from her.

One midnight I had just returned to my flat, still under the spell of the last scene in *La Dolce Vita*, when the telephone rang and Dian asked if Geoffrey was with me.

'He was supposed to have supper over here hours ago,' she said, when I explained I had been alone all evening.

'Perhaps he's with Oliver, or some of his Bond Street chums,' I suggested. 'I'm sure there's nothing to worry about.'

'I feel there is,' she said. 'I rang Oliver and he hasn't seen him. And I rang the Alessandro . . .'

'Look, Dian, perhaps it's an unpalatable thing to have to accept about the man you adore, but it's not unusual for the male of the species to sometimes make a night of it. He may have been in a pub and the conversation was good, and each drink was going to be his last but somehow the hours rolled by. Tomorrow he'll have a terrible headache and you can say it serves him right, or be a ministering angel, depending on how you feel.'

'Sorry I troubled you,' Dian said. 'I'll start ringing the hospitals.' She was hurt that I refused to panic because her beloved had committed one of a young man's commonest offences. Somewhere in the city Geoffrey was enjoying himself, and I could not help grinning as I put down the receiver.

Three hours later the shrilling of the telephone wrenched me from sleep. This time it was Oliver at the other end.

'This is a ghastly time to wake you, dear boy,' he said, 'but we seem to be having a bit of a problem with Geoffrey . . .'

I mumbled something to let him know that I was trying to absorb what he said.

'I've just picked him up from the local nick – it's helpful to have a medical degree sometimes, even if one doesn't practise any more.'

'Was he drunk and disorderly?'

'Nothing as simple as that. I gathered from the duty sergeant that he had been found in an old bombed-out church – St Luke's, I believe. It's quite close to Dian's flat. Of course it's boarded up, but the police visit it every so often to make sure that some meths-drinker isn't freezing to death there, or a lost child . . .'

'What was Geoffrey doing in such a place?'

'That's the question, dear boy. He's in rather an odd state just now, but I'm more worried about Dian. You know how concerned she is about him. I thought perhaps if you came over . . . you know, your calming influence and all that.'

'Can't you put her into a trance or something?'

'Dear boy, this is not the time for frivolity.'

I rang a minicab number and climbed into my clothes, and was just waking myself up with some coffee when the company rang back to say a car was waiting at my door.

Filomena admitted me to Oliver's apartment and took me to Geoffrey's room. He lay on the bed, his hair in wisps over a face that looked so white it reminded me of a Victorian painting of a dead poet . . . Thomas Chatterton.

'If I hadn't rung the police station he would still be in a cell,' said Dian, as though to reprimand me for my earlier lack of concern.

'What's wrong with him?' I asked. 'Not LSD or anything?'

'I'm not sure,' said Oliver. 'When the patrol car brought him in the coppers just thought he'd had a few too many and passed out. There was no charge against him.'

A faint smell of liquor hung in the air, and I saw a streak of vomit on his sleeve.

'Perhaps that's what it was,' I said. 'He must have had a few drinks too many and on his way to Dian's place felt a bit unwell and gone into the church.'

'I think it's something more than that.' Oliver had his fingers on Geoffrey's wrist. 'I'd say he was in a state of shock. His pulse is erratic, but I don't think there's anything wrong physically. Beneath the persona of the rising young artist, the boy is abnormally sensitive. One of our slim gilt souls.' Dian inclined her head in agreement.

Geoffrey gave a little moan and his eyelids opened. I found him staring at me with unnatural intensity.

'You're a furtive little animal, Martin,' he muttered. 'Always the bloody pal . . . always so bloody nice . . . and always so bloody dishonest . . . in Auber all you wanted was to fuck Leila . . . you know I saw you . . .'

His voice faded. Dian regarded me with a startled look – more than that, an expression I could not fathom then, though later I thought it could be dismay.

'Don't take any notice of anything he says,' said Oliver in his most reassuring tone. 'His mind is not under normal control.'

'In vino veritas,' I said.

Dian pressed my hand.

'No,' she said. 'I know what you mean to Geoffrey. In his way, he loves you, Martin.'

'When patients go under anaesthetic they frequently babble things quite alien to their normal personality,' said Oliver. 'Theatre staff are used to streams of four-letter words coming from the most respectable people while they're unconscious. So don't let what Geoffrey said worry you.'

A little colour had returned to the face of the figure on the bed.

'His pulse is settling,' Oliver said a little while later. 'I suggest you take Dian home, dear boy.'

'I want to stay,' she protested.

'There's no need. He's sinking into a normal sleep. I wouldn't be surprised if in the morning he woke up feeling like death but with no recollection of what happened. You'll be more use to him if you are fresh and bright-eyed. He'll need you when I'm away at the clinic . . .'

In the event we persuaded Dian to go home and sleep, and I recalled the minicab to take her.

'Has he ever been found like this before?' I asked her as we sat in the back seat and the two-way radio provided an obbligato of numbers. 'Three-six-zero, three-six-zero . . .' It reminded me of the unearthly radio messages in *Orphée*.

I had to repeat the question before Dian shook her head.

'Sometimes he's been strange and withdrawn, but he's never passed out like this before.' A thought struck her. 'How terrible it would be if the press got hold of the story. Reporters could make a scandal, and ruin his career . . . sorry, present company excepted.'

'It wouldn't hurt his career,' I said. 'Van Gogh's paintings aren't devalued because he cut his ear.'

Beside me I felt Dian shudder.

Next morning was a Saturday, and after rising late I rang Oliver's flat, to be told by Filomena that Mr Geoffrey was resting. Then Dian's voice came on the line.

'He can't remember anything of what happened, but he seems all right and very apologetic,' she said. 'I made him breakfast but he only wanted coffee.'

'He must remember something?'

'Not after going into the old church. He thought it might make a subject for a painting . . . I'm sorry you were dragged out last night. I'll have to go now.'

Curiosity took me to St Luke's that morning. The walls appeared to be undamaged, though scorch marks remained above the boarded-up windows. The bomb blast must have lifted the roof off all those years ago. Grass sprouted from between the paving as I walked up to the entrance, which was sealed with sheets of corrugated iron.

I soon discovered how Geoffrey had got in. The sheet covering a side door, which had probably once opened into the vestry, had been wrenched from its wooden frame and partly bent back – the work of local children, no doubt. I squeezed through and, stepping through the remains of a room without a ceiling, felt like Alice at the start of her adventures.

The area within the blind walls was a wilderness of vegetation. Weeds grew with jungle ferocity as they strained towards the oblong of sky. Various small trees had been self-sown, blackberry tendrils writhed over mossy stone and at my feet there was a profusion of flowers. Someone, perhaps a pensioner condemned to some nearby mini-flat, had tried to grow a garden here.

I could see how this tiny secret world would appeal to an artist. Beneath the east wall the remains of the altar rose above the foliage, decorated with the white bells of convolvulus. This gave an impression of being in a sanc-tuary, and a sanctuary not just for wild plants. I saw a black cat with pale yellow eyes watching me from a broken pillar, and then I noticed several other silent strays. A trace of human occupation was a bluish, sponge-like object which I first thought was an exotic fungus when my toe prodded it. Then I saw that it was a stained loaf, and remembered that drinkers of methylated spirits used bread to filter out the dye and some of the evil taste.

A few minutes later I found what I had been looking for, an Alitalia airline bag which Geoffrey used to carry his sketching materials. Beside it was an empty flask which smelled of brandy and propped against the stem of a towering hogweed was an artist's sketch pad. I picked it up and it was a moment before I understood what I was looking at.

The top of the quick charcoal sketch showed the jagged outline of the church walls. That was quite easy to recognise, but as Geoffrey had continued his work reality ended. In the centre of the page was the Auber mausoleum, and in the grass which filled the foreground lay two children. I recognised myself as the figure bending over a girl without a face.

10

'Stone the crows, cobber, you're a tiger for that stuff,' said the features editor, in his excruciating imitation of an Australian accent.

'It must be the Pommy beer,' I said, screwing the cap on an aspirin bottle. Lately the pains in my back had increased and the little white tablets were the only things which helped. Without being conscious of it, I was becoming an aspirin addict.

'Anyway, the major wants to see you.'

I pulled my tie knot tight, slipped on my jacket and presented myself in the editor's chrome-and-glass office. He carefully retained some old military mannerisms along with his regimental tie and crisp delivery.

'Winter, you want to take over Beryl's job now she thinks she's going on to better things?'

I nodded, fighting an impulse to stiffen to attention and shout 'Sir!'

'You're still single. No thought of settling down to domesticity yet?'

I shook my head.

'Excellent. Once a man marries and starts commuting in from Horsham he no longer gives his best to the paper. He's more worried by having over-reached himself for some semi-detached than he is about *Newsweek*. His wife will play hell over his late hours and the spring will go out of his step. Such men have "mortgage" branded on them like the mark of Cain, and when I sense it I know I'll never get the work I want from them.'

'I think it'll be a long time before I ever think of settling down like that,' I said sincerely.

'Good. I've read a couple of your dummy columns and they aren't too bad. I want the film side built up now the television companies are starting to use movies. Find out what's scheduled and get a viewers' guide going. And let's have a weekly interview with a film personality with the emphasis on entertainment rather than glamour. Try it for a couple of months and if it works out you can do it permanently. Your salary will be adjusted accordingly. All right, Winter?'

Dismissed, I felt I was walking a few inches above the floor as I returned down the olive-green corridor to the reporters' room. I was so pleased that I had to tell somebody, and I dialled Dian's number.

'Hi,' I cried when she picked up the receiver. 'I want to take you and Geoffrey to a celebratory lunch.'

'Oh, Martin, does that mean you've got the film job? Geoff is with the jet-set today, some countess who puts on exhibitions of European artists in New York. Can I come by myself?'

I thought of her use of 'jet-set' as I walked along Charlotte Street to meet her at a small Greek restaurant which we both liked. It brought back the words of the editor of our 'social' (gossip) column who had said to me a few days earlier, 'I hope your chum Auber knows what he's doing with the sort of people he's mixing with these days. It's fine if he's using them for publicity, but may the Great Artist help him if he thinks they're for real. They'll fawn round him while he has novelty value – and then one day when he's been thoroughly chewed he'll find himself spat out.'

'He's far from stupid,' I said. 'But thanks. I'll keep an eye on him.'

'And if he tells you any little items of an opprobrious nature, remember me,' said the editor with a grin. 'It's the silly season.'

It was in fact high summer, and as I sat at a pavement table outside the restaurant I mused again on Geoffrey's luck as I saw Dian hurrying down the street, her auburn hair blowing free and a dress of her own design – a floral pattern in which lilies predominated – floating about her . . . . an embodiment of youthful beauty.

Sometimes I pondered on her relationship with Geoffrey and wondered how much he appreciated the devotion he inspired in her. He usually appeared considerate to her, and I had no reason to suspect that the private side of their love affair was not satisfactory, and yet . . . I was left with a doubt. Since finding his sketch pad in St Luke's I had given a lot of thought to Geoffrey, remembering Wordsworth's dictum that the child is father of the man.

I had removed the drawing from the block, but perhaps meanly I had left everything else as it was. Sometimes I took the sketch out of my drawer and examined it as though it held some hidden truth. One interpretation could be that he had started to sketch the ruined church in the normal way, but as the drawing continued his sense of the present had been overlaid by the past. In some form of abstraction which had led to his collapse among the wild plants, remembered images became the reality he was trying to capture on paper. But what a strange mental state he must have been in.

There was another explanation – that he had deliberately left the picture there for me to find. Was Geoffrey Auber playing some game with us of which only he was aware? It seemed too bizarre, but I decided that if this was the case I would deny him any satisfaction by never mentioning that I had been to St Luke's.

Dian was genuinely delighted with my news. After we had ordered a four stick kebab each, we toasted the future in retsina, which we found a pleasant enough drink after the surprise of the first mouthful.

'Geoffrey will be delighted when I tell him,' she said. 'He's your number one fan, did you know?'

'How is he?'

'No more blacking out, I'm glad to say. But I'm still worried. At times he has a – a feverish quality.'

'Was it Picasso who said that of all problems an artist has to bear fame is the hardest?'

'I think Geoffrey can handle that all right,' said Dian as little plates of hummous were placed before us. 'It would be the same whatever he was doing.'

'Perhaps we take his moods too seriously,' I said, suddenly bored with the subject. 'Even Oliver, who has his fair share of nut-cases, I should imagine, becomes quite reverential when he mentions Geoffrey's depression. But, in fact, he's a golden boy. There must be thousands of young artists who would sell their souls to be where he is . . . rave reviews in the art magazines, pictures being sold in Bond Street, an exhibition planned for New York and another for Tokyo, a feature coming up in the *Onlooker* colour supplement . . . and on top of that he's healthy, charming, and has a marvellous girl friend. I don't think I need worry too much about poor Geoffrey.'

My joking flattery was rewarded with a slight smile.

'It's true what you say. He is a golden boy, but still a haunted one.'

'*Haunted*?' I exclaimed. 'Has the Green Lady followed him to London?' I must have sounded unfeeling to the gentle Dian, but I had no wish for my celebration to turn into a symposium for two on Geoffrey Auber.

'I think he's afraid of madness,' Dian said simply. 'He believes it's a family characteristic, a condition which may not be apparent for several generations and then reappears. I suppose he's anxious because of his father.'

'His father?'

'Geoffrey has hardly ever mentioned him, but I gathered from Leila there was some tragedy. She never went into details. When they want to, the Aubers can be what you journalists call "very private people". I suppose products of ancient families are different from simple souls like us. Perhaps you and I should run away together, Martin. You are so nice and uncomplicated.'

She was smiling as she said it, and I smiled back. How much emotional complication has been conceived by a remark like that?

'Now, no more Auber,' she said, raising her glass to me.

'We're here to drink to the success of Martin Winter, film correspondent – and good friend. Tell me, when will I be able to read your column, and who is the first film star you'll be interviewing?'

The rest of the meal was delightful for us both, and when we rose, and Dian hurried off to rehearse for the Wigmore Hall concert, we were both a little tipsy, not so much from the retsina as from the sun which filled the long old street and the pleasure of each other's company. What we did not realise was that the pattern of all our little lives had begun a subtle change, like the shift in the colours of a kaleidoscope when turned very, very slowly.

The next month was hectic as I worked hard to ensure I would be endorsed in my new job. I visited film studios, was invited to lavish receptions, and on several occasions had a Hilton or Dorchester breakfast with well-known actors and actresses who were passing through London – and I loved every minute of it. As a consequence I saw little of Geoffrey and Dian, though I used the telephone to keep in touch.

On one occasion, which turned out to be very important for me, I rang Geoffrey on Oliver's number only to learn that he and Dian had flown to Stockholm. A gallery had arranged a special exhibition of his Subterraneans, which apparently struck a chord in the Swedish psyche.

'I'm on my own tonight,' Oliver added. 'Why not come over and join me for one of Filomena's simple suppers? To be honest, I feel rather lonely, and you could entertain me with the Secrets of the Stars.' He laughed, but I was touched by his admission of loneliness. When I first met him I would have thought it impossible for this well-to-do character, with his champagne soirées and thriving practice, to feel in need of companionship. How naïve seemed my judgement then, yet had it matured over the past few months? Then I was waiting to feel grown up, believing, like a child, that one day I would be an adult with all the correct adult attitudes. Only as time passed did I realise that such a metamorphosis is illusionary, and that most of us remain children in adult bodies. Was Geoffrey the boy I had known, hiding behind a mask of maturity? And Leila?

I went to see Oliver that evening. I no longer found his blandness and baby smile off-putting, perhaps because I'd had a few glimpses of the person behind his particular mask.

'Martin, dear boy, how kind of you to come,' he said in greeting. 'Tell me you cancelled an interview with Sophia Loren to see me.'

'Oliver, you'll never believe this, but I had to call off a meeting with the Loren to come here.'

'In that case you deserve a drink.'

A moment later, as I sank into one of his enormous easy chairs, he said, 'You look as though you're in agony. Is it the same trouble? You know, I could relieve the pain for you if you'd let me.'

'Post-hypnosis? Wouldn't that be dangerous – not to be able to feel pain?'

'It would be localised to the spot which troubles you. And it wouldn't be permanent. I would have to renew the suggestion every few days. Why not try it? There'll be no going back in time or any experiments that might worry you. Think how pleasant it would be to sit at your type-writer tomorrow without a backache.'

The thought was attractive and I heard myself agree. Oliver immediately dimmed the lights and stood behind me as I slumped in the chair.

'Because I've hypnotised you once already, there'll be no need for the pendulum. I've switched on the tape recorder so you'll be able to hear exactly what happens if you want to. Just relax and get as comfortable as you can.'

I did so, stretching my legs out and laying my hands on the soft arms of the chair. Then I felt Oliver place his fingertips against the sides of my head, between the eye and the ear. The sensation was remarkably soothing.

'Martin, are you relaxed?' asked Oliver softly. 'Good. Now you are going to go to sleep . . . deep sleep . . .'

His words began to flow together, I felt my heavy eyelids shutter my eyes, and then I was falling down into a warm velvet darkness.

Somewhere a pair of hands clapped.

I opened my eyes and felt wonderful. It was like waking from a long dreamless sleep during which every vestige of bodily fatigue had evaporated.

'How do you feel, dear boy?'

'Voluptuous! I don't know what magic you practised, but I am renewed.'

I sat up in the chair and then it struck me that the pain had gone out of my back. Instead of the weary ache there was a sensation of well-being.

'Oliver, how can I thank you?'

'Oh, you know that. You are such an excellent subject I'd like your assistance in some experiments.'

'I certainly owe you something,' I said, walking about the room and stretching my arms. 'I can't remember when I last felt so good.'

'That is one of the effects of hypnosis. Asleep we dream all the time though only the most vivid dreams are remembered, but this ceases in a deep trance. The hypnotist's voice replaces the unconscious which normally sends a continuous stream of dream images into the sleeping mind. The result is a hundred per cent rest and relaxation – a few minutes of hypnotically-induced sleep is equal in restorative effect to several hours of natural sleep.'

'Tell me about these experiments you mentioned.'

'Mental telepathy, dear boy. What the Oxford Dictionary describes as "action of one mind on another at a distance through emotional influence without communication through senses". In recent years there has been a great deal of interest in the subject. In the Soviet Union there have been experiments with a view to using it as a means of communication between cosmonauts in space! So far, though, tests have only worked over short distances, with simple messages such as the transmission of random numbers from shuffled cards.'

I told him how the two Auber children and I had tried such experiments with playing cards when we had become friends at Derwentwater.

'That's interesting,' he said. 'And you and Geoffrey had a particular rapport . . .' He mused for a minute, and continued, 'A long time ago when I was in the Far East, dabbling in some of the esoteric doctrines which flourish out there, it occurred to me that the drawback to telepathy is the human mind. A nice paradox. What I mean is that the mind is so cluttered with extraneous thought that it scrambles the transmission. If one could get rid of this cerebral static the mind of the recipient would receive the projected message as clearly as a coherer receives electric waves in a radio set. Later, when I studied hypnosis, I began to see how this "white sound", as I believe broadcast engineers call it, could be eliminated. Since I began experimenting with telepathy on subjects under hypnosis, I've had some outstanding results.'

'Could you give me an example?'

'As you know, I've hypnotised Dian many times, and she has become an excellent subject. When you first came here you saw me put her under hypnosis by using a pendulum. That was for the benefit of my guests who had not seen a demonstration before. In fact I can hypnotise Dian by telepathy, by sending out a mental command. The moment I will her to go into trance she will do so, no matter what she may be engaged in at that moment.'

'That sounds incredible.'

'Ask her about it when you see her next. An interesting thing about it is that I can do it at some distance. If she is in the next room, or on the floor above, the effect is the same. I believe that I could hypnotise her telepathically at far greater distances, but obviously that would be dangerous. Then, when she is in trance, I can control her without saying a word. For example, I can guide her round a room, make her pick up objects or perform other commands, merely by willing her to do so.'

'That gives you tremendous power over a person!'

'It's one of the things that would be regarded as unacceptable about the experiment – public fear of a latter-day Svengali. All my experiments must be cloaked in the respectability of scientific investigation, so I'm writing a tremendous tome bristling with jargon and tables and graphs and all that nonsense.' A shy look came over his cherubic features as he added, 'I suppose it has become my *magnum opus*.'

By the end of the evening I had forgotten my earlier reservations about both hypnosis and Oliver Penthorne. The easing of my back pain had gone a long way to convert me, and when we parted I had agreed to assist in his telepathic experiments.

'If we could have a session at least once a week I would be most grateful,' Oliver said as we shook hands at his door. 'It will take a little while for you to reach the same stage as Dian, but when you do I'll be able to proceed with my idea of linking two hypnotised minds. Then we shall see. Goodnight, dear boy.'

I was rather disappointed by my following sessions with Oliver as, being unconscious while the experiments were conducted, I missed the fun. But I did see the symbols I had drawn while in a trance state: lines of pentangles, hexagons, letters and figures which Oliver had 'transmitted' to me. The routine was that he would draw these on a piece of card and I would copy them almost instantaneously. He found the similarity between our cards highly gratifying. One odd feature about these tests intrigued us both. When I progressed to writing sentences which Oliver visualised in his mind the words were correct but transcribed in mirror writing. Why this should be puzzled us both, until one evening I emerged from a trance to see that for once my letters were the right way round.

'We've got the answer,' said Oliver delightedly. 'In the past I always sat opposite you, and therefore the images in my mind would look back to front to you – just like a mirror, in fact. This time I sat with my back to you, so when I visualised words they read left to right for you to copy down!'

Mainly for my benefit Oliver began a programme of work on post-hypnotic effect. If my back began to ache at work I merely had to telephone Oliver and when he said a pre-arranged sentence – 'The pain is gone' – I was immediately relieved. This aspect of hypnosis was the most fascinating to me, because, being awake, I was able to appreciate what was happening. On several occasions we tried returning to a past event in a conscious state.

'Is there an incident you would like to experience again – some happy moment you would like to relive?' asked Oliver. Perhaps because Geoffrey was there – he usually accompanied Dian when we had group sessions – my mind turned to the Lake District.

'Yes,' I said. 'My first morning on Derwentwater. I went out in a boat, I can't remember its name . . .'

'*Pandora*,' said Geoffrey almost too quickly.

'That's right. That was certainly a good moment – the lake spread out in front of me, and a glorious sense of adventure.'

'In that case I'll put you into trance for the post-hypnotic command,' said Oliver. 'And then we'll see if it is possible to turn memory back into present reality.' I was so accustomed to the process of hypnosis by now that Oliver merely had to touch my forehead for me to go under. A minute later I opened my eyes and looked about me in anticipation.

'Now, Martin,' said Oliver in his professional tone, 'you are about to row on Derwentwater in . . . *Pandora*.'

Pandora must have been the code word to trigger my illusion because the moment he said it I was conscious of changes in and about me. The walls of the room dissolved into sky, water and a lakeshore. Sunlight sparkled on wavelets slapping against the boat – I was no longer sprawled in an easy chair – and I was filled with childish joy as I rested on my oars and looked at the various tree-covered islands. A breeze ruffled my hair as I watched the *Princess Margaret Rose* cruising beneath the pine-dotted slope of rock towering above the eastern shore.

The odd thing was that although everything was as it had been on that long-ago day – a re-run of an old three-dimensional film through the projector of my consciousness – I was still aware that I, Martin Winter in his mid-twenties, was experiencing an illusion of a morning in my boyhood. I can only describe the feeling as the product of one reality superimposed upon another, rather as photographers sometimes place one negative on top of another to create a special effect.

Oliver was ecstatic when I described my sensations to him.

'Think of the implications, dear boy,' he cried, rubbing his dimpled hands together.

From then on he hypnotised me for longer periods, using key-words to trigger subconscious responses which he recorded on tape while I lay oblivious on his couch.

'I'll let you hear them when the experiment is complete,' he told me. 'It's better that you remain unaware of the form the programme is taking until it is completed, so that there can be no possibility of your conscious mind influencing your unconscious behaviour.'

But I never discovered what our sessions were leading to as the programme was interrupted by my friend's madness.

On the day that Dian was to play in the Wigmore Hall the three of us had lunch at Cranks vegetarian restaurant in Soho. She was obviously nervous, and as Mozart played in the background I tried to make her relax by chatting – I thought amusingly – about a film studio I had visited that morning. Geoffrey remained silent, his face drawn from what I guessed was lack of sleep. He had been working into the small hours of late because his stock of paintings had become so depleted. I sensed that Dian's tension was not entirely due to pre-performance nerves.

Suddenly Geoffrey told me to shut up. His voice was low, yet so intense that it caused a hush among the vegetarians around us.

Dian laid her hand on his and looked at me in a mute appeal not to respond.

'Sorry,' I said lightly. 'I think I'm more nervous about tonight than Dian . . .'

'You make a fine pair,' Geoffrey said. 'Look at you, scared sick in case Geoffrey might make a scene – might tell you the truth for once. You, Martin, hiding behind the role of the nice easy-going colonial boy, and you, Dian, who fell for the fourth temptation . . . you're both so phoney you make me sick.'

This unexpected attack kept me silent, but I felt a rising anger at Geoffrey's behaviour on a day so important to Dian, and it occurred to me, perhaps unfairly as events turned out, that he had chosen to be temperamental because it was the day of her debut.

'Hush, darling,' said Dian, aware of the eyes swivelling in our direction, and to me she added: 'Poor Geoffrey has been under such a lot of pressure to produce more work . . .'

Geoffrey shook her hand from his, and in a deft motion slapped her across the mouth.

Next moment, it seemed, the three of us were outside in Marshall Street, escapees from the English dread of public scenes. Behind us voices were coming to life with 'I say . . .' and 'Wasn't that young . . .'

'I have to go to the Alessandro,' Geoffrey announced abruptly and began walking very fast towards Bond Street, Dian and I following. Not a word was spoken during that stupid trek past Libertys, across Regent Street and through Hanover Square. A terrible unreality seemed to encapsulate that August afternoon. The weather had been splendid, and the bricks of the city, baked by fierce sunshine all morning, were now returning the heat they had stored. People in shirtsleeves or light summer dresses had spilled out of the pubs on to the pavements with their lager-and-limes, and the garden in the centre of the square was littered with girls having their lunch breaks from nearby offices and stores as we passed like three ghosts in a separate dimension. Perhaps it was my imagination, but the rumble of the traffic, the sound of a teenager's transistor, the gibberish squawking from the loudspeaker on a motorcycle policeman's Triumph, the chatter of the pub crowds – all seemed muffled, remote.

Glancing at Dian I saw her eyes glistening, and seeing my look she put her hand on mine. It was trembling violently and I felt a surge of hatred for Geoffrey for doing this to her on this day of all days.

He strode on white-faced, his pale eyes burning with some terrible conviction, until we reached Bond Street, where he halted and faced us. His lips worked for a few moments before he managed to get any words out.

'You two can't deceive me any longer,' he stammered. For a moment I thought he was going to accuse us of having an affair.

'Neither of you . . . neither of you . . .' His words were coming with difficulty. 'Neither of you gives a damn about me – and don't look like that, Dian. Admit the truth. I'm just a substitute for my sister. You both fell in love with Leila, and now all you've got is me . . .' He laughed, or at least made a curious sound which began as a laugh and ended with a sob.

Before we could think of a response, Geoffrey set off towards the Alessandro Gallery. I took Dian's arm to keep her from following him. I thought we had both had enough of Geoffrey for one day, but she pulled away from me and hurried after him. Still haunted by the feeling of insubstantiality, I followed.

When I reached the gallery Geoffrey and Dian were already inside and the girl behind the desk at the far end was saying '. . . and Mr Alessandro is expecting you. He'll be with you in a moment. We sold one of your Castlerigg studies yesterday.'

Geoffrey ignored her and walked to the portrait of Leila which stood on an easel in the gallery window, the reflection of her face merging with the images of the passersby. Then, quite deliberately, he took a knife from his pocket and began stabbing the canvas.

I I

What makes moments of tragedy almost unbearable is a seasoning of farce, and so it was that torrid afternoon at the Alessandro Gallery when Geoffrey destroyed the portrait of his twin sister. As the blade ripped through the canvas the receptionist forgot her Mayfair accent and, with a wail worthy of Eliza Dolittle, shouted, ''Ere, Alec, 'e's gone bloody berserk.' A client who had been standing motionless before one of Geoffrey's Subterraneans leapt to the door and shouted in a Berlin accent, 'Ve haf been hijacked.' Mr Alessandro appeared from the inner sanctum and thanked his dark gods that the ruined picture was for sale on commission only – 'But keep him away from the Hockney. I paid money for that!'

Meanwhile I threw my arms round Geoffrey from behind and tried to hold him, shouting to Dian, 'Ring Oliver!' For my trouble I received a gash across my left palm which later required several stitches at the casualty department of Charing Cross Hospital.

My struggle with Geoffrey ended with the appearance of two policemen attracted by the shouts of the German client. Looking at the frame with its fringe of canvas strips one asked wearily, 'Ban the Bomb or Save the Whales?' The other said to me, 'No need to assault him, sir,' and the moment I released my hold caught Geoffrey in a vicious wrist lock.

'My friend seems to be having a nervous breakdown,' I explained.

'He needs medical help,' said Dian, feverishly dialling the telephone on the receptionist's steel and acrylic desk. 'I'm trying to get a doctor . . .'

'We'll sort it all out at the station, miss,' said one of the policemen soothingly, while his colleague stood at the door of the gallery and spoke confidentially into his Pye transceiver. Almost immediately a police car pulled up at the kerb and Geoffrey, who had not said a word since producing the knife – it occurred to me that he had come prepared – was lifted into the back. Dian asked to go with him, and I was left trying to contact Oliver.

'Please, the carpet,' said Mr Alessandro, pointing to the blood dripping from my hand.

I made my handkerchief into a ball which I clenched as hard as I could, and a few minutes later I spoke to Oliver. He grasped what I said immediately and made no superfluous comment, merely asking where Geoffrey had been taken.

'Savile Row police station,' I said.

'I'll see you there in a few minutes,' he said. As I left the gallery Mr Alessandro was making a statement to a constable, who remarked that slashing a picture of one's sister seemed a bit kinky to him, while his secretary sponged away my blood spots from the cream carpet with 1001.

When I arrived at the police station I found Geoffrey and Dian drinking mugs of tea in a small interview room.

'You a friend of this gentleman, sir?' asked the sergeant who ushered me in. 'Perhaps you can give me an idea of what happened.'

'Mr Auber has been under a great deal of strain recently,' I said. 'What occurred in Bond Street is the result of overwork.'

'In your opinion,' said the sergeant. 'I suppose you wouldn't know if Mr Auber is in the habit of taking drugs.'

'Nonsense,' said Dian, who now looked in a far worse state than Geoffrey.

'It is not unknown for artistic persons to seek inspiration from illegal substances,' said the sergeant drily. 'I believe they were all at it when laudanum could be bought across the counter.'

To my relief the question was dropped when Oliver arrived, for I thought it more than possible that Geoffrey had been taking some drug to heighten his perception as a painter, or as an amusing habit acquired from his fashionable friends. Within a few minutes of Oliver's appearance matters were straightened out. In his most urbane way he explained to the police sergeant that Geoffrey was in need of psychiatric help, and he would personally arrange for him to be admitted to a clinic. As Geoffrey had only destroyed his own property there could surely be no charge brought against him.

Almost before I realised it I was helping Geoffrey into the back of Oliver's Rover while a traffic warden wrote out a ticket. Up till then Geoffrey had remained silent, but as the car drew away from the kerb he lowered his head and a series of sobs shook him.

'Good,' said Oliver, as Dian leant over the front passenger seat to calm him. 'It'll break his tension. Let's go home so that Geoffrey can rest and I can make some arrangements.'

'You didn't mean it about putting him in some clinic,' said Dian, aghast.

'Of course. I know an excellent place in Surrey . . .' Dian looked stricken and stroked Geoffrey's hair all the way to Frognal. My concern over Geoffrey was mingled with concern about her performance and I could see myself ringing up the organisers of the concert to explain that she was unable to attend. But I had reckoned without Oliver.

Once in his flat he told Dian to see Geoffrey to his room and get him to lie down. Then he rang a nursing home called Sayers Grange, just outside Ewhurst, and spoke for several minutes to a psychiatrist whom he appeared to know well. I did not hear what was said but I gathered that he was very concerned about Geoffrey's mental state.

'A private ambulance will be here in an hour,' he said as he replaced the receiver. 'Now to get the dear boy sedated.' He glanced at his watch. 'And then let us see what we can do for our distraught Miss Derbyshire.'

I followed him to Geoffrey's room where with professional care he coaxed my friend to swallow a couple of pills, aided by a glass of soda water.

'I'm sorry,' Geoffrey murmured. He seemed to be quite clear-headed, though at intervals his whole body was shaken by muscular spasms. 'I – I expect this had to happen sooner or later . . . How could it not . . .?' His voice faded as the sedative took effect. Oliver gently placed a blanket over him.

'Let's go downstairs,' he said. 'We could all use a stiff drinkie.' Trust him to call it that in the middle of a crisis.

As we went into the corridor Dian said, 'Oh, I'm going to be sick,' and bolted into the bathroom.

'When we're in the drawing-room just stand behind her and be ready to catch her,' Oliver said to me.

After Dian, chalk-faced and swaying, joined us we went downstairs and into the drawing-room.

'I'm afraid I don't feel very well,' she said. Oliver signalled to me by a jerk of his head, and a moment later Dian's legs seemed to collapse beneath her and she fell backwards into my arms. For a moment I thought she had fainted and wondered how Oliver had been able to warn me.

'Put her on that sofa, dear boy,' he said, going over to the drinks cabinet. 'I told you I could hypnotise Dian by a telepathic command. She's deep in trance, and I'm damned if I'm going to let Geoffrey's little prank ruin tonight for her. I say, what's wrong with your hand?'

After I had arranged Dian comfortably, I opened my fingers on the blood-soaked ball of my handkerchief.

'Nasty,' said Oliver. 'Waggle your fingers. Good, no tendons sliced. It's many years since I gave up doctoring, so all I can do is put antiseptic on it. You must get some stitches in it as soon as you can.'

'I will. It's suddenly started to hurt like hell.'

'Brandy might help a little,' said Oliver, passing me a generous tot. While I drank it gratefully, he stood beside the limp form of the girl on the sofa.

'Dian, you can hear my voice?'

'Yes.' The word came like a breath, faint and far away.

'You will follow everything I tell you?'

'Yes.'

'Excellent, Dian. When you wake you will not give Geoffrey Auber a thought, nor will you recall the events of this afternoon until tomorrow morning. You understand?'

'Yes.'

'When I wake you in a little while you will feel completely refreshed, your nerves will be perfectly steady, and your whole concentration will be focused on playing in the concert this evening.'

'Yes.'

'On waking it will not occur to you that you have been in trance, and your only interest will be preparing for your debut. Now I want you to rest totally.'

'Yes.'

Dian remained asleep until a Citroën ambulance arrived outside the house and Geoffrey, hardly more conscious than Dian, was helped into it and driven away to Sayers Grange.

'My poor patients,' muttered Oliver, glancing at the slim Piaget on his wrist. 'Can I leave Dian in your care once I have woken her?'

'Of course. These days my time is my own provided I meet my deadlines.'

'Oh dear, I must have dropped off,' said Dian with a yawn when she opened her eyes in response to Oliver's handclap. 'But it must have done me good. Is that the time? I must go to my flat and see about my dress for this evening, and have a final run through.'

She sat up, smiling. Gone were the trembling hands, the tear-filled eyes and the haggard expression. I looked at Oliver in admiration.

'Oh, Martin, what has happened to your hand?'

'He was wounded trying to save Beauty from the Beast,' said Oliver. 'Or was the story Hansel and Gretel?'

Later, as I was waiting my turn at Charing Cross Hospital before hurrying to Wigmore Street, I had time to remember his words and they worried me. Why did he mention

Hansel and Gretel? I had never revealed my private nickname for the Auber twins to anyone, unless . . .

'Mr Winter,' called a nurse, and a moment later I had something else to think about.

After the events of the afternoon the artistic decorum of the Wigmore Hall was balm to frayed emotions. Peace descended upon me as I took my seat, surrounded by the long-haired young in jeans and T-shirts and sober members of older generations in formal dress – though an Indian scarf here and an Icelandic sweater there suggested that a few had clung to youthful fancy. Even the pain in my hand subsided to a gentle throbbing as I surveyed the dark polished woodwork and the mural of Art Nouveau figures above the stage on which a concert grand gleamed, waiting for the hands which would bring it into vibrant life. It made me think of an aircraft standing on a runway before breaking free from the mundane grip of gravity.

'The house is nearly full,' said Dian. As her performance was after the interval she sat beside me, and it seemed almost eerie that she made no comment on the empty seat which had been reserved for Geoffrey. Just before the concert began Oliver arrived to take his seat on the other side of Dian, immaculate in well-filled evening dress and, as a concession to modern trends, a velvet bow tie of midnight blue.

'What a rush,' he whispered. 'Some of my patients came back for late appointments when their afternoon sessions were cancelled. I have a sneaking suspicion that my receptionist gave the impression that I had been summoned to Somewhere Very Important. I gather she didn't actually say Buckingham Palace, but . . .'

When it came to Dian's performance there was nothing about her manner to suggest the trauma she had been through a few hours earlier. She gave an impression of total concentration, and her fingers travelled the keyboard with an ease which was later praised in several reviews. When she finally stood up in her sheath-like gown of willow green and inclined her head to our enthusiastic applause, Oliver looked well pleased.

It was over a week before I visited Geoffrey at Sayers Grange. My time had been taken up in ghosting a three-part 'autobiography' of a star famous for his portrayal of ruthless anti-heroes, who in reality lived with his mother in a Dorset cottage and never touched alcohol. To give him a private life in keeping with his cinema persona required a lot of creative writing.

On the occasions when I rang the nursing home I was told tactfully that it might be best to wait a while before making the journey as Mr Auber was not up to seeing visitors just then. Dian was allowed to visit him and she reported that he appeared to be under sedation. He talked very little and then only about trivialities: the quality of the food, the view of the chestnut avenue from his window and how the glitter of Sayers Pond at the end of it made him think of Derwentwater.

He said the same thing to me when I was finally allowed to visit him with Dian. He was well enough for us to sit with him in the garden of the Edwardian mansion whose red bricks had replaced an old Tudor hall at the turn of the century. Fortunately the ancient garden had remained intact and we sat on a rustic bench in a walled garden which, as the scents surrounding us proclaimed, retained many of its herbs. Geoffrey's doctor had told Dian there were obvious advantages in having an enclosed garden, and she found that the smell of sage, rosemary, lavender and other aromatic plants had a remarkably soothing effect on her patients.

'At the moment I feel safe here,' Geoffrey said. 'Wearing a dressing-gown even out here gives one that cosy feeling of being an invalid. But it won't last. Destiny cannot be altered, and Leila and I come of strange stock.' His voice was rising and Dian watched him apprehensively. 'It is our turn to be victims of something that happened in the past, a curse that comes in cycles. Ah, Martin, if one could only break the pattern of those cycles!'

He was close to tears, but he regained control and when he spoke again his voice was less intense.

'It all goes back to witchcraft. Did you know that, Martin? Have you any idea of the horror which took place within the Castlerigg stones, Dian?'

'I only know the circle from your painting of it,' she answered quietly.

'It was strange, sitting there sketching, and all the time I could feel the scream of what had been trapped in the stone, I could sense the column of hatred and agony rising to the sky like smoke from the Devil's factory . . . and all the time I sketched and tried to pretend . . . tried to . . . pretend . . .'

As he ran out of words his right hand made a desperate circular motion until Dian gently took his wrist.

'Geoffrey, old friend, you're making yourself morbid,' I said lightly. 'We might be back at Derwentwater, with you going on about the Weeping Stone of Auber, the Green Lady, and all the rest of the rubbish you used to make up to scare me.'

'Of course,' said Geoffrey. 'I make everything up. I have an over-stimulated creative impulse. Do you understand, dear Dian? Everything is a product of my childish imagination, there is no substance.' Then he turned to me. 'And if that is so, what the hell has put me here?'

No one knew what to say. We sat and regarded an enormous bumble bee hovering over a nearby patch of thyme. On a distant wrought-iron seat a young woman was holding an animated conversation with an invisible friend. From beyond the wall of mellow brick came the pok, pok of a tennis game.

'I am surprised at your lack of curiosity, Martin,' said Geoffrey in a natural voice. His quick shifts of mood seemed to be a symptom of his malady. 'If the roles were reversed I'd be dying to know.'

'Know what?'

'Why I cut that picture in Alessandro's.'

'You'll tell me if you want to,' I said. 'And it may be that at this stage you don't know yourself. Anyway, let's look to the future, not the past.'

'The past controls the future,' said Geoffrey. 'I told Dr Samuels that and she agreed with me. We have a long talk each afternoon. She's so delightfully dedicated. But she's like you – she hasn't dared broach the delicate subject of my little outburst yet.'

'OK, Geoffrey,' I said. 'Why did you take a knife into Alessandro's and destroy an excellent portrait of your sister?'

'It was a gesture. That day I had decided I was finished with art. Well, it's no good just thinking something like that. I needed to underline it with a gesture. I thought it was my best painting.'

'Oh, Geoffrey,' said Dian, suffering for her love. 'Why did you want to stop painting?'

'The shadow of Nemesis was getting darker around me. At night I remembered things in my dreams from before I was born. I felt I was being forced through a very complex ritual, and I thought that if I did something out of character, something utterly different from what would be expected – like throwing away a career just when success was coming – it might break the sequence. Now, of course, I realise that what I did was merely part of the ritual.'

Geoffrey talked for a while in this vein, and I wondered if he spoke like this to Dr Samuels, or whether the airing of these aspects of his obsession were for our benefit.

'Would you like me to get in touch with Leila . . .' Dian began, in one of his sudden silences.

'You want to find out where she is,' he said. 'You'd both love to know. Let her be. She's part of the ritual, too. She might have escaped, but when she had the child . . .'

The last sentence seemed to hang in the air.

'Child?' I cried.

Geoffrey stood up and faced us.

'Yes, child!' he said. 'The child you fathered when you raped her – the fruit of that summer idyll.'

'That's impossible,' I muttered, feeling faint as the possibility of what he said overwhelmed me.

'Impossible?' Geoffrey sneered. 'You were both old enough! Oh, yes, you are part of the pattern, Martin, just like her and me.'

'Geoffrey,' I said, forcing myself to appear calm. 'Why are you inventing this?'

'I was never going to tell you,' he whispered. 'What good would it have done? You came and ruined everything.' He began to cry. Dian and I rose to our feet, but before we could begin to comfort him a young man in an orderly's jacket materialised and took Geoffrey by the arm.

'Time for your Bovril, Mr Auber,' he said pleasantly as he led him off.

For a few minutes Dian and I followed the pebbled paths of the garden, scrunching along with the walking wounded of the modern world.

'I have to go and have a talk with Dr Samuels,' said Dian at last. 'Will you wait here?'

I sat on a garden swing which hung from an ancient oak tree, and looked across to an expanse of lawn on which a group of figures played croquet. Sayers Grange prided itself on having the atmosphere of a luxurious country hotel, a five-star retreat for fashionable people out of sync with reality. A few minutes later I saw Dian walking with a young woman in a loose white coat who gestured continually with her hands as she spoke. Dian led her over to me and introduced her as Dr Samuels.

'Mr Winter, you knew Geoffrey as a boy,' she said.

'Briefly.'

'What do you remember of him as a child?'

'He was highly imaginative.'

'That's our Geoffrey,' she said. 'Anything else?'

'Only a feeling – probably because he and his sister were left to their own devices in a very large old house – I sensed there was something *lost* about them.'

'You mean like the Babes in the Wood?'

'Or Hansel and Gretel.' And as I said it Oliver Penthorne's remark returned to disturb me.

'I was just telling Miss Derbyshire that I'm sure your friend will get perfectly well, though I'm going to recommend he has a thorough course of analysis.'

As I drove back to London in a hired car, Dian said, 'I know nothing about what Geoffrey said, but it was obviously a shock to you. You went quite white. You've been a good friend, Martin, and I owe you this. When we get to Bloomsbury I'm going to give you Leila's address.'

12

The sun disc, magnified many times by the vapours rising from the lagoon, looked enormous poised on the rim of the world. The long launch carrying us bleary travellers from Marco Polo Airport glided on its own white reflection through water stained orange by the sunrise. Ahead the silhouette-city lay as delicate as a mirage, an anachronism of campaniles, domes, and flat palazzo roofs decorated with stone fretwork. I could not have had a better introduction to Venice than this, and I was grateful that, because it was the high season, I had been forced to come by a night flight.

A couple of weeks had passed since my first real news of Leila. Dian had kept her word and given me an address, not of Leila's home but the organisation for which she worked. Oddly enough it was already known to me, though I had had no idea of Leila's connection. At *Newsview* I had received and tossed aside screeds of material relating to an annual film festival the company organised in Venice.

'I don't know her personal address,' said Dian. 'I think her work for World Newsfilm Awards takes her all over the place, but you can be sure she will be in Venice for the festival.'

'Do you write to each other often?' I asked.

'No, every few months just to keep in touch. And to give her news of Geoffrey.'

'Have you mentioned me?'

'No. Will you try to see her?'

I said I didn't know, but in truth I was already scheming to get to the festival in an official capacity.

'I'm not sure if I've done the right thing, telling you her whereabouts,' she said. 'Geoffrey would be angry if he knew. He'd see it as another act in what he calls the ritual.'

'Dian,' I said as gently as possible, 'that talk of rituals is the reflection of Geoffrey's mental state. At the moment you can't take anything he says seriously. Of course, I'm certain he'll get better . . .'

'With all his fire and talent analysed out of him,' said Dian bitterly.

At the office the next day I began my campaign to go to Venice. I knew the idea of newsfilm would not inspire the features editor. He was one of the old school who regarded film festivals as venues for starlets to be thrown naked into pools – several times if the photographers required it.

'G'day, sport,' he said as I went into his office. 'Just back from the black stump, are yer? Bonza to see yer again.'

'I was wondering if I could bring my holiday forward,' I began.

'I thought you were on holiday. Never see you in the office these days.'

'My copy still comes in on time,' I said mildly. 'Look, I've always wanted to go to Venice, and there's a film festival there in a fortnight. If I could go then I might be able to pick up a story or two. I know I'd be having my holiday early, but I think it could be worth it . . .'

'Said like a true free-loader. What's the festival about?'

'Newsfilm. Sequences from film and television news footage from all over the world. There are a dozen categories . . . natural disaster, war, sport, culture and so on.'

The features editor looked at me in mock pity.

'People get enough of that in the dailies and on TV. They want entertainment from us, not doom and gloom.'

'But I might pick up some good stories on how some of the best items were shot. You know, human interest . . . "I could hardly look through the viewfinder for the tears in my eyes." '

'Or "How the rebels held up the execution while I took a light-reading." OK, I'll see what I can do. And while we can't pay for your holiday, if you get some good stories we might consider reasonable expenses. I can't say fairer than that.'

He waved aside my thanks.

'The poor old rag is going through a sticky patch,' he said. 'We may as well take any perks going. By the way, the major told me that you're confirmed as film correspondent. You'll need a wheelbarrow for your pay packet from now on. He likes the copy you're doing, and I think that ghost job on Mike Dennis did the trick. Don't forget you promised to get his autograph for my wife – he's her idea of virile manhood.' He looked down at his paunch with comic resignation.

'Then I won't destroy her illusions,' I said. 'But the nearest thing he has had to a love affair is with his Siamese.'

'Au pair?'

'Cat.'

At lunch time I celebrated by buying drinks all round for my colleagues. Not only had I won the job I coveted but soon I would be on my way to Venice, and I felt that life was going to take another shift.

I did not see Geoffrey before I left. Dian told me, as gently as possible, that Dr Samuels thought I had a disturbing influence on him at the moment. After my visit he had been morbid and withdrawn, and she thought that a nervous depression had been triggered by my presence which might be explained as his analysis progressed.

'Don't take it personally. It's not your fault,' Dian said, her tender heart fearing that her words would hurt me. 'It's true what I told you before – Geoffrey does love you. It's just that everything has got so mixed up.'

We were having an early supper at the Festival Hall, prior to what we sensed might be our last evening together at the National Film Theatre. The Thames and the Embankment opposite were bathed in that luminosity which comes with light summer evenings, and the summer clothing of the crowds dawdling on the terraces below reminded me of my arrival in Wellington, when it had appeared that all its citizens were on holiday.

'By the way, it seems as though I'm going to have a stepmother,' I said, remembering an aerogramme I had received that morning. 'My father is going to make an honest woman out of his friend.'

'I do hope he'll be happy. You'll have to go out and be best man.'

'I'd love to, but Godzone is exactly on the opposite side of the world, and the fares are pretty expensive. But I'll try. I'd like to be there to wish him well.'

'If you go I hope you'll come back,' said Dian in a wistful voice. 'I feel everything is about to alter and it frightens me a little.'

'I suppose change is going on all the time, but we only notice it when something happens to open our eyes to it.'

'I wonder what we'll all be doing a year from now.'

'I can tell you,' I said, hoping to halt the sadness I felt coming over her, which no doubt owed its origin to Geoffrey's mental trouble. 'You will be giving your first recital in the Queen Elizabeth Hall, Geoffrey will be holding his second exhibition in Leighton House, Oliver, of course, will continue to be Oliver and will have acquired more icons, and I will have completed my novel.' For it had recently occurred to me that at last the time had come to start writing for myself as well as for *Newsview*, and an idea for a story had begun to germinate.

We watched a Shell oil barge racing down the river with the tide.

'And Leila? I wonder what will have happened to her?'

And Leila . . . as the airport launch moved gently towards this etching of a city, I wondered yet again if I was mad to come in search of her. The girl I had once thought of as Gretel could no longer exist. It was not a geographical distance which needed to be travelled to find the Leila I had loved as we roved the banks of Derwentwater, but a distance of time. A dozen years separated me from her, and the person I was here to find might have nothing in common with the girl I had lain with in the shade of the Auber mausoleum. Physically, mentally and emotionally she would have altered, just as I had done. What I was doing here was utterly illogical. I was denigrating life by reducing it to the level of a romantic novel.

But why?

I could see what I was doing, but I couldn't understand why I was doing it. Was it because of Geoffrey's wild words in the sunken garden at Sayers Grange? At the time the shock of them was as startling as an unexpected slap across the face, but later I tried to comfort myself – to block the instant guilt which assailed me – by telling myself it was said at a time when Geoffrey was in a state of suppressed hysteria, talking about a family curse and his life's being part of a ritual. Surely what he had said about Leila was also the rambling of a highly sensitive young man thrown off mental balance by a nervous breakdown!

Although Geoffrey had been very friendly since our reunion, sometimes when he was under stress a hidden resentment towards me came into the open. Had that story been inspired by a desire to distress me? If so, it had been effective. While I tried to convince myself that it could not possibly be true, there were times when I found myself in a mental turmoil in case it was. I was certain of one thing: there would be no peace for me until I found out the truth for myself.

Doubts about my journey here faded before my surprise and delight at Venice. Having seen so many illustrations of it in magazines, in holiday brochures and on travel posters, I felt I knew what to expect, but I was unprepared for the impact of the living city. The joy of Venice is that although its appearance has scarcely changed since Canaletto painted it, it is no museum. Today it is one of the few places where crowds of tourists don't look out of place. The city needs them as extras to replace the bright throngs which filled its squares and crowded its bridges in the days of the Doges.

By the time the boat ended its journey at the Molo I had

an admiration for Venice which no criticism from more sophisticated travellers than I has ever been able to shake. And I knew that if ever there was a city to fall in love in, this was it.

Although my suitcase was heavy, I could not resist walking into St Mark's Square. Then, in need of a shower and a rest after my night of travelling, I embarked on a *vaporetto* for the Lido where the festival organisers had made a last-minute booking for me in the small but adequate Hotel Dardanelli. As I lay down to catch a few hours' sleep in my cool, marble-floored room it occurred to me that somewhere close by Leila Auber must be beginning her day, and that tonight I should see her at last.

That evening I stood in a queue of animated people in evening dress, waiting my turn to step aboard one of those sleek, lovingly varnished launches which one sees surging along the Grand Canal, discreetly displaying the name of some majestic hotel along with a rose in a silver holder in front of the white-uniformed steersman. Across the inky lagoon Venice appeared to float in a luminous cloud, its lights diffused by a soft sea mist, while nearer at hand the navigation lights of invisible craft moved like fireflies in slow motion.

At three- or four-minute intervals launches would move out of the dark and briefly tie up for consignments of passengers who embarked with jokes and cries of 'Any more for the *Skylark*?' They were my fellow delegates to the festival – broadcasting officials, directors of news agencies, so-called media executives, television and film company representatives, and mysterious personages who I later learned were referred to by the organisers as 'assorted free-loaders' or AFLs.

When it was my turn to go aboard one of these luxurious craft I did not enter the cabin but stood at the taffrail, savouring the damp rush of air as we raced off, following the curving glitter of lamps which marked our channel.

With the exhilaration words began to form in my mind for the semi-humorous letter I would be sending to New Zealand. 'Dear Dad, Here I am in my white tuxedo being whisked across the Venetian lagoon to a palazzo on the Grand Canal. And who can tell what the night will bring in this ancient city . . . ?'

Indeed, what would it bring?

I was suddenly so nervous that I felt a physical sickness. Up till now I had not given any thought to an actual meeting with Leila. Now it occurred to me that she might not want more than a brief exchange of platitudes.

'*Your name's familiar . . . Derwentwater, wasn't it? . . . small world . . . enjoy your stay . . .*'

There was also the possibility that, should Geoffrey's story be true, she might hate me as the wrecker of her young life. And the child – it would be twelve years old. Would it be with its mother?

'*Martin Winter? Of course I remember you. Come and meet our son (or daughter).*'

I sat down. The laughter from the cabin sounded like mocking jeers. I think that if it had been possible I would have left the launch before it reached its fateful destination but, short of plunging into its wake, there was nothing I could do. Lights from the buildings and cafés streaked the water. Under a sun-umbrella of an outdoor restaurant close to the Rialto Bridge I saw a man and woman – lovers by the way they held hands – raise their glasses to us, and weakly I waved back. A city for lovers, I had thought that morning. Now I thought, what a terrible city to be lonely in.

We passed under the bridge and a moment later there was the sound of waves slapping ancient stonework as our launch came to a stop with reversed engines, its bow almost touching the stern of the launch ahead. Footmen in rococo uniforms helped its passengers to alight. Above them several more stood to attention with flambeaux whose dancing flames played on the eager faces of the guests as they climbed the steps and disappeared into a brightly lit palazzo. A banner proclaiming 'Welcome to the World Newsfilm Awards' was draped above the arched entrance.

The engines of our launch burbled pleasantly as the steersman deftly held our position, and then allowed us to drift against the steps when it was our turn to disembark. Gloved hands made sure I did not slip on the damp step, and I felt the heat of the flambeaux on my face as I climbed towards the ducal doorway. In the foyer beneath a scintillating chandelier a major-domo glanced at my delegate's card and announced to the company in a vast salon beyond, 'Signor Martin Winter.'

The president of the festival and his wife greeted me – a quick handshake and 'So glad you could make it, Mr Martin'. I was processed by several other officials and their fashionably gowned ladies, and then I was free to go in search of a much needed drink. From a gallery above a string ensemble played popular airs which were at times drowned by conversation in a dozen languages, yet such is man's obsession with his own identity that when my name was spoken quietly behind me my ears picked it up in the way that one's name leaps out of a printed page. I turned, and there was Leila Auber.

For some seconds I stood stupidly speechless. This moment, for which I had waited so long, and had been in such fear of a few minutes earlier on the lagoon, was not like any of the confrontations predicted by my over-worked imagination. It was not embarrassing nor dramatic – it was funny.

'You are *the* Martin Winter, captain of the *Pandora*, aren't you?' she asked. Her look told me that she was anxious in case she had made a mistake, though I knew instantly that silver-blonde hair and those eyes which seemed to hold their own light. She was taller and naturally her figure was fuller, but otherwise she was uncannily like the mental images of her I had carried for a dozen years. The greatest difference between them and the Leila before me in her emerald satin dress was a tan of

Mediterranean gold which could never have been acquired on Derwentwater.

'The Green Lady!' I cried in mock horror. She laughed aloud and we shook hands.

We gazed at each other in silence for a moment, then both spoke at once and stopped simultaneously. I joined in her laughter.

'What a splendid setting for a meeting after all these years,' I said, waving at the huge saloon.

'It must have been intuition which made me suggest we hire a palazzo for the reception. Let me look at you. How does the adult Martin Winter compare with the boy who came on holiday to our lake?'

She stood back and surveyed me while, to cover my awkwardness, I took a couple of glasses from the tray proffered by a bewigged footman.

'You've grown taller than I expected – you had a sickly look in the Derwentwater days. Just out of hospital, weren't you? Yes, I'm not disappointed.'

'That's due to the healthy life down under,' I said.

'You left England . . .'

'Yes. Dad took me to New Zealand.'

'That explains . . . Anyway, it seems to have suited you.'

She smiled while I replied with some banal compliment on her beauty.

Taking my arm she led me across the mosaic floor to a gilded couch which had just been vacated by a Japanese couple – he in an immaculate dinner suit which merely served to set off the gorgeous colours of her kimono. A tang of heavy perfume hung in the air, a fading impression of a Hiroshige print.

'Oh, I'm so glad that the Martin Winter on the press list turned out to be you,' Leila said as we watched the carnival throng over our glasses. 'All week I was wondering whether it was a namesake or whether it really would be the Boy grown up. I remembered you had always wanted to write, and that gave me hope. I wonder if I'd have recognised you so quickly if I hadn't been expecting you. Yes, I would, though. Derwentwater seems a lifetime ago, but I'm sure I'd have known you anywhere. You still have that air of innocence, or should I say wonder? Must be useful in your job.'

'Do you live in Venice?' I asked.

'During the festival I stay on the Lido at the Excelsior. That's where it all happens. I often think World War Three would be easier to organise than a film festival.' She put on a comic expression of harassment. 'But just because this is the busiest week of my year don't think you're going to get out of seeing me again.'

'Even festival organisers must have to relax sometimes,' I said, 'and when you do – I'll be there.'

'Good. I'm rather on call here . . .'

'That's exactly what Geoffrey said when I met him at one of his exhibitions . . .'

'Oh, you've seen him . . .'

A young man broke from the crowd and sighted Leila with a look of relief.

'Miss Auber, you are needed so much. It's the East Berlin delegation again . . . it seems that by mistake a waiter put the West German flag on their table. Herr Hinterhauser is shouting!'

'*Sturm und Drang!*' cried Leila, climbing to her feet. 'All right, Gregorio, let's stave off an international incident. Wretched people, spoiling our reunion,' she added to me. 'Look out for me later.'

I nodded. 'Good luck with Herr Hinterhauser.'

Leila vanished into the crowd in the wake of the anxious young man and I strolled round the saloon, admiring the enormous paintings of the city's past magnificence and feeling elated by our meeting. It could not have been more easy and natural, and there was certainly nothing in her manner to suggest that there could have been any truth in Geoffrey's words at Sayers Grange. I took another glass of chilled Chianti and drank a private toast to the next few days, and the fact that I no longer needed to feel like the villain of a Victorian melodrama.

Soon afterwards there was a speech of welcome from the president of the festival, and then we flowed up a staircase of rare marbles and into a banqueting hall to an accompaniment of Vivaldi from the musicians in the gallery. Amid the confusion I managed to find my seat at a long table and saw that the name on the place card next to mine was Y. S. Akkim, a name which – thanks to the National Film Theatre – was not unknown to me. I gave silent thanks to the patron saint of journalists.

Just before the first course was served a small, delicately proportioned and beautifully dressed man came and sat beside me. His greying hair was a mass of curls above a high, smooth brow. His features, like his body, were delicate, his skin the colour of papyrus. His eyes were large and disconcertingly black – the eyes of an old caliph who could be bountiful or merciless as the whim took him. I fancy that Akkim's ancestors were merchants who had cornered the Cornish trade before the bright star hung above Bethlehem.

'Hello,' he said to me, extending a hand. 'I'm Akkim.'

'Yes,' I said. 'You made *Antar – Sword of the Desert*.'

He actually clapped his hands in delight and I saw a coin-thin Piaget watch on his left wrist.

'I am delighted to find someone here who knows my work. Are you connected with news filming?'

I introduced myself and explained that I was a journalist.

'But how do you know about *Antar*? It was never released in Great Britain. The people there have had enough of their own Robin Hood without paying to see the Arabian variety.' He laughed with a flash of attractive teeth, well cared for, regular and neat like himself. 'To be honest, the Arabs weren't all that keen on it either.'

'The message came just too late,' I said. 'The way the price of oil has rocketed will make the Arabs the wealthiest people in the world, and I don't think stories about underdogs and outlaws will have the appeal of a few years ago. But to answer your question, I saw *Antar* at a season of Middle Eastern films put on by our National Film Theatre.'

'It was my last Egyptian film,' said Akkim. 'I am back in Hollywood now.' For a moment a gloating expression flitted across his face. 'Since I was a boy it was my dream to make movies in USA – if you can make movies there you really are a movie maker – and to have an office on Sunset Boulevard. Now I do both.'

We were interrupted by the arrival of the first course, and I took the opportunity to look for Leila. I finally located her at a special table acting as hostess to members of the international jury. I raised my hand and she responded with a funny little half-wave I remembered from what I always think of as the Derwentwater days.

I asked Akkim what he, a producer of cinema features, was doing at a festival devoted to factual filming.

'I am hunting for inspiration – for ideas.' He lowered his voice conspiratorially. 'Listen, Mr Winter, I have been meditating in the wilderness – literally, as I had some work to do in Abu Sabbah – on the way cinema entertainment is going to go this next decade. And I believe that one of the trends will be towards adult fairy tales. People will want the adventures of the prince in search of the king's daughter, magic, monsters, enchantments, and above all the fear of the witch and the unknown. There will be enough mundane fear in their daily lives to make them feel pleasurable relief in fear which they will know is imaginary.'

'And what form would these adult fairy tales take?' I asked.

'Mainly science fiction and horror movies,' he answered, a note of enthusiasm in his voice. 'I have no interest in science fiction – perhaps it is the "science" I am not in sympathy with – but horror . . . ah! Horror! In the next few years I intend to become a merchant of the macabre and the fantastic. I shall restore a debased art form back to the place it held when such writers as Poe, de Maupassant and Bierce were respected as its masters.'

'They hardly wrote fairy tales,' I said.

Akkim's eyebrows arched.

'In that case, Mr Winter, you do not know your Brothers Grimm! All our inherent fears are to be found in fairy tales – fear of the familiar which can suddenly change, fear of the alien, fear of isolation and abandonment, fear of the supernatural. Think of the psychological horror in Hansel and Gretel for example. It is not so much the witch, though she is an excellent character – no, the real horror in that story is the woodman father deliberately losing his children in the wild forest. And do you know the true story of Sleeping Beauty? Not the prettified one served up in Christmas picture books . . .'

He paused.

'Forgive me. I am riding my hobby-horse to death. As I said, I am here looking for inspiration. I thought so much real-life horror might give me a germ of an idea for a movie. To hit on the right concept is the most important factor in making a film. The rest is technicalities. I search all the time. Do you have any thoughts on the subject, Mr Winter?'

Before I could reply a man came up and embraced Akkim. He was introduced to me as a former colleague, and the two men began an animated conversation in Arabic, with frequent apologies to me. To save Akkim embarrassment I chatted to a fellow journalist across the table who was delighted to have an audience to whom he could wax eloquent on the shortcomings of the festival.

Later I met Leila at the palazzo steps and we boarded the same launch to return to the Lido. I could sense her relish of the night breeze and the tranquil water after the strain of the reception.

'I'm sorry not to be talkative,' she said, taking a box of Sobranies from her handbag. 'Remembering you, I'm sure you'll understand. When this festival is over I think I'm going to have a nice quiet nervous breakdown.'

It occurred to me that she might not be aware of her brother's condition. If so, now was not the time to tell her. I took the lighter from her and lit the elegant black cigarette.

'Oh, I needed that,' she said as she inhaled. 'My vice, I'm afraid. I love these, but I don't smoke them in public. Black cigarettes would look a bit much, don't you think?'

She shivered slightly as we entered the lagoon and its chill caught her. She pulled her silver cloak closer about her and leaned against me for warmth.

'If only this were Derwentwater,' she murmured.

13

The first day of the festival was disappointing. My schedule told me that the opening session was for News Documentaries – Culture, and after an hour I found I had seen all I wanted to of Albanian folk dances and American pop art. I had been unable to exchange more than a brief greeting with Leila, whose job it was to see that everything ran smoothly for the judges, and deal with their queries and complaints, but as I headed for the exit I saw her mouth the word 'traitor' at me. It was a relief to find myself blinking in the brilliant light, and I headed to the ferry terminal at the Piazzale Santa Maria Elisabetta. At a small restaurant opposite an elderly waiter and a youthful apprentice stood side by side, smiling, and this made me eager to bring Leila here as soon as she could get away from her duties.

Soon I was on a *vaporetto* churning towards the city, which lay beneath a sky of hot pearl. Landing at the St Zaccaria stop, I strolled along the waterfront to St Mark's Square, where gusts of pigeons swept low over the tourists distributing largesse from bags of peanuts. As well as the cathedral and campanile, the square is famous for its two outdoor cafés – Florian's flanking the south colonnade and Quadri's to the north – whose musicians play alternate numbers. The decision of which to choose for coffee was made for me when I heard my name called and saw Akkim in a pale grey safari suit waving to me from a table in the front rank of Florian's.

'Good morning,' he said. 'You look like an escapee from culture. It will be the war and disaster categories which bring the festival to life.'

He ordered coffee and *aqua minerale* from a waiter wiping tables nearby.

'I'm sorry our conversation was interrupted last night,' he continued. 'But it was an old colleague from the pre-Nasser days when we worked in a Cairo film studio. Now he makes propaganda films, and I am hunting horror.'

He made a wry face at the curious ways of the world.

'And how is the horror hunt going?' I asked. An idea for a story on Akkim was germinating.

'I have not found what I am after. To be frank, I do not know what that is, only that I shall recognise it when I see it. I went to Abu Sabbah to follow up a story about a ghoul which was supposed to have appeared in the Valley of the Jinn. I should explain that a ghoul is a sort of Arabian vampire, which devours the flesh of the dead.'

I nodded, remembering the child Leila reading me a story from *The Thousand and One Nights* in which one of these revolting creatures of Islamic mythology was described.

'And you really went all that way to chase one up?'

'A small price to pay if it had turned out to be what I am looking for,' said Akkim. 'I assure you I didn't expect to find a real ghoul, but I hoped to get something from the gossip and traditions of the villagers who believed one was on the prowl – believe me, Abu Sabbah is a century behind the times. I had hoped this would give me a story.'

'It didn't?'

'No. I decided the concept of a ghoul in a film was not right for the Western mind. One needs to draw on sub-conscious cultural *moeurs* to make a good horror story, and I think a ghoul would only appear ludicrous to Christian audiences. But it wasn't ludicrous to the villagers. They were in terror of it, believing it had been reactivated in a subterranean lair by the recent earthquakes. They even showed me some desecrated tombs which they swore were the ghoul's work.'

'Really?' I said, not quite knowing whether to take Akkim seriously.

'Oh yes. But I am sure it had been done by hyenas.'

He talked until he saw that I had finished my coffee, and then asked whether I would like to explore some of the small *calles*, or alleyways, of the city.

'Perhaps I shall find inspiration there,' he added. 'Who knows?'

We left the square and wandered into a labyrinth of shadowed passages and silent, sun-scorched squares. This was the city on the other side of the façade, strangely quiet after the activity of the Piazza, and populated – or so it seemed at that time of day – by sad cats and a few old ladies in black. We watched while one leaned out of a top-storey window and winched up her basket by a pulley arrangement.

'This is better,' was Akkim's comment. He sniffed, and when I followed suit I caught the tang of dampness denoting a nearby canal. We passed through an archway and there it was: a narrow waterway between towering brick walls, its surface a livid green where a ray of sunlight struck it. A gondolier, his straw hat over his face, sprawled asleep in his craft. The lion's head to which it was moored had probably gazed over the water since the days of Austrian rule.

'What an excellent setting for the sort of film I want to make,' Akkim said as we walked along the narrow footpath above the canal, passing doors whose venerable carving suggested that they must once have belonged in buildings far grander than these backwater tenements. 'Look at those slimy steps leading from the canal to that door in the blank wall. What does that suggest to you?'

'A vampire,' I said, entering into the spirit of the game. 'At midnight a gondola arrives and waits for a beautiful lady to descend the steps. Then it glides silently to the Grand Canal and past the open cafés on the terraces and young men crane forward amazed at the beauty of the passenger seen in the light of a silver lantern . . .'

'Continue, my friend,' Akkim encouraged.

'When the woman in the gondola sees a handsome young man sitting alone, her silent gondolier pilots the boat close to the bank and she tosses him a blood-red carnation, saying one word: "Tomorrow".

'Naturally he is at the same table the following evening, watching every passing gondola, his eyes seeking the one with a silver lantern hanging from a silver chain. At last it appears. The cloaked gondolier pulls up against the steps and with a gesture and a smile the woman welcomes him aboard. The boat then flies like an arrow to the lagoon, heading in the direction of the island of St Michele. There, behind the high wall and under the dark cypress trees, the young man learns what it is like to be loved by a vampire.'

Akkim was about to say something but I raised my finger.

'The next night the young man's table is deserted. The gondolier glides up to the terrace and the lady of the silver lamp tosses another flower on to the table: a white carnation.'

Akkim patted me gently on the shoulder.

'Very good, Mr Winter. You should change your profession so that your imagination may expand.'

I thought that the boy Geoffrey would have been proud of me, and managed to remain silent about the novel which lay half-completed in my desk.

'Oh, what a day!' exclaimed Leila as we sat down at a table at the little restaurant I had noticed opposite the landing stage. 'A week of this and I shall be out of my mind. The judges have been squabbling all the time. One actually turned his back to the screen during the State Occasion session because he disliked the politics of the country which had submitted the entry. And the Third World!

Those African faces under Sandhurst-style caps. The people may be diseased and starving, but those at the top are in love with the ceremonial trappings of the old colonialists. And they proliferate the inherited evil . . . today I got bored watching young kids parading with weapons.

'There! I've had my moan. Now I'm off duty for a few hours, so let's enjoy them while we may. Did you have a good day? I saw you sneaking out during the folk dancing.'

'I spent some of it with a film producer who's just back from some tiny Arabian state where he was looking for ghouls.'

'Girls or ghouls?'

'Ghouls, definitely.'

At that moment the elderly waiter materialised above us with such a benign smile on his pink face that I was reminded of Oliver Penthorne. Leila immediately christened him the Father Figure, and so I thought of him for the rest of my stay.

'So,' said Leila after we had ordered pasta and a bottle of *vino di casa*. 'Alone at last. The time has come for me to hear the story of your life since the Derwentwater holiday, and how it comes about that our paths should cross in Venice.'

For a moment I felt at a loss. It seemed to me that Leila had no wish to assuage my curiosity about her, and I felt that her direct approach was to forestall any questions of my own. I could not believe that this beautiful, cool young woman could be genuinely interested in me . . . I think the reason for my negative view during those first few days in Venice was because I had not yet found my bearings with the adult Leila. For nearly half my life I had been haunted by the image of the young girl I had fallen in love with at Derwentwater, but now we had met again that child ghost was fading before the exorcism of reality. Leila and I were strangers who felt we ought to be friends simply because we had said goodbye to childhood

159

together. Could I have expected this reunion to have been different in any way? Hindsight told me no, but as I sat with a glass of cold clear wine in my hand I smiled at the beautiful stranger and behind my mask mourned the memory she had once given me and which she was now displacing.

I did not want Leila to know that my only intention in coming to Venice had been to see her. If she suspected it I should merely look ridiculous and she would be embarrassed. Yet if I pretended that this was just a routine assignment for me, it would make it difficult to explain my close friendship with Geoffrey and Dian without her guessing the truth . . . I suddenly felt a spasm of irritation. The situation had become a bore. And it was certainly my fault. I was infuriated by my romantic stupidity.

'OK,' I said. Determined to keep it light, I launched into a series of anecdotes about life in New Zealand, my failure as a teacher and my work for *Newsview*. While they gave away nothing about my obsession – at last I admitted to myself that for years I had been obsessed – with her and the House of Auber, my stories did have the virtue of making her laugh as we ate our *spaghetti alle vongole*. The Father Figure stood in the background smiling with approval at our good humour.

When we had finished our supper Leila looked at me with a smile which gave me a pang of regret that dreams did not come true.

'You've been very kind to entertain me like this,' she said. 'I've contributed nothing, I know, but I'm truly tired. It's not just that one gets exhausted during the festival. The last few months of organising have taken their toll. Sorry.'

'I must get you home,' I said. 'Unless you'd like a final drink.'

'Why not? You deserve one even if I don't. May I have a *zambucca* on the rocks? It goes with the setting, I think.'

When our drinks came she raised hers in a toast. Gazing

at me over the liquor, which was becoming opaque as the ice melted, she said, 'Of course, you haven't fooled me – you've talked for a couple of hours – and most amusingly – but you've told me nothing. You're as mysterious as ever, just turning up out of the blue as you did all those years ago . . .'

When we went out into the hot night I led her across the piazzale to where a driver dozed on the seat of his ancient carriage while his horse's head drooped behind the shafts. Across the lagoon the city appeared to lie in a luminous shroud as a fine mist diffused its lights.

'Excelsior,' I said as we climbed into the vehicle, which listed like a boat. The old driver muttered apologetically to his horse and we moved off, creaking sedately along the Gran Viale. For a few minutes we travelled in silence, and then a young man in a scarlet shirt cruised beside us on a white Vespa, rock and roll music crackling from the transistor he wore like a camera. He shouted something to Leila and kissed his fingers, and smiled with amorous suggestion when she replied in Italian. Then he opened the throttle and raced away, his tail-light a dwindling meteor.

'He said we make a good couple,' Leila told me. 'A couple with style is what he actually said. And he was right.'

For a moment she laid her cool palm on the back of my hand.

'It sounded to me as though the word "passion" came into it, too,' I said.

She laughed and nodded.

As we neared the seaward side of the Lido, the clammy mist against our faces not only turned the lamps into a series of haloes but also muted sound, so that we were filled with an isolation which the bent figure on the driver's seat did nothing to allay.

Leila shivered.

'Much as I love Venice, I sometimes find it an ominous place,' she said. 'It's as though the extravagant façade we see by day is a sort of film set behind which there is a secret city. I'm sounding like Geoffrey in his old flights of imagination. Remember?'

I nodded and took her words as a cue to say something I should have mentioned much earlier, something about which I felt a reluctance I only partially understood.

'I did tell you I've been seeing him in London?'

'He mentioned it when he wrote to me. I think he was very pleased.' She sighed. 'Poor Geoff. As soon as this festival is over I must go to England and see him. Dian, his girlfriend – you must have met her – has been very anxious. What evil god created heredity?'

Her words came as a relief. There had been an underlying tension at the thought of having to explain about Geoffrey's breakdown, but obviously she was aware of what had happened. Dian must have written to her, without referring to me or the real reason for my visit to Venice. Looking back, I am surprised at how sensitive I was about this issue, how nervous I was of her opinion.

The driver whipped the reins, and the horse made an extra effort so that we rolled up to the hotel entrance with an impressive rattle of hoofs.

'Thank you so much for this evening,' said Leila as we climbed out to an ominous creaking of leather braces. 'I couldn't have unwound without your help.'

I paid off the driver and walked with her into the foyer.

'Posh,' I commented. She laughed.

'Yes, but only while the festival lasts. I'm here to look after the VIPs, but when they go my coach becomes a pumpkin. See you tomorrow.' She kissed me goodnight – the correct sort of kiss exchanged between friends after a pleasant supper.

I hardly saw anything of Leila during the next couple of days, mere glimpses of her closeted with the jury members or surrounded by anxious people wanting something of her. Our exchanges were limited to handwaves above the heads of delegates. And I had work to do. I wanted to interview several film-makers, including Akkim, who suggested we met for early evening cocktails at Harry's Bar.

The sinking sun had thrown a golden haze over the city when I saw his neat, white-suited figure seated before a tall, garishly coloured drink.

'How goes the search for your story?' I asked as I sat down beside him.

'There are so many ideas, and none of them right,' he said with a sigh. 'You are one of the few people here who haven't pulled a script, or at least an outline, from your hip pocket within twenty minutes of meeting me.'

'One of the hazards of film festivals,' I said. 'If ever I gave you an idea I'd have to be sure it was one you'd like.'

He took a card from an old-fashioned cardcase.

'Here is my Los Angeles address,' he said. 'When the creative thunderbolt smites you, please get in touch with me. Now, do you really want to interview me, or shall we have a pleasant chat?'

I had thought that his visit to Abu Sabbah in search of a monster would make an ideal column for *Newsview*, but I had learned by experience that stories with sensational themes are more likely to crop up casually than develop from premeditated interviews.

'Let's chat,' I said.

'Good. We call this the happy hour back in the States. It's well named; a little oasis of relaxation between the stress of the day and the tension of the night. In Abu Sabbah I envied the simple folk out in the desert. I thought of my life chasing the bitch of success and I decided that they had a much better deal than I. I suddenly understood what it was that made so many Victorian Englishmen go native in the Arabian wastes, and I felt I could have followed their example but for one thing.'

'What was that?'

'They don't have movies in the desert.'

When Akkim and I parted late that evening, just suffi-
ciently intoxicated to feel euphoric, he said, 'Tomorrow is
the Natural Disaster session. There is a remarkable film
which cost the cameraman his life . . . perhaps we'll meet
in the cinema.'

I nodded and, as the *vaporetto* churned away from the
landing stage, watched his white figure shrink with a
feeling of elation. His enthusiasm for film-making had
infected me. After three hours of listening to him I knew
that the novel I had been working on spasmodically in
London was going to be transformed into a film script on
my return.

An hour later I was drifting into sleep when the telephone beside my bed plucked me back to consciousness.
With an effort I picked up the handset and muttered into it.

'Hello. You sound a bit woozy,' Leila laughed.

'I've had a rather good evening with Yousef Akkim,' I
said.

'I thought they didn't drink alcohol in his part of the
world.'

'He's a Copt.'

'There's an answer to everything. The reason I've
woken you from your drunken stupor is that we're running the Natural Disaster category tomorrow and there's a
Japanese film in it you really should see. It's quite remarkable, and could give you some useful copy.'

'Thank you.'

'And the other thing is I want to see something of you.
It's crazy to meet again after a dozen years and then just to
exchange nods across a crowded room. I'm going to make
a break for freedom when the showing ends tomorrow.
Perhaps I can cadge a drink from you.'

Early next morning I went to the temporary press room
and rang *Newsview*.

'Our wandering colonial boy,' said the features editor,
true to form. 'Having a bonza time, are you? Hear the
streets are a bit wet. Now, what can I do for you?'

'I just thought I'd check with you before I phoned my copy through. I've got two or three fairish stories.'

'OK. I'll switch you through to the copy-taker, but I can't promise when they'll come out – or even if they will.'

'What do you mean?'

'Things don't look too good at mill. There's a print strike hanging over us, and that coupled with our falling circulation . . . I don't need to draw pictures. I wouldn't bust a gut getting the story of the year if I were you. Enjoy yourself with the movie moguls and ring me at the end of the week and I'll give you the dinkum oil, cobber.'

After I'd dictated my stories I found a seat in the cinema in a chastened mood. The thought that I could lose my job as a film correspondent so soon after getting it was a sobering one. Mentally I damned the print union. It was said that the old men who did the sweeping up earned more than editorial staff, so what more did they want? Was it a lemming-like death wish? I knew that the publishers would not give in this time. With a falling circulation they might be relieved to close the paper down and score against the union at the same time. I began to feel sick.

But my problems were pushed to the back of my mind when the morning session began. Before the curtains rolled back the festival director made an announcement to the packed house – as Leila said later, 'There's nothing like war or calamity to pack 'em in.'

'Ladies and gentlemen,' he said, and some of the delegates fidgeted with their instantaneous translation headsets. 'This morning we are starting with a dramatic piece of newsfilm so unusual that I think it needs a brief explanation. You will all have read about the violent volcanic eruption in Japan earlier this year. Among the cameramen who went to film the lava flow was Matsu Minimoto. As you will see, he set up his camera on the slope of the mountain to film the approaching stream of molten rock and ash. The flow poured down at an alarming speed, but Matsu was determined to keep filming as long as he possibly could.

'Indeed, he was so dedicated to his work that he forgot the danger, and he kept filming until he was engulfed. Several days later his camera was recovered from the ash which had buried it and by some miracle a laboratory in Tokyo was able to process the film it contained – which will be shown in a minute. When you have seen it I am sure you will join me in asking our international jury to consider awarding this brave cameraman a posthumous citation to be presented to his widow. Thank you for your attention.'

The lights faded, the screen was revealed and the film came up with a brief display of Japanese characters. The news report began with a long-distance view of the cone-shaped volcano with a wisp of smoke drifting from its summit. It was followed by helicopter shots of the crater, out of which incandescent rocks shot up and fell back as though tossed by some titanic juggler, while a tongue of crimson-speckled lava flowed from its crumbling lip. Then, to an obbligato of intense Japanese commentary, we found ourselves looking up a tree-lined valley to a distant line of fire which marked the edge of the advancing lava stream. Trees exploded into giant torches as it touched them, and smoke filled the sky.

This sequence was made up of a series of shots which must have been taken over a period of several hours, showing the lava at increasingly closer stages of its march down the valley. Gasps greeted a shot of the glowing avalanche only a few hundred feet from the camera – a horrible slow-motion roller. But instead of spindrift lurid smoke was whipped from fiery crests, and instead of spray sparks splashed towards the darkening sky. In the next shot it was like a comber poised to break over the camera, smoking ash slithering down its face . . . a shifting slope which reared until it filled the viewfinder, the detail of the debris expanding as it surged to make contact with the lens, and then – a black screen.

The reaction of the audience was one of silent shock. The succession of calamities which followed – floods, fires, earthquakes, hurricanes and other such acts of God – made very little impact after that wall of molten stone, which in one sense had overwhelmed us with its implications just as it had physically buried the camera beneath its cinders.

When the afternoon session was over I sat in the press room tapping out the story of Matsu Minimoto's death and wondering if it would ever achieve print. At last Leila appeared.

'Quick, let's run away before the boss wants me for something yet again,' she said, taking my hand and leading me out of an emergency exit to avoid the small knot of delegates talking earnestly on the cinema steps. The shadows of the palms on the Lungomare Marconi were long as we walked towards her hotel.

'Let's go on to the Excelsior beach,' Leila said. 'I've got a pass, and I haven't had a chance to walk on sand until now. Later I have to go to a reception the Americans are giving.'

She showed her pass to the official at the gate of the hotel's stretch of beach and, passing the lines of bathing huts, we found ourselves a table with a Martini sun-umbrella above it and ordered the drink it inspired. A cool breeze flowed from the Adriatic, sending the last of the sun-worshippers back to the hotel, so that soon we were alone with our drinks and a solitary waiter. Over the water the sky was darkening into a soft blue dusk which blended imperceptibly into the horizon, and the very air about us seemed to reflect a subtle blue quality.

'The blue hour,' I said.

'I love this time of day in Venice,' said Leila. 'There's a hint of mystery – of possibility – about it. Damn this reception. I'd much rather go to the Father Figure and have a plate of spaghetti with you. It's ridiculous that I only see you at odd moments like this. Is there any possibility of your staying on for a few days when the festival is over?'

Leila was wearing a simple white dress which emphasised her tan. In turn her golden skin contrasted with her silver-blonde hair, which she still wore in long tresses, framing a face which though firm and at times determined retained the delicacy that had made my heart turn over in the Derwentwater days. With her long glass poised, the blue air surrounding her and the deserted beach in the background, she would have been an ideal subject for a painter – for Geoffrey? – or for an advertising agency photographer with an eye on the most extravagant magazines. I was so struck by the picture she presented that I did not reply to her question.

She waved her free hand humorously to attract my attention.

'Oh, yes,' I said, returning to reality. 'There's a good chance of my staying on.' After my conversation with the features editor that morning I knew I was likely to have more than enough leisure, and yet would it be so bad? With a redundancy payment I could live frugally and write for myself – at least long enough to finish the script I had begun as a novel.

'. . . and we'd be able to make a trip to Verona. I've always wanted to see it,' Leila was saying. 'I have the use of a little Fiat 600. The company hired it for me. And then . . .'

As she spoke a sudden strengthening of the breeze caressed her hair and drew a strand of it across her face, and I was lost.

For a moment Leila was the child I had rowed on Derwentwater, where so often her wayward hair had blown across her face. Then she brushed the strand into place with her fingers and said, 'Listen, Martin. If I were to sneak away from the reception early we could go for a drive.'

I nodded, but the vision of her a few seconds ago remained with me, and with it came heart-wrenching memory of long-stored emotion, the aching need I had suffered for her, the naïve belief that together we were unique – a whole which was much more than the sum of the two parts which composed it. And with this re-awakened awareness, reactivated by such a simple mechanism – just as Marcel Proust became so monument-ally conscious of times past through the dipping of a biscuit into his coffee – there was another realisation. I was falling in love with Leila again.

14

Later that evening I went to the Hotel des Bains – Thomas Mann's setting for *Death in Venice*, and tonight the venue for a generous reception by the American contingent. Admitted, thanks to my press invitation, to the large suite used for such functions, I wandered among the rich and confident until I found Leila. On the pretext that she was needed urgently at the festival office, I removed her from a hearty gang of studio executives – mere cameramen were never sent to the Newsfilm Awards by their companies. They just provided the entries.

'My saviour!' she laughed as I led her to the lift. 'My, you do look smart in that white jacket.' In the car park she unlocked a little Fiat and asked me to take her 'anywhere quiet'. As I drove south the villas thinned out and, after the little fishing village of Malamocco, the road skirting the lagoon became so lonely that it was almost impossible to remember that one of the world's most famous resorts was only a few minutes behind us.

I saw Leila's face reflected briefly in the windscreen as she lit one of her Sobranies, and a moment later I heard her exhale with satisfaction.

'How lovely to escape into the night, even for a little while,' she said. 'It's like entering another world – did you ever see Cocteau's *Orphée*? Where the poet is driven in a Rolls through the borderland where light and dark become reversed like a negative . . .?'

And for the rest of the drive to the tip of the slender island we talked films. The night, starless because of the mist lying above the lagoon, seemed to press upon us, and it came as a surprise when we saw a bluish glow ahead:

tinted fluorescent tubes illuminating a ramshackle bar with a few battered metal tables and chairs scattered on the hard yellow earth in front of it.

'I'll buy you a drink,' I said, parking beneath a tree whose foliage had lost its colour to the garish light. The only customers were a group of youths in leather jackets drinking from cans and listening to beat music from the radio on the bar, their scooters and a sinister Moto Guzzi lined up nearby.

'Makes a change from the cocktail bar at the Excelsior,' said Leila with a smile as she sat at a table. At the bar I bought a couple of *zambuccas* from a weary-eyed girl and carried them over to Leila with a bottle of *aqua minerale* to dilute them. After a minute the youths gave up staring at us and went back to their music and desultory conversation. At intervals newcomers appeared on roaring machines and others started theirs up and vanished into the night, motors revving at maximum exhaust noise as though racing to some important assignation. Usually they returned after a few minutes, and I realised they were trying to escape the ennui of the evening by cruising up and down the road. They reminded me of the bikers in New Zealand.

'It's the same the whole world over,' I said aloud.

'I'm sure that's very profound,' said Leila. 'Will you let me in on the secret?'

I explained what I had been thinking.

'I suppose you're right,' she said. 'I suppose life is pretty aimless for millions of kids today. Yet a few years ago I used to envy the teenagers I saw hanging about together – at least they belonged to a group, they had each other.'

'That sounds sad.'

'Sad? Yes, I was sad as a young girl. After that summer at Derwentwater life was utterly lonely for a long time. Geoffrey was exiled to some ghastly school, and I had to stay with my aunt, who . . . well, it's over now, but, Martin, how cruel you were not to write to me.'

My words tumbled over themselves as I explained how I had sent letter after letter to be forwarded to her.

'But didn't you get the note I left you? Geoffrey and I were taken away so quickly by our father's chauffeur, but I managed to go to the bathroom and scribble out our address. Didn't Mrs Forster give it to you when you called that day we had planned to go to Croglin? I asked her to send it to the guest house if you didn't turn up.'

'I turned up, but she was in no state to give me your note, and she never sent it to the Ridleys – they would have forwarded it to London, or at least told me about it when I stayed there with Dad that autumn.' I went on to tell her how I had seen Mrs Forster drunk and naked when I entered the House of Auber for the last time.

'Was she alone? Did you see anyone with her?'

'No. But I'm sure I heard something – a man's laugh. Obviously she had been having a private orgy.'

'But you didn't see the man?'

'No. I panicked and ran, just as I did when I thought the Green Lady was after me.'

Leila did not join in my laughter but regarded me with eyes so blue and clear that they appeared to have light shining through them from within.

'Auber should have taught you that nothing is what it seems,' she said suddenly.

'Auber taught me two things,' I said. 'The joy of falling in love for the first time, and the desolation of a broken heart.'

I shrugged and grinned at her, conscious that I was already saying more than I had ever intended.

'I was sure you loved me when we were together, especially as you seemed to be older than your years. Afterwards, when I didn't hear from you – when Geoff and I thought you didn't care – I was so miserable, especially after what happened that day you told me about your friend who died in hospital. But it seems you really were in love, even though you were still only a boy . . .

weren't you? Tell me you were. I've always wanted to believe that.'

Her intensity surprised me. It had not occurred to me that our Derwentwater encounter could have been as significant for her as it had been for me. I felt that in my case there were special circumstances which had created an obsessive emotion before I was mature enough to cope with it, but surely Leila was different.

'Is it important still?' I asked, an almost clinical curiosity briefly overriding my new feelings towards her. She drained her glass with an abrupt gesture.

'Yes, it is. But sitting here, so far away in years and distance from the children we were, you must think I'm crazy to be still affected by that moment in time . . .'

She laughed unexpectedly, her face relaxing.

'"That moment in time"! I'm sounding like a Labour politician on the box! What I suppose I want to convey is that those summer days at Derwentwater were an idyll. I won't bore you with the family background some humorous god catapulted Geoffrey and me into, except to say that happy it was not. I know that doesn't make us unique. You must have had your share of problems when your parents split, but the only happiness I knew as a child was when our mother had to go into a nursing home and Geoffrey and I were shunted off to Derwentwater. That old house and its grounds became a magic kingdom for the two of us. It seemed that at last we could be ourselves. As you know, Geoffrey went mad about the legends of the House of Auber. I think we both lived in the library for the few months before you came. As long as I live I'll never forget that sense of freedom.'

'I think I can understand,' I said. 'After being immobilised for a year in hospital, to be able to wander at will round Derwentwater, to row on the lake, was a feeling I'll never forget either, a joy that can never be repeated.'

'I expect that's why you fitted into our little world so well. We were on a similar frequency. Your arrival made it complete for me: you counterbalanced the enormous influence Geoffrey always had on me. You brought the final ingredient needed for the magic . . .'

'I had no idea.'

'Of course not. Then we accepted everything without analysis. Only now can we look back and dissect. Perhaps we shouldn't do it any more. A dream loses its beauty when you tear it apart looking for significance. I realised that when I was sent to the good Dr Steiner. He was a great dream analyst, and to save my real dreams I used to make up the most outrageous ones to tell him. We both had good fun. Sometimes I used fairy-tale themes. They went down particularly well.' She laughed. 'When I got on to Hansel and Gretel he nearly blew his circuits with delight. "You are a textbook case, dear Miss Auber," he said, in his lovely accent from old Vienna. "You dream about the gingerbread house and the witch, it is wonderful!"'

'That was one dream you didn't make up,' I said.

'How intuitive you are. But I never told him about Sir Galahad who arrived in his magical bark. As I said, you brought the final element to Auber, and that's why I wanted it to be important to you as well as Geoffrey and me. Oh, if one could go back – you don't appreciate happiness fully when you have it. I suppose you believe it's going to last for ever . . .'

'Geoffrey wants to go back – to the house, at least,' I said. 'He's been working tremendously hard to earn the money to restore it.'

'That has been my dream, too,' Leila said with a sigh.

'Hansel and Gretel without the witch,' I said.

'Yes, the witch is no more. Didn't you know? But why should you? Mrs Forster was found dead after we left. In the lake.'

'So that was what the old man meant,' I said. 'When I went back the second time and found the place shut up I met this gardener, but his Cumbrian accent was too much for me.'

'That would be Baites. I think it was he who discovered her. Poor woman, even though she was such a bitch.'

'What happened?'

Leila raised her shoulders.

'Geoffrey and I weren't told the details at the time – and we didn't ask. I'm sure Dr Steiner would have understood our lack of interest – the serpent of death entering Eden. Oh, forgive me, I don't want to sound morbid. Who's this?'

I looked up and saw a beach vendor standing at our table, a gaudy silk tablecloth of Venetian scenes against an iridescent blue background slung over his shoulder and a holdall of African carvings and camelskin wallets ready for our inspection.

'You buy,' he said, the eagerness of his voice an unhappy contrast to the exhaustion of his Levantine features. He jabbed a ballpoint viciously through the tablecloth several times and then demonstrated some quality of the weave by showing that there were no punctures in it.

'Very good cloth, you buy. Lady like?'

The lady watched me with a slight appraising smile.

'What else the lady might like?' I asked.

Like a magician he spread a collection of plastic ivory bangles, worry beads, turtle-shell combs and similar gewgaws on the table.

I wanted to buy Leila something to mark this night – this night when I believed I was starting to find her again – but I saw nothing which might not be received with an embarrassed laugh. Then from his pocket he produced a packet of tissue paper, and, unwrapping it with exaggerated care, he showed me a necklace of blue coral. The colour was so right for Leila that I did not spoil the moment with haggling, and while the pedlar limped to the bar to spend some of his outrageous profit I gave it to her.

'It's perfect, my first present from you,' she said as she examined it closely. 'I wonder from what far reef it has come – the Red Sea, the Seychelles, the Ladrones?'

'It's the second present I've bought you,' I said, and told her about the gold cross I had purchased in Keswick with my holiday money.

'Oh, I wish it had reached me,' she said. 'It would have been a talisman I could have worn during the bad times. You really must have cared, Martin.'

'I never stopped,' I muttered as I stood up and went to buy a couple more *zambuccas*.

When I returned the coral rested in a curve below her throat, and I was well pleased with my purchase.

'I'll treasure it always,' she said. 'It'll remind me of this shabby little bar at the forgotten end of the island where I had my best evening on the Lido.'

She raised her glass in a toast to me and for a while we sat in silence, watching the demented whirl of insects round the fluorescent tubes above the bar.

'You are strangely incurious – or strangely polite,' she mused. 'You never asked why I went for analysis. Anyone else would be wondering if I'd had a mad spell.'

'You'll tell me if you want to,' I replied. 'And I know there's nothing mad about you – a little strange perhaps, a little fey, but never mad.'

'No, I wasn't mad,' she said reflectively. 'It was my aunt who sent me to Steiner. She never understood or even liked me. I'll not go into all that, but, perhaps to punish me in some way, she claimed that the family taint was coming out in me. You see, there is a streak of insanity in the Auber line. Sometimes it skips a few generations and then reappears. It was probably that which inspired the legend of the witch's curse on the family.

'Sadly for my aunt, Steiner decided I was quite sane, but it made me very aware of the danger of being an Auber– I'd be terrified to have a child in case the unlucky genes surfaced.'

She gave a shudder and drained her glass quickly. As I went to the bar again I wondered if it was the 'unlucky genes' which had affected her twin.

'You know, Martin, I can't imagine you as a journalist,' she said as we clinked glasses. 'Putting your foot in the door and bullying confessions out of people. I think you're still shy. I'll make it easy for you – I'll answer anything you want to know. Ask me.'

'All right. Is there a man in your life?'

'Not now. In the past . . . but I seem to be very bad at relationships. Geoffrey and I are Aquarians, super as friends but bad lovers unless we meet exactly the right person. It's odd, but I never thought of asking you . . . you might be married for all I know. It just didn't occur to me. Geoffrey never mentioned your status in that respect.'

'I might have got married once,' I said. 'Coming back to England put an end to that. Absence made her heart grow fonder – of someone else. But it was my fault. I believe that when one loses a lover it's usually because in some way one is inadequate oneself, no matter how unfair it may seem at the time.'

'I'll drink to your coming back,' she said with a smile so warm that it really did make my pulse beat faster. 'And I'll grant you one more question.'

I asked her what she thought was the nature of love. Without hesitation she replied, 'True love is a complicity between two persons trying to outwit fate which, of course, is a hopeless endeavour.'

The night was sundered by the howl of the Moto Guzzi. Vespas and Lambrettas added to the pandemonium and the youths roared away in single file, the noise of their machines drowning their shouts and laughter.

Leila looked at her mansized wristwatch as the last tail-light vanished.

'Dear Martin, you must take me home. It's long past midnight and I have to go to the airport early to glad-hand a delegation from Hong Kong.'

On the drive back to the Excelsior she dozed with her head on my shoulder.

That night was a watershed in what Leila's Dr Steiner might have termed my 'emotional development'. Instead of looking back I had begun to think of a future in which

Leila might be involved, and, perhaps more significant, I started to appreciate the importance of the present. So much of my life had been spent in nostalgia or wishful thinking.

Leila was of the same mind.

Whenever she could steal a few hours from her festival duties we spent them together with the glee of children playing hookey from school. One day, after wandering a labyrinth of narrow thoroughfares until our feet ached, we found ourselves in a deserted square. Thankfully, we sat down at a café table close to the highly decorated coping of an ancient well in the centre. The café itself was closed, its awning cracking in the hot wind, and the only sign of life was a group of somnolent pigeons huddling in the deep shadow.

'You'd hardly think this was the height of the tourist season,' said Leila, tilting her straw gondolier's hat over her face. 'We could be the only ones in the city.'

'As far as I'm concerned, we are,' I said. 'Right now the city is ours, just as Derwentwater seemed to be ours when we were alone on it.'

'Martin, don't keep harking back to that time. Important as it was to us both, it is now that counts. The past cannot be altered, and it will always be there. But we must make the most of today, because today is the frame of our life-film in the camera gate . . . if you see what I mean. The unexposed film – the future – starts now. Oh, how Geoff and I have suffered from the blackmail of the past. I don't want to look back any more.'

'You're right,' I said. 'The wise men of ancient Athens once debated what constituted human happiness, and after six weeks of discussion they arrived at the answer – to live in the present.'

'Wonderful!' she cried, standing up so that the wind pressed her dress tightly against her and I – a traitor to our resolution – was reminded of a younger Leila on wind-swept Cat Bells. 'To hell with original sin!' she added.

I rose and, in a sudden mutual gesture of delight, we

threw our arms about each other, and as we stood kissing in the vast square a gust snatched Leila's gondolier's hat and whirled it over the sunbaked roofs of the city.

The next few days were the most delightful and carefree I have known – 'halcyon' was the word Leila used to describe them. Even the question of *Newsview*'s future ceased to worry me; in fact, I almost liked the idea of being made redundant. Listening to Akkim talk about film-making had unsettled me. Also, there was a possibility that Leila might have to go to Hong Kong for a while, and I wanted to be able to go with her. The company which mounted the World Newsfilm Awards was eager to establish an international film festival in the colony, hence the arrival of a delegation of Chinese businessmen to assess the efficiency of the newsfilm operation. If they approved it would mean that several of the organisers, including Leila, would have to fly out to Hong Kong to set up the complex festival organisation.

In romantic mood I pictured us sharing a small apartment in Kowloon where I would tap away at my scripts while she was at her office. Yet she was reluctant to talk about it.

'You know I only want to live in the present,' she told me as we strolled past the lace shops of Burano. 'Besides, I'm so involved with this festival I can't even begin to think about another.' Instinctively she glanced at her wristwatch. Soon we would have to get back for the afternoon viewing of the war coverage, which proved to be an even bigger crowd puller than natural disaster.

Only once did sex – perhaps an echo from half a lifetime away – cause a brief unease between us. One night, having had supper under the kindly eye of the Father Figure at the Piazzale Santa Maria Elisabetta, we strolled up the Gran Viale to the seafront and the deserted beach of San Nicolo, here to shuck off our shoes and enjoy the sensation of the still warm sand. We rested in the shadow of the sea wall, and as my arms tightened around Leila our kisses and endearments took wing, so that I became almost dizzy with my desire for her. Just as it had by the Auber mausoleum, an automatic pilot seemed to take over my actions.

For some moments Leila responded to my caresses, and my hand slid over silken skin beneath her linen skirt. Her body, until that instant pliant against mine, froze. Her arms straightened out to push us apart and she murmured 'No!' over and over again. I was so swept along by the pulse of my desire that my first response was to hold her more closely. For a few moments it must have looked as though we were struggling together. Then twentieth-century man ousted Old Adam and I rolled away, to lie with my face in my hands while a mean little rage continued to make my heart pound.

'Thank you,' said Leila. 'Oh, thank you. Another moment and . . . please understand, Martin. I haven't been able to arrange precautions yet, and I'm terrified . . .'

'Of getting pregnant?'

'Of course. I'll get everything sorted out, I promise, and then . . . whatever, whenever you wish, my darling. But not tonight. It is unthinkable that I should ever have a child and pass on the Auber malady.'

'Leila, you're perfectly sane. You were passed as A1 by Dr Steiner.'

'I told Steiner only what I thought he wanted to hear . . .' She stood up impatiently, brushing sand from the pleats of her skirt.

'Martin, sorry, sorry, sorry!'

At her words the frustration which had been choking me vanished and we walked to the strip of hard wet sand. From a transistor hidden in the night came the sudden beat of disco music and we began to dance to it, laughing, as wavelets creamed over our feet.

That midnight dance was one of the many clear images which remain of my love affair with Leila – and Venice. What Leila had left of my heart Venice claimed, and I could easily understand how it had attracted succeeding generations of Aubers, how a gondola had been taken to Derwentwater as a love-token of the poets' city.

In the sixties, before advertising agencies found the commercially safe and therefore dull formulae for television commercials, there had been a lot of experimentation in that field, so Akkim had told me in one of his discourses on film art. One of the tricks to convey the maximum number of impressions in the popular thirty-second slot was to show a number of still photographs in quick succession rather than continuous film, a technique known as 'visual squeeze'. Such a series of stills frequently surprised my inner eye after Venice: Leila in the glare of molten glass at the obligatory Murano factory, the hot gloom of the Basilica di San Marco where she added her offering to the tiers of candles, a moment frozen as Leila leaned over a roulette table to put our last chip on No. 27 (it came up), Leila only partly visible through a swirl of opal pigeons eager for their municipal corn ration in the square of San Marco, Leila . . .

Enough. Even today the visual squeeze of memory holds too many advertisements for impossible innocence.

On the morning the festival ended I rang the *Newsview* office half-fearing and half-hopeful of the worst, but, as so often happens, I was to remain in limbo.

'Negotiations have been dragging on,' the features editor said, for once forgetting to call me cobber. 'So we're carrying on as though the old rag is going to last for ever. We've run your story about the ghoul-hunter, centre-spread with some pics we managed to dig up. The major liked it so there'll be no problem over the thief sheet. I may want you to nip over to Milan – there could be a story brewing up about one of our football stars joining the local team, so keep checking in.'

That evening I put on my white tuxedo and joined the delegates waiting at the pier for the launches to carry us to the palazzo for the climax of the festival. As we raced over the black water it was hard to believe that only a week had passed since my arrival in the city: a week in which I had found Leila again, fallen in love with her again and sensed an exhilarating shift in the course my life was taking. Once more I heard my name announced beneath the diamond-bright chandeliers, and this time Leila, in a long gown of midnight blue, ran to me and said, 'I've arranged for you to be seated next to me – you can give me the kiss of life if something terrible happens.'

Her great fear was that the projectionist would show the wrong films when the awards were announced. A silvered screen had been set up at one end of the banqueting hall, a projector placed in a gallery at the other. When the dinner was over the category winners – secret until that moment – would be announced by the showing of their entries. Between each showing the representative of the successful company would receive a silver Hermes figurine from the hands of Italy's most glamorous film star. The Grand Prix presentation – a golden Hermes for the most remarkable film entered regardless of category – would come last, and symbolise the end of the festival for another year.

'Imagine if he were to get the films mixed up,' said Leila as we hurried to the bar for a drink to steady her nerves. 'Usually we'd have the winners laced on one reel in correct order, but the judges only decided on the Grand Prix a few minutes ago and we haven't got an editing table here . . .'

She was tense through the meal, and as soon as liqueurs were served she hurried to the projector to be on hand in case of emergency. Only one film was shown out of order – the unveiling of a monument to some unpronounceable people's hero appeared as the winner of the Natural Disaster category, to the unrestrained applause of ninety per cent of the delegates. My blood chilled in sympathy with Leila, but the rest of the presentation was immaculate.

'And now we come to the winner of the Grand Prix,' the festival director announced from the dais he shared with the dazzling actress. The lights dimmed. Gaudy rays from the projector pierced the cigar smoke above the tables and there was a universal inhalation of breath as a tidal wave of glowing lava filled the screen . . .

Then it was over.

Champagne corks popped at the tables of the winners, salesmen from trade journals hovered round them to book advertisements announcing their success, and electronic lightning washed over self-conscious men holding their Hermes awards.

'Wasn't it dreadful when the wrong film came up?' Leila said, sinking exhausted beside me.

'Don't worry,' I said. 'It was the hit of the evening. Have a drink, darling. It's been a wonderful show.'

Music swept through the hall from the adjoining ballroom and, as soon as Leila had swallowed a reviving concoction of brandy and champagne, we rose to dance.

'It's gone marvellously,' the director told her as we passed his table. 'Our friends from Hong Kong are most impressed.' He raised his glass in a toast to Leila. 'You've been splendid.'

Several people stopped us and thanked Leila for the help she had given them, and by the time we reached the dance floor her eyes were sparkling and the projectionist's error no longer troubled her. Many of the delegates asked her to dance. My eyes followed them over the glass I held meanwhile, and it was obvious that they were praising her work. Later I learned that she had been offered a couple of jobs.

Towards midnight, just as the band had concluded a wild up-dated version of 'Tico Tico', Leila said, 'Martin, I have a surprise for you. You must come with me.'

Throwing her silver cape over her shoulders, she led me to the palazzo's street entrance. Outside, the damp air was refreshing after the heat of the ballroom, the night soothing after the strobe lighting. We crossed the Rialto Bridge, and when I asked to be let into the secret she gave me a mysterious smile and held her finger to her lips in an old gesture.

We continued along streets so narrow they were little

more than passages – and silent except for an occasional yowl from a ghostly cat – then over a bridge and on to a pavement beside a dark canal.

'Here,' said Leila, gesturing to a tall building which seemed to overhang us, its lower windows protected like a seraglio with curving iron bars. 'I just wanted to show it to you.'

'I don't understand.'

'There's a tiny flat on the top floor, leased by the company, where I stay while preparing for the festival. Now it's over I'll move out of the Excelsior, and we can play house . . .'

She turned to me, her face anxious.

'That's what you'd like, isn't it? At last we'll be able to lock the door on the world.'

15

The next day we moved into the tiny two-roomed flat overlooking the canal known as the Rio del Vin. Pigeons lined the sills of its windows, from which we had a panorama of the city's terracotta roofs, and their soft cooing will always be evocative of 'playing house' with Leila.

'We could be two characters in a tale of Hoffmann,' Leila said that first evening when, craning dangerously out of the window, we saw the dark shapes of gondolas and heard the gondoliers taking turns in singing snatches from popular opera.

We turned back into the room, to the candle-lit table on which Leila had laid the ambitious supper she had cooked for us. As we sat opposite each other our talk was trivial but our delight was deep. Hers was expressed by a gentle smile as she watched me – a smile of complicity! And I must have been grinning like a schoolboy, albeit a slightly nervous one. It was not the thought of our first night together which made me anxious, but her beauty.

Never had her features seemed so finely formed as they did in the light of our candles. Standing at table level, they cast an upward glow which emphasised the delicacy of her mouth and cheekbones, and was refracted in her extra-ordinary ice-clear eyes. The Mediterranean sun had given her skin its honey tone but in doing so had claimed the gold of her hair as tribute, so that only the palest hint of it remained.

'Begin the feast,' Leila said.

'It must be the Feast of Pentecost,' I said, pouring wine. She looked puzzled.

'Don't you remember? In Camelot it was always at the Feast of Pentecost that some mysterious damosel enticed one of the knights to undertake a wondrous adventure.'

'Pass the *Aste Spumante*, Sir Galahad. Your quest ends here.'

'I know – I've found the Lady of the Lake.'

'You found her long ago, when you came in a magic craft named *Pandora* and bore a gift of Marmite sandwiches.'

'There certainly was some magic,' I said. 'I never told anyone because I didn't expect to be believed, but I went out on Derwentwater the night before I met you and Geoffrey and suddenly found myself riding that freak wave. What was it called?'

'Oh, yes, I remember. It was one of the stories of Derwentwater, along with the floating island. The bottom wind.'

'That's right. What an extraordinary night it was. Just before the wave came I saw an outdoor masque on the lakeside. There were fairy lights, people in costumes . . . I was looking for the place the next day but I never found it – I found the House of Auber instead.'

'Perhaps the masque had been at Auber.'

'Of course not. You'd have known about it for one thing, and for another the lawn they were dancing on was smooth and Auber's garden was a wilderness.'

'I meant that perhaps you had experienced a time slip – you know, a glimpse of a past event. There used to be marvellous parties at Auber in our grandfather's time, and perhaps the film of time slipped in the projector. Are you psychic, Martin?'

'I hope not,' I said. 'But perhaps I'm telepathic. Remember, Geoffrey and I got some good results when we experimented with cards. Perhaps that's why his friend Oliver Penthorne found me a good hypnotic subject.'

Leila shivered.

'I met that man once. He certainly had a charming manner, but something about him gave me the creeps.

Geoff persuaded me to let him hypnotise me before going to the dentist. It did get rid of the terror I usually feel.'

'I didn't like him at first, either. Now I rather admire him. He certainly got me off my aspirin diet.' I told her how he had banished the pain from my back.

And so our meal passed in inconsequential talk. The candles were starting to gutter when Leila drained the last of her wine.

'The time has come for me to go to bed,' she said. 'Come when you wish.'

She went into the other room. I piled the dishes in the sink, then sat on an old cane chair and looked at a row of Leila's books on a pine shelf. They were battered and obviously well loved, and with the pleasure of recognition I pulled out the Oxford edition of Edgar Allan Poe, whose poems she had been absorbed in when I visited Auber. I opened it where a pressed grass stalk marked her favourite, and taking a verse at random I proclaimed to the open door:

'Thus I pacified Psyche and kissed her,
    And tempted her out of her gloom –
    And conquered her scruples and gloom;
And we passed to the end of the vista,
    But were stopped by the door of a tomb –
    By the door of a legended tomb;
And I said – "What is written, sweet sister . . ."'

'Are you going to read poetry or make love?' Leila called softly. I put down the book, the verse unfinished and the vision it had evoked vanishing as I stepped through the doorway. With two long tresses of hair flowing down over her breasts, Leila reclined in a bed of white-enamelled ironwork and brass ornamentation – a huge battered old bed which, had it been articulate, could have reminisced on the secret joys and terrors, the loves and betrayals, the deaths and births of generations of

Venetians. And now it was our turn to add our story to its chronicle.

Leila shook back her hair over her shoulders. In the dim light the sight of her ivory body shocked me with its perfection, a perfection of which she seemed to be unaware as she threw back the coverlet and gestured me to join her. I slipped out of my clothes and lay beside her and together we sank deep into the engulfing feather mattress as its ancient contours rolled us together. Her limbs were cool about me, but her breasts were warm against my chest and her breath was hot on my cheek. The wine we had drunk, the freedom bestowed by our nakedness, the security of this attic room high above the dreaming city – all this, combined with the ache for her so long buried in my subconscious, overwhelmed me. In the whole world only one thing mattered, to possess her and to drown in her. The flood tide of sexual need swept me beyond reason and even normal desire. If Leila had not wanted me then I would have raped her in the name of a love too intense to contain. But the same immemorial tide had caught her, and looking down on her face I saw her eyes widen strangely as my body shuddered against hers and then – as I experienced the bliss of entry – she encouraged me with a murmur of endearment until an aeon later her back arched and I followed her climactic cry into a vortex of exhausted elation. I had the illusion of seeing our two bodies, doll-sized and dwindling, falling away into a starry void, a little rehearsal for dying. In reality we remained locked together, aware of the hammering of each other's hearts, our skins sheened with sweat, speechless.

At last we rolled apart and, with the formality of tomb effigies, lay side by side. The curtain across the open window billowed as a jaded breeze died among the city roofs.

'Martin, that was worth waiting for,' Leila said in a whisper. She threw aside the coverlet and, glancing down at our bodies, added, 'No deadly nightshade this time.'

'Deadly nightshade?'

'Don't you remember? – that first time some nightshade berries came between us. When I saw myself later on it looked as though I was decorated with woad in the most unlikely places.'

'Geoffrey watched us that day,' I said.

'Of course.'

I turned to ask if it had made him hate me, but Leila's eyes were closed, and moments later I joined her in sleep. During the night we woke several times and made love. Our bodies had developed such a rapport that once we woke to find ourselves already involved in the act. Then, with the dawn, came a slumber so deep that when I opened my eyes to see Leila regarding me with a mixture of tenderness and amusement the last traces of sunset were silhouetting the towers and cupolas of our roofscape.

The days passed in erotic disorientation. We no longer followed the rhythms of night and day but were governed by the primal impulses of our bodies. Sometimes we lay supine and silent through the hot day, moist thigh to moist thigh on the great soft bed, fingers locked, watching the swell of the curtain – then late at night we would roam *calle* and *campo* hand in hand or sit for hours at cafés overlooking the black water of the Grand Canal. Sometimes we felt the need to 'posh up', as Leila put it, and in our evening clothes took the *vaporetto* to the Lido where, after cocktails at the Quattro Fontane, we would eat an enormous supper beneath the approving eye of the Father Figure.

My only discipline was to make a daily telephone call to my features editor, to learn that there had been no developments and that I was to 'sit tight'. Nothing could have suited me better than to remain in the enchanted limbo Leila and I had created within our seemingly timeless cube of ancient brick above the glorious city. Only when I saw the date on a copy of *La Stampa* on a café table did I realise that it was my father's wedding day. We raced to the post office at the foot of the Rialto Bridge to send off a cable, and then discovered it had been yesterday's paper.

We did not talk much. Physical contact was the currency of our love, but there came a time when I wanted more than this two-way possession. It was as though there was a second me competing with my own body for Leila – I was jealous of myself! And this yearning for her elusive inner character took me unawares one evening as we watched the passing parade in the Piazza San Marco from one of Florian's tables. I heard myself say, 'Leila, I want us to get married.'

For a long moment she regarded me with an almost puzzled expression, then, just as I conquered my own surprise enough to continue, she said very quietly, 'Martin, you are extraordinary! Perhaps I should be flattered by your proposal . . . but I believed you understood me better.'

As usual in moments of surprise I could not think of an immediate response, and Leila's unexpected reaction filled me with a vague sense of guilt. For a minute she frowned at her cup of black coffee and then continued, 'I'm being unfair. I suppose I expect people – *you* – to understand my feelings without my having to explain them.' She looked up and smiled faintly. 'It's as though I think you should be aware of my mind through telepathy, and I know that's asking too much – even of you.'

'But surely, if we're in love with each other . . .'

'Why do you want to marry me when you have me already?'

'I haven't analysed it. But I suppose there are several reasons. It's an inherited instinct going back thousands of years which will take more than one generation of liberation to alter. I suppose I want to announce to the world that you are the woman I want to spend the rest of my life with. I suppose I'm trying to prove some-thing to you – that I want to be responsible for you in the future . . .'

'Ah, Martin, if you think like that you should have had a cosy marriage with that girl – what was her name? – in New Zealand.'

I had known that sooner or later we would have to face our first quarrel, but I was taken unawares. This was the last reaction I had expected.

'All along you've known that I'm different – you've said so often enough – and I'd hoped you would have tried to understand . . . Look, Martin, as I see it today there is only one reason for marriage and that's to provide a legal safe-guard for children. But I can never risk having a child – I can't provide you with a family, I can only be your lover . . . isn't that enough?'

Her expression had changed with the intensity of her words. The serenity to which I was accustomed except during the act of love had changed to something I could not fathom then but which I recognise retrospectively as anguish. Neither of us heard the band playing close to us; we enveloped ourselves in sullen silence. My surprise had been replaced by a sad anger. I was suddenly sick of the Auber preoccupation with the past and their so-called family curse. Hadn't I heard enough about it from Geoffrey, who had fallen in love with his own morbid fancies? What I had not expected was that Leila should share his obsession.

'When I saw that newsfilm of the lava flow I thought of you,' Leila said. 'You are emotionally so like the Japanese cameraman . . . so intent upon your own role, so *focused* on the world as you see it through a tiny viewfinder, that you have no conception of the forces about you . . .'

She paused, and then added impatiently, 'Can't you say something?'

'Yes,' I said. 'I don't see why there should be all this drama because I was so insensitive as to propose, nor do I see why, like Geoffrey, you find it necessary to act like a character in a Shakespearean tragedy because you come from a family that has some childish legends woven in with its ancient privileges. Perhaps the truth is that while I might be all right for a brief encounter in Venice, I'm not good enough to marry an aristocratic Auber – and I think that's why any discussion of the future has been tabu.'

'Martin, I never thought you'd be capable of thinking such a ridiculous thing.'

She was genuinely shocked, and her tone was as embittered as mine. She stood up and hurried into the crowd. I sat for a moment aghast that a pleasant evening could have turned so sour in so short a time. I desperately wanted to put things right, to pacify Leila, to conquer 'her scruples and gloom' as Poe had said in the verse I had read aloud the other night. I rose to hurry after her but was held up when the waiter came forward to be paid. Finally I found her on the Molo, a slender figure alone in the light of old rose-glassed lamps. I put my arm round her and for some time we stood watching the prows of moored gondolas in front of us rise and fall as the wash from a passing launch struck them.

I began to apologise but Leila said, 'Hush.' Then she added, 'I'm taking you for a ride tomorrow . . . let's go home now.' And we did, feeling a curious sad tenderness towards each other for the hurt given and received.

During the night a single sob woke me from a dream-haunted sleep. I lay still in the stifling darkness, aware of Leila awake and equally still beside me. It seemed incomprehensible that we should lie in silence like this, that the joy of our bed had deserted us, but one thing I did understand was that this sea change was not due to the words spoken at Florian's. They were merely symptomatic of something deeper and darker which had come upon us.

And I cursed myself for not having the perception to say

something which would conjure back the happy mood of twelve hours ago. I was dismayed at the way the compass needle of a relationship can swing so far off course in an instant, that a mere minute can divide a state of content from one of bewilderment and loss. This train of thought made me feel contempt for the self-pity I was dangerously close to seeking refuge in. There was nothing unique about what I was feeling. Similar situations must be happening all over the world – the lover eagerly opening the last letter he will receive from his mistress, the wife looking up from her book as her husband clears his throat to announce his departure for ever, the sudden revelation to the young couple that they had been in love with love and not each other.

These night thoughts were more desolating than the dreams I had just escaped from. I put out my hand to Leila and her strong slim fingers pressed it against her breast.

'It's my fault, Martin,' she whispered. 'All my fault. How could I have expected you to understand?'

There was nothing I could say. The only contact possible that night was to make love, which we did with the cruel passion of despair.

It was a relief to leave the apartment in the morning before the heat haze gathered over the city. As Leila drove the little white Fiat on to the causeway linking Venice to the mainland the vastness of the pale watercolour sky lightened our spirits after the claustrophobia of the night, and I began to enjoy a feeling of escape as we cleared Mestre and headed west on the autostrada.

'Can I ask where we're going or is this a magical mystery tour?'

'We're going to see someone,' Leila replied lightly. 'Light a cigarette for me, please, darling. They're in my handbag.'

Taking out the black box of Sobranies I felt encouraged

by her tone. The tension of last night had gone out of it, and I dared to hope that what had happened was perhaps nothing more than one of those emotional squalls which are inevitable when two people suddenly come into such intense contact as Leila and I.

Ahead, the road began to shimmer in the harsh sunlight. Water mirages appeared only to vanish as we neared them, and we had to open the windows as the heat from the great plain smote us like a gust from a furnace door. Several times we stopped at motorway cafés, first for black coffee to revive us from the exhaustion of the night, later for *aqua minerale*.

Towards noon we passed Vicenza and left the autostrada to drive north along a less strident route which wound into the Dolomite foothills. For lunch we stopped at a roadside restaurant masquerading as an alpine chalet, and as we ate our salads on the terrace we could see a distant lake silver in the noon glare.

'Our destination,' Leila said. It was the last time she spoke for a while, and I sensed the unease in her preoccupation when we resumed our journey. As the little car juddered gamely along a secondary road I was treated to vistas of the lake literally flashing between the trees which lined it. Catching sight of two weathered pillars – one still had a mottled lion atop it – Leila slowed and turned between them. I had a glimpse of a sign on one of the wrought-iron open gates, but I only managed to make out the word 'ospedale' before we were climbing a gravelled drive towards a large stuccoed mansion overlooking the lake. We parked beside a row of cars and Leila led me across a withered lawn to the entrance. From here there was an excellent view of the lake and the hills surrounding it, while on the far shore I could make out the roofs and campanile of a village.

I turned and followed Leila into a large reception hall. When the house had belonged to a wealthy family in the previous century it must have been ornate and gilded, but now it was bare and whitewashed, its only decoration a plain wooden crucifix on one of the walls. Beneath it an elderly nun in a white habit was seated at a desk on which a small switchboard looked embarrassingly modern.

At the sight of Leila the nun's finely wrinkled face broke into a warm smile and she welcomed her in fast Italian, to which Leila responded fluently. Once she looked towards me and asked a question, and Leila nodded. Not knowing why we were here made me feel awkward, and when the nun led Leila up a staircase I did not know whether I was expected to follow.

'Come,' said Leila. 'If you love me, come.'

As I climbed the stairs the nun turned and, obviously making an effort to recall words she had learned a long time ago, managed to say to me, 'He . . . tranquil.'

Reaching the top of the staircase we followed a long white corridor, passing a series of doors which were identical apart from the Roman numerals painted on their panels. At XXI the nun produced a ring of old-fashioned keys and inserted one in the lock. Another nun appeared, wheeling a trolley piled high with clean bedding, and our guide signalled her to join us as the door swung open. I followed Leila inside. The two nuns stood in the doorway with downcast eyes, still as statues except for the rosaries clicking through their fingers.

Like everything else in the building the room was an unrelieved white. There was a white coverlet on the bed, which was bolted to the floor. The inflatable easy chair by the barred window was white, and the stooped man sitting in it was dressed in white pyjama-style clothes, very loose and with tapes instead of buttons. He did not take his gaze from the shimmering lake beyond the window when we entered, nor was there any reaction when Leila gently laid her hand on his shoulder and said, 'Father.'

If she had not said anything I would have still recognised their relationship. The patient, despite the ravages of time and his malady, still retained a certain delicacy of feature – what I thought of as the 'Auber look' – and beneath shaggy eyebrows there gleamed a pair of pale blue eyes which had been reproduced in both his children. Remembering my visit to Geoffrey at Sayers Grange, I had the curious fancy that I could be repeating that visit forty years on.

Leila, her gaze never leaving his lined face, sat on the edge of the bed, and we waited in silence. At last he tore his eyes from the lake scene which had absorbed his attention. His mane of fine silver hair turned and then a faint look of recognition appeared.

'Helen,' he said, confusing his daughter with his wife.

'Roderick,' she responded.

'The children?'

'They are well.'

He sighed and his eyes were drawn back to the window. The only sound in the room came from the two rosaries. Minutes dragged by. Twice Leila made an attempt to recapture his interest but his eyes only narrowed as though there was something on the lake demanding his concentration. Finally the nun spoke in Italian – I guessed she was saying that there would be no alteration in the patient's present disposition – and Leila stood up. Her movement reminded Roderick Auber of her presence.

'On a day like this,' he said, with a languid wave to the village at the far end of the lake, 'I can see Keswick very clearly.'

'I had no idea,' I said as the Fiat left the grounds of the asylum. 'How long has he been here?'

'A dozen years,' said Leila. 'That's one of the reasons I found a job in Italy. I don't know what I'll do if the Hong Kong project goes through. Light me a cigarette, would you? I always feel a little ragged after these visits.'

While I did so she said, 'I know I must have seemed absurd to you last night. That's why I brought you here today to see for yourself . . .'

'But, darling . . .'

'You see, his malady is in the Auber genes. Sometimes it skips several generations, but it lurks in the blood, waiting to make an appearance. It's as though there's some truth in the legend of the witch's curse. There was a verse about it, supposed to have been said by the witch just before they put a torch to the faggots in Castlerigg circle, but I can't remember how it goes. Geoffrey found it in an old book on Cumbrian folklore in the library at Auber. I think we were secretly rather proud of belonging to a "cursed family" – there was something Byronic about the idea. As it turned out it was more like Stevenson.'

'Jekyll and Hyde?'

'Yes. Our father became periodically dangerous. It was kept from Geoffrey and me as much as possible when we were small, but things fell into place later on. The strain caused Mother to have a nervous breakdown and when she had to go into a nursing home we were sent to Derwentwater. Now he's much less violent – something to do with the decline of the sexual urge, I've been told – he's only likely to be dangerous at full moon. I know that sounds like an old wives' tale, but the moon definitely has an influence on him.'

'Leila, I'm very sorry about your father,' I said carefully. 'And I'm sorry for the effect his mental illness must have had on your life, and I do think I understand how you feel about it. But you are completely sane, and . . .'

'Oh, yes, the Auber syndrome only comes out in the males. The witch had nothing against the Auber women. She was one herself!' She laughed briefly, so that I did not know how seriously she took the tradition. 'No, my fear is that if I had a son he might take after his grandfather or, if not he, then his son. After some of the dreadful things that have happened down the generations the buck has got to stop, and it stops with Geoff and me. We are the last of the Aubers.'

For a while we drove without speaking, each busy with our own thoughts.

'Wouldn't it be easier if he were in England?' I said at length.

'He was in Venice when he went totally mad. You know our family had an affinity with the city, especially in the last century. So when our father fled England he came here with a sort of homing instinct. You see, dear Martin, it's not just that our father is mentally ill – he's a murderer.'

'He served a sentence?'

'Oh, no, he was never even charged. The police had their suspicions, but for the sake of all concerned they came to an arrangement when it was learned that he had been certified insane in Italy. They would take no action provided he never returned to England, and since then the trustees of the estate have paid for him to be cared for at the asylum.'

'Did it happen at Derwentwater?' I asked with a sudden inkling.

'Yes. Mrs Forster was his Cumbrian mistress. He stayed alone with her at Auber when we were suddenly sent away . . .'

Mrs Forster – her normally puritan hair hiding half her face – was sprawled on a faded chaise-longue. *She had no clothes on and was careless about keeping her legs together. Bottles stood on a little circular table nearby, and she was regarding the glass in her hand with a lopsided grin. Then, from a hidden part of the room, there came a man's laugh.*

'You told me her body was found in the lake. I thought you didn't know what had happened.'

'As children we weren't very interested – probably we didn't want to know. But we found out when we grew up. She had drowned in Derwentwater all right, by the boat-house I took you to one day. At the time the public thought she had committed suicide while drunk – she was well known for her drinking, but she hadn't fallen in by herself, or the police didn't think so. She was wrapped up in a tapestry and there were marks on her body which suggested she hadn't been alone. And the only other person at Auber when she died was our father, though he had left for Venice by the time the body was found. There's no doubt he did it – he had attacked Mother and I believe another woman, his London mistress, had had a near escape. It all fits in with the Auber tradition – the curse was that Auber men would destroy those who loved them . . .'

As she lapsed into silence a picture came into my mind of Geoffrey in the Bond Street gallery tearing her portrait to shreds.

16

When we approached the causeway the sky curving above the city was deep rose, the hue so often seen in Venetian glass and perhaps inspired by such evening light. By the time we reached the Piazzale Roma it had been transmuted to an indigo setting for the evening star. The events of the day had provided a release. We were emotionally drained, but now that we were in familiar territory we were elated by a sense of peace with each other.

Our evening in the flat was delightful. We shared the cooking of a simple supper, drank a little too much red wine with it and, having watched the nightly procession of gondolas pass beneath our window, drifted towards sleep in each other's arms. I believed a vital element had returned to our relationship – friendship, which is the necessary counterpoint to passion.

'And it makes no difference?' murmured Leila. 'What I told you, it makes no difference?'

I told her I was relieved she had been able to tell me, but already her eyes had closed.

In the morning we strolled to the main post office where I put through my call to *Newsview*.

'Stone the crows, sport,' the features editor cried. 'You were supposed to check in yesterday.'

'Something came up,' I said.

'I'll bet. Now you race to Milan and get an in-depth story on Paul Alexander, late of Spurs, and file it in time for this week's edition. Getting to Alexander may be difficult – he'll be preparing for his first match with his new club. We're arranging for a local freelance photographer called Bruno Farina to help you. Better write down his number . . .'

A couple of hours later I was watching the hazy Lombard Plain flowing past my carriage window, thinking of yesterday's journey on the autostrada. In the space of an hour I had learned more about the Aubers than I had in the whole of my previous contact with Leila and Geoffrey. And though nothing had been resolved I had a far deeper understanding of my lover, whom I was still determined to persuade into marrying me.

With an arrogance it now embarrasses me to recall, I was convinced that by patience, psychological insight, and if necessary the help of an analyst, I could alter Leila's persona – that through my devotion the dark fears which lurked beneath the cool surface of her nature could be exorcised. I would devote myself to the realignment of Leila as the person I believed she was destined to be before she was influenced by the tragedy of her father. Fool that I was, I did not realise that we love most intensely where we have the least perception, nor that the human penchant for remoulding the objects of our infatuation is the inevitable prelude to broken dreams.

On reaching Milan I was greeted by Bruno Farina, who explained that as the result of the furore over his joining the Italian club Paul Alexander was difficult to contact. Bruno had hopes of tomorrow; meanwhile, if I'd like to have an evening on the town . . . As it turned out we did not locate the errant soccer star until the following night. I wrote up the story on the train next day through the mists of a hangover from a wild drinking party at Alexander's glossy penthouse, at which Bruno took pictures which he swore were front page material.

As soon as I arrived in Venice I telephoned *Newsview*.

'I think I've got the story you want,' I told the features editor. 'I had to drink myself stupid to get it, and I still feel dreadful . . .'

'Sorry, Martin,' he said, 'but your touching devotion to duty has been in vain. *Newsview* has had it. The management and the print union couldn't agree – yesterday a strike was called in the machine room and our masters retaliated by killing the paper with remarkably little regret. The father of the chapel has agreed the redundancy payments, and we're closing our desks. Sorry, cobber.'

Now that I knew for certain I had no job to return to my brave ideas of writing independently deserted me, leaving a physical sickness as I realised just how much I had enjoyed my work and the camaraderie of my fellow journalists, and what a sense of security had been inspired by my monthly pay cheque. The sense of loss made me eager to talk to Leila, and I hurried to board the *motoscafo*. As it churned away from the landing stage I tore up my story and scattered it over the white and green wake, and my career as a journalist was over.

The black-shawled old lady on the second floor regarded me with her customary hostility as I toiled up the narrow stairs to our apartment, and she continued to glower up the stairwell while I banged on the door and called to Leila. When there could be no doubt that she was not at home I fumbled for the key, black motes whirling before my eyes as a taunting reminder that last night's debauch had been in vain.

Inside I made myself a cup of coffee and sat with some unease in the room which was tidy and very still. Did the first hint of alarm rise from my subconscious then? Or was it just being alone for the first time in the silent apartment which made me feel that its character had undergone a subtle change? I felt menaced, and anxious to find my lover.

I hurried down the stairs, still under scrutiny from the old woman, who seemed to spend her life at her open door, and then I was thankfully hurrying from the Rio del

Vin and on to the bustling pavements. From the San Zaccaria I took the *vaporetto* to the Lido. It had occurred to me that Leila was likely to be at the Palazzo del Cinema on some festival business. But when I reached it I found it closed and deserted, its World Newsfilm Awards poster replaced by those for a James Bond film.

A salty wind gusted from the sea, whip-cracking the flags of all nations in front of the nearby casino. The noon sun had sent the Venetians to their siesta and the tourists into the marble-floored cool of their hotels. The only moving figure on the long hot esplanade, my physical aloneness seemed symbolic of my emotional state. I tried to control my panic with logical arguments – the shock (and I had to admit that it was a shock when it actually happened) of losing my job had upset my equilibrium so that the fact that Leila was not in the flat had assumed ridiculous proportions in my mind. She was probably shopping, or going about her post-festival duties in some other part of the city. It would be neurotic to fear a repetition of her disappearance from Derwentwater half a lifetime ago . . . and yet, despite my logic, the fear remained.

That evening, I sat at an outdoor café table overlooking the Grand Canal. I had spent the afternoon in a vain pilgrimage to different spots in the city where I thought there might be a chance of encountering Leila, a search through the geography of our affair which only aggravated my apprehension. At dusk – at our beloved 'blue hour' – I had returned briefly to the apartment, but it was filled with the same silence that I had found on my return, and I left hurriedly. I was already finding a haunting element in places of old familiarity – but it was I who felt like a ghost. I would not go back to the flat until midnight, when Leila was sure to be there. Even if she had driven out of Venice, perhaps taking the opportunity to pay another visit to the lakeside asylum, she would surely be back by then.

★

Just after twelve I was walking in the direction of the Rio del Vin. I had begun to feel more cheerful, and an almost erotic excitement grew at the thought of finding Leila in bed, her fine-spun hair shimmering on the pillow.

As I climbed the stairs the door of the second-floor flat opened and the old woman regarded me with contemptuous irony (or so it seemed) as I went past. Poor old creature. How empty her life!

I unlocked our door, snapped on the light and found the place deserted. My overnight bag still lay on the floor where I had dumped it. A tap above the sink dripped as monotonously as it had when I'd left. I looked through the bedroom door and saw the curtains billowing with the exhausted airs which the hot stone of the city sucked from the lagoon. Not a hint of Leila.

Now I felt real panic, no longer for myself but for her. Loss of memory, illness or an accident, abduction! Anything was possible. A wild idea came to me. I would try one course of action and if that failed there would be nothing for it but to go straight to the police. I hurried to a hotel overlooking the Grand Canal where my NUJ card, followed by more acceptable lire credentials, induced the night porter to let me use the telephone.

'Hello?' came a voice at the other end of the line. For a moment I did not recognise it.

'Dian? Dian Derbyshire?'

'Yes. Martin? Oh, how nice to hear your voice, even at midnight. You must be ringing about Geoffrey . . .'

'No, I'm not. Actually this must sound rather odd, but I was wondering if you had any idea where Leila might be.'

'Of course. She arrived here today – to see Geoffrey.'

'You mean, she's in England?'

'Are you all right, Martin?'

'Yes. It's just that it's a surprise to me. I've been away in Milan, and . . .'

'Then you don't know – about Geoffrey?'

'At the moment I'm rather confused. What's happened to him?'

'It's terrible. This morning he tried to commit suicide.'

There was a silence. I could picture her struggling to control her voice. No wonder she had sounded so strained.

'At Sayers Grange . . . he . . . he got on to the roof . . . and jumped . . .'

'Is he all right?'

'He missed the concrete path below and landed on soil, thank God. He broke several bones and he's severely concussed – he was still unconscious when I rang Sayers an hour ago.'

'And Leila?'

'It was a most extraordinary thing. She just *knew* that Geoffrey was in terrible trouble. She was actually on her way to England before . . . before he fell. It was amazing intuition; I suppose because they're twins.'

'Dian, did Leila say anything about me . . . us?'

'Only that she was upset you hadn't told her how serious Geoffrey's condition was . . .'

'But she knew. I was certain she knew. I thought you . . .'

'I'm just telling you what she said. Martin, what's wrong? Please tell me.'

'Where is Leila?'

'She's staying at a hotel near Ewhurst, to be close to Geoffrey. She's very shocked but somehow she's managed to keep her usual calm. Oliver Penthorne took her down to Surrey. He's been a tower of strength, but I do wish you were here. I'd like to put my head on your shoulder and burst into tears . . .'

For a while I listened to her talk about Geoffrey, how until today she had believed he was well on the way to recovery. Then I wished her goodnight and rang off. At least I would not have to go to the police to report a missing person.

I was so weary, and so dazed by Dian's news, that when I entered the apartment for the last time I just kicked off my shoes and threw myself on to the bed in the dark bedroom. In the morning I must arrange to return to England, and give Leila what moral support I could. As I moved my head I felt something smooth against my cheek, and heard the faint crackle of paper. Switching on the dim bedside lamp I saw a folded piece of paper on the counterpane with 'Martin' printed on it in Leila's hand. Obviously she had propped it on the pillow for me to find, but the breeze which made our curtains belly like sails had blown it flat, and I had missed it when I had given the bedroom a cursory glance that morning.

For a minute I sat on the edge of the bed holding the folded paper. Somehow I sensed that it was not just a note explaining that she had an impulse to return to her brother. And I had the childish fancy that the die would not be finally cast until I had actually read the contents. To prolong this moment I did something I normally did not do – I lit one of Leila's black cigarettes.

'Now for the moment of truth,' I said finally and unfolded the paper. And moment of truth it was.

My poor Martin,

In a few minutes I am leaving for the airport to return to England. Geoffrey is in great need of me. This has hastened the inevitable, but perhaps it is best that it should happen suddenly this way. While you were away I finally admitted to myself the necessity of ending our relationship. Over these last few days my feeling for you was genuine enough, but I cannot live with the guilt of my unfairness to you – involuntary though it is. To continue would be a hundred times more unfair.

The pain which, knowing you, you must be suffering now is a light price to pay to avoid the anguish of the future. The gods were cruel to lead you across Derwentwater, and then bring you to this sad city. Did you have an inkling of my situation, or does it seem crazy? Best to think of it that way.

Martin, there is no future for us. I do not want us to

meet again. It would add pain to pain and achieve nothing else.

I must go. L.

A banal postscript told me what to do with the key when I left the apartment.

I re-read the words which told me so little of the cause but broke my heart with the effect. I knew Leila well enough to recognise their finality.

'Why?' I cried aloud as an impotent anger seethed through me. I crumpled the paper into a ball and hurled it into a wastepaper bin in the corner. After a few minutes – or hours – I lit another cigarette and, unable to resist the urge to read the note once more, to gain some crumb of comfort I might have missed, I put my hand into the bin to retrieve it. Instead my fingers closed on something agonisingly familiar, and I withdrew the blue coral necklace I had given her at the bar on the deserted end of the Lido. Memory of that happy moment returned with sickening treachery to contrast with the way this symbol of that night had been thrown away like trash.

('From what far reef has it come?' Leila had asked. 'The Red Sea, the Seychelles, the Ladrones?')

I slumped back on the bed with the beads lying across my upturned palm. The despair with which the discovery filled me brought a humiliating warmth to my eyes. I knew I was about to go out of control, that in a moment I would not be able to stop myself crying out.

Without hesitation I pressed the glowing end of the black cigarette against the inside of my wrist. There was a tiny hiss as the soft skin shrivelled, and an acrid smell in my nostrils as I remorselessly ground out the butt, leaving an ugly ash-smeared pit where wrist and palm met. The physical pain shooting up my arm at least neutralised my agony of mind, and I managed to contain the lunatic desperation which had been about to over-whelm me.

Panting, I fell back and wondered if I was indeed insane to let another's action affect me so deeply, and through the chaos of my mind echoed the best known single word from Leila's book of Poe's poems.

Nevermore!

17

The little girl in the long Victorian dress emerged from the winter woodland. The branches of the naked trees which curved to meet above her head hinted of witches' fingers poised to pluck at her. Above them the louring sky was filled with the menace of approaching night. She began to cross the forest clearing, pushing her way through clumps of withered weeds.

Suddenly she halted and gazed with childish curiosity at something lying on the ground before her.

'Poor scarecrow!' she said, starting off again, but with her eyes swivelling on the terrible figure – almost a skeleton but not quite – which lay sprawled in tattered cerecloth.

'Poor scarecrow, poor scarecrow,' she chanted. Then, losing interest in the emaciated object, she began skipping along the track which vanished into the opposite wall of trees.

The camera moved away in a POV shot until it focused on the figure. Its skull-like head turned, and it raised itself on one spindly arm. Then, with uncanny agility, it climbed upright and with a curious loping action began to follow the dwindling form of the child . . .

The *Danse Macabre* theme music swelled and the action froze for the credits to roll. Cameraman. Sound-mixers. Best boy. Script girl. Miss Silver's hairdressers. Film accountant. Action effects by Tufguys . . . the extraordinary collection of experts required to make a film.

Akkim, fastidiously dressed in tropical-weight suit and the open-necked shirt required by Hollywood convention, touched a remote control. The lights came up in the preview cinema of his Bel Air house – as yet he was not ready for Beverly Hills. There was silence as the guests, all of whom had been involved in the making of *Croglin*, eyed him, trying to hide their anxiety. His production manager, who had organised the catering, waited for the verdict which would require the opening of either French Champagne or Californian Sparkling.

'Son of a bitch!' Akkim breathed, letting fall his gold-braceleted wrist as though his strength had been drained by the film's first showing. 'That's one fine son of a bitch! There won't be a dry seat in the house. I'm deeply grateful to you all.'

We lay back in our seats, luxuriating in the knowledge that he liked it – that Akkim, the gentle-voiced dictator, the terrifying perfectionist, had admitted he was pleased. The hired Mexican waiters began circulating with glasses of Moët on their silver trays.

'Ever since I was a small boy sneaking into fleapit cinemas to see Frankenstein or the Wolfman I've wanted to make a horror movie,' Akkim said. 'And now it is accomplished. This new concept in the handling of tradi-tional themes will be a breakthrough. Bob,' he turned to the cherubic director, 'you have an understanding of menace which amounts to genius. That scene on the moor will make them shit.'

'Even though I played it a dozen times, it made my heart go bump when I saw it tonight,' exclaimed the star of the film, Sonia Silver.

'You were magnificent, baby,' Akkim said automatic-ally, and I could not help smiling as I remembered how he had once declared in quiet desperation that 'the Silver bitch isn't enough of an actress to wear the Minnie costume at Disneyland!' But Bob Hart's directing had always saved the scene, and on the screen Sonia's innocent beauty heightened the atmosphere of fear he built up during the film.

Akkim raised his glass in my direction.

'And let us not forget that in the beginning was the

word,' he said. 'Congratulations, Martin, on your first feature script.'

His words gave me deep satisfaction. I followed the guests out to the large patio illuminated by the underwater lamps of the pool, where steaks sizzled on barbecue grills to the accompaniment of the *Croglin* theme music. The night was warm and heady with the scents of Akkim's immaculate garden, just discernible in the reflected glow of the Los Angeles sky. I sought a recliner by the edge of the pool and watched the throng over the bursting bubbles of my drink.

'Picture of a solitary genius,' came a voice and, turning, I saw Tash seating herself beside me, carefully balancing a plate of steak and salad and a glass of champagne. In the curious light she had that clear-cut attractiveness I had noticed in so many American women since my arrival in California six months earlier. It glinted on the sun streaks in her dark blonde hair and the gold flecks in her large eyes. Her deceptively simple white dress – claimed to have been bought in a temporary fit of insanity on Rodeo Drive – set off the bronze of her skin. By profession she was a freelance film production manager, and I had liked her from the moment we met, when she said with a generous smile, 'I'm Vera Tashlin. My great-grandaddy was a gunfighter and I shoot from the hip. That's what Akkim pays me for.'

During the filming I had not seen much of her because I was usually in my room in the Sportsman's Lodge hotel, rewriting scenes over and over until Akkim declared himself satisfied, frequently with the original version.

'Another film, another dollar,' Tash said. 'What are you looking so thoughtful about? On a night like this you ought to be getting drunk and leaping into the pool – not palely loitering.'

'I was just thinking how all this began,' I said, waving towards the euphoric group surrounding Akkim. 'It's an interesting exercise for an author to try and pinpoint the actual moment when his book – or script – started its life.'

'So what triggered off *Croglin*?'

'I was sitting on an island in an English lake called Derwentwater when I was a boy, and a friend told me the legend.'

'It's a neat story, but I didn't know about its being a legend.'

'It's supposed to have happened about a century ago.'

Tash's eyes gleamed with interest.

'You mean, there really was a night-walker at Croglin?'

'So it's believed in Cumbria. Of course, I had to adapt the story, create more characters, introduce a love interest, change the original characters from Australians into Americans. And alter the end, of course. In real life . . .' we both laughed over the phrase '. . . the Cranswell brothers burned the vampire on a pyre in the churchyard.'

'But the end you've given it allows Akkim to make *Son of Croglin* if it's a box-office success.'

'There's no question of *if*,' said Akkim, appearing above us. 'Tash has said she likes it and she's the one person here whose opinion I value. She isn't full of Hollywood crap – she shoots from the hip. And wait until the press sees it – you'll have your picture in the *Reporter*. Ah, Martin, it's been a long year since we met in Venice. It was destiny that our paths should cross . . .'

If it was destiny it was also my salvation, I thought. The morning after I had found Leila's letter I had decided on two things, to run away so that I would not be tempted to make a pathetic fool of myself, and to become a scriptwriter. To this end I returned to London to collect my redundancy money and give up my flat, and the only friend I contacted before flying to New Zealand a couple of days later was Dian Derbyshire. We had a strained, and on her part tearful, meeting. She could tell me nothing more about Leila – or, if she could, my haggard appearance which so upset her kept her tactfully silent.

'Oh, Martin, we've both been made so miserable by the Auber twins,' she said as I left. 'Perhaps we're natural victims. I should try and escape like you, only Geoffrey will need me when he's better.'

'He'll have Leila,' I said with unpremeditated cruelty. 'And there is your work,' I added hurriedly. 'Bury yourself in it. I'm going to.'

It is often said that time is the great healer, but in New Zealand I discovered that unrelieved work can at least provide emotional first aid. I stayed with my father and his new wife for a few days and then rented an old *whare* – something halfway between a hut and a house – overlooking a remote and magnificent headland named Castlepoint because of its rock bastions against which the Pacific thunders. Here, apart from trips to the nearest town for supplies every few days, I devoted myself to writing a film treatment which, when I was finally satisfied with it, I sent to Akkim.

Apparently it was the story he had been looking for, and he invited me to Los Angeles to write the full script under his guidance. I stayed for the shooting in order to be able to do day-by-day revisions and, to my gratitude, learn about film technique. The year had been so full of new experience that most of the time I had managed to stifle my sense of loss. Nor had I allowed myself to attempt to contact Leila, although at times, when I'd had too much to drink and nostalgia filled my heart, it took a painful effort not to reach for the telephone. Apart from a dutiful monthly letter to my mother, my only contact with my London life had been to send Dian a card of the *Queen Mary* at Long Beach, to let her know that I was well and 'working in pictures' in L.A. And if I am honest I hoped this news would reach Leila, though why I could not easily explain.

'. . . and, as I have said, horror films should be adult fairy tales,' Akkim was saying. 'They provide catharsis for the terrible everyday fears of modern life. They must come of age. There's no need to lead in with axes and ketchup. Our opening – just those helicopter shots of moorland and overcast sky – makes the hairs on your neck spring to attention.'

'Bob has a great feeling for mood,' I said.

'The man's a genius, but it all came from your script; it was your concept. Before you leave L.A. I want to talk to you about your ideas for a treatment for my next film. I hope you've got some. Excuse me, please. There are people I must thank.'

'Wow!' laughed Tash as Akkim joined a group at the far end of the pool. 'Who's teacher's pet?'

'I am,' I said, catching a couple of glasses of champagne from a passing tray. 'Yet I can hardly believe that I'm at a Hollywood party celebrating a film I wrote, chatting to a production manager, who, on the basis of her looks, should have been the star.

Tash smiled.

'You English are so delightfully perceptive.'

'Am I bustin' in?' asked Bob Hart, imitating a high-wire act along the edge of the pool.

'Yeah,' said Tash. 'But I'll circulate while you good buddies tell each other how fantastic you are. But – like the Croglin vampire – I shall return.'

'That was General MacArthur,' said Bob, taking her place on the recliner. 'That Tash makes me wish I was younger, lighter and had some hair. But at least Akkim's happy. He's on long-distance to the money men . . .'

Inevitably, we began to reminisce about the making of the film, about incidents which seemed disastrous at the time and now, seen through the glow of champagne, were merely hilarious.

'I hope we work together on another,' he said, climbing to his feet when disco music replaced the *Danse Macabre* on the hifi system. 'I reckon you must have grown up in Spooksville to write the sort of stuff you do. You're too authentic.'

His words had a curious effect on me – his words and the sparkling wine I had drunk, no doubt. A vivid memory caught me unawares. For a moment I was once more running in terror of the Green Lady out of the House of Auber, down the yew avenue towards the mausoleum and Derwentwater beyond. And for those few seconds the sun glinting on the Cumbrian lake was more real than the blue luminosity of Akkim's pool. Laughter and music were replaced by the wind that sounded like surf in the woods.

Then I was back in Bel Air and about to hurry in search of Akkim when Tash left the whirl of dancers and, still swaying voluptuously, placed her hands on my shoulders.

'I guess you'll need a lift to the Sportsman's Lodge,' she said.

'I guess I will,' I said, joining her in the dance. 'But before I go I'd like to have a word with Akkim about an idea . . .'

'This is not the time,' she said. 'Lo! 'tis a gala night . . . and Akkim is either on the phone to his Mid East buddies or in the clutches of La Silver, who no doubt expects him to yell "Hi ho" any minute. Not in his most receptive state, I'd say. Leave it for now. We'll dance a bit and then go cruising. OK?'

'OK.'

We danced along the terrace and then lost ourselves among the gyrating guests. I could feel the beat of the music physically; coloured strobe lights which had been rigged up by Sparks turned us mauve and green and red by the instant, and through the hot air I caught the acrid tang of Colombian Gold – only the best wine and weed for such a celebration. At last Tash and I could dance no more and, to a pleasant chorus of mutual congratulation and farewell, she led me to the horseshoe drive where her sleek yellow Vega was parked.

'It's always a bit sad,' she said, settling herself behind the wheel.

'Sad? I feel the opposite – elated that it's all in the can.'

'I know. I'm sentimental. I see people of different skills come together, work together, bitch together and maybe play together – an instant family – and suddenly it comes to an end. We go our different ways.'

'I hadn't thought of that – that I may never see most of these people again.'

As the car glided along an avenue of flowering trees, I asked Tash what she was going to do now that her contract with Akkim Films Inc. was completed.

'I've some location work to do for a Western in Arizona,' she said. 'And you?'

It was a question to which I had no definite answer. I had been so engrossed in the making of *Croglin* that I had given little thought to what would happen after it was completed.

'I'm infatuated with California, so I don't want to go home yet,' I said. 'Perhaps I'll rent a simple shack out in the desert and get to work on my non-electric typewriter which amuses everyone so much, and watch the sunset over the hills. A simple, pleasant life.'

'And lonely. But you'd be lucky to find a shack without a jacuzzi. Things have changed since the gold rush.'

Laughing, she touched a button on the car's stereo. A smooth deep voice announced, '. . . real joy can always be found at the heart of your FM dial, 'cause that's FM99, and that's K-JOI, where you get Cloud Nine music – and more of it.'

We listened to the sound of K-JOI's 'singing strings' and heavenly choirs while the car climbed a gently curving road. On reaching the top of the incline Tash braked and swung the car round so that it skidded to a stop in a parking area. A constellation of lights burst upon my unsuspecting eyes.

'I give you the San Fernando Valley,' cried Tash, delighted with the dramatic effect.

'It's like being in a space ship,' I said, recalling a childish notion.

'Right now we *are* in a space ship! You writing guys are supposed to be great at the suspension of disbelief. What are we in?'

I laughed. 'A Vega spacecraft. Heading for the Milky Way.'

For a while we sat listening to a misty version of 'Laura' and watching the winking lights of an aircraft as it climbed its electronic trail from Burbank.

'Tell me, Martin old sport – are you gay?' Tash asked suddenly.

'No. Why?'

'I just wondered. Whenever we met on the set I tried to provoke your interest – always with zero result.' She sighed comically. 'I must be losing my appeal. Or is it just your English reserve?'

'I've been rather fraught since – since I came to L.A. My first film and all that. Now I feel free again, and that's why I thought I'd head for the desert.'

'It never occurred to you to head for me, right? All that languishing I did in vain!'

'I think you're making this up. The night and K-JOI are getting to you.'

'Martin,' she said seriously. 'There was more to your moods than the making of *Croglin*. Did it have anything to do with the beautiful girl Akkim told me you were in love with in Venice?'

I shrugged.

'Venice was an age ago . . .'

'And I think it's been an age since you had any real fun – you know the stuff, f-u-n? It's good for you.'

She started the car and before long we were driving along Ventura Boulevard. When she finally pulled up in the forecourt of the Sportsman's Lodge she said, 'Seriously, Martin, you ought to play. Why don't you come with me to Arizona? I can combine work with pleasure, and you'll see real desert . . .'

'Tash, I'd be delighted to come with you,' I said, suddenly pleased with myself for making the decision.

★

After the Delta flight landed at Tucson airport I hired a Ford Mustang, and soon we were driving through the afternoon heat towards Tombstone. Ahead the highway was perfectly straight, a black line ruled through the heart of the desert. I was fascinated by the extraordinary vegetable sculpture dotted over the plain – the saguaro cactus. Many were as big as trees and would have been taller than men when Napoleon's armies were rolling across Europe. But I was most surprised by the terrain itself. I suppose I had imagined deserts were always composed of sand, great seas of the stuff, their waves petrified into dunes like the deserts of Australia, or the Sahara. Here the surface was covered with sage, stretching like a purple carpet to the low mountains bounding the horizon.

Tash inhaled the air which flowed through our open windows appreciatively.

'The smell of the Old West,' she said.

'Did you really have a gunfighter for a great-grand-father?'

'Sure. We're going into his territory – Tombstone, Nogales, the Gila Desert. His name was Bill Tashlin. He made his reputation by shooting down a famous outlaw named Joshua Noon. So be warned, Martin.'

'If I see you reach for your six-gun I'll run for my life,' I told her. We were both in a holiday mood, though this trip meant work for Tash. I remember we laughed a lot on that journey, and played her Poetry Game.

'Did you study poetry at college?' she asked.

'Yes. I was an enthusiastic member of the Poetry Society.'

'That's neat,' she said, clapping her hands like a child. 'I loved poetry in school, especially the rumpty-tumpty kind. It's a pity that the modern poets intellectualised it out of existence. The only poems today are the words of some pop songs. Let's play the Poetry Game. I'll say a line and you have to follow it. If you can't I get a point, but nothing too obscure. OK?'

'OK.'

' "My name is Ozymandias, king of kings . . ." '

'Shelley!' I said. 'A poem about a huge broken statue in the desert. I know, 'Look on my works, ye Mighty, and despair!" '

'Too easy. Your turn.'

The time passed pleasantly and the hot tarmac disappeared steadily beneath the bonnet as I kept the car exactly at the speed limit, having no wish to fall foul of the Highway Patrol. When we ran out of inspiration for the game we sat in companionable silence, Tash watching the sun sink towards the mountains which sent blue shadows racing across the plain.

'I saw a Western some years ago about the OK Corral,' I said. 'Wasn't that in Tombstone?'

'Yeah. The shoot-out between the Earps and the Clantons took place there. In books and TV movies the Earps are always shown as the good guys, but when we go to the Boothill cemetery tomorrow you'll see that not all the citizens of Tombstone thought so.'

Some time later Tash said, 'Look,' and pointed to the west. The sun was sinking behind the rim of the world in a conflagration of citron and crimson. The mountains became deep purple silhouettes against a band of orange. Even the air had taken on a violet quality when we reached the Good Enough motor lodge, named after the silver mine responsible for the foundation of Tombstone.

A few minutes later I was carrying our suitcases into the cabin she had reserved for us.

'I hope the idea of sharing doesn't upset your delicate susceptibilities,' she said, with a slightly mocking smile. 'Since we women have been liberated we reserve the right to be as predatory as the male of the species.' She had already investigated the small drinks refrigerator and I gratefully took the rye on the rocks she handed me.

'I must warn you, I have rather bizarre tastes,' she continued as we raised our glasses in a mutual salute. 'Like, I sometimes like to be kissed . . .'

I took her in my arms.

'The flagellation can come later.' She laughed as I bent my head to kiss her.

For a moment we clung together, then she gently pushed me away.

'I may be kinky but necrophilia is not one of my pleasures,' she said, seating herself on one of the twin beds and taking up her whisky. 'You're like the walking dead, Martin.'

I stretched out on the other bed and gloomily eyed the ice in my glass. As usual I hesitated over a reply.

'Listen, Martin, today if you bed a girl you don't have to be madly in love with her. Nor is there any longer the danger that she's going to use a roll in the hay to trap you into the unholy state of matrimony. Since the Pill has altered the history of the world marriage is no longer the prize it was once, and the message is that sex can be fun. So why not relax and let the good things happen?'

I felt foolish, and ashamed of my churlish lack of warmth. Looking at her attractive profile against the last bloody smear of the sunset I wondered what man would behave as stupidly as I. And yet . . . and yet . . .

'I think it's a question of a malady lingering on,' I said, and she smiled good-naturedly at my words.

As I ordered drinks for Tash and myself in the Crystal Palace saloon I was struck by the thought that the big, intricately etched mirror behind the bar in which I saw myself had once reflected the likeness of Johnny Ringo. The bar had not altered since Tombstone's heyday, and one could feel the weight of the town's free-wheeling history.

Over our drinks Tash told me about her assignment.

'The idea of the film is to give the other side of the coin in the famous feud between Earp and the so-called out-laws,' she said. 'It'll be called *The Clantons*, and my job is to do some research and to make a report on the location. You see, the town was divided between the Earps and the

Clantons. One newspaper, the *Tombstone Nugget*, was partisan towards the Clanton faction, while the *Tombstone Epitaph* supported the Earps. The *Epitaph* is still in business.'

Tash, who had already done some background research on Tombstone, kept me amused with her stories of the little mining town a hundred years ago, before its silver lode ran out. Among its population were gunfighters such as Doc Holliday, Johnny-behind-the-Deuce, 'Buckskin' Frank Leslie, Curly Bill Brocius and others, who were buried in the cemetery we would be visiting – the real-life characters on whom Hollywood has built a complete mythology.

At last we stepped out into Allen Street and found that the warm air was perfumed with the heavy scent of roses.

'Tombstone's present claim to fame is that it has the world's largest rose bush,' said Tash. 'Back in 1885 someone in Scotland sent out a little Lady Banksia to her daughter, and today it covers five thousand square feet!'

I expressed polite amazement, but my interest had returned to something which had been on my mind all day. That morning, as I was leaving the Sportsman's Lodge, a friendly desk clerk had handed me a letter which had been sent on by the publishers of the defunct *Newsview* to my father's address in New Zealand. He had duly re-addressed it and added another set of stamps.

'That's done some travelling,' said the clerk. 'If you don't want the stamps, sir . . .'

'I'll give them to you later. I haven't time to open it now,' I answered, and as I rode in the airport car I decided I would not open it at all. The original postmark, dated a month before, read 'Keswick', and the handwriting was Geoffrey's. To read that letter could be the opening of a Pandora's box of memories and mysteries I wanted to remain safely in the past, yet I did not have the courage to throw it into a rubbish bin. Now the feel of it in my pocket tempted my curiosity – which was quickly neutralised when I remembered my last night in Venice.

Tomorrow, when I was alone, I would burn it and the temptation would be gone for ever.

We drove back to the motor lodge. By now a silver-dollar moon was high enough to flood the desert with eerie light, silhouetting the cactus semaphores which soared out of the sage as enigmatically as Easter Island statues.

'Let's stroll,' said Tash. 'You can tell me the story of your life – or at least about your malady. Was it something to do with the girl in Venice?'

'Yes,' I said. 'But it wasn't just a love affair that went wrong. It was something which went back to when I was a boy. I can't understand why I allowed it to affect me so deeply . . . in fact I have wondered whether it wasn't due to some mental aberration . . . but anyway, let's not talk about it. This is too lovely a night for morbid introspection.'

'Don't you believe it,' cried Tash. 'I majored in psychology at UCLA. Tell me. I have a feeling you've kept it bottled up for too long.'

'I've never discussed it with anyone,' I admitted. 'There aren't many understanding people about . . . In fact there's only one person I could have told, but it wouldn't have been fair because she's in love with Leila's brother.'

'Let's sit,' said Tash.

We seated ourselves close to a joshua tree on a bank which gave us a view across the plain. Sage brush rustled as a breeze sighed over it. When we heard the cry of a hunting owl Tash took my hand, and suddenly I was overwhelmed by my desire to talk about Leila and Geoffrey. I felt that in one verbal outpouring I could rid myself of the spell they had laid upon me.

'It all began when I came out of hospital as a boy,' I began, and continued for the next hour.

With what relief I finished my tale!

At last, I had been able to translate so much unspoken emotion and memory, so many futile hopes and obscure fears, into ordinary words which cut away the mystique clothing my obsession.

'So that's what ails thee, wretched wight,' improvised Tash. 'Alone and palely loitering . . .'

Remembering our game from the afternoon, I added, 'The sedge is withered from the lake, and no birds sing.'

We laughed, and how good it was to be able to laugh now that I had talked my incubus into the open. The Church knew what it was about when it introduced the confessional, and no wonder psychiatry had to be invented when religious faith began to weaken.

'Those Auber twins must be something else,' mused Tash. 'If anything, you should feel sorry for them, the victims of an old inbred family.' She saw everything in primary colours.

'Yes, but what I've never been able to understand is why this shared neurosis – however they got it – should have had such an effect on me over the years; why my boyhood crush on Leila didn't fade as these things normally do.'

'Here comes the old UCLA instant analysis,' said Tash. 'To me, an outsider, it is quite obvious how it happened. There were a number of factors which combined to make you vulnerable so that those experiences at Derwentwater left a traumatic imprint on your subconscious. The lake itself was clearly a symbol of your need. First, let us consider the boy Martin Winter who had been hospitalised for a year and therefore was more than usually receptive – as you yourself said. Also, Martin Winter was an only child, and most only children have a deep desire for brothers and sisters. Leila and her brother – what's his name?'

'Geoffrey.'

'Leila and Geoffrey were twins – the strongest bond between children of the same parents. To Martin Winter, whose loneliness for his peers was underlined by the death of his best friend, they were the ideal brother and sister, and when they allowed him to enter their secret world he felt he'd achieved an instant family. This was heightened when his awakening sexuality was focused on the girl, so that his first love experience had more than a hint of incest about it, a powerful factor in his involvement.

'And there was something else which may have made Martin so ready to blindly accept every aspect of his new family. It was not long before his mother and father parted, and for some time their strained relationship must have affected him . . .'

'No,' I interrupted. 'I wasn't aware of it. When my mother left it came as a great shock.'

'Martin probably had a subconscious inkling that all was not well between his folks and, as is not unusual, he may have assumed a sense of guilt over the situation. The beauty of your "Auber family" was that there were no adults involved and therefore nothing to take the blame for. At Derwentwater Martin found the answer to all his emotional requirements, but the sudden ending of this world created a trauma. Aspects of his development were frozen and his involvement with his surrogate family remained to dominate his emotional life. How's that?'

'You make me sound like a text-book case,' I said. 'I'm sure a lot of it is correct, but I feel it's not just that simple. What I can't understand is why my second encounter with Leila should have been so emotionally shattering.'

'I guess that was just an old–fashioned broken heart. After all, the woman you met in Venice was not the girl you had known at Derwentwater but someone you happened to fall madly in love with who, for her own neurotic reasons, walked out on you. Tell me, Martin, when you were a boy did you worry in case you'd made her pregnant?'

'No. According to schoolyard mythology it couldn't happen the first time.'

'And it was the first time?'

'Of course. I told you.'

'But are you certain you took Leila's virginity? Was there any proof?'

'I've always taken it for granted.'

Tash looked at me sideways in the cold light.

'Maybe things weren't exactly what they seemed,' she said cryptically.

I shrugged. What did it matter? 'Strangely enough, many years later I did worry in case she'd had a child.' And I went on to tell her about Geoffrey's accusation during his nervous breakdown.

'And how did you find out it wasn't true?'

'Leila would have told me in Venice if it was.'

Tash laughed. 'Poor Martin. You don't understand women, do you?'

'No,' I agreed cheerfully. 'But what man does?'

She stood up, brushing sand from her denims. Then, with my arm round her, we began walking towards a distant speck of green light – the neon sign which was our guide back to the Good Enough motor lodge.

'Thanks for listening,' I said. 'It seems you can't bottle things up for ever, and you gave me the opportunity to put it into words. I'm very grateful.'

'It was fascinating to get a glimpse into a scriptwriter's soul,' she said lightly. 'Anyway, listening is one of the functions of a friend – and that's how I see us, as good friends, so don't think I'm going to add a new complication to your life. Right now I put friendship at the top of my priorities. It's more compassionate and more enduring than love – at least that's my experience. And if you detect a bitter note it's because I'm still recovering from an unfortunate bout of marriage.'

When we returned to our cabin I brought out the whisky bottle, and settled beside her as she brushed her hair. I poured myself a drink and said, 'To friendship and fun.' She put aside her brush and held out her glass, and, with her penchant for Victorian poetry, quoted:

> 'Ah, my Beloved, fill the Cup that clears
> Today of past Regrets and Future Fears . . .'

The following morning I went to the office of the *Tombstone Epitaph* to do some research for Tash while she began her reconnoitre of the town. A production manager has the most exacting task in film-making. One oversight or mistake on his or her part can send the company's expenditure soaring beyond its budget. Tash's present job was to make a highly detailed report upon which the producer and director could plan their shooting schedule. She told me that she had to check on the availability of accommodation for the film crew, the position of power sources at sites to be filmed, municipal permission to close certain streets for filming, the weather averages of the past few years and a hundred other items. She even logged the positions of shadows at various locations by going round with her Polaroid camera at different times of day.

Meanwhile I enjoyed being back in a newspaper office, following the familiar procedure of searching through old files of yellowing newsprint. I found the report of Tombstone's famous shoot-out in the edition of 27 October 1881, and I began to copy it into a notebook. 'The liveliest street battle that ever occurred in Tombstone took place at 2.30 p.m. today, resulting in the death of three persons and the wounding of two others, one probably fatally. For some time past several cowboys have been in town, and the fight was between the city marshal, Virgil Earp, his two brothers, Morgan and Wyatt Earp, and Doc Holliday on one side, and Ike and Billy Clanton and Frank and Tom McLavery on the other . . . the fight was over in less than a minute.'

As I made my notes during the drowsy morning I was intrigued that such a minor skirmish – at least in comparison with the urban shoot-outs which have become such routine news in the latter twentieth century – should have captured the imagination of generations around the world. It has been the inspiration for thousands of magazine stories, books, television plays and films, and now Tash was working on its latest resurrection.

At noon we met and, after a pizza pie at a motel restaurant, walked out of town to Boothill graveyard. This was the original Boothill, whose name became generic for cemeteries all over the Old West.

'See what I mean about local attitudes towards the Clantons?' said Tash as we passed through a gate in a wall which reminded me of the dry-stone walls in Cumbria. She pointed to a monument erected to the memory of the Clantons and their friends who had died at the OK Corral. A legend in large lettering stated that they had been 'murdered on the streets of Tombstone'.

Together we walked along the rows of markers and read the brief epitaphs . . . 'Margarita, Stabbed by Gold Dollar', 'Teamster, 1881, Killed by Apaches', 'Charley Storms. Shot by Luke Short. 1880', 'Geo. Johnson. Hanged by Mistake' . . . Only one – that of a Wells Fargo agent – was in verse:

> Here lies Lester Moore,
> Four slugs from a .44,
> No Les, no more.

'To work, to work,' Tash cried, unslinging her camera and taking out her compass to note the bearing of each shot. While she began systematically taking her instant pictures, I stretched out with my back against the rough wall. The desert wind rattled the spiky crucifixion thorn which grew round the graves, and I felt beautifully relaxed in the heat. Thanks to Tash the moment I had been dreading for so long – the completion of the film work which had been an anodyne against my inner loneliness – had passed with unexpected ease. Although I agreed that Tash's view of the causes of my obsession with Leila Auber was logical, I still sensed that there had been deeper and more mysterious influences which I would probably never fully understand. However, the very act of talking to her about it had given me a sense of liberation. And our happy night together, free from emotional tension, had endorsed that feeling. Tash asked for nothing but friendship and in return gave it with such warmth that I could hardly credit my good fortune. Perhaps, at last, I was learning to follow Leila's precept about enjoying the present.

Thanks to this new-found sense of well-being the letter addressed in Geoffrey's hand held no apprehension for me. Yesterday I had decided to destroy it unread, today I was going to satisfy my curiosity. I took it out of my pocket and, as Tash wandered further and further away among the graves, I tore open the envelope and unfolded the single sheet of pre-war rag paper with a faded crest and the words 'Auber House', a flimsy relic from happier days.

'Dear Martin,' Geoffrey had written in a minute yet nervous hand.

Time passes, and I am home again and looking out over Derwentwater, which today is leaden beneath cold rain. Apart from a limp (which I must confess was the result of my own folly) I am recovered from the malaise that must have been so distressing for my friends, and for you, my oldest friend. Apologies for my behaviour about which, mercifully, I can recall very little.

I no longer paint, nor do I care that I do not paint. *Sic transit gloria mundi*!

My world has taken a turn and my time is spent in monumental study since Oliver Penthorne set me upon a journey into a whole new region of infinite possibility. And this is one of the reasons which has prompted me to contact you. I have heard a rumour that you are doing wonderfully well as a writer for the cinema, but your address is unknown and I am sending this letter with the desperation of a marooned mariner launching a message in a bottle.

The message is this: Martin, when you are able to rest from your labours come and spend some time at Auber. You will be fascinated, I promise, by the nature of my work, and I would be delighted, of course, if you were to play some part in it. Also you might find the old place conducive to your literary efforts. With self-confessed selfishness, I am in need of your companionship.

I know that you will at least appreciate the sincerity of this *cri de coeur*.

When I reached the signature, bold compared with the rest of the script as a result of signing paintings, I folded up the letter and returned it to my pocket. I stood up amid the alien graves and thought: You knew it would be impossible for me to refuse. But, Geoffrey, this time I shall come on my terms.

The Mustang cruised along the highway towards Tucson. On either side of the ribbon of melting tarmac the desert rippled under the blaze of the noon sun and reminded me of driving on an Italian autostrada. I felt regretful that Tash's work in Tombstone had come to an end. As she'd predicted, it had been fun – a commodity I had been greatly in need of.

'Are you still going to rent a desert home?' Tash asked.

'I don't think so,' I answered. 'I've an idea for another horror film which would take me to England for a bit. I want to discuss it with Akkim when we get back to L.A. How does *The Murder Room* grab you as a film title?'

'I'd have to think about it. You're keen to get started again.'

'It may sound naïve to a hardened film professional, but the *Croglin* script was the most exhilarating thing I've ever done. I loved being a journalist, but I was only writing about things that had happened. In a script you make them happen. I'll never forget seeing the first rushes. There on the screen was my story made flesh!'

Tash laughed. 'You'll get a god-complex, like all authors! Everyone in a film sees his own part in it as the most important. The sound mixer doesn't think about the quality of the plot, or an actor's performance. For him the film stands or falls on the quality of the sound recording.'

'Anyway, I'm hooked on film,' I said. 'I was lucky to meet Akkim in Venice.'

'Apart from your little emotional difficulty, you seem to be a very lucky young man indeed. Especially for one who on the surface appears rather innocent.'

'It's just colossal charm combined with genius.'

Tash said a rude American word.

After a while she chanted:

> 'And slowly answered Arthur from the barge:
> "The old order changeth, yielding place to new . . ."
> "And God fulfils Himself in many ways . . ."'

I responded. ' "Lest one good custom should corrupt the world." Tennyson.'

'OK, you know the English poets. Now let's try some American ones.' Tash thought for a minute.

> 'And I said – "What is written, sweet sister,
> On the door of the legended tomb?"
> She replied – "Ulalume . . ."'

I had laughed when she began, because here was an American poem I did know, but when she reached the last word I saw the colour of the sky change. From hot blue it took on an overcast hue. The road turned from black to the green of grass, and on each side dark trees reared . . . and running towards me down this avenue was Leila with her pale hair flying.

'Look out!' I screamed as the Mustang was about to run her down. I wrenched the wheel and the car slewed off the road, skidding over the sandy soil of the desert until its front wheels dropped over the edge of an arroyo and it stopped so abruptly that my temple cracked against the windscreen and I lost consciousness briefly.

'You tried to kill us! Are you mad?' The adrenalin released by the shock of the accident made Tash turn on me in anger as my eyes opened.

Was I mad?

As I held my head in my hands I remembered how the road had changed into the yew avenue at Auber, how Leila had become part of the hallucination. What had happened to me?

'Are you all right?' Tash .asked in a more controlled voice. 'What the hell happened, Martin? The road was clear . . .'

I tried to remember. She had started the Poetry Game. She had quoted a couple of lines from Poe, one of Leila's favourite poems when I had met her at Derwentwater.

An alarming suspicion grew. I remembered how Oliver Penthorne had used trigger words to induce hypnotic effect. Was the name Ulalume, a word unlikely to be heard in ordinary conversation, a verbal control which had been implanted in my sleeping mind? If so, I was determined to discover whether it had been left latent in my subconscious by accident – or by design.

To Tash's consternation I began to shudder.

18

And so I returned to Derwentwater.

Arriving by coach at Keswick I was surprised to find how little the town had altered since I had first seen it with my mother and father, and with the manuscript of *Black Days in Dark Ages* across my knee. The grey houses, the narrow streets and the dominating church spire were exactly as I remembered. In Los Angeles I had soon felt at ease. I liked a place where people worked to enjoy themselves rather than to exist, the domestic architecture reminded me pleasantly of New Zealand, and I was involved with film people whose enthusiasm I wholeheartedly shared. Yet, as I walked past Keswick's Moot Hall into the market place, I had a tremendous sense of home-coming. New Zealand, London and California receded. I was back in territory which held an old familiarity for me.

Perhaps it was this which decided me against going to the House of Auber immediately. Following my acceptance of Geoffrey's invitation he had replied that I was welcome at any time, and, as no actual day had been set for my arrival, I would be able to have a little time to myself before once more exposing myself to the old allurement of Auber. My eye caught the blue and red of a Routier sign at the entrance of the King's Arms, and I was lucky enough to get a room there.

After I had unpacked and changed into comfortable, 'worn-in' clothes which I had brought with the idea of some fell walking, I set out to rediscover Derwentwater. Following Lake Road, it only took me ten minutes to reach the Boat Landing, where there were jetties for the sight-seeing launches – I was pleased to see that the *Princess Margaret Rose* was still making her circular voyage – and rowing boats for hire. It was late afternoon and the lake surface was a dazzling mirror under the slanting rays of the sun, turning the boats into black silhouettes against the brilliance.

The rowing boat I hired was of the elegant, highly varnished type one associates with Jerome K. Jerome.

'Watch out if you're going to be on the water for a while,' said the attendant, nodding to the west as he handed me the oars. I turned and saw a line of dark cloud above the hills which, with the climatic capriciousness of Lakeland, could rapidly spread across the sky. He reminded me of the time he 'shut up shop', and gave a mighty heave so that the craft surged from the shore leaving arabesques of quicksilver in its wake.

Turning towards Derwent Isle – it seemed impossible that so many years had passed since I had last rowed round it – I saw the bright triangular sails of windsurfers, and realised that the sport had not been invented when my father brought me here. I rowed on past the Ruskin memorial, and then headed towards the centre of the lake. Childishly I kept my eyes on the transom, wishing to renew my acquaintance with the old landmarks from the best possible vantage-point.

At last I rested my oars and looked up to see the mass of Skiddaw soaring against the bright sky. Allowing the boat to turn slowly, I feasted my eyes on the Great Wood and beyond it the towering rock wall known as Falcon Crags. The shore line flowed past as the bow swung round the compass, so that soon I was looking down the lake to the marshland surrounding the mouth of the river Derwent where the Auber twins and I had taken *Pandora* when we went to see the Lodore Falls. And then, past St Herbert's Island, I recognised Cat Bells with particular affection, and beneath it the woods lining the western shore which hid Auber from view.

Auber!

Recollection returned of how I had found what I thought of then as the 'secret inlet', tied up to the tilting jetty and pushed my way through brambles and willow-herb into a domain whose enchantment changed all too soon to bewitchment. How would it look now? Would its atmosphere, which once I had found delightfully mysterious, now merely be that of a neglected old house? Would it have shrunk in size, as happens too often when adults revisit childhood's vistas? I decided to row round the lake and find the inlet, and then see how much my own eager imagination had contributed to the mental picture I carried.

I had just started to pull on the oars again when a sail-board hissed through the water ahead of me, and the young man riding it deftly lowered the sail so that it bobbed beside me.

'Hey, mate,' he said in a South London accent, 'do you know where the floating island is supposed to be?'

'Down the Borrowdale end of the lake,' I said, pointing south.

'Is it really a floating island?'

'It's supposed to surface every three or four years,' I told him. 'One year the Girl Guides planted a Union Jack on it and claimed it for England.'

'They would. Ta, mate.'

He raised his shark-fin sail and scudded away. As I settled to the oars again I noticed that the same wind that filled his sail was driving the cloud which had clothed the horizon across the sky. Though most of the lake still glittered, the water along the western shore was dark beneath its menacing shadow. It was as though nature was providing a theatrical effect for my first glimpse of the old house.

The sun still warmed me and this, coupled with the unaccustomed exertion of rowing, produced a light sweat. I found it pleasant after the long period I had spent at my typewriter in the air-conditioned room at the Sportsman's Lodge. Consequently, when the boat crossed the shadow frontier, I shivered suddenly as its chill struck me. I found that I was opposite Abbots Bay at the south-west end of the lake and I began to follow the shoreline north in search of the inlet, trying to identify landmarks which would give a clue to its location. All I recognised was the dense wall of trees lining the margin, and I permitted myself the passing fancy that Auber had vanished like a mirage and I was in *Pandora*, late for tea with my parents at the guest house.

There was the germ of a story idea in this, but I did not have time to develop it. Glancing to where the shore curved into a shallow bay I noticed a gap in the foliage, and there was my secret inlet. As I manoeuvred towards it my damp shirt caused another shivering fit and I paused to put on my windcheater, the boat gently drifting into the inlet and chafing against some rotting piles which were all that remained of the jetty I had once leapt off in a fit of terror.

I jumped over the bows on to the muddy strip and tied the painter to a branch which had fallen under the weight of winter snow. Then I straightened up and looked along the yew avenue to the old grey house. The avenue itself was more choked with weeds than I remembered it. Here and there saplings waved as the forest gently sought repossession, and the mausoleum appeared like a square, weathered rock rising out of a sea of greedy vegetation. Beyond the avenue the once-lawned terraces were now waist high with rank grass, which rippled as a cold wind gusted down from the fells and made the woods on either side of the yew walk sigh and whisper conspiratorially.

The House of Auber was exactly like the picture I had carried of it. Time had not shrunk it or dimmed the curious effect of *concealment* which it had always had upon me. I began to push my way through the briars and hog-weed and willowherb to get a clear view. If anything its tall walls appeared greyer – older – than I remembered, the gabled roofs steeper and the bulk of the peel-tower more forbidding. It was, in fact, more like the subject of an illustration in a book of Victorian fairy tales – 'The Ogre's house stood alone in the enchanted wood.' The effect was heightened by the colour of the sky above it.

The oppressive cloud, which now cast its shade over the whole of Derwentwater, had taken on a sickly purplish hue which made Auber appear at its most sombre – sinister, I should say. Everything had become dull, dark and soundless, and this gave me a sense of insufferable gloom. And I suddenly wondered whether this was caused by the melancholy vista, or by the uneasy notion that perhaps it had been a mistake to leave California.

As though in answer to my thoughts a scribble of lightning etched itself against the gloomy sky, and for a fraction of a second the lancet windows of the ancient house came alive as they reflected bluish fire, before fat raindrops began to make the leaves and fronds through which I had been wading bob and quiver. Another flash unzipped the cloud and the downpour began. Pulling my collar tight, I threshed my way back towards the boat, where I could shelter beneath the trees which overhung the water's edge. Before I dived for shelter beneath a weeping willow I took one more look at Auber through the lancing rain. High in the peel-tower a square of yellow light suddenly appeared, and I realised that someone was now occupying the Murder Room.

The next day was brilliant. When I caught glimpses of Derwentwater from Keswick, where I went shopping for a local gift to send to Tash, I found it hard to equate its sparkle with the dismal, rain-swept waste I had rowed back across last evening, water slopping over my shoes. I still felt a strange reluctance to continue to Auber, and dawdled in the town on the pretext of sending a colourful postcard to my father and seeking a suitable scarf of Herdwick wool for my mother. Towards noon I decided it would be unfair to arrive unannounced so close to lunch, and having bought a packet of sandwiches I enjoyed a picnic meal on the lake-shore.

For a while I was infected by the holiday atmosphere, the children eager for a launch ride, the bright triangles of the windsurfers, the young couples strolling hand in hand close to the water, and the harassed family groups into which the latter would soon be transformed. How pleasant this aura of lakeside relaxation, and what a contrast to my destination on the far side of the lake – as different in mood as today's sunshine was to yesterday's storm.

At last I forced myself to get up off the grass, and walked back to the hotel to collect my bag with the feeling that my brief vacation was over. A taxi took me over the bridge spanning the river Derwent where it flowed out of the lake, and along the road on the high ground of the western bank, giving me a view over the treetops of the water which, at the moment, was of an unexpected Mediterranean vividness, as though the blue of Como or Lugano had been transferred to Cumbria.

'Auber, you said?' The driver glanced at me. 'Hardly ever any call to go there. I've heard that years ago it used to be one of the big houses on the lake, if you get my meaning, but now they say it's near derelict. A pity someone don't buy it and turn it into a nice private hotel. I'd better slow down, because I don't rightly know the gateway.'

It struck me how strange it was to be approaching Auber by road. In the past my journey to it had always been by water, and this had added to my sense of its isolation. It had never occurred to my young mind that it would be accessible by car like any other house. Suddenly I saw its square tower and jumble of roofs rising above the woods surrounding it, just as it had been pointed out to me by my father on Cat Bells long ago.

'We're close,' I warned the driver.

'This must be it,' he said a few minutes later, pulling up by an old-fashioned gate whose woodwork was hidden beneath grey lichen. Beyond it a rutted track – one could no longer dignify it with the name of drive – curved away through old trees whose trunks were equally lichened.

The driver regarded the ruts, filled with mud from last evening's downpour, with distaste.

'I needn't have polished my car this morning if I'd known I was coming here,' he grumbled, adding – in case I had not got the message – 'I really need chains to get through that lot.'

'Don't worry, I'll walk.' I paid him, and hauled my grip off the back seat.

'Good luck,' he replied, and accelerated away.

I had a tussle with the gate, and then walked carefully down the path, which sloped steeply as it wound through the woodland. In some stretches the trees, which had not been cut back for many years, met overhead so that I had the impression of passing down a tunnel of dim, greenish light. At last I slithered through a belt of enormous rhododendrons and found myself on a weedy courtyard in front of Auber's main entrance.

'Martin!'

I turned, and saw Dian Derbyshire hurrying across the cracked flags. Her gown of burnt umber silk seemed to float about her and she held an armful of arum lilies, a perfect model for Tennyson's maid of Astolat.

'Martin!' Lilies were scattered as she impulsively put her arms round my neck and kissed me. 'Oh, it's good to see you here,' she said, standing back to regard me while I picked up her flowers. 'You don't look any different.' She sounded surprised.

'People don't change much in a year,' I answered. 'You look as lovely as ever.' And I meant it. Against the worn stone walls of Auber and its tremendous iron-studded door she appeared like a beautiful heroine in an ancient legend. I had the feeling the twentieth century had been left behind at the gate of the domain.

'Come and see Geoffrey. He's been looking forward so eagerly to your coming.' She took my arm, smiling. 'We can't get through the front door. The key was lost years ago, Geoffrey says.'

We walked on the once-gravelled paths round the side of the house, past pedestals holding urns out of which a profusion of weeds sprouted, the satyrs' faces on their sides half obscured by moss. I asked her about Geoffrey.

'He's quite recovered,' she answered. 'But you'll find a change in him. He's withdrawn at times, and very intense about his work . . . you'll see. Your being here will do him the world of good. I come up from London for a few days whenever I can.'

'And your music, Dian?'

'It's going well. That's what keeps me in London half the time. I must say I feel guilty about not being here permanently, but Geoffrey is adamant that I don't miss my master classes with Bruggeman.'

I thought I detected an unease behind her words, and I felt this was emphasised by her evident relief at my arrival.

As we entered the old kitchen she said, 'I'm so thankful you answered Geoffrey's SOS. It couldn't have been easy for you after what happened . . .'

'SOS?'

'Oh, yes. I've always told you, you mean more to him than you've ever realised. He's needed a friend . . . you.'

'And Leila?'

'She went back to Italy when their father died.'

'I had no idea.'

'Well, you have rather been out of touch. Your host is Sir Geoffrey now.'

'I had no idea about that, either.'

'He doesn't use the title.'

I think she expected me to ask more about Leila, but I had no wish to know anything further then. The metallic foliage in the balustrade of the great staircase *ting*ed as we climbed past it. The house was as still as I remembered it. The years I had been away were but a minute in its long history. When we came to the door with the bas-relief of the chained ape on its central panel, Dian paused.

'I'd like it if you and I could talk – just the two of us – sometimes,' she said. 'Geoffrey spends hours at a time on his studies . . .'

'Of course, Dian.'

I was wondering what I should find on the other side of the door. My only recollection of the room which had been closed for generations was of mouldering tapestries and massive pieces of furniture shrouded in cobwebs. Therefore I was startled when Dian pushed the door open and I saw that the Murder Room had been transformed into a combination of comfortable modern study, complete with soft leather armchairs and glass-topped tables, and sound recording control room. Although it was summer flames danced above fragrant logs in the stone fireplace with its heraldic devices, and I noticed that the hangings had been removed from the walls, which were now lined with cork to deaden sound.

At the far end of the room, his halo of fine hair catching the sun that streamed in through the large square window, Geoffrey reclined on a sofa, a leather-bound book in his hands. He looked well, yet a blue scarf round his neck gave a hint of the invalid.

'Geoffrey, may I present Martin Winter?' said Dian.

He looked up over his book, then with a cry of welcome climbed to his feet and, limping slightly, crossed the floor (a deep-pile carpet hid the paint stain which had sent me fleeing in horror) and took my hand in both of his.

While he expressed his delight at seeing me, and his gratitude that I should have made the journey, I saw now that I was close to him that his face had altered. He appeared to have aged more than the year which had elapsed since I had last seen him, giving him a worn look which emphasised the delicacy of his Auber features. Ascetic was the word which sprang to my mind.

'We must drink to our reunion,' he cried, and went to one of those small refrigerated cabinets that film producers and public relations men regard as essential in their offices.

'This has been chilling ever since I knew you would be paying us a visit,' he said, producing a bottle of champagne, so cold that its surface misted in the warm air. A minute later we raised our glasses to each other.

'Last time I tasted this was at a party in Bel Air,' I said.

'Little did I guess that I would be returning to Derwent-water so soon.'

'You must tell us everything about Hollywood,' said Dian enthusiastically.

Close to the low armchair in which I sat was a table piled high with books, and while I chatted I eyed their spines for some hint of Geoffrey's new interest. Some volumes I recognised as very curious – *The Subterranean Voyage of Nicholas Klimm* by Holberg, for example, and rare editions of Robert Flud, Jean D'Indagine and Eymeric de Gironne. Among these were dry-looking tomes on local history, and several modern works on philosophy and the occult.

'And what's this?' I gestured to the electronic equipment which included a sound-mixer, turntables and several very costly tape recorders.

'When I came out of Sayers Grange I found I had lost the desire to paint, a talent I had begun to prostitute anyway,' Geoffrey said. 'And so I turned to my other love – music. With this equipment I can compose my own *musique électronique*. I can't comment on its worth, but at least Dian – our real-life working musician – says it's been very therapeutic for me.'

Dian smiled. 'It's not the sort of music I was trained in. And it's hard to describe, but . . . it's genius. Please, Geoffrey, let Martin hear some.'

Geoffrey nodded and refilled our glasses.

'I must confess I acquired a taste for this at Oliver Penthorne's soirées,' he said, settling back on his sofa while Dian expertly fitted a spool on one of the tape machines. She then adjusted the controls on a console, and I was aware that several speakers placed in different parts of the room had come alive.

'Now,' she said, sitting down with a grave anticipatory smile on her lips. 'This piece is entitled *Etude*.'

A few seconds passed, and then came a high sound of remarkable purity which seemed to hang in the air about us. I could not attempt to describe it in words because my knowledge of music is negligible. All I can say is that for me it conjured up a vision of a great crystal wand, a glittering stalactite in a cavern of velvet blackness. On and on it went, until its resonance became almost unbearable. Then it faded into a silence which was gently broken by tiny sounds like the lapping of water on a stone, the murmur of a distant bee, the hiss of a breeze through grass, and I realised that Geoffrey had recorded these from nature, editing and emphasising them with his complex equipment. Soon the natural sounds grew louder, and a rhythm began to emerge which was interwoven with snatches of strange electronic sound. Sometimes thunder rolled from the speakers, crashing across the delicate tonality as the piece continued.

Music? I could not say. Certainly it was not the old-style *musique concrète* of the clashes and squeaks variety. I had never heard the like of it before, and, however it might be categorised, I had to agree with Dian's use of the word genius. At last it came to an end with the same great crystalline note that had opened it so effectively.

I was sincere in my congratulations. Geoffrey smiled faintly and said that he was working on a 'Derwentwater' symphony whenever he could spare a few hours from his studies.

'What are you studying?' I asked.

And, remembering his obsession with the past when his nervous breakdown was upon him, I was apprehensive when he answered, 'I'm trying to get back in time.'

The room I had been allotted was in one of the wings adjoining the original peel-tower, a wing I had not entered when I had been a visitor to Auber as a boy. The room bore all the traces of the house's former grandeur, the carpet was now threadbare but had been woven in Pekin, my bed was a graceful four-poster, and on the escritoire beneath the window a monogrammed folder of faded blue Morocco still contained yellowed writing paper and monochrome postcards for the use of guests. I put my portable typewriter on the desk and looked forward to working there because, by raising my head, I had a view down the avenue – Leila's 'alley Titanic' – and of the woodland foliage which always gave me the impression of pressing against the walls of ancient yew. I decided I could not have a more ideal place to work once I began on my new script.

The routine at Auber fell into place immediately. Because Geoffrey worked into the early hours he slept late and we did not meet until lunch time, after which we spent some time together, often outdoors on an old bench near the double row of classical statues which had been brought back from Italy by the ancestor who had fallen in love with Venice. During the afternoon Geoffrey returned to work and we met again for dinner, after which the three of us listened to his tapes or watched soap operas on television. Then Geoffrey, sometimes assisted by Dian, went back to work once more. This arrangement could not have suited me better. It gave me plenty of time to ponder upon the work ahead, to catch up on reading which had been sadly neglected, and to enjoy myself.

To the latter end I asked Dian to drive me to Keswick in her old but cherished dark green Morris 1100, and went in search of a second-hand boat. With little difficulty I found one which might have come from the same boatbuilders as *Pandora* of boyhood memory, and I rowed this across Derwentwater with great satisfaction, mooring it by the old boat shed which housed the gondola – and where, I suddenly remembered with a twinge of repugnance, Mrs Forster had been found floating.

To begin with we were all reticent, and out of some unspoken tact Leila's name was not mentioned. At times I could see that Geoffrey was hovering on the edge of an apology for his behaviour before he was taken to Sayers Grange. Dian had her own preoccupations, though she worked hard at being a hostess. In the evening candles were lit on the long table in the enormous oak-panelled dining room, their soft light reflecting on the Auber silver.

And even when she had not been able to provide a gastronomic meal – often we managed happily with fish fingers and frozen peas or bacon and eggs – at least a good wine was always brought up from the cellar, and we observed the niceties of a dinner party, concluding with port. And to cover the introspection of my two companions, I told anecdotes about my experiences in Los Angeles.

'It's thanks to you that I went there,' I said to Geoffrey at our first dinner. 'You told me the Croglin legend on Otterbield Island, and I based my script on that.'

'So I did,' he said reflectively. 'I had a penchant for old legends in those days, and now I'm trying to get to the bottom of some of them.' I remembered the piles of books on local history and folklore I had seen in his study.

'In every legend there must be a grain of truth,' he continued. 'I can't imagine people ever sat down and said, "Let's invent a legend." No, every tradition, no matter how fantastical, was inspired by *something* at *some time*. It's an alarming thought.'

'How does Geoffrey seem to you?' Dian asked me one morning as we took a stroll on the overgrown terraced lawn.

'I find it hard to believe he's the same man I saw at Sayers Grange,' I said. 'His recovery his amazing.'

'I'm so glad you think so. Of course, your arrival has really cheered him up. He used to have long periods of being withdrawn, when he sat alone in his study for hours with his tapes playing and a faraway look in his eyes. At times he hardly knew me, and I was scared it meant his illness was recurring. I should have recognised the danger signs the first time – like when he went into the derelict church to paint – and now perhaps I'm *over*-alert.'

'That's only natural, when you care about him so much,' I said. 'The Aubers are not quite as ordinary mortals.'

'As you know to your cost. I'll never forget how you looked when you came back from Venice.'

'There's been a lot of water under the Bridge of Sighs since then,' I said lightly, not wishing to have a conversation about Leila. 'What's all this work Geoffrey's doing?'

Dian's fingernails left a reflective groove in the lichen covering the ample belly of a satyr.

'He's researching his ancestors,' she answered slowly.

'Is he trying to make up a family tree?'

'No, there's no need for that. The Aubers are well documented, you've seen the ancestral portraits all over the house. No, it seems he's trying to find the answers to some of the things which were supposed to have happened long ago.'

'Like the famous family curse,' I said relentlessly. She did not answer.

'You're worried that this is a symptom of the obsession with the past he showed when he had his breakdown.'

'Yes. I know he's made a wonderful recovery, but I'm scared this may be some kind of relapse. He's always been rather haunted by his family traditions.'

He's not the only one, I thought grimly, remembering Leila's words in Venice. Without thinking I rubbed the white scar on the inside of my wrist.

Dian said, 'Please keep a careful eye on him when I'm down in London, Martin. You have a good influence on him, and he really does need you.'

'You say that, but I'm not so sure. I haven't spent that much time with him. In London I felt I was an admirer standing on the fringe of his circle.'

'That was because he had been taken up as a promising young artist. He was lionised a bit and I rather think he loved it, but people have probably forgotten him by now. Except for Oliver, of course. But, as I've told you before, you mean a great deal to him. He said once, half-jokingly, that he must have known you in another life, seeing how easily you fitted in when you first came to Auber. He and Leila had never made any real friends until then, poor things. And something else that worries me is that he's under great financial pressure.'

245

My interest quickened.

'Now that he's inherited Auber there's a problem with death duties. All the money he earned from his paintings has gone, and it's likely that the house will have to be sold.'

'Then perhaps it was lucky I came.'

'Yes, you can give him moral support,' she said, taking her own meaning from my words. We went down the broad garden steps to a path I had made going down to my boat between dark patches of nettles alive with butterflies, and docks, wolf's-bane, cowparsley, nightshade and other flourishing examples of British weeds. Sometimes puff-balls exploded into white dust beneath our feet, and here and there there was an agitation in the damp greenery as a toad catapulted out of our way.

'In his letter he mentioned I could help him in his work,' I said. 'Have you any idea what he may have meant?'

'No, but perhaps he wants to draw on your journalistic skills for the research. I'm sure he'll tell you as soon as you're settled in.'

We approached the mausoleum.

'When I first came here in spring Auber was everything I imagined from hearing you and Geoffrey speak about it,' Dian said. 'Ancient, hidden, a little desolate, a little beautiful . . . and I sometimes find it a little sinister, too. Whenever I see that old tomb I feel as though a goose is walking over my grave.'

'The morbid musings of an artistic soul.' I laughed. 'Now for me it has a quite different connotation.'

I did not add that here I had lain with a witch child whom, in return for the fairy gold of her love, I allowed to cast a glamour over me which had only faded this last year.

'What is your connotation?'

'I once sat on the steps and ate Marmite sandwiches,' I said, laughing. 'I'm sure it was those sandwiches that endeared me to Geoffrey.'

★

One evening I sat in Geoffrey's study – I could no longer think of it as the Murder Room – with an after-dinner drink in my hand. In some other room Dian was practising on her silent keyboard. Geoffrey sat riffling through photostats of documents in the British Museum library which had arrived from his London researcher that day.

'Geoffrey,' I said. 'I am going to make a proposition which I hope you will consider very carefully. I understand that the future of Auber may be in doubt . . .'

He sighed in agreement.

'. . . and this could be an answer to the problem. It's not for me to discuss the financial arrangements – that would best be arranged between your solicitor and Akkim – but before I left L.A. Akkim gave me to understand that you would receive a very generous amount of money if you agreed. But he also realised that a certain family delicacy might make you refuse. I think he has the idea that an English gentleman would prefer bubonic plague to publicity, and I rather encouraged the notion as it gives you a better bargaining position.'

'Martin, get on with it. I'm all agog.'

I explained that after the completion of *Croglin* it had occurred to me that the story of Auber's Murder Room could be adapted into a good horror script. Not only that, I had suggested to Akkim that to give the film extra interest it should be shot in the actual locations where the events took place. This would also save a lot of expense in set-building.

'You mean, he would want to stage re-enactments in the house and grounds?' said Geoffrey, his pale eyes alight with interest.

'Right. And you would be paid for permission to turn your home into a virtual film studio for several weeks, and for your collaboration on the story which I would turn into the script. When you've thought it over . . .'

'I can tell you now,' he said. 'I'd go along with anything that would save the house. Your proposition is like the arrival of the US cavalry when the homesteaders are down to their last cartridge. As for the legend of the Murder

Room, that comes into the research I'm doing and I'd be delighted if you could help me with it.'

'Is that what you were suggesting in your letter – help with research?'

'Not exactly. What I had in mind was a fascinating project involving Oliver Penthorne, but it would be better if I leave it to him to put you in the picture. He's coming up here soon.'

'It'll be interesting to see Oliver again. There's something that I want to discuss with him rather badly.' My tone of voice caused Geoffrey to glance at me sharply.

'Have you ever heard of the Bloxham Tapes?'

Thinking that Geoffrey was suddenly turning the conversation to music, I shook my head.

'Never mind. Oliver will explain everything.'

The next day Dian drove me to Keswick in her little car. Auber's telephone had been disconnected for many years, and I wanted to let Akkim know of Geoffrey's approval of the Murder Room project, subject to financial agreement. Dian appeared to be in two minds over the idea. While she was delighted that Geoffrey's financial problems could be solved, the focus on his family legend worried her.

'I'm just afraid that in his present mental state it might increase any morbid fancy,' she said.

'It might have the opposite effect, act as catharsis. Once he sees it go through the process of film-making he won't be able to take the Auber tradition so seriously. It could put everything into perspective.'

Dian turned to me with a wry smile.

'One can get a bit tired of the Auber tradition.'

'But you put up with it.'

'It's funny what hoops love will put you through.'

Mentally I agreed with her.

Poor Dian, I thought. If you did but know it you're far too good for Geoffrey.

I wondered what happiness she got out of the relationship

apart from a certain masochistic gratification in looking after an unstable young man. At Auber Geoffrey treated her kindly – always smiled most charmingly when she did anything for him, praised her cooking extravagantly, and was quite jolly at times – but surely lovers want something more than kindness. There was still a remoteness about him which did not encourage emotional intimacy. Although I was not sure, I had a suspicion that Dian did not even share his bedroom, but had a guest room of her own in the opposite wing to mine.

I shrugged. It was none of my business. Perhaps Dian guessed what I was thinking.

'I can't help it. Geoffrey's in my blood,' she said. 'I've only felt that way about one other person.' For a moment her wide eyes looked into mine with an expression I could not read. 'How much nicer if I could have fallen in love with you. You're so even and uncomplicated, or so it seems. So easy-going and unambitious, yet without visible effort you got on to Fleet Street when you wanted to, and then became a scriptwriter in Hollywood where the competition must be terrible. I've only seen you upset once and then you were cool about it. Please be around when I need someone to pick up the pieces.'

I was amused by her view of me. If only she knew of the turmoils behind the façade.

At Keswick post office I copied out a long cable to Akkim which I had composed on my typewriter, then we went shopping. Dian was returning to London the next day, and she was planning an ambitious meal for her last evening. Thoughtfully, she also bought extra supplies which Geoffrey and I would need when we were on our own.

That evening, over Dian's *coq au vin*, Geoffrey asked me, 'Do you believe in predestination?'

'Very reluctantly, I find I'm forced to.'

'I remember you and I had this conversation a long time ago,' Dian said. 'I think it's a horrible idea. I want to be captain of my fate.'

I repeated the views I had expressed in Dian's flat while she looked on nervously, fearing the direction of Geoffrey's chain of thought.

'So you believe that while we have the illusion of free will, the only true freedom man has is in his attitude to preordained events,' said Geoffrey when I had finished.

'Right.' (A form of affirmative I had copied from Tash.)

'But supposing his attitude could nudge the cycle of events to cause an alteration in future cycles?'

I am sure Dian remembered as well as I did the bizarre explanation for ending his artistic career that Geoffrey had given us at Sayers Grange, for she became over-busy with the Cona coffee-maker.

'Ah, that supposes that existence is a series of cycles,' I said lightly.

'Not identical cycles, as some Eastern philosophers believe,' Geoffrey answered seriously. 'Rather I see time as – how shall I put it? – a spiral. Each coil of the spiral is identical in shape, yet they cannot be exactly the same because each is in a different relation to the others, and, unlike a series of definite cycles, they're part of a continuous process. So I imagine events recurring endlessly, but each time with a fractional variation. The problem is to influence that variation . . .'

'Who wrote, "The road runs in a circle, but looks straight"?' Dian interrupted.

I shook my head but Geoffrey said, 'I know the verse but not the poet. Let's see . . .

'The road runs in a circle
But looks straight,
As straight as the horizon looks
Although the world is round.
So we fear to meet ourselves, face to face,
Yesterday's smile a mockery on our lips.'

This quoting of poetry brought Tash vividly to mind, and remembering her easy companionship I wondered again if I had made a mistake in leaving California. When my attention refocused on my companions I heard Geoffrey's voice. '. . . and only by mapping the past would it be possible to influence the course of the future.'

19

The following day Dian left for London and I settled to work. If I was to write a full length film script based on the Murder Room I must find the necessary material, even though I knew that by the end of the day it would probably have been adapted and angled and altered almost out of recognition. So I joined Geoffrey in his research on the early Aubers, and I must say I thoroughly enjoyed the hunt for facts, or even inklings of facts, through dusty volumes which had been undisturbed in Auber's library for generations.

Geoffrey's notes provided background on the early history of the family. The first Auber to settle in England was Sir Gilbert d'Auber, one of the knights-of-fortune who came from France with William the Conqueror. Duke William had persuaded the Pope to proclaim a holy crusade against England, which meant that mercenaries from all over Europe could be recruited to swell William's ranks in return for promises of land and loot. After the Conquest the new king found Cumbria a difficult region to control, and when his patience was exhausted he razed Carlisle. Sir Gilbert was one of the knights given land in the area in return for keeping the locals in subjection, and no doubt Auber was one of the most hated names in this remote corner of the kingdom for several generations.

The descendants of Sir Gilbert remained loyal to their sovereign, keeping the Saxons under control and acting as a buffer between Celtic reivers from the north and the softer lands to the south. They prospered, and their wooden palisaded hall was replaced by the grim peel-tower as their estates increased.

'The deterioration in the Auber fortunes began towards the end of Elizabeth's reign,' Geoffrey told me. 'That was when the curse was put upon the family.'

Certainly it was in late Tudor times that the decline started. Times were changing and feudal families were losing their importance, added to which was the Aubers' sympathy for the old faith. Later it was their Jacobite tendencies which continued the process.

While Geoffrey was absorbed with his notes and photostats in the old Murder Room, and I spent hours in the library which had impressed me so much as a boy, telexes were passing to and fro between Akkim and Geoffrey's London solicitor. Telegrams brought by a youth on a red Post Office motorcycle kept Geoffrey abreast of the negotiations, and he became more and more confident that an agreement would be concluded which would remove his financial burden.

In moments of elation he would limp up and down his study telling me in extravagant detail how Auber would be refurbished.

'I can't wait to get work started on the gardens,' he cried while I watched him with amusement. 'An army of men with scythes – tractors if necessary – to clear the jungle, and then there'll be lawns again, green as a billiard table and smooth enough to play croquet on. And the rose garden – did you know there was once a rose garden and a walled herb garden? – that'll be brought back, and replanted, and the yews can be cut into shape. And the lily pond! It used to be on the lower terrace, but it's full of rubbish. And a new jetty . . .'

He paused and looked at me with his pale blue eyes shining in a way that I have only seen in one other person: his sister.

'Martin, to celebrate Auber's return to its proper state I shall hold a celebration, a party such as my grandparents used to throw.'

'You should have it in costume. Then Akkim could film

it as background material and there'd be expenses towards the cost.'

'Brilliant! A masque!'

'Wait for the contracts to be signed before you send out the invitations.'

But, after Dian's departure, I found that Geoffrey's periods of elation were interspersed with moods of sombre introspection when he would brood alone for hours in his study, his notes and photostats discarded, and only his most melancholy tapes playing over his audio system. To my attempts to cheer him up he would respond in monosyllables or with brief and enigmatic sentences.

'I dread the events of the future. Not in themselves, but in their results,' he remarked once when I walked in with a tray of coffee.

'Geoffrey, you're becoming morbid.'

He looked at me for a long moment, and then said quietly, 'You've read the works of Edgar Allan Poe?'

'As much as I ever want to,' I replied with a grimace.

'Martin, I'm not fit company today for man or beast. Go out on the lake in the sunshine and forget about my gloom.'

He turned away to his console, and from the speakers came an improvised dirge whose synthesised notes told me more about his mental state than I could have learned by talking to him for an hour. It was obvious that Geoffrey's mind was not as stable as Dian and I had believed, and I wondered if these fits of despondency were the prelude to another mental breakdown.

'See you later,' I said as cheerfully as I could, and left him hunched over the console with his wild harmonics surrounding him. Outside the house drizzle filled the grey air, but I preferred it to the atmosphere of the house, which in my imagination had absorbed Geoffrey's melancholia. Putting on my windcheater, I strode through the dripping vegetation which might soon fall before Geoffrey's scythes, and wondered if I would not prefer

Auber to be hidden in this Gothic wasteland rather than rising above baize lawns and obedient ranks of roses. I decided to enjoy the place as much as possible while it was in the state I was accustomed to, and not think of the future. Once Akkim had finished here I would be leaving with the technicians, and I would probably never see Auber again. Its magic would have been transferred on to the screen, and for me the old enchantment would be gone.

I reached my boat which, since it did not have a name painted on it, I now thought of as *Pandora II*. After bailing out the accumulated rainwater – more rain falls on the Lake District than on any other area of Britain – I rowed out on Derwentwater to look for the floating island which had once so excited my imagination. The fine rain hid the opposite shore and the islands, and ensured such a silence on the water that the creak of the rowlocks was a vulgar intrusion. Despite the damp and dimness, my spirits rose as the bank became an imprecise shadow in the mist, and I realised with a slight shock of surprise that I was still a little vulnerable to Geoffrey's shifts of temperament; and with the knowledge came sympathy for Dian's anxieties.

Following the shoreline, I rowed south. Although I was probably foolish to go on such a quest in conditions of such poor visibility, it did not really matter whether I located the island or not. It was an excuse to get on to the lake. My fingers were eager to start typing the first draft of the script – the first of many drafts, possibly – but as yet I did not have enough material to begin. I needed to know how the Auber curse came about, the characters involved, and its connection with witchcraft. And now I was wondering how the mysterious island could be worked in.

This curious feature of Derwentwater, which floats to the surface every three or four years in a bay opposite the Lodore Falls, was first mentioned in a book on Cumbrian history and antiquities by William Hutchinson in 1794. Not having seen the phenomenon himself he wrote: 'The tale with which travellers are amused, of a floating island, appears on strict examination to be fabulous.' But Jonathan Otley, a clockmaker who became one of the earliest Lakeland geologists, was far less cavalier with the centuries-old tradition of the island, and when reports reached him that it had surfaced in 1814 he set out to investigate. He found that it was about half an acre in size and about six feet in depth, being composed of vegetable material and peat on which a covering of clay soil allowed wild plants to take root.

The popular explanation of its appearance is that in particularly warm weather decaying vegetable matter on the bed of the lake generates so much marsh gas that a huge slice of it becomes buoyant and rises to the surface, where it remains for a period of several weeks.

I might not have found it that morning had not the weather changed with the unexpectedness one associates with Cumbria. The rain had turned to mist through which fingers of pale sunlight now probed, giving me enough landmarks to cross to the bay where the river Derwent flows into the lake. For a moment the Lodore Pier loomed up and I swung away into the centre of the bay. There, turning my head, I saw the island steaming gently as the dampness surrounding it dissolved.

It was only a foot or so above the water but it looked substantial enough, its surface mottled with the greens of grasses and sedge which had seeded themselves there. As I rowed closer I saw patches of bursting methane bubbles at its margin, and decided that this must be responsible for the island's Will o' the Wisp, inspiration for several eerie legends.

For a moment I considered landing, but its shores were quaking slightly and I knew it could be dangerous. A man might sink through the topsoil and be sucked down into the saturated peat just as if he had stepped into a morass. No matter, I rowed away well satisfied with what I had found. There was certainly the possibility of setting a dramatic scene there.

When I returned to Auber I sensed immediately that something had changed. In a moment I realised that the great clock on the landing – whose tick Leila's grandmother had likened to the heartbeat of the house – had been set going for the first time this century. As I listened, both hands reached twelve and there came a sound which was loud and deep and exceedingly musical, but of so peculiar a note that I began to imagine how effective it would be on the soundtrack of my film.

In the middle of the chiming Geoffrey appeared at the top of the stairs, waving a telegram.

'Martin, the contract has been agreed,' he shouted, all trace of his earlier moroseness gone. 'Your Akkim will be here in three or four weeks. I can't tell you how grateful I am.'

I congratulated him, and then reminded him that I had to get a script written before Akkim's arrival. '. . . so I'll need to know everything I can about the Auber tradition.'

'Of course. It's time we got down to it,' he said, leading me to his study. 'The problem is that it's mostly hearsay. The story of the curse was handed down from generation to generation. Unfortunately our father thought it was a lot of nonsense and refused to talk about it – now, of course, I can understand why. I believe you saw him . . . in Italy.'

'Yes, Geoffrey.'

We entered the study and he gestured to the piles of books.

'I've been trying to discover what really happened,' he said, 'but so far without much luck. However, I've got a lot of material on the effects of the curse, which was manifested every so often by a male member of the family's becoming unbalanced.'

He went on to explain that it was 'a constitutional family evil', and in the past had resulted in the death of a spouse or a lover 'through accident or mad design'. He looked searchingly at my face, seeking, I knew, for my reaction to this in view of the fact that I had seen him in a clinic for the mentally disturbed.

I merely shrugged and smiled back at him.

'By facing up to these old stories, by finding out everything you can and then seeing it processed into entertainment, you'll lay the ghost which has been haunting you and your sister,' I said. 'Not even family curses can last for ever, and in his way Akkim will exorcise this one. You'll see how ridiculous the whole business is.'

For a moment his face resumed the sombre look it had worn that morning.

'It will take a lot besides your friend Akkim. I think I can see how to free myself from my role in the ritual, but I need to know more . . .' His voice trailed away and he seemed lost in thought.

'And so do I,' I said briskly. 'No script, no film.'

'Of course,' he said, blinking. He picked up a black notebook.

'Thanks to my research, I have details of what you might say were the effects of the curse.' He turned the pages of the notebook at random. 'During the Civil War Sir Gilbert Auber fatally wounded his wife when a pistol he was priming before joining the Royalists accidentally exploded . . . Sir Richard Auber murdered his wife by cutting her throat, which gave rise to the story of the Green Lady haunting this room. He managed to keep the crime secret and married the woman he had fallen madly in love with, but when she committed suicide – legend says inspired by visitations of the Green Lady – he went completely insane, and told how he had hidden the body of his wife in a wood by the road so that her death had been accepted as the result of an attack by footpads. In 1870 John Auber, a younger son and a promising artist, created a family scandal by setting up a household in Bloomsbury with his favourite model, the daughter of a Covent Garden porter. For some mysterious reason she died soon afterwards of an overdose of laudanum. And then there was . . .'

'It's a dismal list,' I interrupted, 'but it doesn't prove that a curse had been laid on the family. From what little I've read of English history I imagine many aristocratic families have had their share of misfortune down the centuries. Perhaps there never was a curse of Auber, and the similarity of the tragedies is pure coincidence. I'm starting to wonder whether it wasn't events which gave rise to the tradition of the curse rather than the other way round . . .'

I was going on to say that hereditary mental instability was not all that uncommon, but I stopped myself in time. My job was to find out what I could of the Auber legends without encouraging Geoffrey's morbidity. Surprisingly he responded to my argument with a smile, and I was pleased to see that the good humour caused by the conclusion of the negotiations with Akkim remained.

'I may be able to supply proof about the curse which will convince you,' he said, putting away his black book, 'but we must wait for Oliver's arrival. In the meantime I'll read you this extract from Braithwaite's *Anecdotes and Traditions of Notable Families in the North of England*, published in 1773. It'll give you something more to go on.'

He took up a large, superbly bound book illustrated with fine engravings of country residences, and opened it at a marker.

'"I found there to be another quaint legend concerning a malediction placed upon a family when my journeyings took me to the small town of Keswick, that which has been noted for the manufacture of pencils since the illustrious reign of Queen Elizabeth, on the north shore of a dismal stretch of mere known as Derwent Water in an uncomfortably remote valley in the County of Cumberland,"' Geoffrey read. '"On the west bank of Derwent Water, sequestered among woods which provide not only privacy but complete seclusion for its occupants, stands an ancient tower mansion known as the House of A——, which, if my informants be reliable, has more than once been defended against bands of pillagers from Scotland whose unwelcome forays into the Kingdom of England were so providently brought to an end at Drummossie Moor by the military determination of the Duke of Cumberland.

'"To return to the House of A——, whose appearance struck me, when I ventured upon the mere in a craft of dubious reliability, as having a quality of atmosphere sympathetic to the grotesqueries of the local story-tellers who are in great demand during the long evenings of winter at the rural inns of this comfortless region. On beholding the bleak walls and vacant eye-like windows of this ancient mansion as the shades of evening drew on, I was conscious of an utter depression of soul which prompted me to make inquiries as to its history on my return to Keswick.

'"Here I was introduced to a schoolmaster who had some local reputation as an antiquarian and, flattered by the interest shown by some person from the outer world, regaled me with some preposterous myths of the district including one about a floating island which might have been more appropriate to the fanciful narrative of Gulliver than to a man charged with the responsibility of instructing the young even of this outlandish place.

'"Touching on the House of A——, this venerable Homer informed me that a curse had been placed on the family who had possessed it for centuries . . ."'

'At last,' I exclaimed.

'"'. . . and on my pressing him he recounted what little he knew of the matter which I faithfully copied into my journal,"' continued Geoffrey, who appeared to be relishing the author's verbose style. '"I was informed by my worthy schoolmaster that in Tudor times a master of the House of A——, having married a lady of wealth for pecuniary advantage, tired of her as was the wont of wicked story-book barons and therefore plotted how to be rid of her without incurring opprobrium. In order to achieve his base object he denounced his wife to the authorities on a charge of witchcraft, expressing the deepest horror and sorrow at the discovery of her demonic practices.

' "In the trial which followed witnesses testified that the mistress of A—— had been seen by them in strange company performing a ritual in a circle of ancient stones which had been erected by the Druids on a lonely hill with an unsavoury reputation of ancient paganism. Other witnesses came forward with more fantastical statements (from what I heard I considered that they were at odds with each other to furnish the most outrageous testimony). but I shall not waste ink by recording them. Suffice to say that one of the mildest charges was that the lady had a familiar imp in the form of a small ape who at her bidding would carry poison to her enemies.

' "Despite the lady's protestations and explanations, she was found to be guilty of the crime of which she was charged, which was regarded very gravely at that period in history when the passing of the Witchcraft Act of 1563, following threats of a magical nature to the person of Queen Elizabeth, created a climate of fear and suspicion, and an abhorrence of those believed to engage in diabolical pursuits. The unfortunate victim was sentenced to death although in later times she was held to be innocent, it being considered that she had been falsely accused, as in the case of Lady Janet Douglas of Glamis Castle who was burnt at the stake following the accusation of a kinsman who later confessed to calumny.

' "The place of execution was sited in the Druid's circle, according to my threadbare authority, as an example to other would-be witches and warlocks, and to demonstrate the power of the righteous over the forces of Satan. The prisoner was bound to a stake in the centre of the ring, but before the faggots could be ignited she called down a curse upon the House of A—— that from time to time a madness of its lords should be responsible for the destruction of those who held them dear, just as she was about to die at the instigation of her husband, so that each inheritor would be in fear of the family bane falling upon him."'

Geoffrey paused and then went on to read how the author, mistrusting the old antiquarian's account which at best was 'a mere old wives' tattle', endeavoured to find some historical reference which might throw light on the origins of the legend. He consulted old records at Keswick, Penrith and Carlisle without discovering a single sentence to corroborate it, except that in the sixteenth century one of the masters of the House of A—— did marry twice in quick succession and there was a curious lack of information about his first wife and the manner of her death.

' "And with this slight crumb of information I resigned my interest in so ambiguous a subject, especially as it is a not uncommon ingredient in folk tales of the North Country and Scotland where the logic and reason now so prevalent in the south of the kingdom is slow to circulate," ' Geoffrey read in conclusion. ' "In truth I endeavoured to pay my respects to the current owner of the House of A—— but was informed that he and his family wisely spent much of their time in more salutiferous climes. Thus, deeming that at best the legend was the import of some itinerant fabulist, I continued on my journey to Lowther Castle whither I had the honour to be invited by Sir James." '

Geoffrey put down the Braithwaite and looked at me with raised eyebrows.

'From my point of view it has possibilities,' I said, 'but you must admit it is rather nebulous. Is there any confirmation that there was a witch-burning in the Castlerigg circle? You'd think there must be some sort of record of that.'

'Not necessarily,' said Geoffrey. 'Technically the execution would have been illegal. English law, following the Elizabethan Witchcraft Act, stated that the penalty for witchcraft was hanging, not burning as in Scotland and on the Continent. But it was not unknown, especially in isolated areas, for the mob to take the law into its own hands and burn a witch. Such unofficial punishments would obviously be left out of the records.

'Well, all we can do is sift through the material we have,' I said. 'After lunch I'll carry on in the library.'

'I have a feeling you'll get all the confirmation you need. I can see how it'll enhance the film if it's based on fact rather than fiction. But first let me take you down into the cellars and you can choose a wine worthy of celebrating the promise of Akkim's gold!'

Geoffrey's elation did not last for long. His spells of brooding returned, but now they were marked by a quiet intensity, a suppressed excitement over something about which he would not, or could not, talk to me. For whole days he abandoned his papers and sat recording his synthesised sounds on to tapes, distorting, replaying and blending on different tracks, and then synchronising them on to a master recording of his often eerie compositions. These, I knew, would fascinate Akkim, who was always on the search for soundtrack material.

While such moods were upon Geoffrey I was glad to be working away from him in the old library, where I systematically searched the shelves for likely books. As yet Geoffrey had only examined a quarter of the several thousand volumes lying under a patina of fine dust on oak shelves which had been installed soon after the young Victoria was enthroned, and whose burden had rarely been disturbed since. It was work I enjoyed. The sweetish smell of decaying leather bindings, of rag paper and vellum, which welcomed me in the mornings gave me a sense of excitement as I began the day's hunt.

When I became bored with my lack of success I went to work at the typewriter in my room, gazing over its keyboard down the avenue stretching through the woods to the glimmer of silver which marked the lake. Not infrequently this vista would lure my mind away from the job in hand, and I would become lost in contemplation of the restless treetops which I fancied shared a corporate life. Sometimes I imagined the wood resenting the house and avenue as alien factors set in its heart. Perhaps it was this which sometimes made me feel that the dark old yews, themselves equally alien to the surrounding trees, were the walls holding back the thrust of the wilderness.

Annoyed with myself for such childish imaginings I would return to the Olympia and rattle off a few lines at high speed before some new aspect of the view beguiled my attention. Looking back, I believe those moments were inspired by the knowledge that Auber – *my* Auber – was about to change. Geoffrey's new-found money and Akkim's film unit would transform it from my realm of lost content into a fine, well-groomed house overlooking Derwentwater. Its secrets would be shared with millions of people through the medium of the film – and where would the ghosts of childhood go?

I felt that the coming change would mark the end of an era in my life, that in the future things would be completely different. Most likely I would settle in Los Angeles to work, and thoughts of Tash came frequently to mind.

It was in my room that I typed material for Akkim: a revised outline of the Murder Room story which I had given him in Bel Air; the suggestion that he might get good footage at the masque which Geoffrey was so keen on; the possibility of incorporating the floating island, provided it was still afloat when the time came for filming; and my advice to film Auber while its grounds were still overgrown and the house retained its desolate air for an evocative title sequence. I waxed enthusiastic over the cellars Geoffrey had shown me when we went down for the wine to celebrate the news from his solicitor. They were illuminated by a line of old-fashioned electric light bulbs which had been strung along the curved ceilings before the Second World War. The yellow light illuminated walls of roughly dressed stones from whose ancient mortar nitre hung like moss.

Geoffrey led me under a low archway into a circular room with a vaulted ceiling – I believe it is called an under-croft – which made me think of a subterranean dome.

'Where does that lead to?' I pointed to a metal-bound door set in the wall between dusty wine racks.

'I believe it's the entrance to the tunnel,' said Geoffrey, peering at the bottles through ancient webs which appeared to have caught nothing but dust. 'It was a so-called secret passage in the days of Catholic persecution, useful for smuggling fugitive priests out of the house. Of course, at that time the entrance was hidden, and I believe it came out somewhere near the lakeshore. My ancestors used to keep their choicest wines locked away in there. As children we were warned not to try and open the door. It was said to be dangerous, and the exit had been sealed long ago. Didn't we show it to you when you used to play here?'

I shook my head.

Geoffrey laughed. 'No, perhaps not, after the Murder Room incident! How does this Medoc take your fancy?'

In my description of the cellars for Akkim, I concluded, 'They are straight from *The Cask of Amontillado*.'

Several days later I woke to find bright sunlight stream-ing through my window. The low-flying clouds and rain squalls so frequently attracted by the combination of lake and mountain had vanished, and the scenery outside had a brightness about it that made it impossible for me to spend a morning in the library. Instead I threw on my clothes, gulped a mug of instant coffee in the old kitchen which had not altered since I sat at its enormous table with the Auber twins, and then set out for a hike over Cat Bells.

On my return I recognised Oliver Penthorne's Rover parked in the old courtyard. My pulse rate increased with the adrenalin of anger as the thought of the hypnotist recalled my car swerving off the Tucson highway. I had a lot to say to Oliver.

Rounding the side of the house I saw him standing beside Geoffrey, both men gazing over the swaying weeds which covered the terraced lawns. He was wearing Austin Reed casual clothes of a pale blue that seemed to emphasise the babyishness of his plump features.

'Martin, how marvellous to see you after so long!' He came quickly to me with an outstretched hand. 'Tell me, is your back all right these days?'

His welcome and concern for my health seemed so genuine that I was momentarily disarmed, and I found myself shaking his smooth hand warmly.

'So we're all together again,' he said as Dian, who had been his passenger, appeared from the kitchen. Her dreamy smile further disarmed me, it would be churlish to create a fuss now. Later, though, I would have it out with him.

The opportunity came when we found ourselves alone together in the study after lunch.

'What's wrong, dear boy?' asked Oliver. 'You seem a trifle *distrait*.'

I invoked a formula I had worked out for occasions when I was angry but could not find the words to introduce my complaint.

'I must tell you what's on my mind, Oliver.' My tone focused his innocent blue eyes on my face. 'I want to ask you a question about something which I believe happened when I was a hypnotic subject at your flat.'

'And a damn fine subject you were. You and Dian were the best . . .'

'Did you leave any command words inplanted in my subconscious?' I demanded. 'Words which you thought might be useful if you ever wanted to continue with your experimenting – words which, in effect, gave you power over me?'

Oliver's face became grave.

'Go on,' he said quietly.

'The trouble with control words is that they can be accidentally triggered, with the result that I might have

266

suffered a very nasty accident. It's not funny to be the subject of post-hypnotic suggestion when you're on an American highway.'

'What was the word?'

'*Ulalume*! A word from a poem which was a favourite of Geoffrey's sister when she was a girl. And this brings me to the second point – what exactly was the nature of your experiments with me? Was it Geoffrey's idea to probe into the emotions I felt when I first visited Auber?'

'My dear boy . . .'

'Why was it that when I heard that word I had a vision of the child Leila running towards me? Had you both been checking on my relationship with her? Did you record my one-sided conversations with her so that brother Geoffrey could substitute a tape machine for his binoculars?'

My anger was in full spate, and to my surprise Oliver sat down suddenly as though overcome by sudden weakness.

'Listen to me, Martin, please,' he said, holding up his hand as though to stem my words.

Here they come – the excuses and the charm, I thought, but it also occurred to me that I was achieving nothing by my outburst. I turned away and watched the play of the sunlight on the treetops moving with a sea-like swell under the fresh breeze. The window was open, and from thousands of branches and billions of leaves came a continual muted sound like distant surf.

'It greatly distresses me that you should think I was responsible . . .'

'It greatly distressed me when the car went skidding over the desert,' I interrupted as I felt a reprise of my resentment.

'That I can well understand, dear boy. But let's examine the situation objectively. First, those sessions at Frognal – in which I found your co-operation absolutely invaluable to my research – were all taped, and if you have any anxiety about the nature of the experiments you can have everything played back.

'Second, it's quite true that "Ulalume" was a control word. I believe it was suggested by Geoffrey simply because it was an unusual, made-up word he had heard from his sister. I knew that the word must have connotations for you, but for my purposes "Derwentwater" would have done as well in regressing you to childhood. Of course some completely neutral word would have worked, but I've found that when there's an association it does help the type of experiment I was conducting.'

He paused, and I continued to watch the surge of the foliage.

'I never cancelled the control word,' Oliver continued. 'If you remember there was no reason why I should at the time. Despite the . . . unforeseen interruption I assumed that our sessions would continue. But it would have been pointless anyway. I had implanted the word into your subconscious with the command that you would only respond when I – the hypnotist – used it . . .'

'But supposing you let others use it during your experiments?'

'My dear boy, I told you, you can hear the tapes any time you wish.'

'They're down in London.'

'Yes. But let me continue. To remove your distrust of me, I am afraid I must discuss your personal life. As a boy I gather you had a crush on Geoffrey's sister. When you met her again in Venice your boyhood feelings were renewed and you fell in love with her. Sadly, Leila Auber felt unable to continue the relationship and this affected you deeply, so deeply in fact that you ran away. Forgive me. I don't mean that in a derogatory sense, but you did quit this country hurriedly.

'The event had been traumatic for you, and though you overlaid it with new experiences, your emotional commitment to Leila remained. Now, as you know, you were an excellent hypnotic subject because you have, whether you're particularly aware of it or not, what I can only describe as a certain "psychic vision" – a highly developed imaginative capacity, if you prefer. Do you see what I'm getting at?'

'No,' I said, although I had an inkling of what was coming. I would let him spell out his glib explanation.

'When you were driving and heard that evocative word, you had a vivid emotional response which, with this unusual imaginative capacity of yours, projected itself into a hallucination of an idealised image. Don't you understand, dear boy? The word would have had that effect even if it had never been used in our experiments. I can only conclude that something had occurred in your life which made you particularly susceptible . . .'

His words ran on smoothly, and I remembered how a vision of Auber had disturbed me on Lake Waikaremoana when Dawn and I spent our first night together. And when I found a brief spell of comfort and happiness with Tash during our visit to Tombstone her chance use of 'Ulalume' was enough to revive the old enchantment. It seemed that when I believed I was escaping, a shadow of the past arose to haunt me.

It was an uneasy line of thought, but had Oliver's explanation been the truth? Still watching the trees, and half listening to his relief that the matter had been cleared up, I sensed that only a thin curtain of time separated me from recognising the reality of my bond with Auber.

20

Dian, who always had an eye for effect, had dimmed the lights of Geoffrey's study so that the main illumination was provided by the flames dancing above the hissing logs in the ancient fireplace. Outside a wild wind was racing and every so often a gust in the chimney would puff aromatic smoke into the room, reminding me of campfires in the New Zealand bush. For a while the after-supper conversation had been desultory. Each of us had a glass of port and his or her own thoughts. I noticed that now Dian and Oliver were here the tension which I had felt radiating from Geoffrey was easing, and in the firelight his face looked unusually calm beneath the fine hair which floated rather than fell about his face.

'I think the time has come, Oliver, to tell Martin the nature of your work,' he said at last. 'I've been rather reluctant to talk about it myself, knowing you could explain it so much better, but my cryptic references must have been frustrating.'

Oliver nodded, and his expression was that of a man about to enjoy describing a pet project.

'A while before you left England my research into the possibilities of hypnotism had suddenly taken an exciting turn,' he said, holding up his glass so that the fire created crimson sparks in the port. 'Until then I had had the feeling that everything I tried went so far and no further. I was very interested in telepathic phenomena associated with hypnosis, but when I pursued the subject I reached a point beyond which it was impossible to go. Perhaps that's why no really serious work has been done on it in the past

– that coupled with the slight air of charlatanry that has always dogged it. But with you, Martin, a whole new area presented itself for exploration, and that was regression. As you know, in its simplest form it was the taking of a person back through subconscious memory to a specific point in his or her earlier life.

'For demonstrations one would usually choose a birthday as a convenient point. It made a good party piece for a grown woman to be waxing enthusiastic in a childish lisp over a doll her father had just given her. When I tried it with you I realised there was a great deal more to this aspect of the work. What sparked it off, I think, was that unfortunate time when you relived a sequence in hospital – a sequence which was chosen by your subconscious self rather than by me.'

'I wonder why I went back to Henry's death, rather than some happy moment,' I said, remembering the horror I had felt when Oliver wrenched me back to consciousness.

Oliver gave one of his delicate, ambiguous shrugs.

'Perhaps it was an attempt to rid yourself of a painful memory,' he said. 'I recently cured a man of a speech complaint by taking him back through a road accident in which his mother was killed when he was five. It was a ghastly ordeal, but at the end of it he no longer stuttered. The ghost of the trauma had been laid.

'Anyway, Martin, your experience gave me cause for reflection, and I realised that I had overlooked something so obvious as regression for proper investigation. So, using Dian and you as my subjects, I began a systematic programme of research, and around the time you went to Venice I was getting results which hinted at an extraordinary possibility – the regression of a person to experiences before physical memory.'

He paused reflectively while I tried to understand what he was getting at.

'Meanwhile, a hypnotherapist in Cardiff named Arnall Bloxham had been following a similar line of inquiry, and had achieved remarkable results. He recorded subjects giving vivid descriptions of past existences – the Bloxham Tapes.'

'You mean, those people had been regressed into previous lives – previous incarnations?' I asked, as the significance of what Oliver had been saying struck me.

'Arnall Bloxham's a Christian who believes in reincarnation, so that would be the interpretation he put on his experiments. Of course, there are other theories, some rather sceptical. A popular one is that the subjects had at some time in their lives – perhaps as children – been fascinated by particular periods in history, though this may have been genuinely forgotten later on. Then, under hypnosis, there's no real regression but a fantasy against a background of historical fact dredged up from the memory store – a case of wishful thinking, if you like. The technical name for this is cryptomnesia. Of the four hundred cases Bloxham taped, many are striking for their historical detail.'

'What's the answer to the cryptomnesia argument?' asked Dian.

'One is when someone comes up with a piece of verifiable historical information which it would be utterly impossible for him to have heard of. An astonishing example of this was the case of Jane Evans, who under hypnosis became a Jew named Rebecca living in York towards the end of the twelfth century. The tape began with a description of her family and life in a northern part of the city where the wealthy Jews lived. Her husband, Joseph, was a well-to-do financier. She then went on to describe an anti-Semitic riot which we know took place in 1190. Her words changed into the present tense and she described what was happening moment by moment.

'In the hope that the Christians wouldn't spill blood in their own holy place, many of the Jews took refuge in a church just outside the city gates, which has been identified as St Mary's at Castlegate. Jane Evans, as Rebecca, told how she and her children went down into the crypt when the mob entered the church. She became almost incoherent with fear when her daughter Rachel was taken from her, and then she was silent, apart from uttering the word "dark" twice.

'The story was so terrible, and so authentically described, that it was hard to imagine it was an invention. There is, of course, information available about the massacre – in which the chroniclers wrote that a hundred and fifty Jews died – especially as a royal army was sent from London to punish those responsible, take hostages against further lawlessness and to levy heavy fines on the citizens of York. However, an error in the story was soon spotted – there was no crypt in the church where Rebecca was killed.

'Then, six months later, when the church was being converted into a museum, the workmen found a crypt under the chancel.'

Oliver paused to let the significance of his words sink in.

'Another possible answer could be termed genetic memory,' he resumed. 'The hypothesis is that genes might carry memories down the generations as well as the blueprint for each individual, and that what happens in regression is that this memory bank is tapped.'

'That sounds more likely than reincarnation,' I said.

Oliver turned his baby-blue eyes upon me in surprise.

'I'd have thought you'd have seen the flaw in that argument immediately. Think about one of Bloxham's most successful cases: a man called Graham Huxtable, who was regressed to two centuries ago when he was gunner's mate on a frigate. He described his life on the ship, sometimes using archaic slang which was only understood when the tape was played to naval historians, and ended up with the ship going into battle. From his last screams it was obvious that he was killed by having his leg shot away.'

'Of course,' I said. 'No genes carrying that experience could be passed on, they'd die with him.'

'Exactly.'

273

'So what do you think?'

Oliver raised his shoulders again.

'So far I understand the effect better than the cause,' he said. 'My experiments lead me to believe that there's a vast area as yet beyond our comprehension. I think we need to understand a great deal more about the nature of Time. At the moment we can't explain it, any more than we can really imagine an endless universe.

'The difference between my work and Bloxham's is that, while his subjects talk at random of things which happened before they were conceived, I have been attempting to *direct* my subjects into specific areas of what we think of as the past. I've been working on the premise that regression is not taking a person back to an incident in an earlier life, but "tuning them in" on an event actually experienced by another person – or even a group of people – at the time.'

He smiled at Dian.

'Under hypnosis your powers of telepathic reception were magnified. What I'm trying to do is magnify what's sometimes referred to as psychic power, because I'm sure that when we fully understand regression we'll also have the answer to ghosts and other so-called supernatural phenomena.'

I suddenly remembered the books on the occult I had seen on Geoffrey's table.

'I believe that when someone sees a phantom he is having a moment of what I might term natural regression. I'm trying to control regression, and I've found that it's intensified when the subject's mind is cleared of extraneous thought by hypnosis. You can perhaps see where this is leading, Martin.'

We sat in silence for a while.

'Were any of your regressions as dramatic as Boxham's?' I asked.

'No. Bloxham said that most of his tapes were of deadly dull ordinary people who lived and died having done nothing whatsoever, and I found the same.' He laughed.

'Have you ever noticed how people who are hooked on reincarnation tend to have glamorous past existences? – always the pharaoh's daughter, never the Nubian slave! My brief experience of regression makes me think that if there is anything in the reincarnation theory, one's a million times more likely to have been a peasant than a princess.'

Another silence fell.

I was not surprised when Oliver broke it by saying, 'I'd like to try a regression experiment with you, Martin.'

A look of expectation crossed Geoffrey's face and he sat forward in his chair.

'You mean, you think it's possible for me to experience some previous event at your direction, and not merely undergo a Bloxham-type regression? So in effect I would become a time traveller?'

The expression smacked a little too much of science fiction for Oliver's taste.

'Let's say you'd become conscious of certain things which happened long before your birth.'

'Why me?'

'Because you're one of the best hypnotic subjects I have ever worked with, and because you have an element of the psychic in your make-up. An ideal combination for what I have in mind.'

'And that is to discover if there was ever a witch-burning connected with the House of Auber.'

'Precisely.'

If what Oliver said was true the thought was exciting. To go back into the past, to actually see something that had occurred centuries ago, struck me as as important as man's lunar landing – one was a conquest of space, the other a conquest of time. But I was not going to let Oliver, and obviously Geoffrey, think they had won too easily.

'Why not Dian?' I asked. 'It's over a year since I had anything to do with hypnosis, and – as you know, Oliver – I've had reservations since then. And although you say

275

there's something psychic about me, it's not something I want to cultivate.'

With distaste I remembered the spiritualist meeting I had attended with Dawn in Wellington, and the weeks of anxiety I had suffered until I received proof that my mother was still alive.

'It has to be you, because of your affinity with the House of Auber,' said Geoffrey. 'Don't you see? You're in tune with the place, with its history . . . Martin, haven't you ever wondered about the sense of familiarity you had with Derwentwater when you were a boy, and how from the first minute you were at home with Leila and myself – one of us? Since then I know you've never been free of the spell of Auber. It came over when you were under hypnosis . . .'

Oliver gave Geoffrey a warning glance.

'. . . and hasn't it struck you as something very unusual?'

Frequently! I thought.

'You're suggesting that I lived here in a previous life?' I asked with a suitable note of amusement in my voice. 'When you were a Norman lordling and I was a Saxon serf?'

Dian giggled.

'You may laugh, but I'm certain you have a past association with Auber. I've told you about my belief that events occur in continuous cycles . . .'

'And you think I was on a previous cycle?'

'Would you be interested in making an attempt?' Oliver interjected.

'Perhaps,' I said doubtfully.

'I think you could find it very rewarding. I've discovered that it's possible for a subject to be conscious of the experience, so you wouldn't have to rely on a tape to know what happened. You would actually have the sensation of living through it.'

'It's a wonderful improvement,' Dian said. 'Oliver tried it with me when we were working on childhood regression. Before that you went off and then when you were awakened you were told how you'd acted or heard your words replayed. This way it's as though the present-day you is back in the role of the child, or almost. It's not exactly like life, but like life with the edges fuzzy.'

'How does it work?' I asked.

'It's so simple that I was furious it hadn't occurred to me before,' said Oliver. 'Now I'm using the technique on my patients, with very satisfactory results. Basically the idea is to begin the regression in the normal way, then put the subject into a type of post-hypnotic state which allows him to be aware of the experience. Of course, in normal regression the subject, though conscious of events, obviously can't influence them. With pre-conceptual regression there might be a possibility of a certain . . . *flexibility*. However, if you agree, Martin, I'm certain we'll begin to learn a little about the process – and, being conscious, you'll have every safeguard.'

'Or the illusion of having every safeguard,' I said. We were both thinking of our conversation that afternoon, and Oliver looked at me with apprehension. I allowed a minute to pass, then said, 'All right, I'll try it.'

'Splendid,' boomed Oliver.

Geoffrey, now smiling, poured more drinks and said, 'Can we do it tomorrow?'

'There's no reason why not, if Martin's agreeable,' said Oliver. 'We should go to the site where this burning took place.'

'If it ever took place,' Dian said sombrely, and I could well understand her anxiety.

'If we go to Castlerigg early in the morning we should have the place to ourselves,' Geoffrey continued enthusiastically.

At the name of the stone circle I suddenly remembered something my father had said the day we picnicked in the shadow of the megaliths.

'It's rather weird, isn't it? As if there's something brooding here . . .'

*

Cold. Bleak and bitter cold was the first thing I was aware of. Frost-rimmed tussock-grass cracked beneath the feet of the people plodding sullenly up the gentle hillside, their steaming breath rising in columns to mingle in a cloud which hung behind us in the still air. The sky was a sickly white, opaque with the threat of snow and diffusing the winter sun which I guessed had just risen.

I was conscious of walking in this silent procession, the head of which was obscured by a wall of mist rolling down the upper slopes. Certainly there was nothing dreamlike about the experience, and yet it could not be likened to everyday reality. Going over it in my mind afterwards I realised how apt was Dian's description of the state as being fuzzy round the edges.

To begin with I had no memory of how I came to be there, and surprisingly I felt no anxiety about it. I was merely tramping through a near-silent world of white frost, mist and sky. Yet before I had gone far I was conscious of foreboding, a hint of evil to come through which ran a tiny thread of excitement.

I regarded my companions, who remained silent except for a muttered curse when one slipped on a patch of frozen mud. All had heavy woollen cloaks about them, and I was surprised at the lack of colour in their dress, the cloth grey or brown depending on the natural shade of the wool. When I discussed it with Oliver later he said, 'It's only since modern dyes were developed in Victorian times that the world has become intoxicated with colour. Before then plain folk, especially outside the main cities, were very drab indeed. Coloured cloth was expensive, and synonymous with rank and wealth. Probably the brightest colours a villager saw in his life were those in the stained-glass windows of his church. What an impact they must have had on people who had nothing but natural colours about them!'

Another thing I noticed about those panting along beside me was their smell, an odour of bodies unwashed from one year to another, and, as the constant sounds of flatus testified, the results of a diet of semi-putrid meat, salted fish and coarsely ground grains. I moved from the middle of the ragged procession and walked to one side of it, but no one seemed to take any notice of me. A minute later we were enveloped in white mist through which we moved like shadows.

When we emerged from the clammy vapour I was able to see that the procession was led by some men on horseback, followed by a farm cart pulled by a team of heavy shires. A chair had been tied between the rails of the vehicle and on it sat a figure wrapped in a filthy blanket. Sometimes the ponderous hooves of the horses slid as they attempted higher ground, and then the carter's long whip would flick over their flanks and the figure jerk like a marionette as the cart swayed and jolted. Behind me stragglers were emerging from the mist wreaths like dark phantoms, and I saw that a number of them were women with children clinging to their skirts.

The going was steeper now, and several times the cart got stuck. The horsemen waited impatiently while the whip cracked like pistol shots, and men seized the spokes of the clumsy wheels to roll the cart onward. I hurried forward and looked up at the woman seated on the chair, but a corner of the blanket was over her head like a shawl so that I could only see some tresses of reddish hair.

On one occasion when the cart paused a tall man in a long black coat with a white clerical stock and a broad-brimmed hat low over his face climbed on. He began to read in a harsh voice from his book, but the prisoner turned her back towards him.

Someone called, 'You waste your breath, parson. She only likes prayers backwards.'

'And not only prayers, I'll be bound,' bawled another. 'Hey, witch, is it true that Satan's prick is like ice?'

At the sound of their voices a chittering noise came from the back of the cart, but I was unable to see what it was.

Suddenly the horses found their footing and the vehicle jerked forward. The clergyman lost his balance and there was a growl of laughter as his legs went from under him and he found himself sitting on the floorboards.

The horsemen riding nearby were well muffled against the cold, but they were as sombre as the folk who trudged behind the cart, their eyes on the frozen ground before them. I passed and, standing to one side, looked about me. The surrounding fells, their upper slopes white against the wan sky, were familiar – Castlerigg Fell to the south, Lonscale Fell with Skiddaw looming behind it to the north, while to the north-east lay the gaunt outline of Souter Fell, once better known as the Hill of Demons.

For a while I watched the gap-toothed faces passing, old before their time with boils or rashes, yet all with serious expressions matched by their silence. When the main body had passed I fell in with the stragglers, the lame, the elderly, and mothers with babies. In the east a luminous patch of sky suggested that the sun was climbing. The cold continued to numb me, and the air was so icy that it felt as though it was burning my throat, yet there was something about it which I found exhilarating. Before long the incline became more gradual, and then the leading riders and the swaying cart moved on to a stretch of level ground. Those around me surged forward, and as they reached the smooth, frosted turf a strange sighing sound came from them. When it was my turn to climb on to it I saw the object which had inspired this. The people gazed at it with expressions of awe while the cart continued to trundle forward.

It was a heavy stake standing about eight feet high, close to a group of megaliths forming an 'inner sanctuary' within the ring of boulders which made up the Castlerigg circle. By the stake were a couple of men in leather aprons who grinned awkwardly up at the riders like workmen seeking acknowledgement for a job well done.

'It were hard to plant it right with the ground froze solid,' said one.

'Get the firewood round it,' one of the mounted men answered, distaste in his voice. 'Be quick. The sooner this sorry business is over the better.'

While brushwood and small logs were stacked at the base of the wooden pillar, the people stood just outside the circle as though there were invisible barriers stretched between the stones now sparkling with hoar frost. A rider trotted his horse over to the cart, where the blanketed figure still sat on the chair, turned away from the stake on which everyone else's eyes were fixed. At his order several men lifted her out and, half supporting her, brought her into the circle. From somewhere in the crowd a drummer began a slow but regular beat.

I pressed forward to the front line of spectators, to stand with my shoulder pressed against one of the ancient stones. Its coldness soon began to numb my arm.

'Here's the rope to bind her,' said one of the carpenters, throwing down a coil beside the pile of wood.

'Fool,' said the horseman who appeared to be in charge of the proceedings. 'That will burn before she does. Go to the cart. There's a length of chain in it.' The man went, and returned pulling a long chain behind him. The horseman nodded to the men surrounding the prisoner and immediately her blanket was snatched away. She stood in a white shift, her feet naked on the cold earth so that it was no wonder she trembled.

'Come, madam,' called the horseman.

A man moved to support her, but she shook his hand away and walked towards the stake, her long hair hiding most of her face.

'Ah, God pity the poor sinner,' said a voice beside me, and turning I saw a young woman with tears in her eyes. ''Tis hard enough being a woman, and what do men know of the temptations that come to us?'

As she spoke I saw lice crawling in her hair.

The remorseless beat of the drum continued as the prisoner was made to climb on to the pyramid of firewood and stand with her back against the stake. She made no resistance as the chain was wound round and round her waist. Behind her I saw a series of sparks as someone tried to ignite a torch with a flint and steel.

When the chaining was complete the horseman walked his horse into the centre of the stones and, bringing forth a roll of parchment from under his cloak, began to read: 'Madeline Auber, you have been found guilty on the following counts . . .'

He turned irritably to the crowd and shouted, 'Stop that damned drum.'

It fell silent and he continued, '. . . you have been found guilty on the following counts: That you did make a pact with the Devil, that you did consort with witches in this place, that you ordered your imp named Ape to poison innocent folk, that you did raise a monstrous wave on Derwentwater, that you did constantly sour the cream of Goody Forster, that you did have unholy intercourse with demons, that you had a teat in your secret part to give suck to your familiar, and that you did bewitch and beguile your lord and husband.'

His voice went on flatly, the dead tone of officialdom. Now I could see the prisoner's face, which would have been of great beauty were it not for its ivory pallor and the blue shadows beneath her eyes. Her teeth were chattering, as were many of the spectators', but she managed to hold an expression of contempt for those about her.

'. . . and therefore, in accordance with Holy Writ which states "Thou shalt not suffer a witch to live", you have been brought to this spot, where your pact was made with Satan, to be put to death as a punishment and an example.'

'You know you speak false, Master Reeve. 'Tis I that am being murdered . . .'

'Silence, witch. Your chance to speak was at your trial.'

The parson stepped forward and stood before the woman, holding up his book as though to protect him from the forces of evil, his face resolute as though he believed he was challenging Lucifer himself.

'Witch, now is the time to repent, for your hour is nigh. Admit to your sin against God and man . . .'

The woman took a shuddering breath and, closing her eyes and clenching her hands, said in a choking voice, 'Parson, I do have something to say.'

The man in black stepped back as though her very words might contaminate his immortal soul.

'Say on.'

Around me the people craned forward to catch whatever the prisoner might say within minutes of her immolation. Making a supreme effort, the lady Madeline said clearly, 'My husband, whom I have loved faithfully all the time of our marriage, has placed me in this plight for reasons that he knows in his heart, and which you will all know some day. For his betrayal of my life and honour, I curse his line.'

She opened her eyes wide and her voice rang over the stone circle.

'I curse the House of Auber so that sons of my husband's sons, until the name of Auber is no more, shall destroy those who love them. A blight will hang over the family, and each heir shall tremble lest the madness fall upon him, and each wife shall fear to bear a son . . .'

A murmur, part fear and part anger, rose from the crowd, and the parson hurled his book at the prisoner's face.

'Enough,' cried the reeve, angrily spurring forward. 'Fire up, Rob.'

Another murmur rose with the pillars of breath into the freezing air as a man in a blacksmith's apron approached the sanctuary stones and applied a flaming torch to the kindling at the base of the log pile. A trickle of blood dribbled from the lady Madeline's nose where the holy book had struck her, but she retained more dignity than the parson who scrabbled through the white smoke coiling at her feet to retrieve it.

'I curse the House of Auber so that its children shall fear

the madness of their fathers. I bequeath them my pain and my husband's treachery . . .'

'Be quiet or I'll have you gagged,' the reeve shouted. 'Why isn't it alight, Rob?'

'It's the wood, Master Reeve. It be wet.'

'It matters not now, my curse is said,' said the lady Madeline. 'No power can alter it. My death shall be the bane of Auber.'

She began to cough as smoke from the damp faggots rose about her.

'Oil, you fools,' cried the reeve. 'Why haven't you got the oil?'

A couple of men ran to the cart and one returned with a small cask, the other with a box covered by a lattice. With a new impression of horror upon that which was making me sick, I saw a small brown hand appear between the lathes as though reaching for something it could not quite grasp. Surely not a child? Then the frightened chattering told me that the captive was a monkey.

The box was thrown on to the pile of wood, and I saw the little hand wave frantically through the tendrils of heavy smoke curling over it. The measured beat of the drum began again.

The man carrying the cask, encouraged by curses from the reeve, pulled out the bung and splashed its contents over the faggots.

'Husband!' shouted the prisoner. 'Come forward and see your work . . .' Another coughing attack drowned her words, and turning my head I saw one of the horsemen at the far end of the circle turn his horse and gallop away.

The man with the torch reapplied it to the smouldering oil-soaked wood and little flames began to dance over it. Hot air lifted the smoke and I could see the prisoner again, pulling against the chain as the heat seared her. There was a puff of steam at her feet as fear made her lose control of her bladder.

With horrible speed the burning oil ignited more wood. The lady Madeline screamed as flames rose about her legs, and the scream seemed to hang like a raw, tangible thing beneath the white sky. And at that moment, as though in reply to her agony, several snowflakes drifted down.

'More oil,' yelled the reeve. 'She can't burn piecemeal. Make it blaze!'

Obediently the men threw the remaining liquid on to the fire and a column of flame seethed upwards.

Until then I had been unable to tear my eyes from the pyre, but a speeding-up of the drumbeat made me turn my head to the crowd. It was the children who began the dance. Edging past the stones, they joined hands and capered in several ragged rings. Oblivious of the cries from the fire, their eyes shone with excitement. The drummer, an itinerant entertainer by the look of his particoloured costume and bell-fringed cap, ran into the centre and beat louder and faster. Then the spectators, released from their awe, surged forward and with linked hands began to leap in concentric rings round the bonfire. Snowflakes fluttered down like confetti.

Nausea swept me – that smell! – and I had to lean for a moment against my megalith. Then, as though an outside force was controlling me, I found myself stumbling through the gleeful dancers until the heat hit my face and halted me. I gazed up at the prisoner through the smoke and flame, and saw that most of her shift had been burned off. Flesh on the lower part of her body was charred.

For a moment the fire from the oil exhausted itself and I found myself looking directly into her face. For a few seconds – seemingly endless in memory – she held my gaze while her blackened lips twisted with her efforts to speak. The blaze leapt up again, her hair ignited in a rush of flame, her eyes melted, and then all was hidden by a fire-fringed curtain of greasy smoke.

I turned and fled, side-stepping cavorting peasants until I blundered into a standing stone. My last recollection was of sliding down its icy surface as my legs collapsed beneath me. The thickening snowflakes turned to black and I was engulfed by darkness.

21

I awoke to find myself lying on a Black Watch tartan rug, my shoulders against one of the sanctuary stones in the Castlerigg circle. Despite the heat of the summer sun I was trembling with cold. The sky, apart from a small flock of celestial sheep hurried across it by a warm westerly breeze, was the clear, delicate blue that is one of the most attractive features of the Lake District. But as I gazed upwards it brought me no pleasure – in my mind's eye it was superimposed by a jerking figure surrounded by flame.

'They were dancing,' I said. 'Even the children were dancing . . .'

'Martin, are you all right?'

I lowered my eyes and saw Dian kneeling on the turf beside me. Beyond her Oliver and Geoffrey stood looking at me with concern.

Although the fresh breeze sung softly among the stones, my nostrils and throat seemed to be full of a stench which made me turn my head from Dian and retch.

'They didn't get the fire lit properly,' I said, wiping my mouth on my hand. 'And they burned Auber's Ape.'

'He's had a bad shock,' I heard Oliver say as my head lolled back and I watched the clouds above the stones. Strange to have picnicked here without an inkling of the horror which had once taken place. Did I expect some invisible monument? I do not know, but remembering Geoffrey's painting of the Castlerigg stones I recognised his awareness of some past evil here.

'Have some of this, dear boy,' said Oliver, proffering a slim silver flask. I nearly choked on the neat cognac but it seemed to clear the odour from my mouth. I began to think more clearly, remembering the drive in Oliver's car, now parked by the National Trust sign, then settling by the tallest stone in the sanctuary while Oliver prepared to hypnotise me. He had swung the crystal pendant as he had in his Frognal flat, but I had no idea of how he 'talked' me back to an event which we had thought might have occurred centuries before. A portable tape machine was still recording, so I could learn about the technique later.

Just now the horror of the witch-burning was still upon me. Unlike the memory of a nightmare, which fades so quickly on waking, every detail remained as clear as if I had watched the actual event a few minutes earlier. But had I? Had I gone back in time like H. G. Wells's *Time Machine* character? Or had I seen a 'psychic' replay of the lady Madeline's death? In my shocked state they were questions I could not cope with. I would leave it all for my debriefing with Oliver.

'I think I'd like to go home,' I said. 'I don't feel all that good.'

The two men helped me to my feet and we began a slow march to the road, Dian following with the rug and recorder. A young couple with rucksacks watched my unsteady progress and the man asked politely if there was anything they could do.

'Thanks, no,' I said. 'Just a nasty touch of déjà vu.'

'Poor thing,' I heard the girl say.

Gratefully I sank into a rear seat of the car. How good the smell of the leather upholstery, how comforting the sound of the V8 engine! I wanted the reassurance of familiar twentieth-century things. Oliver exchanged a puzzled look with Dian when I asked him to play one of his Glen Miller tapes over the stereo system. Moments later *Moonlight Serenade* filled the Rover. Looking about me as we glided down the narrow road I saw the unchanging outlines of the fells that less than an hour ago I had seen as they had been four centuries earlier. And the enormity of what had happened hit me. I had been directed to witness a specific event which had taken place in the past. The possibilities this opened up made my thoughts spin.

'I know you're not feeling very well at the moment,' said Geoffrey, turning round in the front passenger seat, 'but can you tell us – was there . . .'

'Yes, Geoffrey,' I said. 'I heard Madeline Auber curse your line before she was burnt alive.'

In the days which followed activity at Auber accelerated to a frenetic pitch. Workmen began essential work in the house under the supervision of Dian. Post office engineers reconnected the telephone, and a boat-builder from Windermere enthusiastically refurbished the gondola while a gang of carpenters built a new jetty. I had to assert myself to postpone the arrival of landscape gardeners, explaining that Akkim wanted to have the gardens filmed in their wilderness state.

Since the Auber curse seemed to have been confirmed by my regression in the Castlerigg circle Oliver and Geoffrey spent long hours in their respective rooms, Oliver hard at work documenting my experience and developing his theories from it, and Geoffrey seeking background material to the witch-burning with an intensity which bordered on desperation. To this end I spent the daylight hours in the library, poring over documents which seemed mainly concerned with feoffs, manorial rights and deeds going back over the centuries. When I came across a bound volume of sermons or a treatise on heraldry by some scholarly member of the family it seemed like light relief.

The four of us now met only at dinner, and it seemed that the forthcoming arrival of Akkim – when Auber had to be ready for filming the masque and I had to have a working script prepared – hung over us like Nemesis.

A few days after my regression I was at work in the library when Dian carried in a coffee tray.

'Elevenses,' she said cheerfully. 'Mind if I have mine with you, or shall I be interrupting?'

'I'm delighted to be interrupted,' I said. 'I'm not making any headway here. Geoffrey's more likely to find something in his outside material.'

'I heard from Leila before I left London,' said Dian, seating herself opposite me. 'She's coming back to England for a few days to settle her affairs before going to Hong Kong.'

'I'm glad it came off for her,' I said.

'I just thought you might like to know.'

'Not really, Dian.' I could not explain my feelings, so I just shrugged.

'Sorry.'

'Don't be silly. And don't look so serious. If you can spare a little time from the redecorating, you can help me go through this pile of books. Ignore any in Latin or Greek; they'll be classics in the original language.'

'I will if you promise not to tell Geoffrey,' she said with a laugh. 'Poor boy, he's so anxious for the house to be ready for his masque that I'll get the sack if he thinks I'm slacking.'

I pushed a pile of books towards her, several of whose covers were held in place by twine tied round them.

'Geoffrey is rather intense about it all,' I said.

'I wish he could relax as he used to do in the old days. There were times in London, before his breakdown, when he was quite easy-going and rather good fun. Remember?'

I nodded.

'Now he's absolutely *taut*. He's hardly been sleeping. Thank goodness Oliver has given him some sleeping pills. He says they'd knock a horse out, so I hope they do the trick for Geoff.'

'I hate to say this, but I've had the impression over the last few days that he's working up to some sort of crisis. I'm rather relieved that you and Oliver are here.'

She said nothing more, and we settled down to work our way through the books which crowded the table. After half an hour Dian held up a small leather-bound volume containing handwritten pages.

'This looks promising,' she said. 'It's called *The Ape of Auber and other Family Anecdotes*, and it was written by the ancestor who spent most of his time in Venice. Geoffrey told me he's buried there. This is what he said in the preface. "This collection of traditions is not for vulgar publication but for the edification of forthcoming members of the Auber family, for I do believe that unless they are set down they will be lost in an age that so resolutely turns its back upon the past. Such tales may seem unrefined to present literary taste, yet it is my belief that the strength and character of families is largely due to traditions forged in more stalwart days . . ."'

'I get the idea,' I said. 'What does he say about the ape?'

Dian turned the brittle pages covered with well-disciplined lines of sepia copperplate.

'He must have written all this with a quill. Ah, here we are.' She read how an early scion of the family 'took the Cross' in 1189 and departed on the Third Crusade. When he returned from the Holy Land he brought a monkey, causing great consternation among the locals, who had never seen such a creature before. To the knight's amusement, the general opinion was that it was an imp from the land of Prester John. He proved that his pet had no Satanic connection by taking it to church one day, incidentally outraging the priest.

The animal was cherished by the Auber household when it was learned that he had saved his master's life. Apparently it was his shrieking which had woken him in time to defend himself against a band of Saracen assassins who penetrated the camp under cover of night.

' "When the knight inherited the Auber estates he incorporated the monkey, then known as Auber's Ape, into the family coat-of-arms, together with the motto that has given much cause for puzzlement down the years – *He without Honour beware the Ape*.

' "During the years which followed it was usual for a monkey to be kept by the family, but this custom ended tragically when the lady Madeline Auber was accused of witchcraft and the pet of the time, a great favourite of the unfortunate woman, was held to be her demonic familiar. The execution of the lady Madeline was a shameful episode even by the superstitious standards of those uncouth days, and has been the basis for a proliferation of conflicting legends. Indeed, it is so unlikely that the truth of the sorry matter can be ascertained today that I have omitted it from these pages . . ." '

I swore in my frustration.

Dian laughed, and said, 'All is not lost. Listen to this: "Howsoever, should you have some scholarly interest in the ancient scandal, dear reader, I would recommend the work by my ancestor Edward Auber, which gives the most accepted account." '

'And?' I said.

'That's all.'

'He doesn't give the name of Edward Auber's work?'

'No. He goes on to a new chapter on the role of the Aubers in the Wars of the Roses.'

I looked round the large library, its walls lined with books from floor to ceiling, and rows of free-standing bookcases taking up most of the floor space. Geoffrey had told me that there were between six and seven thousand volumes here, and to his knowledge no serious attempt had been made to catalogue them.

'So we have to hunt for Edward Auber's needle in this literary haystack,' I said. 'We may as well get started.'

It took us two days to find the work of Edward Auber, which turned out to be a small mouldy book hidden among legal documents in one of the library's muniment chests. What the author of *The Ape of Auber* failed to mention was that it was printed in Latin. My heart sank at the further delay until Oliver, who had joined in the hunt, said, 'I'm afraid my Latin is rather rusty, but they do say you never quite forget it. If I can get hold of a Latin dictionary in Penrith I'm sure I could get the gist for you.'

'No need to go to Penrith,' said Dian. 'I came across some Latin grammars and a dictionary yesterday.'

'I'll get to work immediately. I know your impatience, Martin, but don't expect miracles.'

Oliver hurried away to begin translating. I was relieved that my stint in the library was over. Since the telephone had been reconnected I had had several calls from Akkim, who sounded very enthusiastic about the project, no doubt because *Croglin* was being well received by distributors. As a result I had arranged for a small film unit to come from London to shoot the grounds of Auber while they were still wild. The unit was arriving today, and now I would be able to give it my undivided attention.

Dian was equally thankful to be out of the library. Her most pressing task was to organise a group of musicians who specialised in playing early English music on replicas of Tudor instruments to perform during the masque.

'Geoffrey's determined to make it an unforgettable night,' she told me. 'You should see the costumiers' catalogues which have arrived. And the invitations printed on vellum. And as well as period musicians, I've got to get hold of tumblers, jugglers and a fire-eater.'

The film unit, consisting of director, cameraman, focus-puller and several assistants, arrived during the morning.

'Blimey, it looks like Frankenstein's castle,' said the cameraman, watching morosely while his equipment was unloaded. From then on the conversation, as is the way with film crews the world over, was purely technical. Even during their lunch break they talked of nothing but focal lengths, filter combinations, and the merits of different makes of equipment.

'You want it spooky?' the director said to me. 'Should

be easy in this place. We'll shoot some of it day-for-night. Perhaps you'll take me round and show me what you want. A zoom on those gargoyles would be effective. And all those tangled weeds down there'll make the house seem like the Sleeping Beauty's palace.'

I was exhausted by the end of the day. 'I'll phone through the lab report the day after tomorrow,' the director said, before his car lurched away through the rhododendrons.

I went indoors in search of a drink. The telephone chirruped; it was Akkim ringing from Los Angeles to ask how the shooting had gone.

'I'm very much looking forward to seeing you next week,' he said finally. 'I met Tash today, and she sends her love.' He laughed. 'She wanted me to quote a couple of lines of poetry, but I've forgotten them. Pity she's tied up with that Western; otherwise I'd have her on *Murder Room*.'

'My love to her, when you see her,' I said.

'OK. I hope your script is superb.'

'So do I.'

I was going through the usual period of disillusion which with me comes halfway through a script when I wonder how a film could possibly be made from it. Now cold fingers of panic were closing on me. Akkim would soon be here and so far I had nothing I would be happy to show him. *Croglin* had been so much easier to write. There was a good plot; here was just a basic idea and lots of atmosphere but as yet no story.

At supper I felt less gloomy when Oliver announced that he had the basic outline of Edward Auber's account.

'It's not a word-for-word translation, but it'll give you an idea to work on. Gracious heaven, their relationships were just as entangled then as they are today – though today we tend to burn people only by remote control.'

After we had eaten we followed our usual practice of going to the Murder Room study. A fire was burning in the grate even though it was the height of summer. As I followed the others through the doorway, the sight of the carving of Auber's Ape on the panel brought back a sickening memory from my Castlerigg experience – the pathetic little hand waving above the box.

'You look a little peaky, dear boy,' said Oliver, passing me a drink.

'I've been sleeping badly,' I admitted. 'And when I do I have ghastly dreams.'

'Very understandable,' Oliver said. 'I could give you a sedative if you think it might help.'

'Thank you, doctor, it might. I don't want to be too ragged when Akkim gets here.'

When we had settled ourselves I found that the cheerful flames flickering above the log in the fireplace were as upsetting as the carving of the monkey, and I turned away, hoping that the others would not notice my nervous state. Geoffrey's suppressed tension was quite enough for the moment.

Oliver put on his heavy black-framed executive glasses and opened a notebook.

'It's quite a melodrama,' he said. 'I haven't got an actual date for these events, but I gather it was some time towards the end of the sixteenth century. The head of the household was Sir Piers Auber, who had found his inheritance in an impoverished condition due to what were termed "political payments". Although the text didn't elaborate, I would guess that the family had had to buy protection from court officials while the country was going through its anti-Catholic convulsions.

'It seems Sir Piers was very presentable, and proficient in the Elizabethan requirements. He could pen a sonnet or fight a duel with equal aplomb, and apparently he was a highly accomplished lutist. His younger brother Aylward, to whom he was very attached, was also a man of talent. His interest seems to have been in play-writing, and when he came of age he left Cumbria to try his luck in London. As the younger son there was obviously little future for him at Auber.

'Another character in the drama is referred to merely as Rowena. She was an orphaned relative of the brothers who spent her formative years at Auber, where she was very much a member of the family. This, however, did not prevent Piers and Aylward from having strong feelings for her as they grew older.'

Oliver paused and, catching sight of Geoffrey's face, I was amused at his avid expression. Such a story was the stuff of his obsession with the Aubers' past, and I sympathised with Dian, who feared anything which excited his imagination in this direction.

'This triangle didn't lead to any conflict,' continued Oliver. 'I guess from the tenor of the text that Rowena was more partial to the younger Auber, but it's not actually stated. The author was rather circumspect over certain matters. I'm sure he wrote in Latin because he didn't wish his ancestors' antics to become a source of amusement for the *hoi polloi*. Indeed, from the tone of his work it seems as though he regarded himself as something of a serious historian, and therefore felt compelled to write in the dullest possible style.

'However, if Rowena was attracted to Aylward, it certainly didn't stop him leaving Derwentwater for London.'

'Perhaps he was going to come back for her after he had made his name at the Globe,' Dian said.

'Ever the romantic,' said Oliver with a smile. 'I should imagine that Sir Piers, with his brother out of the way, entertained thoughts of marrying Rowena – even picking my way through the dull Latin I gained the impression that he felt a grand passion for her. But if those were his plans, he had to abandon them when he inherited the House of Auber. In order to save the family fortunes he married the lady Madeline Norbury who, on the death of her father, had become the sole owner of a tidy estate in Cheshire.

'The lady Madeline was what would have been described in my parents' day as a bluestocking. Certainly she was not one to stay in the solar and do needlework. Her father had been a scholar, and she had been taught Greek and Hebrew, but this didn't make her immune to natural emotion. It was her tragedy to become infatuated with her husband.

'Once her lands had been sold up and Auber was solvent again, Sir Piers quickly tired of her. For one thing she had not become pregnant immediately after the marriage, and he shared the Tudor obsession with having an heir. For another he was still in love with Rowena who, with Aylward away in London peddling his plays, seems to have reciprocated, because before long she was with child.

'It was this which set Sir Piers upon his drastic course. Madeline had played her part in rescuing the House of Auber, and could be dispensed with. He acted immediately because he wanted to marry Rowena so that the child could be born as his legal heir. One night when an entertainment was being held here, he denounced Madeline as a witch to the reeve and the local parson. Sir Piers claimed that, as a God-fearing and loyal subject, he could not countenance his wife's trafficking with Satanic powers.

'She was held in the cellars while evidence was accumulated against her. This included a number of books written in "unChristian characters", regarded as *grimoires* by the superstitious. Most likely they were Greek and Hebrew texts.

'Another damning piece of evidence was the behaviour of the Aubers' pet monkey. Being very fond of his mistress, the animal found some way of entering the cellar in which she was imprisoned – or it was put there while she slept. However it got there, her guards claimed that it must have materialised by magical means, and it was therefore held to be her imp or familiar.

'Because of her title Madeline did not have to stand trial in public. She was judged in the "largest room in the tower", which I think points to this very room.'

Oliver paused for breath, and none of us could refrain from gazing around with morbid interest.

'At the trial there were plenty of witnesses eager to testify against her. A yeoman farmer whose cows had died of disease claimed that he had seen the "witch's imp" stealing over his land to poison them. A woman who had been delivered of a deformed child claimed that she had been overlooked by Madeline, and a shepherd swore that he had seen her with "dark companions" at the Druids' circle. No one bothered to ask why he had kept quiet about it until the prisoner was on trial.

'There's a tedious amount of similar material, though out of respect for his class and feelings Sir Piers was not required to give evidence against his wife. Her fate was finally sealed when a pricker was brought down from Dumfries .. .'

'A pricker?' Dian queried.

'A pricker was a woman skilled in finding so-called Devil's marks, usually some minor irregularity like an extra nipple or even a large mole. Such things were also known as Devil's paps, as it was believed they were used by witches to suckle their familiars. Another pricker's test was to blindfold the victims and run needles into their flesh – hence their name. If they found a spot where there was no pain response it was regarded as a sign of guilt. In fact if you take a needle and prick yourself very gently you will soon find tiny areas with no nerve endings beneath the skin where the needle can be pushed in without discomfort. Anyway, the pricker from Dumfries found a secret teat on Madeline and that sealed her fate.'

'How barbarous they were in the old days,' exclaimed Dian.

'Historically speaking, it's not so long ago,' Oliver said. 'The last official witch-burning in Scotland took place in 1726.'

'So the lady Madeline was found guilty and burned at the Castlerigg circle,' said Geoffrey.

From where I sat I could see that he had gone pale, and

his light eyes had a feverish look which I hoped Dian, who was gazing pensively into the embers, had not noticed.

'That's right,' said Oliver. 'She was taken to the stake early on the morning after she was pronounced guilty, presumably to prevent her appealing to a higher court at Carlisle. In those days remote places like Derwentwater had little contact with the outside world, and tended to be laws unto themselves.'

'The curse,' said Geoffrey. 'Did the author mention the curse?'

'Oh, yes. I've no idea where his source material came from — some contemporary account since lost, I shouldn't wonder — but his account tallies remarkably with what Martin told us. He even makes the point that the fire was slow to start. As far as the curse that the prisoner laid on her husband's family was concerned, it was identical to what Martin heard.'

'What a perfectly horrible story,' said Dian with a shiver. 'Was that the end?'

'There was a little more. Sir Piers married Rowena almost immediately and she was subsequently delivered of a baby son, before "the natural length of her time", as the text put it. The child grew up to inherit the House of Auber, and it was his son who murdered his wife, giving rise to the Green Lady legend. That was only one of several tragedies put down by the credulous to the lady Madeline's malediction.'

'Not just the credulous, Oliver,' said Geoffrey. 'I'm an Auber, and I know.'

It was the only occasion I have seen the urbane Oliver Penthorne lose his temper.

'Geoffrey, if you really believe an unfortunate woman was able to alter the course of history by crying out *in extremis*, then you're as superstitious as those who brought her to her death.'

Then Geoffrey said something, quite coldly, which I have pondered upon since. '*But if she was a witch . . .*'

'Was there any mention of the playwright brother?' asked Dian swiftly.

'Indeed,' replied Oliver, regaining his accustomed calm. 'He returned soon after the birth of Rowena's son, but we're not told what her reaction was to his home-coming. Whatever she felt had little bearing, because his visit ended in tragedy. According to the text he was drowned in Derwentwater. A "monstrous wave" was believed to have sunk his boat. This, of course, was seen by the locals as a manifestation of the lady Madeline's vengeance.'

'Thank you, Oliver!' I said. 'At last I have a *raison d'être* for the story. With luck I might just get my script finished in time for Akkim's arrival.'

'I hope you won't think me rude, but I'd like to be left alone,' said Geoffrey. 'I have a splitting headache. I've been sleeping rather badly.'

'Of course,' we murmured. Dian tried to be comforting but was politely rebuffed, and we left. As I followed the others down the spiral staircase I caught the strains of one of Geoffrey's wilder tapes.

'Feel like a chat?' Oliver asked me when we reached the hall, now filled with the sonorous tick of the great ebony clock.

'All right.'

'If you come into the kitchen I'll make some coffee,' said Dian. 'I wonder if Geoffrey would like some.'

'I should leave him to rest,' said Oliver in a voice so soothing that I'm sure it was cultivated for his patients. Presently he and I sat facing each other across the huge kitchen table.

'Do you mind talking a bit more about your regression?' he asked.

'I thought you'd got everything I could remember about it on tape.'

'New questions keep coming to me. We're on the

threshold of something utterly extraordinary. I don't think you quite realise . . .'

'But I do. It's just that I want to distance myself from what I saw before I get involved again.'

'That's understandable, dear boy. It was obviously a horrific experience. But one thing I do need to know is whether any of the people took notice of you or spoke to you. You can see the implications.'

'Surely,' I said. 'Was I actually there, like someone returning to a previous incarnation in which he would have been visible – or was I seeing a re-enactment, like the Battle of Edgehill phenomenon?'

'Yes. Were you in any sort of contact?'

'It may sound silly, Oliver, but I don't know. No one spoke to me, but then they didn't speak to each other. I was certainly walking along with them . . .'

'Did you notice anything about yourself that was strange? What were you wearing?'

'I felt like me. But I was so absorbed in what was happening that I didn't take any notice of my clothes. I was just there, and it was very cold and the mob was very smelly, so it wasn't just a visual thing.'

'But did you have any sort of communication with anyone?'

For a moment I was about to tell Oliver of the sensation I had experienced when I looked up at the lady Madeline's face and for a fraction of a second had thought there was some recognition, but without quite understanding why I decided to keep it to myself, for a while, at least. Perhaps I wanted to think about it without outside theories to distract me.

'No, I was just an observer,' I said. 'Everything was real enough, though in a way I can't explain there was the feeling that something was . . . slightly out of kilter. And there was one odd thing I've just remembered.'

'Yes?'

'It probably sounds stupid, but I was breathing deeply going up the hill, and it seemed that the air was richer.'

'Fascinating!' exclaimed Oliver. 'Don't you see? Before the great upsurge in combustion in this century – one jet across the Atlantic burns several tons of oxygen – the air did have a much higher oxygen content. You would have hardly been aware of that seeing a vision.'

Oliver rubbed his pudgy hands like an excited child.

'How lucky I was to find you as a subject! Gracious heaven, what will this lead to?'

'An eye-witness at Runnymede,' I said lightly. 'A spectator at the Crucifixion!'

'Why not?'

Then, as though embarrassed by his enthusiasm, and the sensational line his thoughts were taking, Oliver changed the subject, and when Dian served the coffee he was telling me of a 'really stunning' icon of St Michael he had bought at Sotheby's before leaving London.

For a few minutes the three of us chatted inconsequentially to cover our preoccupations. Oliver was exhilarated by the various theories occurring to him on regression, Dian's thoughts were obviously with the lonely occupant of the Murder Room, and I could not get my mind off my script.

'I must get to my typewriter,' I said, and Oliver accompanied me along the passage to my room.

'I'm rather concerned about our friend,' he said. 'I fear he could be heading for another breakdown. Half the time he's in a world of his own – and what a world, if his music's a reflection of it. I'm sure Dian's right when she says it's genius, but to me his recent tapes have an element of the macabre about them.'

'I don't suppose I've helped by raking up the old family scandals,' I said. 'It could be a great mistake to have returned to Auber.'

'If it hadn't been for you, estate agents would be trooping through the house with their prospective clients, and that would have been worse for Geoffrey.'

I said goodnight to him and, putting a new sheet of paper in my portable, began the revised version of the script. Now the most dramatic scene would not be culled from my imagination but would be straight reportage. But how many among the millions who would enjoy the film's gothic escapism could ever imagine that?

During the next few days I saw little of my companions, remaining closeted in my room to write the complete *Murder Room* script. Sitting hunched over my typewriter for hours at a time caused a nagging pain in my back, and at times I was tempted to ask Oliver to ease it by hypnotherapy. But I resisted. At the moment the opening scenes of the script were keeping my Castlerigg experience shockingly vivid and I felt an emotive distaste for hypnosis.

Dian, who supplied me with coffee, kept me up to date with the progress on the restoration of Auber and preparations for Geoffrey's masque. A Freeman cruiser, which I had hired on Akkim's instructions as a camera platform for filming from the water, was now tied up at the new jetty. Stage electricians had come to arrange the lighting in the reception rooms and set up strings of coloured bulbs outside.

'I hate to think how much this is costing,' she said one afternoon. 'A truck-load of liquor has just arrived. Thank goodness I've got everything arranged with the Elizabethan quintet. Now Geoff wants drapes to match the lighting effects in the house.'

From my window I saw the grounds being transformed. A motor-scythe left straight swathes up and down the avenue between the yews. Men with rakes piled up the greenery and burned it, so that all day columns of pearl smoke rose above Auber like Indian signals. On the terraces below my window landscape gardeners unrolled bolts of turf like green carpeting. Sprinklers flashed in the sunlight above these instant lawns. A couple of youths had full-time jobs with scrubbing brushes and Vim, removing the grime and lichen from the statuary. I was fascinated to look out each day and see more and more figures of **gods** and satyrs restored to their original whiteness. A tree surgeon had been employed to cut back the great yew hedges so that they became smooth dark walls making contrasting backgrounds for the pristine statues.

Auber was changing before my eyes and I wondered if Geoffrey had any regrets now that he had embarked on the process. And Leila? If she was to return to this miniature stately home would she miss the wildness?

I had a day to revise my script before Akkim arrived in a hired Jaguar. He was staying at the luxurious Lodore Hotel on the opposite side of Derwentwater. I was relieved to see that he was favourably impressed when I led him up the grand staircase to Geoffrey's study.

'I saw the rushes in London,' he said. 'They certainly had an atmosphere of gloom and desolation. Hard to believe this is the same place. Tash is spitting mad that she's not working with us. I promised her I'd entice you back to L.A. when *Murder Room* is shot. What's that weird sound?'

'It's Geoffrey's *musique électronique*,' I explained. 'I'd like you to hear some of his pieces. Might be useful for the soundtrack. Incidentally, he's Sir Geoffrey now, but there's no need to curtsey.'

'Look at that monkey on the door,' Akkim said, as we arrived at the top of the spiral stair. 'It almost seems to give you the evil eye.'

' "He without Honour beware the Ape," ' I quoted.

'How's that?'

'You wait until you read the script,' I said, and opened the door. We were greeted with a crescendo of thrilling sound which I recognised as part of Geoffrey's uncompleted 'Derwentwater' symphony. He was reclining on his white sofa by the window, the sunlight catching his silken hair. Both men looked at each other with a hint of suspicion. Neither fitted the mental picture the other had formed, but Akkim's natural charm soon put Geoffrey at ease, and when we began a tour of the grounds he became unusually animated.

'This is the Weeping Stone of Auber,' he said, pointing to a block which had been built into the old peel-tower wall. 'Did Martin tell you about it? It was taken from an old monk's hermitage on one of the islands, and when doom is about to overtake the House of Auber it exudes tears.'

'Is that right?' said Akkim. 'It might make a nice touch. Maybe we could fit a pipe behind it and get it to weep for the camera.'

'No need for that,' said Geoffrey. 'It's wept often enough by itself.'

I touched it and felt dampness under my fingertips, and decided there was probably some quality in the stone which caused condensation.

Akkim looked everything over with a critical eye, and by lunch time pronounced himself highly satisfied. He was also impressed by Dian. In a long dress of dark green silk and a little jacket of sumptuous brocade, she was an illustration of *The Lady of Shalott* come to life. (I often thought of Dian in terms of Tennyson.) Akkim took us to lunch at his hotel, and then he ran the others back to Auber, explaining that he would like to spend the afternoon on the script with me.

Driving away from Auber, he said, 'I'd like it if you could show me the real Croglin places.' And so I found myself gliding along the route over which I had once made a lonely pilgrimage by bicycle.

'What beautiful countryside,' he said of the Eden Valley. 'You can have no idea of the hunger people from my part of the world have for soft greens and gentle rain.'

As we drove slowly round the Croglin area, comparing the reality with the film sets we had used, Akkim said, 'If I'd known there was all this available I'd have shot *Croglin* here. At least *Murder Room* will have authentic settings. After the party tomorrow I'm off to London to get the casting and the main crew sorted out, but at least we'll have the masquerade in the can. Tell me, is Sir Geoffrey always so high-key?'

'The search into his family background has been upsetting for him.'

'Is that right? But the curse and everything happened so long ago!'

'Sometimes I think Geoffrey has got himself on to a different timescale.'

'At least I admire his taste in women. Now we'll go back to the Lodore and have a look at your script.'

It was nearly eleven o'clock that evening when, replete with fine food and wine, I bid Akkim goodnight at the gateway (now renovated) to Auber. As I watched the tail-lights dwindle and then vanish round a bend, I still enjoyed the satisfaction of knowing that the *Murder Room* script had won my producer's acceptance. In the back of my mind had lurked that spectre of doubt which stalks the mental backroads of so many authors – would I be able to repeat the success of my last story or had it been a one-off? Now, thanks to Akkim's generosity in voicing his approval, I knew I should be able to continue to live by doing the work I liked best.

A full moon rode high in the clear sky, illuminating the lake and fells with such cold, pure light that I was amazed at the detail of my surroundings. Stones and trees were so finely etched in monochrome that I saw them as the quiddity of their cruder daytime substance. Following the newly gravelled drive through the trees I walked through a dappling of silver, and felt disappointed when I reached the house. It was just the night for strolling.

As I entered the kitchen I was aware of something that had an old familiarity and yet for a moment I could not define. My mind skittered back over the year to when I lay on a soft bed in a stifling little apartment overlooking a

Venetian canal, watching the curtain billow and fall in the languorous breath of the city.

Of course. It was a smell: the pungency of a black Sobranie.

'So, Martin, you had to return to Auber.'

At the sound of that once-loved voice I turned. At the doorway stood Leila.

22

'I've been waiting for you,' Leila said. 'Will you walk with me?'

'Of course.'

We stepped outside and the scent of grass was about us as we crossed the new damp turf. Without a word we went down the ornamental steps to the next terrace, where statues gleamed against the yew walls like white ghosts. At the end of this lawn there was a garden seat fashioned from a long slab of white stone resting on ornate pedestals, which gave us a view down the alley Titanic. Leila sat down and pulled her hooded cloak about her. In the background an eternally smiling nymph reached amorously towards her.

I cursed myself for not being able to think of something appropriate to say, but as only banalities came to mind I remained silent.

'I need a cigarette,' said Leila, producing the black, gold-lettered box. When she tried to light it her hand trembled so much that I took the lighter from her and held the flame to the tip of the Sobranie.

'It's not caused by seeing you,' she said. 'I've had a difficult session with my brother.'

Instinctively I looked up at the bulk of the peel-tower against the crystalline sky. A square of light showed that Geoffrey was still in his study.

'I wonder what you feel, seeing me,' she continued. 'I know I made you unhappy, and I couldn't make you understand.'

'It was a year go,' I said. 'Time the healer, and all that.'

'It was a hateful way to break with you,' she continued as though she had not heard me. 'I suddenly knew Geoffrey was going to do something terrible, but that wasn't the whole reason I fled, leaving you that note. You see, I was a terrible coward. I knew what I had to do for both our sakes, but I also knew that if I saw you again face to face I shouldn't have the courage to go through with it.'

Don't talk like this! a voice inside me was crying out. A year has gone by and I have survived being alone. Other lovers lie in our old bed watching the curtain. Other lovers drink wine in the little restaurant on the Santa Maria Elisabetta piazzale. The Father Figure smiles kindly upon them and forgets them as he has forgotten us.

'I admired your courage, Martin,' she continued. 'For a long time I was afraid of what would happen if you came after me, of false reconciliation which would lead to yet another parting. But you had the strength to recognise the inevitable, and for that I was grateful.'

'I just ran away. And I discovered that physical distance is a help. It removes the temptation to do something immediate out of desperation.'

She nodded.

'I hope you're right. I'm going to Hong Kong this week.' She drew on her cigarette and then turned to me. Her hood slipped back and in the moonlight it seemed that her hair had finally decided to become silver.

'I shouldn't have talked to you like that,' she said. 'It's not what I wanted to see you about. I want to warn you . . . to ask you to leave Auber. Cancel this film, or shoot it somewhere else, but go.'

'That's impossible,' I said in a voice which showed my astonishment at the intensity of her last words. 'I have no control over the filming. I just wrote the script. But . . .'

'Then go yourself – tomorrow, before this wretched masque. And take Dian with you!'

From my expression she realised she was not making

309

sense to me. For a minute she sat silent beneath the nymph stooping to embrace her.

'Let's walk some more.'

'If you wish.'

She laid her hand lightly on my arm and like a sedate couple in an old print we promenaded down the yew avenue, the stalks of the newly scythed grass springy beneath our feet. Although intrigued by her words, I said nothing. One thing I had learned as a journalist was that people will always talk if you give them time.

As we neared the mausoleum Leila said, 'Do you realise that Geoffrey is mad?'

'He seems to have been under strain, and I know Dian is afraid of another nervous breakdown – but mad? No, I don't think so. Would he have been able to plan the restoration of this place and carry on composing if he was?'

'Martin, he's been mad ever since he slashed my portrait in Bond Street. The treatment at Sayers Grange gave him a façade of normality, but deep down Geoffrey is insane. By that I mean he no longer thinks along parallel lines with the mainstream of humanity. He sees the world very differently from us, and that's being mad, isn't it?'

'Some might say it was an artist's vision,' I said.

Leila did not speak as we passed the ivied walls of the Auber tomb.

'Martin, you know how there's a mental rapport between twins?' she said at length. 'Remember how good Geoffrey and I were at telepathy . . .'

'How good the three of us were.'

'. . . and in Venice, a few hours before he threw himself off the roof, I knew he was in danger. A little while ago I became aware that another crisis is approaching. More than that, I felt his madness within myself. But this time the mental violence was not directed inwards. I just know it'll be outward, against others. Against you.'

'Me?'

'Yes. In the love-hate feeling Geoffrey has always had for you, the hate is becoming uppermost. I see you don't understand, but you must believe me. I sense the tortured processes of his mind, and it's enough to make me crazy, too. That's why I'm so relieved to be going to Hong Kong, and I don't think I'll ever come back.'

Out of the trees ahead of us something swooped with wings spread and a wide-eyed face made ghostly by moonlight. An owl was hunting.

'Martin, I came up from London for no other reason than to warn you. Doesn't that prove I'm in earnest?'

'Of course I believe you're in earnest, but I'm not sure I understand what you're in earnest about. I do believe that you've picked up vibes from your twin which are very distressing for you. But that doesn't explain why you think I'm in danger. I mean, if the worst happened and Geoffrey did get violent there are others here beside myself, and Oliver has medical experience. When you talk about Geoffrey's hating me I can't believe you. There are times when he's very sombre, but he was like that when I got to know him in London, and I've always put it down to the eccentricity of genius. But hatred . . . no, I can't accept that.'

'You should take my word for it,' she said calmly. 'I had a long, unhappy session with Geoffrey before you got back. I tried to talk him into a reasonable state of mind. It was useless, but it certainly revealed his feelings about you, and everything is coming to a head tomorrow. Do you know how he regards this masque?'

'A celebration of the re-occupation of his family home.'

'Martin, you know his obsession with the past's repeating itself . . . he sees it as a re-enactment.'

I admit I began to feel uneasy at her words.

'You're sure?'

'It came out tonight. He sees certain characters from the past being re-invoked at what he called a nodal point in time. Apparently some experiment you went through with Oliver has reinforced his conviction, so if you do stay I beg you to keep an eye on Dian.'

We had reached the jetty. On one side of it was moored the white cruiser for tomorrow's filming, on the other the repainted gondola rocked slightly with the ripples. The sight of it brought impressions of our time in Venice flooding back. We stepped aboard and sat facing each other on the upholstered seats. Leila's words certainly made me draw parallels between the little group of us at Auber today and the characters in the drama which had led to the placing of the curse on the family. But – ridiculous thought! – if Geoffrey were as ruthless as his forebear Sir Piers, he could have no motive for harming me.

Leila lit another cigarette and gazed over the water.

'I'm afraid I haven't made out a very good case,' she said finally. 'But I truly did come to Auber because I'm desperately worried for your safety. You'll be thinking it's me that's mad, and perhaps I am to expect you to take notice of me after what happened in Venice.'

'Not for the first time, I'm a little mystified,' I said. 'I seem to be involved in a game of which no one's told me the rules.'

'That game is called Life,' said Leila, with a hint of her old humour. 'Martin, do you remember the cameraman who was engulfed by lava? Now I see you in the same situation: so absorbed in your work that you don't realise the danger.'

A breeze rippled across the lake and on the bank the trees whispered. Until now I had been surprised, and gratified, at my calmness over this unexpected reunion, but a certain angle of her face, as beautiful as ever and turned to alabaster by moonlight, caught me unawares. For an instant I saw her again as my Leila, the girl I should be waking up beside in the mornings, who, in response to my love, briefly gave me that sense of intimacy I had wanted all my life. I felt this like a physical pain, but before I could put it into words the nostalgia was swamped by a sense of lost illusion, and by the realisation that if our relationship had been real it would not have ended as it did. For an instant I was back in the apartment on the Rio del Vin with a cigarette poised above my wrist.

Strange, I thought, how a fleeting facial expression or a whiff of tobacco smoke could conjure up such an emotional reflex. It also struck me that with her talk of danger Leila had no more escaped the family neurosis than her brother.

'Perhaps we should go back,' I said. 'Tomorrow is going to be a hell of a day.'

'Martin, if the only way to convince you means that you lose whatever shreds of feeling you may have left for me, then so be it,' she said in a voice so low that I had to concentrate to catch her words. 'You deserve to know the truth.'

Whose truth? I wondered, but I was not prepared for what Leila said next.

'The reason for Geoffrey's hatred is that after we left Auber that summer I had a child.'

Her words seemed to hang in the air while I sought to adjust to this shift in perspective.

'So Geoffrey was telling the truth . . .'

'He was terribly unhappy and jealous about it. You see, he was my first lover . . . Poor Martin, you never guessed,' she added with a sigh, and before I could ask the questions which crowded to my mind she began describing her childhood with her twin. I gained a picture of a large and ugly house south of Waberswick on the Suffolk coast – its remoteness emphasised by vast sky and seascapes – of a highly-strung mother unable to make contact with her children, and a father they adored because he was not above romping. But as they grew older he appeared to be less interested in them, and his absences in connection with his work became more frequent.

When the twins were old enough they went to school in the nearby village. Although they found it difficult to mix with the other children, who sneered at their lack of the local accent and their 'stuck-up' ways, it was a relief to spend the days away from their silent mother and the grim widow who acted as a part-time servant.

Their refuge was in each other's company. At weekends and school holidays their greatest delight was to go off together over the empty beaches and explore the marshes stretching windswept and desolate behind them, watching wildfowl and transforming the reedy wastes into their own secret world – a mutual act of imagination which they later repeated at Auber.

As Leila spoke I visualised two small children walking hand in hand on a deserted shore, the only living things in a world of grey wind and vast space.

As time went on, Leila said, their father stayed away for longer and longer periods and, frightened by the animosity they saw he bore their mother, they welcomed his absences. Finally, after periods of domestic strife which the children could not then understand, their mother found sanctuary in a nursing home. The Suffolk house was sold, and their father took them to Auber. Putting them under the reluctant care of his 'Cumbrian mistress', he then departed for Venice.

A new life began for Leila and Geoffrey. In the library the boy delved into books on the history of Derwentwater, local folklore and family chronicles. It was the latter which gave them the notion that they were not 'ordinary children' but, as twin inheritors of the Auber traditions, a pair with a special and secretive destiny. The house and its overgrown grounds became an enchanted domain in which they found a freedom they had never experienced before.

There was also fear in this domain: fear of a future in which they might be parted; fear of their father whose violence against their mother had alienated them; and, in Geoffrey's case, fear of some nebulous doom hanging over the family – the result of his poring over old tomes in the library.

'Geoffrey and I had always loved each other,' said Leila. 'Being twins, and in each other's company all the time, it seemed that we were part of each other. No one else existed for us here, and I suppose it was inevitable that as we moved out of childhood our love took on a sexual expression. Geoffrey made love to me several times before the enormity of what we had done struck us. In our way we were too sophisticated to see anything sinful in sex, but as a Catholic our mother had brought us up very strictly, and the sin of incest was something we knew about and couldn't cope with. It might sound extraordinary to you, but guilt made Geoffrey impotent. At the time we were both relieved – it insured us against temptation, and our relationship returned to normal.

'Then you appeared on the scene, and you just seemed to fit into Auber. Geoffrey was delighted to have the friendship of a boy at last. But you can understand his jealousy when he realised how fond I was of you. He saw us making love that day, of course, but he was clever at hiding his feelings – something we'd both learned at school, I suppose. And the strange thing was that even when I told him I was going to have your baby, even though he suffered the hell of a jealous lover, he still liked you. You may have thought about the effect the Auber twins had on you, but you probably didn't realise the effect you had on us. You were our first real friend from the outside world.'

'Leila,' I broke in. 'Tell me, the child . . .?'

'A boy. Please, let me tell you in my own way. You see, I had to tell Geoffrey it was yours, and also my aunt, who regarded me as a harlot – her word, in fact. There was no point in dragging my brother through the agony of guilt and family punishment, but the fact is, Martin, I'm convinced I was already pregnant when you and I made love.'

'You mean, it wasn't my child?'

315

'You'll be relieved to know it wasn't. It was Geoffrey's, of course – product of an incestuous union.'

She gave a bitter smile and drew hard on her cigarette. When she saw that I was about to ask questions she continued. 'It was a ghastly time. As you know, when our father returned to Auber we were sent to our dragon of an aunt. And when it became obvious that I was pregnant she acted as though I was the original Scarlet Woman – especially as she must have heard about my father's going insane by then. The inquisition I was put through! Geoffrey was sent away to avoid contamination with his fallen sister. Since we were Catholics abortion was out of the question, and it probably wasn't legal then anyway. So I gave birth in a home run by nuns, but the baby didn't live many months – not unusual in such cases, I understand.'

For a moment her voice was unsteady, and it seemed that her eyes glistened.

'I used to wonder if it was a punishment for our sin, this congenital weakness in my son. You can imagine the construction Geoffrey would have put upon it if he had known the truth. But I would have lost the child anyway, because my aunt had arranged for him to be adopted. It was a sad time, Martin. And having to have sessions with Dr Steiner didn't help.'

She was quiet for a minute. I felt it would be crass to bring out the questions that were tumbling about in my mind.

'So that's the background to Geoffrey's complex feelings towards you. Logically he can't allow himself to blame you for falling in love with me; emotionally he blames you for the end of the idyll between us. Until your arrival I was his world, and vice versa. Of course, as the years passed everything receded and, in our different ways, Geoffrey and I tried to put our childhood behind us. These things will be the death of me,' she added inconsequently as she lit another cigarette. 'Does this make my behaviour in Venice any more understandable?'

I remained silent.

'So, that's what lies behind my attempt to get this masque called off, for Geoffrey's sake and yours. You know his theory of things happening in cycles but being a little bit different each time around? When I used to visit him at Sayers Grange he talked about being part of a ritual, and how he was striving to alter it. In the end he became so desperate that he tried to take his own life.'

'But he's improved since then,' I protested. 'He's perfectly rational, even if he is tense at times, and he has his music now . . .'

'I told you I know – I feel – what's going on in his mind. He is mad. It breaks my heart to say it, but it's true. If you can't call off this masque, and I can see it's probably gone too far to be stopped, can't you go away?'

'I could never explain to Akkim. Besides, if anything should happen I'm likely to be more use here.'

Leila stood up in the boat and looked down at me.

'Even if you think what I've said is crazy, do you wonder that I should be concerned about you?'

'No,' I answered. 'I think I understand.'

She frowned, and added, 'And there's nothing else you want to know?'

A few minutes ago there had been so many questions; now they seemed pointless. I knew there was one she would expect me to ask – had she let me make love to her by the mausoleum in order to prepare Geoffrey for the lie she was going to tell him, or had it been the act of love I had thought it was?

'Let's leave everything just as it is,' I said. 'Shall we go back to the house?'

She stepped out of the gondola and I followed her, and we walked up the avenue in the moonshadow cast by the yews.

When we went into the house Leila slipped off her cloak, and I saw that she was wearing a small golden

317

cross at her throat. Seeing me looking at it she smiled slightly.

'Yes, it's the one you sent me all those years ago,' she said. 'Old Baites the caretaker must have shoved the envelope into the kitchen drawer where Geoffrey found it. I think he was very amused at your letter, but at least he had the grace to give me the cross. I shall always keep it.'

'Why did you throw away the coral necklace when you'd said the same about that?'

'To convince you that our relationship was at an end. I knew you'd see it, and I'm afraid I bargained on your sentimentality.'

Before we parted at the grand staircase as the clock above us announced midnight, Leila took my hand.

'Goodbye, Martin. Thanks for the cross.'

'You're not staying for the masque?'

'I don't think so. I'll probably take a taxi to Carlisle and catch one of the Glasgow to London Intercities. But first I'm going to see Geoffrey again. If I can't convince you, I must have one last try at reasoning with him.'

Halfway up the stairs she turned and leaned over the balustrade.

'Lock your door, Martin.'

'Leila, this is ridiculous.'

She shook her head sadly.

'You forget . . . what I told you in Italy . . . about our father.'

The fine metal foliage with its fabulous bestiary stirred as she hurried out of sight. I went to the kitchen and took half a bottle of vodka out of the refrigerator to carry to my room. Rarely have I felt such a need for a drink.

When the alarm bleeped my eyes open I found that, although I would never have got to sleep without the vodka, its after-effect at six in the morning was horrid.

Knowing that the film unit would arrive soon from its lodging in Keswick, I still had to exert all my willpower to get out of bed and blunder into my antiquated bathroom. Having cut myself shaving, and still feeling as though my skin did not fit my body, I went to the kitchen to make myself a mug of instant coffee.

Apart from the heavy tick of the clock, the house was silent and I wondered whether Leila had stayed overnight or had caught an early-morning train. I rather hoped she had gone. At the moment I had no wish to be reminded of last night's revelations. They were something to think about later. Today I would concentrate on nothing but filming.

'A good morning to you, Martin.'

Through the kitchen door came Akkim, immaculate in his expensive casual clothes and radiating good health and enthusiasm.

'It looks as if it's going to be a splendid day, and the weather report promises a clear night. Will you ask the charming Miss Derbyshire to see me about getting the musicians' clearances signed?'

As I handed him a cup of coffee, he said, 'You aren't sick, are you? You look as if you need a transfusion.'

'A bad night. A mixture of belated truth and vodka. The result is a hangover and a conviction that truth – like beauty – is only in the beholder's eye.'

'Damn right. Here come the guys.'

We went outside to where a number of men in anoraks were looking about them speculatively. The unit director, who had already supervised the earlier sequences of Auber, and the chief lighting-cameraman came forward to meet Akkim. Together we walked on the gravel path along the side of the house to where half a dozen estate cars and vans were parked. Over a plan of the grounds I explained the location of the musicians and where the dancing would take place. While Akkim and the director discussed camera angles, and the placing of lighting units, members of the crew unloaded the equipment. On the generator truck the electrician connected up heavy-duty cables which his assistants unrolled in the direction of the terraced lawns. From the lighting van a number of massive flood lamps – known as 'brutes' – were unpacked, and once more I had the feeling of controlled chaos which goes with 'setting up'.

'Let's stroll down and see the cruiser,' suggested Akkim. 'What I want is an over-the-water shot from the lake to the inlet, then a very slow zoom up the avenue to the house, finally focusing on the lighted window of the Murder Room.'

'That'll take some rehearsing,' said the lighting-cameraman morosely.

'You've got all day to get your shots figured out.'

'I thought Wilberforce had abolished slavery.'

Wreaths of early mist still hung in the avenue as we walked down to the lakeside. Thanks to the clean air, and the anticipatory excitement of filming, I began to feel better, and before long my hangover had settled down to a mere throbbing headache. While the others inspected the Freeman cruiser, and the cameraman became more despondent, I looked down on the gondola and decided this was not the time to think of Leila and her extraordinary conversation. Luckily I was soon so engrossed in the preparations for the evening that even if I had wanted to there was no time to ponder on lost illusion.

During the morning rails were laid for a tracking shot which Akkim was particularly keen on, only to be dismantled and reassembled in a different location after he had looked through the viewfinder and decided it was not what he wanted after all. The brutes were set in place, and even in daylight they blazed like so many suns. Amplifiers which would carry the music of the Elizabethan quintet to the far reaches of the domain crackled spasmodically into life, and the sound engineer moved from site to site checking sound levels on his Nagra recorder.

Indoors, the kitchen had been taken over by outside caterers, and when Akkim and I went to the reception rooms a camera dolly was making dummy runs from apartment to apartment while the focus-puller rehearsed the different lens apertures he would need for the varying light levels. Dian had followed Geoffrey's wishes and the rooms were draped with hired hangings whose colours toned with the dramatic lighting. Even the windows had been covered with coloured film to enhance the effect. The first room through which the guests would pass was hung in blue, and vividly blue were its windows. The second was purple and the third green throughout, while the great hall was shrouded in black velvet tapestries that fell down the walls in heavy folds to a carpet of the same hue, but here the colour of the windows did not correspond with the decorations. The panes were a deep blood colour.

Akkim was delighted.

'Think of what a good editor will be able to achieve by intercutting these shots,' he enthused. 'We should get a red spotlight on that clock face . . . where's the sparks? And someone tell Chris I want a track of its tick-tock. It's like a heart beating. Eerie!'

'That's why I put it in the script,' I said smugly.

We were so busy during the day that I saw hardly anything of the other members of the household. Oliver remained in the seclusion of his room, doubtless still writing up his conclusions from our experiment in regression. Once I glimpsed Geoffrey's silhouette at the Murder Room window, gazing over the activity in the grounds. Like me, Dian was fully occupied with preparations for the evening.

When the sun hung low over Cat Bells and the shadow of the peel-tower raced along the avenue, the film unit took a break. Cameras were swathed in their covers and the men trooped to the house for a meal and to change into their costumes. Akkim dawdled behind with me at the jetty – the setting up of a camera on the boat had been difficult – and surveyed Derwentwater, now reflecting sunset clouds.

'I think this is one of the most tranquil places I've ever

seen,' he said. 'Fortune must favour your friend, to give him a house like Auber in such a setting.'

'He's inherited a lot of problems along with it. And I don't just mean the financial kind – your fees have taken care of that!'

'The last of his line, isn't he? I wonder if he'll marry that very attractive girl who is so devoted to him. He's probably not easy, but that's a great attraction to some women. He would be feared in the part of the world I come from.'

'Feared?'

'Yes. The fellahin would say there was a touch of the afrit about him, with those pale eyes. Do you think Geoffrey has the Evil Eye?'

I laughed.

'Only when it turns inward.'

'He's the brother of that beautiful girl you were so enamoured with in Venice. She has the same eyes.'

'They're twins.'

'It never worked out for you.' It was a statement rather than a question.

'No.'

'What a writer needs is someone like Tash, someone with a sense of humour and a generous heart, someone who will understand what he is trying to do and forgive him for it, and above all someone who will not suffocate him with her problems. Forgive me if I speak without tact, but I should imagine anyone attracted to a member of the Auber family would have to be an audience for some heavy drama. Tash, on the other hand, would be in the front row with you, sharing the popcorn.'

'I think I'm getting the message.'

Akkim smiled.

'If I did not have a wife – even though she prefers Alexandria to Bel Air – I would be in hot pursuit of Tash. She understands movies.'

We turned and strolled past the mausoleum towards the house.

'Tonight it will be fairyland, Martin,' Akkim said. 'A very dangerous place. A world of lights and illusions, of camera tricks and masked actors dancing to a script which keeps changing. Sucked into a black box through Merlin's crystal and trapped on a magic ribbon, it is their fate to perform their parts on an eternal carousel.'

He laughed at his flight of imagination, but I thought how Geoffrey would have approved if he had heard it.

23

'One by one the guests arrive, the guests are coming
   through,
The open-hearted many, the broken-hearted few.
And no one knows where the night is going,
And no one knows why the wine is flowing . . .'

To make a final check of the sound system the recording
engineer, an enthusiastic admirer of Leonard Cohen,
played one of his cassettes over it, and the sad voice of the
singer-poet filled the dark grounds of Auber. At the touch
of a switch hundreds of coloured lights glowed in the trees
like multi-coloured fruit.

'Beautiful,' cried Akkim. With the unit director we
stood at the top of the garden steps which led down from
the terraced lawn. Neither Akkim nor I had ordered
costumes for ourselves, and had chosen ones which fitted
near enough from the hampers of apparel provided for the
film crew. The result was that the producer – appropriately, according to some – was dressed as a Grand
Inquisitor. I had put on a grey monk's robe, the hood of
which tended to fall over my eyes. Like everyone else we
wore the obligatory masks.

'Light up the brutes,' said Akkim, and the Harlequin
unit director spoke into his pocket-sized transceiver.
Immediately a number of lamps in strategic places blazed
forth, pushing the night back to the woods. On the lawn
below us the camera crane rose majestically while a
piratical cameraman checked the scene through his
viewfinder.

Leonard Cohen was replaced by live music from the

Elizabethan players, who were placed in a floodlit portico specially erected for the occasion.

'It's out of our hands now,' Akkim said. 'I'm going to check the interiors and then I'm going to enjoy myself. It's not often you get to be at a party like this.'

We entered the house, where catering staff, dressed in mulberry livery with a golden A emblem, were ready to serve drinks. As we passed from room to room the lighting changed dramatically, until we entered the great black-draped hall where a spotlight turned the clock face into a scarlet moon.

'Where did Sir Geoffrey get his ideas from?' Akkim asked.

'As children he and his sister were greatly influenced by Edgar Allan Poe,' I answered.

'I think Edgar Allan Poe would have loved him.'

A locksmith had made a new key for Auber's main door, which led into the hall, and here Geoffrey stood welcoming the trickle of guests which had already begun to arrive. He was dressed in the extravagant doublet and hose of a Florentine prince. The toes of his shoes turned up at an angle that was the rage in the sixteenth century, and at his side the hilt of his poniard flashed with glass gems, as did the theatrical jewellery on his fingers. Beside him stood Oliver, a rotund Caesar in a purple-edged toga.

The guests gazed about them in amazement as they entered. Rumours of Auber's transformation had been rife after the invitations had arrived at the home of Cumbria's oldest families, but I could see that the appearance of the house and the princely hospitality were far beyond their expectations. They laughed in astonishment as they walked through the music-filled rooms, while servants, entering into the period atmosphere of the masque, pressed drinks upon them at every turn.

A letter had gone out with each invitation to explain that filming would be discreetly taking place, and that only costumed guests would be admitted. Those who turned up in evening clothes hoping that their social standing would exclude them from the edict had to deal with Oliver's assiduity. On a table beside him lay a pile of dominoes, and these he pressed upon them with determined charm. Only one couple got past him. A local lord in an ancient dinner jacket followed meekly in the wake of his wife, a stout woman with a voice of such aristocratic pitch that she could stop a hound in its tracks and shrivel a shop assistant at twenty paces.

Seeing this, Akkim stepped forward and, with the bow and smile that his forebears had used to win favours from caliphs, suggested that they would feel more relaxed in dominoes.

'I am Lady Lanercost, and I'd like to know who you are to tell me what to do.'

'My name is Yousef Akkim, your ladyship, and I must ask your pardon for not realising that you're in a character role.'

As she turned and led her husband to the door a number of guests, realising the freedom bestowed by their disguise, broke into applause.

The unit director came up to Akkim.

'Problem,' he said. 'The fellow steering the cruiser can't keep it steady enough.'

'I'll come,' said Akkim. 'Back home I have a Chriscraft at Del Ray.'

I went with him to the jetty and sat with my back against a tree as he expertly reversed, swung the cruiser round and headed out into the lake. The bow pulpit had been removed and a camera was mounted on a stocky tripod. Lights powered by a row of linked heavy-duty batteries had been fitted on the cabin roof for a sequence Akkim wanted of the gondola gliding over the water. But now, with the moon newly risen, the cameraman's task was to film Auber from the lake.

When the Freeman was a couple of hundred metres from the shore Akkim lined it up with the house and then throttled back, holding it steady while the cameraman crouched behind his camera and experimented with his zoom lens.

Faintly across the water I heard him call, 'Camera running.' And the cruiser began its run towards the shore. Knowing they would be making several takes I left my tree and began to walk up the alley Titanic. The grounds ahead were bathed in light and already guests, led by members of an Old English dance society, were forming up on the top lawn. Other guests sat with their drinks beneath the statues or wandered the grounds, laughing and talking and enjoying their anonymity.

The night was still young but I could already sense a gala spirit in the air. Enough alcohol had been served to make the masquers ignore the cameras and lights, and as I came closer to the couples promenading with their glasses of sparkling wine I caught the currents of sexuality generated by the new-found freedom their masks bestowed upon them. In a mask one could whisper – and listen to – outrageous things that could never be said face to face, and the unknown masked partner allowed erotic fancy to run riot. And for the romantic of heart there was the dream that behind the silk was the lover-friend one had awaited for so long, who had remained on the edge of dreams despite the stain of the world.

Several times as I strolled beneath the fairy lights strung along the yew trees forms emerged from the shadows and warm, strange lips sought mine, but with a joke about a monk's vow of chastity I continued on until I was caught up in a throng of carnival characters, each robed in the trappings of his or her fantasy, surrounding one of the entertainers. Between the heads of a centurian and a pixie I watched him haul a sword blade from his gullet; then, seizing a small brand, he ignited his breath and sent a gust of flame whooshing over the heads of the revellers. By the yellow light I recognised Oliver standing to one side.

'*Pax vobiscum*, my son,' I said, laying my hand on his shoulder. He was startled to see my austere figure behind him, my hood covering my masked face.

'Martin, you did give me a turn,' he said as more dragon fire flared above us. 'Isn't this absolutely splendid? Your charming Akkim must be very pleased.'

'And Geoffrey, I hope.'

'I hope so too. It's such a fitting re-establishment of Auber, but poor Geoffrey.' He sighed.

'What's wrong with Geoffrey?'

Oliver put his hand on my arm and we walked away from the fire-eater along a path gaudy with Chinese lanterns.

'Geoffrey has a fit of the remotes,' Oliver said. 'He spent the day locked in his study. Each time I went to his door there was no response to my knock. All I could hear was his 'Derwentwater' symphony being played at full blast.'

'He seemed all right when he was welcoming his guests.'

'It was like being close to an automaton. He was very correct but I felt . . . ah well, it reminded me of how he behaved sometimes at my flat before he had the breakdown. He was there physically but one had the impression that his mind was roving in some other dimension. I pray that tonight passes without incident. The excitement could trigger off something unfortunate. We have to face the fact that our friend's behaviour does suggest an increasing tendency towards schizophrenia. It was something they were afraid of at Sayers Grange.'

'At least he looks all right at the moment,' I said, pointing to where Geoffrey – accompanied by a camera dolly running on rails laid at the side of the lawn – was making what I can only describe as a triumphal progress. Electricians swung the brutes in his direction so that he appeared in an aura of light. It sparkled on his theatrical jewellery and gave his peacock-blue cloak the iridescence of a butterfly's wing. Although he was masked like the rest of us, there was no mistaking the fine, pale gold hair which floated round his head. Behind him, like a knot of courtiers escorting a medieval king, walked some of his old friends from the London art world who had received first-class rail tickets with their invitations, and some members of the younger country set obviously dazzled by 'this artist fellow's' grand style.

I looked for Dian among them, but as her costume had been kept a secret I could not tell whether she was there or not.

The music faded, the flame from the fire-eater was extinguished and the chatter of the guests died as Geoffrey limped to the balustrade of the garden steps.

'Prince Geoffrey the Magnificent,' I heard Oliver mutter.

'My friends,' said Geoffrey, turning to the crowd. 'I thank you for joining me in this celebration to mark my return to my ancestral home. As you know, it has been neglected, but even the destiny of the Aubers can change, and after tonight it will be free from shadows of the past. Now the evening is still fresh, and there's plenty of time to enjoy ourselves before fireworks signal the unmasking.'

Applause rippled. Hands holding glasses raised them in Geoffrey's direction. Music filled the air and dancers resumed the dance. Rays of light which had been focused on Geoffrey dimmed . . . and a spasm that I can now only describe as horror swept through me, so intense it was like physical nausea. I had to turn away and retch.

'I say, dear boy,' Oliver said from a great distance as I slumped on the path while Chinese lanterns danced about me. I could not reply. Insane imaginings, shot through with a sensation of hatred, made my pulses thud. Rage, too long controlled, was coupled with a frantic impulse to sever spider strands of ancient terror which were suffocating me.

However I try to describe that sensation, it can only sound melodramatic. For a few seconds I had shared Geoffrey's feelings. Somehow I picked them up, just as as a boy I had picked up his mental images of playing cards. And I knew why Leila had come with her warning. How much more vivid her impression of her twin's disordered mind!

When I became aware of myself again I saw Oliver kneeling beside me.

'You'll get grass stains on your toga,' I said stupidly. He helped me to a rustic seat in a newly planted arbour.

'Steady, Martin,' he said. 'Try and tell me what happened.'

'I don't know. Some sort of telepathic flash . . .'

'What do you mean?'

'I can't explain. You're the one who's always talked about my bloody psychic perception. This must have been it. All I know is that Geoffrey is about to blow his mind.'

'But why should you have suddenly felt that?'

'Because he must have thought of me,' I answered. It was only later that I realised the import of my words. 'Look, Oliver, let's worry about the mechanics of this later. The point is, Geoffrey is dangerous – or about to be. I know when he was normal he was a gentle enough soul, but remember I saw him shred Leila's portrait in Bond Street. He was attacking her in absentia. You know the family curse that has haunted him – that when madness comes to an Auber he destroys those who love him. And don't forget that his father was suspected of murdering his mistress.'

'I never knew that. Poor, tormented Geoffrey . . .' Oliver paused and then, as he saw the implication of my words, he exclaimed, 'Dian!'

'Exactly. Try and find her, Oliver, and I'll follow Geoffrey. As long as I'm near him nothing can happen.

There was no sign of Geoffrey on the lawn, so I hurried to the house, turning my head constantly in the hope of glimpsing a princely figure among the merrymakers. I was filled with a sick panic because I knew that it was up to me to prevent some hideous calamity. And if it occurred it would be my fault for dismissing Leila's words as typical Auber fantasy.

I entered the house through open French windows, and

in a room which had been hung with crimson drapes I found myself swept into a frenetic crowd of disco dancers. Here the Elizabethan music which still filled the grounds was replaced by heavy metal pop music to which red strobe lamps pulsed in rhythm. The dancers – pierrots and cavaliers, queens and flower girls, jesters and Salome – threw wild shadows on the walls as they gyrated millisecond by frozen millisecond. But this was no setting for a prince of Florence and I shouldered my way through the throng, the music drowning the protests at my desperate passage.

From room to room I hastened, and several times I approached tall disguised ladies in the hope of hearing Dian reply, but she remained hidden among the several hundred guests. My alarm for her grew agonisingly with a visual memory of Geoffrey's knife slicing the canvas in the Alessandro gallery. When I had been through all the reception rooms, luminous with intense colour, I tried the library, but wisely its massive door had been locked. Next into the chapel, which was in darkness except for moonlight shining faintly through stained-glass saints. But it was not deserted. The sound of hoarse breathing guided my eyes, once they were accustomed to the heavy dusk, to the altar, where two figures in dominoes and slightly darker than the dusk fulfilled an erotic fantasy.

I returned to the hall. The ebony clock tolled the hour with such brazen notes that couples seated on the grand staircase paused in their laughter and kisses until the last echo of the chimes died. Then laughter returned and kissing became more passionate. Stepping round them, I ascended the staircase. If Geoffrey had been mingling with the revellers downstairs I would certainly have recognised his striking costume and the handsome head which his mask did nothing to disguise. After the floodlights and the disco strobes the upper corridors were dim, though even here I saw phantom figures gliding in search of refuge from the music and laughter and the hot, winy air.

At the bottom of the spiral staircase leading to the

Murder Room Columbine sat in a window recess, outlined by starshine. As I paused she held out a rose, which I took before running up the stairs. Then, rose in hand, I found myself facing the carved door with the trepidation I had felt as a boy daring myself to enter.

I pushed the door and it opened on its recently oiled hinges. The only light flickered from the fireplace and as I approached it I saw that a female figure in a domino lay on a steel and leather couch. The domino's hood and mask hid her hair and features, but I told myself it had to be Dian. But as I put forward my hand to touch her shoulder I saw firelight glint on a tiny golden cross hanging on a chain outside the folds of the robe.

'Ah, Martin, I'm so glad you came,' said Geoffrey from the shadows. 'I was bracing myself to seek you among the mob.'

He came forward and stood by the fireplace, his voice so friendly – so good-natured – that I wondered if my fears were the result of some mental disturbance of my own.

'Poor dear,' he said, gesturing to the figure on the couch. 'A victim of the wine, but she'll be all right after a sleep. Tell me, is Akkim happy?'

I nodded, still unable to relate my fearful imaginings to my old friend standing so normally in the cosy light of the logs.

'Good. I must thank you again for making all this possible.' His voice trembled slightly as he continued, 'It's the most important day in my life. It's not only my return to Auber we're celebrating, but what will be a change of direction – an escape, if you like, from my hex. Ah, little did we guess when you came ashore how it would turn out! But this is no time to brood. Tonight you must join me in a very special toast in a very special port which was laid down by my grandfather before he went to fight for king and country. There's only one bottle left, and I've kept it for such a night as this.'

My eyes wandered about the room, expecting to see the bottle, white with dust.

'It's not here. To carry it up the stairs would have ruined it by stirring up the sediment. No, it must be drunk in the cellar. Come.'

He turned to the door and, with a quick glance at the gently breathing girl on the couch, I followed. *If* there was a hint of truth in my wild suspicions, all would be well as long as I could keep an eye upon him.

'No need to go through the giddy crowd,' he said, leading me to a door at the end of the corridor. This he unlocked, and in the feeble light of an unshaded electric bulb I saw steep wooden stairs leading downwards.

'This was for the use of the servants,' Geoffrey explained. 'Careful you don't trip over your gown.'

His words were so commonplace that again I felt disconcerted by my earlier suspicions. Then the picture of him destroying the portrait returned. I wished I was away from Auber, back at Castlepoint listening to the surge of the Pacific while I sat at my typewriter, or wandering desert trails with Tash. What a fool I had been to become involved with Auber again merely to get a film script out of it!

'Here we are,' said Geoffrey. 'This door leads straight into the undercroft.'

He switched on the lights and I followed him out of the stairwell, but instead of making for the racked bottles he turned to the door of the tunnel. He took a lantern down from a peg and lit its candle.

'Our finest wines were kept in here, out of the way of temptation.' With a huge antique key he unlocked the oaken door. As he held the lantern high I saw several steps leading down to the flagstones of the square-cut tunnel. With a flash of recognition I realised that here was the original for Geoffrey's Subterranean paintings.

He set the lantern on a narrow shelf and motioned me to sit on an empty crate. From a cobwebbed rack he withdrew a dark bottle which he placed on another crate. I watched in silence while from his pocket he produced two small glasses, a piece of gauze and a metal instrument which he deftly ran round the neck of the bottle just below the cork.

'Uncorking it in the normal way would only stir up a cloud of sediment which would take over a year to settle again,' he said, and smartly tapped his instrument against the glass so that the top of the neck was neatly flicked off. I held the gauze over the glasses while he painstakingly poured the port through it. Its aroma, trapped for decades, filled our nostrils pleasantly.

Geoffrey raised his glass and sipped the dark red wine tentatively.

'Very good,' he pronounced. 'It's fitting to have such a drink at such a significant moment. Tonight, Martin, I'm going to free myself from the pattern which has been the bane of our family down the ages. After tomorrow there will be no curse of Auber, no fear, no madness. Largely thanks to you, I realised how the pattern can be altered.'

'Really?' I said in a neutral voice.

'Oh, yes. It was through Oliver's regressing you at Castlerigg that I got the proof of how the curse had come about. You see, it would be impossible to alter the cycle if I did not understand it first.'

He held his glass to the candle so that it looked like a huge ruby in his fingers.

'Of course, the experience must have made you realise your role in the pattern.'

'My role?'

'Now, Martin, don't play the innocent. You're involved in this as much as I am. Surely that's obvious. How else could you have had such an instant affinity with Auber, with Leila and me? Or, for that matter, how do you think it was possible for you to experience such a remarkable regression if you didn't already have some connection with those past events?'

As Geoffrey spoke my alarm grew, but I tried to keep my voice light and conversational as I said, 'So you believe we all played our roles here in a previous incarnation. For example, you see me as the younger Auber . . .'

'. . . who loved Rowena and died in the lake,' concluded Geoffrey, carefully pouring more port. 'No, it's not exactly like that. You – Martin Winter – were not a member of the family in Tudor times any more than the Geoffrey Auber you see before you was once Sir Piers. But you and I, and Leila and Dian, are the present-day manifestations of a pattern which was created then. All my studies lead me to believe, and this should amuse you as a scriptwriter, that we're like actors condemned to play certain parts laid down generations ago. We're not the original cast, but, allowing for modifications in succeeding productions, we're destined to play similar roles to the first actors. Until one performer learns the trick of altering the plot.'

'I see. But you mentioned Dian . . .'

'She has her role. She was drawn back to the Auber drama just as you were.' He laughed with sudden bitterness. 'As a young and impressionable girl she fell madly in love with Leila. It was only when Leila left England and Dian realised how hopeless it was that her affections were transferred to me. Oh, yes, Martin, she's involved like the rest of us.'

'Amazing,' I said. I believed that as long as I could keep Geoffrey talking he would be no threat to Dian. I hoped that it would give Oliver time to find her and take her to safety in his car.

'Why "amazing", Martin? I'm surprised that, with what Oliver calls your psychic perception, it's not clear to you. Surely, looking back, you must see the parallel between you and Sir Piers's younger brother who wanted Rowena for himself.' He gave an unsteady laugh. 'You don't really imagine it was Derwentwater's bottom wind that caused his death, do you? From the moment you arrived here you were drawn to Leila, weren't you? Oh, yes, I know exactly what you felt. I've heard what you said to her then.'

My face must have expressed my shock, for a gloating smile showed beneath Geoffrey's mask.

'Yes. When you were Oliver's subject last year he once gave me control of you while he was working with Dian on one of his endless telepathic experiments in another room. It gave me a wonderful opportunity to . . . tamper with Oliver's commands.'

'So that explains the post-hypnotic effect . . .'

'"Ulalume"? I thought it appropriate. And so is the other word I implanted, as you will see. Ah, your glass is empty.' He poured more port.

'Oliver explained to me once the value of emotive connotations in hypnotic control words. "Ulalume" was associated strongly with Leila. I wonder if you can remember what other word would have affected you in those days. I'll tell you in a minute, because the night draws on and I must complete my work. It will look like an accident, and it would only be you who could say otherwise.'

'Accident?'

'Come, Martin, you must realise . . .' He suddenly lost control of his voice. It rose in pitch and echoed down the tunnel. 'I'd have to do this even if you hadn't taken Leila from me that summer. But when I remember seeing the two of you . . .' A sob halted the flow of his words. 'I saw you on her like a rutting animal . . .'

'Stop, Geoffrey,' I said sharply. 'There's something you should understand. All these years you've believed an illusion. Leila never had my child. Ask her.'

He gulped several times to regain control of his voice.

'She told me that last night,' he said finally. 'She was trying to protect you with a lie. Again, it's you who's come between . . . But it's over now. Your role is finished, Martin. It was down here the lady Madeline was brought on the night of Sir Piers's masque, and it is here that you will ultimately be found. Death by misadventure, the coroner will say.'

The gloating was back, and his rapid change of mood was as it had been in the herb garden at Sayers Grange.

'No one will see you alive again. Tonight you will disappear, and at some later date you will be found here, in your monk's habit, an empty bottle beside you. It will be obvious that while you were here drinking yourself insensible on my best port someone must have closed the door and turned the key, unaware that you lay unconscious in the darkness. So simple and so sad . . . and of course no signs of violence.'

He drained his glass, put it into his pocket, and then poured the remnants of the port on to the damp flags. I began to climb to my feet.

'Martin,' said Geoffrey, standing halfway up the steps leading to the door. 'I want you to hear this word – *Henry*!'

For a moment the face of a dying boy, a bubble forming on his lips, appeared before my inward eye. And for a moment I was racked by guilt, but that, too, faded.

'It's no good, Geoffrey,' I said. 'I made Oliver neutralise any possibility of command words. I wouldn't let him regress me otherwise. Didn't you wonder why I showed no reaction when you said "Ulalume" just now? You have no power over me. Let's go and find the help you need.'

I had completely underestimated Geoffrey. Without thinking, I bent to pick up the candle lantern, and at that moment he brought the bottle swinging down on me. Mad he might be, but he could still calculate the precise spot on which to strike. I felt the blow exactly where my vertebrae had been infected by tuberculosis when I was a boy. The pain was so intense that I could not even cry out. My knees buckled beneath me and I collapsed to the floor. Waves of agony flowed along my spinal nerves and I lay as though paralysed, only dimly aware of the rasping of a key in the heavy lock.

As the tide of pain ebbed two thoughts became uppermost in my mind. The first was disgust at my stupidity in not pretending that Geoffrey had put me in a hypnotic coma. The second was that in his plan for my demise to appear accidental he had left the lantern burning with a couple of inches of candle in it. Its steady yellow flame gave me a crumb of hope. I managed to heave myself into a sitting position, and then, very slowly, my shoulders rubbing the tunnel wall, stood upright. For several seconds the candle provided a pyrotechnic display, and then the dancing lights slowly merged into one. I drew a deep breath and risked a step forward, and was relieved to find that while the blow had been agonising it did not seem to have done any physical damage. More than anything I wanted to sit down on the box and rest for a few minutes, but the thought of Dian kept me on my feet.

'It will look like an accident,' Geoffrey had said. I wondered if he had hypnotic control over her, and I was filled with desperation that I knew I must channel if I was to escape. As a matter of course I climbed the steps to the door but it was firmly locked, and since it was two inches thick I knew it was pointless to try attracting attention through it. And who would be in the Auber cellars to hear me?

I picked up the lantern and began to walk along the tunnel. I remembered that it had been used as an escape route for Roman Catholic priests, so it must come out somewhere. At no time did I feel much anxiety for myself. I had noticed the dampness of the floor and I knew that I should be able to survive for a long time by licking the flagstones. It was the thought of what Geoffrey might be doing which made me determined to escape before the candle guttered out.

The passage ran straight ahead, disappearing into shadows which retreated as I advanced in my little pool of light. I guessed it must be leading towards the lake as the dampness increased and drops of moisture began to glisten on the roughly dressed stone of the walls. Here and there the brick ceiling had given way and I had to clamber over piles of dank earth, but I did not come to any cave-ins as I had feared I might. And then the shadows retreated no further. I had reached a blank wall. A number of stone blocks, presumably left over from the building work, had been piled up by long-dead masons. I sat on them and tried to think what to do next, and it occurred to me that they might serve some purpose, such as steps. Raising my lantern I looked at the ceiling, which was festooned with ancient webs, and gave a shout of relief when I saw that a slate slab had been set in a moulding of brickwork.

Climbing on to the blocks, and pressing against the slate, I was rewarded by feeling it give slightly. At least it did not have a great weight of earth piled over it. I took several deep breaths, and then heaved upwards with every ounce of strength I could muster. The slab rose easily and a cascade of dust set me coughing as I pushed it to one side. The dryness of the dust, and the fact that the candle flame never wavered, told me that the yawning oblong aperture did not lead to the outdoors.

I picked up the lantern and, placing it on the ledge above me, hoisted myself through the space, to find myself inside the Auber mausoleum. Tiers of dust-covered coffins, the earlier ones decorated with ornate carving, were ranged round the walls, and a couple stood on the floor. The lid of one of these had succumbed to dry rot and as I held up the lantern the skull of a departed Auber grimaced at me.

Stepping over the caskets, I examined the bronze doors. Faintly through their panels I heard a voice over the sound system. 'Buffet supper is now being served in the house.'

Only a thin sheet of metal separated me from the world of laughter and buffet suppers, but at last it began to dawn on me that unless I found a way out the Auber mausoleum could become my last resting place.

The doors were held together by a heavy brass lock which I knew I had no hope of opening, but as I raised the lantern, in which the candle was now alarmingly low, I saw that the left hand door was fastened in position by a long bolt slotted into a hole drilled into the stone lintel. A similar bolt fitted into a hole in the threshold. I almost laughed at the simplicity of it. I pulled back the bolts and put my weight against the door which, with a screech of corroded hinges, slowly opened.

A girl in a catsuit, hanging on the arm of a matador, gave a shriek as she saw my cowled figure emerge from the tomb.

There were few figures on the lawns now, most of the guests having gone inside for their supper, but as I hurried up the alley Titanic I felt immense relief as I saw a tall girl in a medieval gown standing between a Grand Inquisitor and Caesar at the foot of the garden steps.

'Martin, what has happened?' asked Oliver, when I panted up to them. 'You're filthy.'

'Thank God you're safe,' I said to Dian. 'Have you seen Geoffrey?'

'This poor girl has spent most of the time making sure everything ran smoothly in the kitchen,' said Akkim.

'You look terrible,' said Dian as I threw back my hood and sank on to a stone seat. My friends looked on anxiously while I pulled off my mask and threw it to the ground.

'Geoffrey needs help,' I said, and went on to relate what had happened.

'And did you really think he wanted to harm me?' asked Dian incredulously.

'He said as much . . . that his work would look like an accident.'

'He must have been referring to his plans for you,' Akkim said.

'No. It was something he was going to do after he left me. Something to reverse the events around the lady Madeline's death.'

'Then Dian is in no danger,' said Oliver calmly. 'Obviously Geoffrey, in his present mental state, must equate her with Madeline, just as you were equated with the younger brother of Sir Piers. The curse said it would be those who loved the Aubers who would be the victims of the inherited mania. Geoffrey must reason that if he is to change the pattern the object of *his* love must be sacrificed. It must be Rowena rather than the lady Madeline, which by the present-day cast suggests . . .'

'Leila!' exclaimed Dian, distraught. 'I suppose I've always known he loved her best . . .'

'At least she's out of harm's way,' said Oliver.

But I was on my feet again.

'She was in the Murder Room. At first I thought it was Dian, until I saw her golden cross. She was asleep. Did he ever try to hypnotise her?'

'She'd never let him,' said Oliver. 'He's most likely used some of the pills I gave him.'

'We must find them,' I said. 'I'll go to the study and see if she's still there.'

Akkim took out his transceiver.

'I want all the lights turned up and all the crew to look for Mr Auber,' he said into it as I set off to the house at an awkward run. Again I had to fight my way through a delirious whirl of guests. After panting up the spiral staircase I saw that the Murder Room door was open, and the glow from the fire showed it to be deserted. Geoffrey must have taken her down the servants' stairs.

It was unlikely that he could stage an accident in a house packed with people, so he was probably somewhere in the grounds. The pain in my back was a constant reminder of the ruthlessness of his intention.

When I returned to the terrace I found the grounds brilliantly lit. Akkim stood at the top of the steps, directing the operation through his transceiver.

'No luck yet,' he said as I reached him. 'I've got Jim up on the camera crane with the telephoto lens.'

'I'm going to start searching the woods,' I began, but Akkim held up his hand. A tinny voice chuckled from the transceiver, 'I've just seen Mr Auber, boss . . .' Chuckles again. 'He's carrying a girl down to that black boat at the jetty. She looks like she's had a skinful . . .'

I did not wait to hear another word. I leapt down the steps and raced along the avenue, my arms waving as I tried to throw off my robe.

And I knew suddenly that long ago, from a boat out on the lake, I had seen myself running like this.

When I reached the jetty the gondola was gone, but I soon saw its silhouette on the moon-spangled water. I began a desperate search for the oars belonging to

Pandora II, and, when I found them propped against the trunk of a weeping willow, I untied my boat and began to row as I had never rowed before.

Over the stern I saw a dozen rockets scrawl fiery trails above Auber before exploding into a thousand drifting stars. The firework display to herald the unmasking had begun.

Glancing over my shoulder, I saw that Geoffrey was rowing easily, in the style of a gondolier, across Derwentwater. As yet it seemed he had no idea he was being pursued. I realised he was heading for Lodore, and this urged me to greater effort. An accident involving two people who had had too much to drink, fatal to one, would not be unlikely on the floating island.

It was the roar of the Freeman's engine starting up which made Geoffrey look back, and in the greenish light of rockets exploding over the lake he saw me, and increased his speed. My frantic breath burnt my throat as I endeavoured to hold the distance between us, but every stroke brought fresh agony to my back, and I began to fear that the sleek gondola was gaining on me.

With its camera lights blazing, the cruiser turned from the jetty and followed us. Turning my head again I saw that Geoffrey was now only a hundred yards from the dark shape of the island. He had begun to tire, too, for now I was definitely closer to the gondola.

'Geoffrey! Stop! It'll be all right,' I shouted, but my words had no effect. Perhaps they were drowned by the rumble of the Freeman which was coming up fast, Akkim at the wheel.

It must have been this which prompted Geoffrey to ship his oar and step down into the craft. The space between us decreased as he bent down. Then he straightened up and heaved a limp figure over the side.

A few more strokes and I was near enough to the spot to dive. As I did so I had a glimpse of Geoffrey thrusting on his oar, then I was swimming down through the cold water until the weeds at the bottom slid past my legs, trying to entangle me in their slimy grip. Appalled at the odds against finding Leila in this blackness I surfaced for air, and saw her floating face down a few yards away.

Thank God I have always been a good swimmer. With a couple of strokes I reached her and turned her on her back, and was towing her in what I hoped was the direction of *Pandora II* when the white cruiser loomed beside me and paused as Akkim expertly threw it into reverse. Hands reached down over the side, gripped Leila by her domino and hoisted her aboard. As an afterthought someone helped me to heave myself up. In the cockpit she was laid across the stern seat, and lake water gushed from her mouth as Oliver pressed her ribs with all his might. Moments later her eyelids fluttered and she took a shuddering breath before vomiting more water.

'She'll be all right,' he said. 'Are there any rugs in the cabin?'

Akkim kicked the long gear lever and pressed down the throttle control so that the cruiser surged forward. One of the crew swept the lake ahead with a powerful searchlight. Suddenly the gondola was caught in its beam as Geoffrey drove its high fretted prow into the soft margin of the island. He raced the length of the craft and leapt on to a patch of grass, and then began running towards the centre.

'Son of a bitch!' Akkim swore, almost in awe of the figure scrambling from one patch of vegetation to another. Seconds later our bows wedged themselves into the bank beside the gondola.

'Keep the lights on the bastard,' he yelled. 'Come on, Martin. We've got to reach him before he gets caught in that mire.'

Throwing off his costume, Akkim lowered himself over the side to the quaking shore and I was about to follow when the man behind the lamp gave a cry of disgust. In the white beam we saw that Geoffrey was up to his waist in a patch of peat between some reed clumps. As we watched, he slid lower, his masked face turned to us and his mouth open in a mixture of astonishment and appeal. A moment

343

later his head sank out of sight, but for several seconds his arms remained, waving. Then the surface of the island closed and there was nothing – nothing! – to mark what had happened.

The man with the searchlight began to sob. Then came the ultimate horror. On the stern seat Leila's eyes rolled upwards and her quivering lips moved. From her mouth came Geoffrey's voice. 'Leila, help me . . . it's *dark*!'

Postscript

It is Christmas night and the Southern Cross is blazing above me as I sit at an old table outside my *whare*, listening to surf music and watching the luminous rollers explode against the Castlepoint rocks. Today I finished this account of my strange enchantment which began on the shore of Derwentwater. What an exercise in catharsis!

Now, thanks to a bottle of whisky and the isolation of my headland, I can enjoy a sense of tranquillity at last. Perhaps tonight will be free from dreams. Yet one thing still haunts me from my re-examination of my past – that moment in the stone circle when, whether in a vision or in some strange reality, the smoke parted and for a second it seemed there was a look of recognition on the face of the woman at the stake.

Was it my horrified imagination, or did she see me as someone she knew in her own timespan? Or did I appear as a confirmation of the bane she had called down on the House of Auber? At least her curse is ended now; the Auber line expired with Geoffrey.

After his death Akkim, troubled by possible publicity and his own deep superstitions, scrapped his plans for *Murder Room*. In his last letter he said he was about to shoot a vampire film in Venice.

I left Derwentwater before the estate agents drafted their *Country Life* advertisements for Auber's sale and flew to New Zealand, where I returned to Castlepoint to spend my days in solitude and my nights at my typewriter.

This morning a Maori shepherd rode through the heat from the sheepstation some miles away. When he learned I had not availed myself of the owner's invitation to

Christmas dinner, the kindly fellow turned up with my mail and a bottle of Bells as a joint gift from his mates.

Tonight I have been drinking it and reading my letters by the light of a hurricane lamp surrounded by a carnival of insects. The post included a card from Tash depicting a Las Vegas night scene, a sad affectionate note from Dian with a programme for her first solo concert, and an embossed Christmas card from Oliver Penthorne, who added a line that he had found a publisher for his book on hypnotic regression.

One letter remains. I need to drink more whisky before I read it. Meanwhile, I shall enjoy the surf and the stars, and the hard-won freedom to be myself. Then, when I am drunk, I shall open the airmail envelope, bright with Hong Kong stamps and addressed in her unmistakable hand.

Fiction

GENERAL

☐ The House of Women	Chaim Bermant	£1.95
☐ The Patriarch	Chaim Bermant	£2.25
☐ The Rat Race	Alfred Bester	£1.95
☐ Midwinter	John Buchan	£1.50
☐ A Prince of the Captivity	John Buchan	£1.50
☐ The Priestess of Henge	David Burnett	£2.50
☐ Tangled Dynasty	Jean Chapman	£1.75
☐ The Other Woman	Colette	£1.95
☐ Retreat From Love	Colette	£1.60
☐ An Infinity of Mirrors	Richard Condon	£1.95
☐ Arigato	Richard Condon	£1.95
☐ Prizzi's Honour	Richard Condon	£1.75
☐ A Trembling Upon Rome	Richard Condon	£1.95
☐ The Whisper of the Axe	Richard Condon	£1.75
☐ Love and Work	Gwyneth Cravens	£1.95
☐ King Hereafter	Dorothy Dunnett	£2.95
☐ Pope Joan	Lawrence Durrell	£1.35
☐ The Country of Her Dreams	Janice Elliott	£1.35
☐ Magic	Janice Elliot	£1.95
☐ Secret Places	Janice Elliott	£1.75
☐ Letter to a Child Never Born	Oriana Fallaci	£1.25
☐ A Man	Oriana Fallaci	£2.50
☐ Rich Little Poor Girl	Terence Feely	£1.75
☐ Marital Rites	Margaret Forster	£1.50
☐ The Seduction of Mrs Pendlebury	Margaret Forster	£1.95
☐ Abingdons	Michael French	£2.25
☐ Rhythms	Michael French	£2.25
☐ Who Was Sylvia?	Judy Gardiner	£1.50
☐ Grimalkin's Tales	Gardiner, Ronson, Whitelaw	£1.60
☐ Lost and Found	Julian Gloag	£1.95
☐ A Sea-Change	Lois Gould	£1.50
☐ La Presidenta	Lois Gould	£2.25
☐ A Kind of War	Pamela Haines	£1.95
☐ Tea at Gunters	Pamela Haines	£1.75
☐ Black Summer	Julian Hale	£1.75
☐ A Rustle in the Grass	Robin Hawdon	£1.95
☐ Riviera	Robert Sydney Hopkins	£1.95
☐ Duncton Wood	William Horwood	£2.75
☐ The Stonor Eagles	William Horwood	£2.50
☐ The Man Who Lived at the Ritz	A. E. Hotchner	£1.65
☐ A Bonfire	Pamela Hansford Johnson	£1.50
☐ The Good Listener	Pamela Hansford Johnson	£1.50
☐ The Honours Board	Pamela Hansford Johnson	£1.50
☐ The Unspeakable Skipton	Pamela Hansford Johnson	£1.50
☐ In the Heat of the Summer	John Katzenbach	£1.95
☐ Starrs	Warren Leslie	£2.50
☐ Kine	A. R. Lloyd	£1.50
☐ The Factory	Jack Lynn	£1.95
☐ Christmas Pudding	Nancy Mitford	£1.50
☐ Highland Fling	Nancy Mitford	£1.50
☐ Pigeon Pie	Nancy Mitford	£1.75
☐ The Sun Rises	Christopher Nicole	£2.50

Fiction

HORROR/OCCULT/NASTY

☐ Death Walkers	Gary Brandner	£1.75
☐ Hellborn	Gary Brandner	£1.75
☐ The Howling	Gary Brandner	£1.75
☐ Return of the Howling	Gary Brandner	£1.75
☐ Tribe of the Dead	Gary Brandner	£1.75
☐ The Sanctuary	Glenn Chandler	£1.50
☐ The Tribe	Glenn Chandler	£1.10
☐ The Black Castle	Leslie Daniels	£1.25
☐ The Big Goodnight	Judy Gardiner	£1.25
☐ Rattlers	Joseph L. Gilmore	£1.60
☐ The Nestling	Charles L. Grant	£1.95
☐ Night Songs	Charles L. Grant	£1.95
☐ Slime	John Halkin	£1.75
☐ Slither	John Halkin	£1.60
☐ The Unholy	John Halkin	£1.25
☐ The Skull	Shaun Hutson	£1.25
☐ Pestilence	Edward Jarvis	£1.60
☐ The Beast Within	Edward Levy	£1.25
☐ Night Killers	Richard Lewis	£1.25
☐ Spiders	Richard Lewis	£1.75
☐ The Web	Richard Lewis	£1.75
☐ Nightmare	Lewis Mallory	£1.75
☐ Bloodthirst	Mark Ronson	£1.60
☐ Ghoul	Mark Ronson	£1.75
☐ Ogre	Mark Ronson	£1.75
☐ Deathbell	Guy N. Smith	£1.75
☐ Doomflight	Guy N. Smith	£1.25
☐ Manitou Doll	Guy N. Smith	£1.25
☐ Satan's Snowdrop	Guy N. Smith	£1.00
☐ The Understudy	Margaret Tabor	£1.95
☐ The Beast of Kane	Cliff Twemlow	£1.50
☐ The Pike	Cliff Twemlow	£1.25

Fiction

SCIENCE FICTION

☐ More Things in Heaven	John Brunner	£1.50
☐ Chessboard Planet	Henry Kuttner	£1.75
☐ The Proud Robot	Henry Kuttner	£1.50
☐ Death's Master	Tanith Lee	£1.50
☐ The Dancers of Arun	Elizabeth A. Lynn	£1.50
☐ The Northern Girl	Elizabeth A. Lynn	£1.50
☐ Balance of Power	Brian M. Stableford	£1.75

ADVENTURE/SUSPENSE

☐ The Corner Men	John Gardner	£1.75
☐ Death of a Friend	Richard Harris	£1.95
☐ The Flowers of the Forest	Joseph Hone	£1.75
☐ Styx	Christopher Hyde	£1.50
☐ Temple Kent	D. G. Devon	£1.95
☐ Confess, Fletch	Gregory Mcdonald	£1.50
☐ Fletch	Gregory Mcdonald	£1.50
☐ Fletch and the Widow Bradley	Gregory Mcdonald	£1.50
☐ Flynn	Gregory Mcdonald	£1.75
☐ The Buck Passes Flynn	Gregory Mcdonald	£1.60
☐ The Specialist	Jasper Smith	£1.75

WESTERNS

Blade Series – Matt Chisholm

☐ No. 5 The Colorado Virgins	85p
☐ No. 6 The Mexican Proposition	85p
☐ No. 11 The Navaho Trail	95p

McAllister Series – Matt Chisholm

☐ No. 3 McAllister Never Surrenders	95p
☐ No. 4 McAllister and the Cheyenne Death	95p
☐ No. 8 McAllister – Fire Brand	£1.25

Fiction

CRIME

☐ The Cool Cottontail	John Ball	£1.00
☐ Five Pieces of Jade	John Ball	£1.50
☐ Johnny Get Your Gun	John Ball	£1.00
☐ Then Came Violence	John Ball	£1.50
☐ The Widow's Cruise	Nicholas Blake	£1.25
☐ The Worm of Death	Nicholas Blake	95p
☐ The Long Divorce	Edmund Crispin	£1.50
☐ Love Lies Bleeding	Edmund Crispin	£1.75
☐ The Case of the Sliding Pool	E. V. Cunningham	£1.75
☐ Hindsight	Peter Dickinson	£1.75
☐ King and Joker	Peter Dickinson	£1.25
☐ The Last House Party	Peter Dickinson	£1.75
☐ A Pride of Heroes	Peter Dickinson	£1.50
☐ The Seals	Peter Dickinson	£1.50
☐ Gondola Scam	Jonathan Gash	£1.75
☐ The Sleepers of Erin	Jonathan Gash	£1.75
☐ The Black Seraphim	Michael Gilbert	£1.75
☐ Blood and Judgment	Michael Gilbert	£1.10
☐ Close Quarters	Michael Gilbert	£1.10
☐ The Etruscan Net	Michael Gilbert	£1.25
☐ The Final Throw	Michael Gilbert	£1.75
☐ The Night of the Twelfth	Michael Gilbert	£1.25
☐ The Blunderer	Patricia Highsmith	£1.50
☐ A Game for the Living	Patricia Highsmith	£1.50
☐ Those Who Walk Away	Patricia Highsmith	£1.50
☐ The Tremor of Forgery	Patricia Highsmith	£1.50
☐ The Two Faces of January	Patricia Highsmith	£1.50
☐ Silence Observed	Michael Innes	£1.00
☐ Go West, Inspector Ghote	H. R. F. Keating	£1.50
☐ Inspector Ghote Draws a Line	H. R. F. Keating	£1.50
☐ Inspector Ghote Plays a Joker	H. R. F. Keating	£1.50
☐ The Murder of the Maharajah	H. R. F. Keating	£1.50
☐ The Perfect Murder	H. R. F. Keating	£1.50
☐ The Dutch Shoe Mystery	Ellery Queen	£1.60
☐ The French Powder Mystery	Ellery Queen	£1.25
☐ The Siamese Twin Mystery	Ellery Queen	95p
☐ The Spanish Cape Mystery	Ellery Queen	£1.10
☐ Copper, Gold and Treasure	David Williams	£1.75
☐ Treasure By Degrees	David Williams	£1.75
☐ Unholy Writ	David Williams	£1.60

Fiction

HISTORICAL ROMANCE/ROMANCE/SAGA

☐ A Dark Moon Raging	Aileen Armitage	£1.50
☐ Hawksmoor	Aileen Armitage	£1.75
☐ Hunter's Moon	Aileen Armitage	£1.95
☐ Blaze of Passion	Stephanie Blake	£1.75
☐ Callie Knight	Stephanie Blake	£1.95
☐ Daughter of Destiny	Stephanie Blake	£1.75
☐ Fires of the Heart	Stephanie Blake	£1.50
☐ Scarlet Kisses	Stephanie Blake	£1.50
☐ So Wicked My Desire	Stephanie Blake	£1.75
☐ Unholy Desires	Stephanie Blake	£1.50
☐ Broken Promises	Drusilla Campbell	£1.75
☐ Silent Dreams	Drusilla Campbell	£1.95
☐ Stolen Passions	Drusilla Campbell	£2.25
☐ Tomorrow's Journey	Drusilla Campbell	£2.25
☐ Raven	Shana Carrol	£2.50
☐ Paxton Pride	Shana Carrol	£2.25
☐ The Far Morning	Brenda Clarke	£1.50
☐ The Fifth Jade of Heaven	Marilyn Granbeck	£2.25
☐ The Ravensley Touch	Constance Heaven	£1.75
☐ Sutton Place	Dinah Lampitt	£2.25
☐ Captive Bride	Johanna Lindsey	£1.50
☐ Fires of Winter	Johanna Lindsey	£1.50
☐ Paradise Wild	Johanna Lindsey	£1.50
☐ A Pirate's Love	Johanna Lindsey	£1.25
☐ Wild Flowers	Pamela Redford Russell	£2.25
☐ Curtain Call	Rona Randall	£2.25
☐ Dragonmede	Rona Randall	£2.25
☐ The Eagle at the Gate	Rona Randall	£2.25
☐ The Ladies of Hanover Square	Rona Randall	£2.25
☐ Glenrannoch	Rona Randall	£1.75
☐ Full Circle	Judith Saxton	£2.25
☐ The Glory	Judith Saxton	£1.95
☐ The Pride	Judith Saxton	£1.95
☐ The Splendour	Judith Saxton	£1.75
☐ The Fields of Yesterday	Robert Tyler Stevens	£1.50
☐ Shadows in the Afternoon	Robert Tyler Stevens	£1.50

Zenith

☐ The Voices of the Dead	Autran Dourado	£2.50
☐ My Double Life	Sarah Bernhardt	£3.25
☐ Pages from Cold Point	Paul Bowles	£1.95
☐ A Walk Around London's Parks	Hunter Davies	£3.50
☐ Behind God's Back	Negley Farson	£2.95
☐ The Way of a Transgressor	Negley Farson	£2.95
☐ A Small Yes and a Big No	George Grosz	£2.50
☐ A Child Possessed	R. C. Hutchinson	£2.50
☐ Johanna at Daybreak	R. C. Hutchinson	£2.95
☐ March the Ninth	R. C. Hutchinson	£2.95
☐ Shining Scabbard	R. C. Hutchinson	£3.50
☐ Recollection of a Journey	R. C. Hutchinson	£2.95
☐ The Stepmother	R. C. Hutchinson	£2.95
☐ 5001 Nights at the Movies	Pauline Kael	£5.95
☐ Days of Greatness	Walter Kempowski	£2.95
☐ The Hill of Kronos	Peter Levi	£2.95
☐ The Confessions of Lady Nijö	Lady Nijö	£2.95
☐ The Brendan Voyage	Tim Severin	£3.50
☐ Tracking Marco Polo	Tim Severin	£2.75
☐ The Dark Lantern	Henry Williamson	£3.50
☐ Donkey Boy	Henry Williamson	£3.50
☐ The Dream of Fair Women	Henry Williamson	£2.50
☐ The Pathway	Henry Williamson	£2.95

NAME...

ADDRESS..

....

Write to Hamlyn Paperbacks Cash Sales, PO Box 11, Falmouth, Cornwall TR10 9EN.

Please indicate order and enclose remittance to the value of cover price plus:

U.K. CUSTOMERS: Please allow 55p for the first book, 22p for the second book and 14p for each additional book ordered to a maximum charge of £1.75.

B.F.P.O. & EIRE: Please allow 55p for the first book, 22p for the second book plus 14p per copy for the next seven books, thereafter 8p per book.

OVERSEAS CUSTOMERS: Please allow £1.00 for the first book plus 25p per copy for each additional book.

Whilst every effort is made to keep prices low it is sometimes necessary to increase cover prices and also postage and packing rates at short notice. Hamlyn Paperbacks reserve the right to show new retail prices on covers which may differ from those previously advertised in the text or elsewhere.